PENGUIN BOOKS
YELLOW LIGHTS OF DEATH

Benyamin has published seventeen books in Malayalam, including seven novels, three short-story collections, a travelogue and memoirs. His most famous work, *Aadujeevitham*, is a bestseller in Malayalam, and has been translated into many languages like English, Arabic, Thai, Nepali, Oriya, Tamil and Kannada. It is a textbook for many universities, and has received the Kerala Sahitya Akademi Award in 2009, and was longlisted for the Man Asian Literature Prize 2013 and shortlisted for the DSC Prize for South Asian Literature in 2014. The Arabic translation of the book is banned in Saudi Arabia and the UAE. His other major works include *Euthanasia*, *Pravachakanmarude Randam Pustakam*, *Akkapporinte Irupatu Nasrani Varshangal* and *Manjaveyil Maranangal*. His latest work, *Al Arabian Novel Factory*, is banned in the UAE.

Sajeev Kumarapuram has served editorial stints in reputed media houses, including *Times of India*, *Miami Herald*, *New Indian Express* and *Businessworld*, and now specializes in infographic design, which enables him to equitably distribute his love for two forms of expression: lines and letters. Raised in Thiruvananthapuram and living in New Delhi, the thirty-three-year-old has donned plenty of hats in his career—an award-winning investigative reporter, a columnist, an artist, an illustrator and a photographer. *Yellow Lights of Death* is his maiden attempt at translation.

YELLOW LIGHTS OF DEATH

BENYAMIN

Translated from the Malayalam
by Sajeev Kumarapuram

PENGUIN BOOKS

An imprint of Penguin Random House

PENGUIN BOOKS

USA | Canada | UK | Ireland | Australia
New Zealand | India | South Africa | China | Singapore

Penguin Books is part of the Penguin Random House group of companies
whose addresses can be found at global.penguinrandomhouse.com

Published by Penguin Random House India Pvt. Ltd
4th Floor, Capital Tower 1, MG Road,
Gurugram 122 002, Haryana, India

Penguin
Random House
India

First published in Malayalam as *Manjaveyil Maranangal* by DC Books,
Kottayam, 2011
First published in English by Penguin Books India 2015

ISBN 9780143420897

Typeset in Sabon LT Std by R. Ajith Kumar, New Delhi
Printed at Repro India Limited

www.penguin.co.in

MIX
Paper from
responsible sources
FSC® C047271

To all my friends

1

Udayamperoor

WE DIDN'T HAVE to ask for directions at Udayamperoor; the descriptions in Andrapper's book were detailed and accurate enough. There were scores of churches along the right side of the road. The oldest one among them had a board that said, 'Oh, Gervasiuses and Protasius Kandeesangals, please pray for us.' Next to it stood an antique stone cross guarded by figurines of a winged lion, a vulture, a bull and a man. Half a furlong ahead, on the left, was Kochuparu Stores, where we halted for some refreshing lemonade. Nearby was a large ground with the Nadakkavu Bhagavati temple at the centre. We took the road that forked towards the right and headed east. It was there that a dog ran across in front of our vehicle. A few minutes later, I saw tall brick walls that reminded me of a heavily guarded prison.

'We have reached,' I said. My voice betrayed my apprehension.

Anil slowed down the car and stopped on the unpaved sidewalk.

Close to the gate was a small stone slab embedded in the wall. If Andrapper hadn't mentioned it in his book, I probably wouldn't have noticed it. It was covered with moss. Slowly, I deciphered the faded letters: Valyedathu Veedu! I had butterflies in my stomach. But I kept a lid on my emotions. The gate was wide open. Anil drove inside. An ancient, double-storeyed mansion came into view. The courtyard was paved with white pebbles. In front of the majestic building was a *pala* tree, which looked like it had stood there for centuries. We parked the car in its shadow.

A man jogged out of the front door towards us.

'We are here for the rites,' said Anil, getting out of the car.

'Was it booked in advance?'

'Yeah . . . I had called last week.'

'OK. Please come in.'

He guided us into a spacious reception and started checking a logbook. We were the only people in the room. I was surprised because I had expected a large crowd.

'In whose name was it booked?' he asked, furiously flipping through the pages.

'Anil Vengode,' I replied.

'You've brought the cash, right?' He must have found Anil's name in the register.

'Yes.'

'Then, please place an amount not less than 10,000 rupees here, with prayers,' he said, pointing to a brass plate on a teapoy. Anil placed there an envelope that had Rs 10,000 in notes and a one-rupee coin.

The man covered the money with a red cloth. 'This will remain here,' he said. 'If you are not convinced by the results, you can take it back when you leave.'

This is a good practice that should be followed everywhere, I said to myself.

'Please be seated, I'll call you soon.' He closed the logbook and stepped inside.

Like every other traditional old house, the reception room was chock-a-block with rich woodwork. Sculptures, figurines, photographs in large frames, a small flowerpot, an old wooden bowl and a telephone stand. It was evident that a gifted interior designer had been at work. Nothing was missing. Nothing looked out of place. This is my ideal reception room, I told Anil.

After a while, a young man stepped out. 'Meljo!' I whispered, half to Anil and half to myself. 'Photocopy,' Anil murmured.

'Are you the people who called last week?' he asked.

'Yes.' We rose slowly.

'What is the case?'

'We are searching for someone.'

'Come,' he welcomed us inside.

When Anil picked up his bag and camera, the young man said, 'Leave these things here. Nothing is permitted inside.'

As we walked inside, he asked, 'Where are you coming from?'

'Thrissur,' I lied, looking at Anil.

'There are a lot of abbeys in that area, then why here?'

I wavered for a while, not knowing what to say. Anil came to the rescue. 'His father's been here, and what he needed was done,' he said. 'Hence the belief.'

'The old priest is still there, I hope,' I added.

The young man turned and stared at me. 'No, Appachan died recently,' he said. 'I'm in charge now. Don't you have faith in me?

'What happened to him?' Anil and I asked in tandem.

'Don't you have faith in me?' his voice betrayed a seriousness and maturity beyond his age.

'Nothing like that . . . I was just curious about the doctor,' I replied.

'Then, please stand in front of that lamp and pray with your eyes closed. I'll call you,' he said, pointing towards a flickering stone lamp. He stepped inside another room and closed the door.

Even as I pretended to pray in front of the lamp, I surveyed my surroundings.

This must be where the festival described in Andrapper's book had taken place. Only then could someone have witnessed it from the upper floor. I looked up. Which was the room where he had been hiding that night? From where had he seen the whole thing? What happened to him after that?

Meljo, the new custodian of Valyedathu Veedu, I whispered to myself. I won't leave without getting satisfactory answers to these questions—I swear before this stone lamp!

A few minutes later, Meljo returned. There was a red cloth wrapped around his waist and a towel on his shoulder.

'Take a little oil from the lamp, smear it on your forehead, and follow me,' Meljo said.

He took us to a prayer room. It resembled the altar of a small church. There were plenty of candles and lamps lit in front of a statue—a woman adorned with garlands.

I recognized her. Thaikkattamma! The goddess of Thaikkattu!

I looked at her and prayed without thinking. Anybody could have mistaken her for the Virgin Mary. But the skin tone was dark. The face didn't display love or tenderness. It was full of fury.

There was a wick lamp flickering at the centre of the room. Meljo asked us to sit before it, and took the spot opposite us.

He touched the lamp and prayed. He meditated for a while. Then a barrage of questions started.

'Do you know that Thaikkattamma rules the land and water of Udayamperoor?'

'Yes, we know,' I said.

'Do you have faith in Thaikkattamma?'

'Yes, we have faith.'

'Do you have faith in the powers of Thaikkattamma?'

'Yes, we have faith.'

'Do you have faith that Thaikkattamma will fulfil your pursuit?'

'Yes, we have faith.'

'Have you come to Thaikkattamma to wish misfortune upon anyone?'

'No.'

'Are you aware that Thaikkattamma blesses in abundance if pleased and flares up in fury if angered?'

'Yes.'

'Do you have faith that Thaikkattamma will appear before this lamp and to us?'

'Yes, we have faith.'

'Do you have faith in Thaikkattamma?'

'Yes, we have faith.'

'Do you have faith in Thaikkattamma?'

'Yes, we have faith.'

'Do you have faith in Thaikkattamma?'

'Yes, we have faith.'

'Now, repeat this prayer as I chant:

Hail gracious Mother, almighty Thaikkattamma,
To thee we pledge our body, our soul and our thoughts,
And our actions, our life and our death.
O Mother, Thaikkattamma, queen of the Nazarenes,
Beyond anything, with all our heart,
We hold thee close to us.
With the blessings of your Lord Jesus,
Grace us with thy presence, we beseech thee,
Despise not our petitions.
(Both of you think about your petitions.)

Hail gracious Mother, almighty Thaikkattamma,
By the power of your Father and our Lord Jesus,
Pour forth mercy and blessings towards us.
Gift us all thy blessings, we humbly pray
O Mother, Thaikkattamma,
Grace us with thy presence, we beseech thee,
Hear and answer our petitions.

He chanted some more prayers and hymns for a while.

'Now, tell me. Why have you come?' he asked as he stretched both his hands and placed them together above the lamp.

'One of our friends is missing. We want to know where he is.'

'How long has he been missing?'

'For almost a year.'

'Where is he from?'

'Diego Garcia.'

'Diego Garcia!'

'Yes.'

'What is his name?'

'Andrapper.'

He withdrew his hands in a flash, as if he had burnt his fingers, and blew out the lamp.

'What happened?' I asked anxiously.

'Thaikkattamma doesn't like to know where he is now. That's all. Get up!' He was already on his feet.

'No.' Anil pulled me back as I was about to rise. 'We need to know where he is. We paid good money to find that out. We are not leaving without the truth.'

'You can take the money back when you leave. Don't argue against the decisions of Thaikkattamma.'

'The money wasn't paid to be returned, but to fulfil our need. Whether Thaikkattamma likes it or not, Meljo, you will have to tell us the truth.' Anil was adamant.

All of a sudden, Meljo rushed towards one of the doors and rang the bell next to it. We could hear the commotion inside. All the doors to the prayer room were latched on the outside.

'Tell me the truth. Who are you? Why did you come here? What is it that you want?' he asked in a soft but angry tone.

I wavered a bit, scrambling for answers. Once again, Anil came to the rescue. 'Meljo, we haven't promised anyone that we will return from this trip alive,' he warned. 'But some of our friends know that we were headed here. So don't try to scare us off. I'm Anil. This is Benyamin, a writer. We are Andrapper's friends. We are searching for him and that's how we landed here. We need clear answers.'

'Here! What's his connection to Valyedathu Veedu?' Meljo feigned ignorance.

'Nothing at all?' asked Anil. 'Meljo, don't try to fool us. We know you. We know this house. We know all about Andrapper's ties with this house. This is the last place that he visited. Don't lie to us in front of the family deity, Thaikkattamma.'

Meljo deflated visibly. He went and opened the door, gesturing at those guarding it to leave. Then he asked us to follow him.

He led us back to the reception room. 'How do you know him?' Meljo asked as he sat down. 'What's between him and you two?'

'The novel that he was writing—*The Book of Forefathers*—is with Benyamin. It has all the details of his life. He has elaborately described the roads he had taken and the places he had visited. Valyedathu Veedu plays a prominent role in those pages.'

Meljo looked defeated; resting his chin on his hand, he said, 'I've also been searching for that cheat for so long . . .'

'Cheat?' That took us by surprise.

'Yes. He promised me and my Valyapapan that he would return soon. We waited for a long time, but he didn't come. We rang him up many times, but he didn't pick up the phone. He deceived this family. He betrayed our love for him.'

'No, Meljo. If what he's written in the book is true, he didn't cheat you. He left meaning to return,' I said.

'How did you get hold of his book?' Meljo wondered.

'I'll tell you.'

Sipping the tea that his servant brought, I began to narrate parts of the story to him.

THE PREFACE

ONE FINE MORNING, I received an email from a stranger. Its contents went something like this:

Dear author,

I have bittersweet emotions as I write this mail. I happened to read your novel that was published recently. I consider it one of the best novels I have ever read. I'm still enjoying the hangover of the experience. Reading it inspired me with strength and energy. I can draw upon them to face any challenge.

I'd like to meet you someday. I have a story to tell. I strongly believe that if you listen to the story, you won't be able to resist the temptation to write about it. In fact, it is a story that I wanted to write. But due to unforeseen circumstances, I don't think I'll be able to write it.

Of late, I have been living under immense stress. I have no clue what's going to happen tomorrow. In such a situation, I don't think I can write anything. I assume you write about the desert heat sitting in an air-conditioned room. Nothing wrong in that. Stories are not penned by those who experience them, but by those who listen to them. Only they can write stories.

To acknowledge that you have read my mail, please update your Orkut status message to: 'I don't believe for a moment that creativity is a neurotic symptom' (Aldous Huxley). I'll understand from it that you have read my mail. Please don't try to reply to this address. This is a disposable email ID. Within an hour, this account will disappear.

Because of some personal issues, I cannot reveal my identity or give you my real email address. Hope you will understand.

Wishing you all the best to write more wonderful works.
—A reader

Honestly, I didn't give much importance to the mail. For starters, I don't take such fraud mails seriously. I believe that people who can't reveal their identities don't deserve any consideration. Another thing, after my last novel was published, I have been bombarded with dozens of mails from readers who wanted me to hear their stories. Each one of them bored me to death with their clichés and repetitions. I felt sick at the very thought of reading another one. On top of that, I had a lot of pending work. So I didn't bother too much about that mail.

I had forgotten all about it. Months later, I got another mail from a different account.

Dear novelist,

I don't know whether you remember me. I had sent you a mail some months ago. I mentioned that I had a story to tell you. But I'm afraid that the mail must have got lost in the hundreds that reach your inbox every day.

I'm going through days that are a hundred times more stressful and terrible. I have forgotten the story I wanted to write. But I tried my hand at writing about my life. About the experiences I had to endure and the situations I had to face. There is no order or chronology to it. I just scribbled something. I've kept them as notes. I've no clue whether the jottings are in the form of an autobiography or a novel or an essay. But whatever has been written, there is no exaggeration in it. No imagination either.

Dear author, with much affection, I send you the first part of my life story. Whenever you get some free time from your busy schedule, please have a look. You'll definitely find it useful.

Unfortunately, I won't be able to send the remaining parts of my story. There are many reasons for it. One, you ignored my request to acknowledge the receipt of my first mail. Two, because of that, I don't know how considerate you are about my life and words. Three, if by any chance, you misplace it, my life story will be lost forever. Four, if you are a coward, you will hand it over to the police. That will endanger my life further.

So, I'm sending the remaining part of the story to the people mentioned in the story, and who I think are trustworthy. If the first part piques your interest, you can collect the rest from the others and combine everything. My autobiography will be complete only when all the parts are together. Again, due to reasons of security, I don't wish to disclose my identity or theirs. Please don't think that I don't trust you. As you read, you'll understand my reasons.

Dear author, it was my dream to write a novel and see it become the best and most read novel ever published in Malayalam. How many years have I wasted on that dream! But my destiny did not want me to become a novelist. My destiny held something else.

If you ever succeed in collecting the parts of my story, don't turn it into a novel. Publish it as my autobiography.

I hereby grant you the rights to it through this email. I certify that my family, friends or any other person will not have any ownership of it. If someone asks for evidence, tell them that my act of sending the first part to you is proof by itself. I really hope to meet you in person someday.

With love,
—The one who wanted to be a novelist

When I received the second mail, I was in the middle of spinning the yarn for my upcoming novel, *Nedumbassery*. It had so completely occupied my imagination that I had time for nothing else. So, once again I ignored the mail. Two more arrived and went past me. I managed to complete ten chapters of *Nedumbassery*, and then I was hit by the cursed writer's block. Despite my best efforts, the story would not move forward.

The characters were fighting over who would narrate the rest of the story. In all probability, it was a symptom of the distress that I was going through. Neither the characters nor I could escape from the struggle. The novel was stalled. The writing came to a halt. I was frustrated. For days, I could do nothing. I randomly picked up books to read, but I was unable to focus on them.

One evening, while browsing through blogs, I suddenly remembered that old mail. Curious to know about the mysterious sender's life story, I searched my inbox and finally dug up the mail and downloaded the attachment. They were scanned images of handwritten text. I started reading it.

THE BEGINNING

I HURRIED HOME through the narrow streets of Seleucia. I was shivering, as if caught in a polar vortex, my hands glued to my body. Just a while ago, I had been wandering in an alley when a story idea dawned on me. The visuals were still buzzing in my head. Some snatches of dialogue were crystal clear, more beautiful than I could ever think of. If even a word moved left or right, the whole beauty of the sentence would be lost. These words were oozing out of some unknown corners of my heart.

I walked as if I was on a mission, unwilling to be distracted. I didn't bother to pause over anything or pay notice to the sights of the street. A couple of acquaintances walked past. I did see them from the corner of my eye, but I didn't acknowledge them. If I'd stopped to talk to them, they would have dragged me into the usual chit-chat. The words that I'd been guarding carefully in my mind would have leaked out. Some strangers looked at me in amazement. They were probably wondering whether it was as cold as I was making it out to be. Or they might have thought that I was sick. I didn't worry even a bit about what they were thinking.

A friend did stop me in my tracks. He shook my hand and asked me how I had been. How was my job? How was my family? I stammered and answered in monosyllables. And because my answers were not satisfactory, he probably said to himself, 'Oh lord, what happened to him!' Somehow, I escaped.

When I reached the Krishnaswami temple, another friend waved at me from the other side of the road. I didn't pay any heed. Then he made a teasing remark: 'Da, don't think so much. Our lives are not worth such lofty thoughts. Even Derrida wouldn't have thought so much while walking . . .' The mere mention of Derrida had me on the verge of laughter. Well, how the hell does he know about Derrida? Is he a voracious reader or did he catch it from the speech of some intellectual? Or did he overhear one of his smarter friends talking about the famous philosopher?

Then I promptly went back to my beautiful words. I repeated them in my head. No, nothing has been lost. My mind remembered every single thing. It knew every situation. My god! Some of the dialogue . . . the scenes . . . what were they? I had stumbled upon a metaphor that no one had used before. What was it? Like a ghost house . . . No, not that. Like a ghost form. No. It was something else. Something that fit the sentence perfectly like a glove. Oh god! I'd forgotten it. It was lost forever!

I cursed myself for not carrying a pencil or a piece of paper. I wanted to knock on some door, any door, and beg for a pen and some paper, and scribble the lines from my memory then and there. But how would people react to this madness? If I had been a famous writer, I could have got away with anything. If I had walked into a stranger's house with such an odd request, they would have welcomed me and made me use their writing table to note down whatever was on my mind.

They would have served me strong cardamom tea, maybe even some banana fries, and left me in silence. After some time, when I'd finished jotting everything down, a shy girl would have come up to me blushing, to ask if she could read it. My handwriting would have made me hesitate for a moment, but I'd have offered it to her with pride. As she received it with trembling hands and started reading, her family would have gathered around her quietly. The magic of my words would have given them goosebumps and made their body hair rise like that of a fighter cock's. Then, for a long time, they would have proudly narrated the story to their neighbours and friends.

And when my novel got published, one of the first copies would have been bought by the family. When I pass that house on some later day, the same girl would have run to me for an autograph on the book. When I returned it with words of love, she would have kissed it as a holy book. Thereafter, she would have kept the novel in their prayer room. Before she took it in her hands again, she would have purified herself with a bath. She wouldn't have let anyone touch it without cleaning their hands.

Swaying and staggering, I reached home somehow. Loud noises could be heard. Chettathi was watching TV with a friend and speaking louder over the noise. 'Please reduce the volume of both the TV and your chat, I have to write,' I begged her.

'Oh, a writer . . .' she laughed at my plea with contempt.

Well, she didn't know that I was writing a novel and some lines from it were playing hide and seek in my mind, like a nervous cat. 'Please . . . switch it off . . . for a little while. Let the world be peaceful. Just for a little while.' I begged her, clutching her feet. They must have been shocked and scared by my behaviour. They hastily turned off the TV.

They must have suspected that I'd gone mad. But they didn't know about the beautiful lines hidden in my mind like a playful cat.

In that wonderful moment when the world fell silent, I entered my room and wrote the first lines of my novel.

I hurried home through the narrow streets of Seleucia. I was shivering, as if caught in a polar vortex, my hands glued to my body . . .

DREAD OF DEATH

ONE FINE MORNING, I got a phone call.

'This is Das!'

I didn't recognize the voice.

'Mohandas Purameri,' he elaborated.

The name sounded familiar, but I was still not sure.

'I don't know if you remember me. We were together at the Parana literary group. And also at my photo exhibition . . .'

Oh, Mohandas! He's a fairly well-known photographer in Pentasia. I remember once attending an exhibition of his work, and commenting that it was among the best that could be found in such a place. But it's better not to recall the Parana literary group. It was a union of twenty-five of us to protest against the five-star culture of senior writers . . . It had budding talent from all the languages spoken in Diego Garcia. For Malayalam, there was Mohan, Jayendran and me. It was a big craze then. We used to refer to it as a postmodern literary co-operative, etc. But one by one, each of the members started hiding behind the flanks of various writers' forums. They were the smart ones. They got good reviews in magazines, and won endowments and awards.

'I called suddenly because a story of mine was published in the *Diego Daily* on Valentine's Day. Have you seen it? If you haven't, please try to get it and read it . . .'

I hadn't seen it. If I've to read all the stories published everywhere, I'll need to be on 24x7 like the banks' ATM ad. So I just skim through the titles. Sometimes, at the most, I read a paragraph, that's all. Jayendran used to say that for every novel that I got down to reading, I allowed a margin of fifty pages. From that point onwards, it was the duty of the writer to take me forward. But those days are gone. Now, if you can't buy a reader in the first five pages, then it's impossible to get him.

'*Diego Daily* gave a full page for my story, which opposes Valentine's Day celebrations. Our Rajanbabu sir liked the story very much.'

Diego Daily is the most prominent newspaper in Diego Garcia, and the only morning paper. The rest are eveningers—lousy ones that print TV news from the mainland. The *Daily* devotes one page each for every major language in Diego. It's a unique language daily. A whole page for a story—that too in Malayalam—is not a small thing.

'A doctor from City Hospital is going to translate it into English because he likes the story . . .' Mohandas kept on talking without waiting for replies. I felt disappointed. How many stories have I written! They had romance, history, sex, politics, criticism, but none of the editors sent me letters, no reader praised my stories. No one translated them into any other language. Here, a story, which I would have passed on, is getting translated into English. What had I got wrong?

'I called you to say something important. I'm writing a novel! You must have heard that *Pentasia This Month* is conducting a contest for the best novel. It can be written in any language. I'm going to submit my manuscript. Without winning awards, today's novels can't gain popularity.'

'What's the title of the novel?' I asked just for form's sake.

'Archipelago.'

My disinterest in listening to him till then gave way to shock. I was really shocked. 'When I said I'm writing, I meant I've completed three-fourths of it. Shall I read you a part of the first chapter?' he asked.

'No, perhaps another time.'

I disconnected the phone in fear.

Archipelago! You won't believe me, but really, really, that's the title I'd decided for my own novel. I had dreamt of it for a long time. How can a novel based on these islands have a name better than that! Pity, he had stolen that title. Oh god, was he also writing on the same subject and along the same lines? I have always dreaded that. After I get an idea for a story, I fear that someone in some other corner of the world has got the same idea and that he is competing with me in writing the story. So, I hurry up to finish the story and publish it before my faceless enemy does. Those were just fears, but the case of Mohandas was not like that. He had come very close to my subject. Now when I start writing my novel, it'll not be my enemy who will be writing the same story hiding in some unknown corner of the world, it'll be you, Mohandas Purameri! Only you. I'll be competing neck and neck with you. I'll finish writing the novel before you. I'll find a title better than your Archipelago. I'll win the contest. I ran to my study and doggedly began to write.

CUSTOMS OFFICER

ON A DAY when I got bored of writing, I took a boat to Port Louis. It is a small harbour town in Diego Garcia. It takes hardly fifteen minutes by boat from Seleucia to get there. Beyond the narrow alleys to the jetty and the bustling shops and St. Martins lay the main road to the port. Along the two-kilometre stretch are shady trees and open-air coffee shops, adding to the beauty of Port Louis. Tables and chairs spill onto the brick-laid road. Food is cooked fresh right in front of you. The aroma of coffee and ghee! It is my favourite hangout. I can sit in a corner, sip coffee and contemplate in peace. I can observe the arrivals and departures of the port workers, the hustle and the bustle. I can overhear the traders' and exporters' mathematics and mutterings. From these, I can find something for my novel. It is not being solitary in a room but being in a crowd that makes for better thinking. In each person's rush and panic and pain, there is a story. If I sit alone in a room, what story will I get; all I will be doing is staring at an empty mind. In any case, Momma wouldn't let me stay idle at home. 'What? Has Valyapapan's disease caught you too?'

I had hardly sat down after ordering a butter coffee when I heard someone call out. About four tables away, a young woman was waving at me. I didn't recognize her at first. She got up and walked up to me—Jesintha! I stood up in surprise. She was with me till Class VII at St. Joseph's. A Tamil. She had changed completely. Jeans, T-shirt, shades. There was only a distant resemblance to the dark, petite girl of my memory.

'How many years has it been! I'm amazed. We live in such a small place and still it took so much time for us to meet again!' She pulled up a chair and sat close.

'Really! It's not those who're far, but who're near who are difficult to meet. You're still in Peruntheruvu, aren't you?'

'No, we moved to Cornish two years ago. I was in Sri Lanka before that. I completed my higher studies there.'

Cornish! I was surprised. It's the area of Diego's newly rich. A man-made island filled with the villas of ministers, movie stars and businessmen. Jesintha there? I remember her family.

She must have perceived my astonishment. 'I'm currently with the port. A smart customs officer can now live at Cornish.' She smiled and got up. 'It's time to get to work. We'll meet again.' She strode past.

I was incredulous. Does a customs officer in Garcia earn enough to settle in Cornish? The bribes wouldn't be much—Diego is not a country with many restrictions or taxes. The Diego government allows free import of all products. The customs is just for name's sake, that's all. How was she earning so much? There must be something. I was unaware of the changing times. Was it the 'lag' from my education in Thiruvananthapuram, as everyone says?

DIVISION A

MOMMA WAS SWEEPING the house in the morning. Things were scattered outside. She was cursing the men in the family for letting the house get dusty and dirty. Once it was a family where women did not even look at the men. It's only during the heyday of a family that the men are held in esteem. Otherwise, they are destined to be abused by the women.

In the trash heaped outside, I spotted a photograph. One taken during my upper-primary schooldays at St. Joseph's during Class V. I picked it up and dusted it. I grieved that it had aged in such a short time. Some of the faces were lost, but none were unrecognizable. Partly through the photo and partly through memory, they were knowable. There was Sseri sir. In faded attire. He was our Malayalam teacher for a long time. A hard-core fan of Cherusseri's poems. His name was Surendran. We called him Sseri sir. He had come from Kerala to Diego to teach Malayalam. He was a native of Payyannur.

The first language in our school was English. French, Malagasy, Tamil, Divehi, Malayalam or Sinhala could be chosen as one's second language. Most would opt for their ancestral tongue as their second language. I chose Malayalam. That's how I ended up in Sseri sir's class.

Next in the photo was our class teacher, Monica D'Souza. She was a Goan, if I remember right. She was in the school only for a short time. Then the headmaster, William Hodges. He'd enter the classroom with the customary line: 'When I was in Ethiopia . . .'

There was Jesintha in her earlier form, in a wrinkle-free dress, deadly serious. There were eighteen of my classmates. I went through the faces and tried recalling the names of each one of them. To the left of Sseri sir were Anita and Supriya. To the right of William Hodges were Alexy and Jyoti. Behind them, standing in a row: Vinod, Babu, Senthil, Jesintha, another girl whose name I couldn't recollect, and Rahim.

Behind them, on the bench: I couldn't remember the first girl, then Leena, me, the boy next was an African, couldn't remember his name, Bilal, Seyfu, couldn't remember the next boy either, little Anita, and at last Daniel D'Silva.

Gopal P.V. was the only one missing in the photo. And from the world. A month before this photo had been taken, he died in a major boat accident, with sixty-three others.

I'd met Jesintha the day before. Here I was, with ambitions

to become the first novelist of the Malayalam Diaspora. And where was the rest of the class? Almost everyone of us had been together from Class I to X. We were in Division A, known to have the smartest boys and girls in the school. I'd already forgotten four names out of the nineteen. Would I be able to recognize them if I met them? Anita, Leena and Jyoti were the best not just in the class, but in the school. After them came Senthil, Vinod and Supriya. Seyfu and Babu were the brats of the class, and the best of the worst. Supriya was a good dancer. Anita used to sing and speak well. Vinod was talented in painting, and Rahim in acting. Where were they now? Where had they gone, what had they become, within these short years? We had predicted and dreamt that Anita would become a doctor, Leena a lawyer, Supriya an actress, Daniel D'Silva with his deep voice a radio anchor, and Rahim a stage actor. Had our predictions and dreams come true? If not, who had become what?

The curiosity of the first days turned into a strong desire later on. I had to find out. I had to know where each of them were and what levels they had reached in this short period. It may have been the amazing growth and change in Jesintha that stimulated my search. The rest of my days were spent thinking of a way to find them.

ORKUT

ONE WEEK OR a maximum of ten days—I thought I'd find all of them within that time. Such a small place. Walk twice through some four alleys and all of them will be found. That's how lightly I'd taken it. But I failed to find even one. Finally, I did a search on the social network, Orkut—the most advanced, convenient and simple means available. After an elaborate search, I managed to find just one person: Alexy. He was running an Ayurveda physiotherapy centre at Seychelles. I contacted him. He had no updates on anyone. It was like his life had been wholly transplanted from Garcia to Seychelles. He was that distanced from Garcia.

Even though I knew that only one per cent or so of our friends could be present on such social networks, I started a community there by the name of my school: St. Joseph's, Seleucia. I waited for days hoping that some of my classmates from some corner of the earth would become its members and thus I could get in touch with them. Many of my juniors in school joined the community, but not a single member from my class. And this was supposed to be the age of such school–college social gatherings. Especially after a movie on it came out in the mainland! Using new technologies, people were finding their oldest friends and arranging get-togethers. I felt deeply disheartened. Why was it that only my classmates were averse to such gatherings? Weren't they aware of these technological utilities? Didn't they use them? Had we all become so outdated that we could not figure out the virtual world?

But I didn't lose hope. I decided to meet Jesintha again. I was sure that through her, I'd be able to find at least one more person. For the next two days, in the hope of meeting her, I went and waited for long hours at the coffee shop in Port Louis. Either she didn't come on those days or I had missed her. I cursed myself for not asking for her mobile number when I met her last. However, I caught her on the third day, sitting under a tree. She ran towards me, saying, 'Hi!' She was with a friend. We ordered coffee, and while we were waiting for it, I casually asked her about our classmates. No idea where they are, she gestured. I shared my curiosity with her. Where will we go to find them—she was puzzled.

We can easily trace someone from a faraway village in a large country, she said, but to find even a single known person in the narrow streets of a town is next to impossible. In a village, every person is 'marked'. You could go to a particular location to find a particular person. Mostly, from birth to death, their location stays the same. But in a city, anyone can be anywhere. People keep moving all the time. Especially in places where there are temporary migrants and tenants. They come, they go. The whole demographic could change within a year. Go to any church. The ones whom you saw last year won't be the ones whom you'll see the next year. Go to any street. The ones who were there last year may not be there the next. Diego, too, has this dynamic character. It will be difficult to find our classmates and arrange a reunion.

I had to accept her hypothesis, sadly.

It was then that an incident happened, about four tables away from us. There was a gunshot. A person shuddered and fell to the ground before my eyes. People who were talking to him till then ran off in random directions. I saw one of them quite clearly. A couple of workers chased them, but none were caught.

Jesintha and I were among the crowd that flocked around the wounded guy. I tried to catch a glimpse of him. He was lying under the table. Some people pulled him up from there. He'd been shot in his chest. There was blood splattered all over his face. The crowd waited for the ambulance to come. Some started leaving the place.

'They shot a person in the open, in a public place, and fled. No one could catch them despite so many of us being here,' I said morosely. 'The Public Security will catch them,'

Jesintha said briskly. By then, the ambulance-boat had reached and he was shifted to it. It was a speedboat. It sailed away within minutes.

In a short while, the place returned to normal, as if nothing had happened. Jesintha returned to her seat and took up her coffee. I went and sat next to her. I no longer felt like drinking coffee. My mind was awash with the terrible incident. To witness someone falling to a bullet! But more than that, what baffled me was how quickly the crowd had overcome the incident. I would have been placid if it had happened in Mumbai or Karachi or Iraq. They were used to it. But here in Diego? To my knowledge, it was the first incident of its kind. Someone getting shot in a street! Had our people become so insensitive as not to get affected by that?

The Public Security officers arrived at the spot and started their investigation. They began by asking the people in the cafe to describe the incident. All of them shied away from it. When I was about to get up, Jesintha stopped me, pulling my hand. 'You don't go there and get involved. Let the Public Security do their job. We have not seen the incident. We have come here just now.'

'But, Jesintha, when such an incident occurs in our island, isn't it our duty to help the Public Security team? Shouldn't we give them the information they need?'

She made a face and then smiled. 'Yeah, right . . . our island . . . there is still a huge contest about who owns this land. Our island! Whatever. Anyhow, more than knowing who the killers are, you'll be stunned to know who the victim is.'

She got up, her bag on her shoulder. 'In your search for your classmates, the number has been reduced by one. The person who got shot was Senthil from our class.' She said it nonchalantly and walked away with her friend.

THE FACE OF DEATH

SENTHIL? OH MY god! And then Jesintha walked away so casually? In our class, Senthil, Jesintha and Daniel D'Silva were the Sri Lankans. Senthil and Jesintha were good friends. They used to come to the school and leave together. Both of them lived in Seleucia's Tamil colony, Cherar Peruntheruvu. Now, it was as if she didn't even care a bit for him; she had stood among the multitudes as an onlooker—and refrained from being even an eyewitness before the Public Security. He was among the smartest in our class. Though we didn't have any career prediction for him, nobody had thought he would end up being shot dead in the streets.

Though Jesintha was cavalier about what had occurred, I couldn't set it aside without knowing what had happened to Senthil. I left straight for City Hospital. All I could think about during the boat journey was Jesintha, not Senthil. Who would have thought she'd react like that?

How did she know so quickly that it was Senthil who got shot? How long had I stared at that face, hoping for a hint of life? I never realized it was him. And was she aware all along that Senthil was there? Then why didn't she tell me? I was more struck by Jesintha's reactions as an onlooker than by the mystery behind the gunning down of Senthil. If that was Jesintha's normal response to such an incident, then it is terrible how unfeeling the times have made us. If that wasn't her normal response . . . if she had some ulterior motive . . . was she . . . involved in the murder?

I had to sweat a lot at City Hospital to get any information about him. I finally got to know that he was in the ICU. It was easy to figure out that it was just a medical formality. A medical hypocrisy—to show that all attempts had been made to save him, when, in reality, he had dropped dead long back! As I'd supposed, he was shifted to the mortuary without much delay. When they brought the body out, I lifted the sheet and looked at the face another time. Though Jesintha had said it was Senthil, till that moment I had my doubts. But now I was certain. Despite the coagulated blood, I could easily identify the Class V face! When the corpse was brought out, there were two Public Security officials accompanying it. As the only person who went there looking for Senthil, I was stopped and questioned thoroughly. They were rude to me. Not many in the town had heard the news. Hence, they wanted to know how I came to know about it. I tried bluffing, saying a friend had told me, but they didn't let me get away with that. Jesintha's warning wouldn't let me admit that I had indeed witnessed the incident. I couldn't explain my behaviour. But while standing before the Public Security officers, I felt it was the right thing to do.

They asked a lot of questions such as how I knew him, what my relationship was with him, when I had met him last, etc. Finally, only when I told them my address did they loosen up. At least, some of them still remembered the influence the Andrapper family had in Diego Garcia. Even then, they let me go from the hospital only after warning me that I would be called if they needed me.

While I was walking down the hospital corridor, I ran into a friend from my Thiruvananthapuram days. Johnny. We used to go to the mainland together. And also return together, after the vacations. That was the connection. He had also studied in a college in Thiruvananthapuram.

Honestly, he had been nowhere in my memory till then. I had often reminisced about my life in Thiruvananthapuram, those journeys and those days. But not even once had his face sprung up in my mind. It's surprising. I didn't spare a thought for a person whom I had known for three years. He and all the things related to him had disappeared from my mind. Many such faces and incidents have been lost to us for eternity, haven't they? Some of those faces would have been of our dearest ones, those whom we have respected the most; some of the experiences we forgot had probably affected us deeply. How does the mind erase such things?

With these thoughts in mind, I deliberated on my life for a long time. I tried to walk through each and every moment in the past. I didn't succeed much, but I recollected a train journey from my childhood. In that crowded compartment, I had travelled squatting on the floor. Though there are no trains in Diego, I was sure that it was not a dream. I asked Momma about that journey. When we would drop anchor in Kanyakumari, we used to catch a train to a relative's house in Alappuzha, but never in anything but first class, Momma asserted. She couldn't even imagine a journey sitting on the floor. I asked everyone at home about such a trip. If I had gone on a journey at that age, it couldn't have been alone. Some elder would have accompanied me. But no one knew of any such journey. So, when or to where did I make such a trip? All I could manage to gather was that it was either a dream or a journey made in my previous life.

Anyway, I could recognize Johnny as soon as I saw him. Not just that, I even managed to retrieve the memories of those days.

'I'm with the hospital administration,' Johnny said. 'Why are you here?'

I told him.

He took me to his office. Served me coffee. Inquired about my house and job and marriage. I quipped that the house was where it always was, and that nothing had happened with job and marriage.

'Why would someone like you who sits on cash need a job?' Johnny was half serious, half joking. There was a tint of jealousy in his question. A common envy that one who has to work for a living feels for another who doesn't. When I was about to leave, he held my hands. 'Nonetheless, we have travelled together for ages. Please tell your family to arrange a promotion for me. You guys have good contacts. You can get it done.'

Not knowing what to say, for a minute I stood bewildered. Then I said OK, nodding my head.

GEOGRAPHY

DIEGO GARCIA IS a land of lagoons. Located 1600 kilometres away from the Indian subcontinent, which we islanders refer to as the mainland, at 7°19'S latitude and 72°25'E longitude, Diego Garcia is the largest land mass in the Chagos Archipelago that also include Eagle, Three Brothers, Egmont, Nelsons, Salomon and Danger. Our neighbours are Tanzania, Madagascar, Mauritius, Seychelles, Zanzibar, Maldives and Sri Lanka. The islands of Pentasia, Seleucia and Venecia, often called the Three Sisters, constitute our hub. Then there are the small islets, more than forty of them, including Sarthe, Cordoba, Parana, Sao Paulo, Bahia, Mahala, Bourdon, Messia and Messina. Our prosperity lies in the lagoons that blanket the island. The dry land rim, with a width of 2.4 kilometres, separates the fresh water from the sea. Lagoons divide our cities. Lagoons are our pathways. Our lives are moored to the lagoons. Houses that extend into the lagoons; front yards that walk up to the lagoons; shops that open up to the lagoons; churches with steps leading up from the lagoons; temples that face the lagoons; mosques that summon to prayer beside the lagoons; schools ... offices ... hotels ... bars ...

Pentasia on the western-most side is the capital of Diego Garcia. The Senate Hall and other main government offices are in Pentasia. It is twenty-five kilometres long and up to three kilometres wide. Serpentine, it lies in the Indian Ocean. The Port Louis harbour is at its western end. The other two islands are smaller. The eastern island of Venecia has the St. Raphael International Airport. Seleucia in the middle is the main residential area.

In Diego, cars can be found only in Pentasia. That too, very few, and mostly used for official purposes. Other motor vehicles are rare. Some use cycles, some bikes. Canoes and boats are our primary mode of transport. There'll hardly be a house without them. My house has six canoes, four small boats and three speedboats. A long time ago, it seems the family had 400 canoes, sixty boats and four vessels. All that grandeur disappeared before I was born. On 13 May 1973, to be precise.

It was on that day that the French transferred Diego's administration to the British. Before that, the Andrapper family were the real lagoon moguls of Diego.

According to recorded history, most of the people now in Diego Garcia are migrants or their descendants. Most of the migration to Diego took place from Kerala, Tamil Nadu and Andhra Pradesh from the mainland, and Sri Lanka, Mali, Mozambique and Zanzibar.

The world-famous explorer Vasco da Gama, who set off from the West in search of black gold, first landed on the shores of Diego Garcia, mistaking it for Malabar. 'Here we have reached, friends . . . the land we've been searching for. That shore . . .' exclaimed da Gama as he jumped into the waters and ran to the shore. But he was to be disappointed soon. In his log entry, he described Diego Garcia as deserted: a wasteland of lagoons and swampy bayous, a place that gave us hope of our destination and which killed our joy.

We have been here for ages, we are the sons of the soil, the land belongs to us; it was our ancestors who battled da Gama with stones and slings to stop him from setting his foot here, and it is because of that shame and anger he wrote that there were no inhabitants: These are the claims of the Dhivehi-speaking Chagossian tribes that echo from the mikes during every election campaign. On hearing that, my Valyapapan has a way of emerging from the top floor and walking down, dragging his feet. What follows is a string of abuses, facing the lake. 'Sons of bitches! All your fathers had been entrapped and brought from the African wilds by my forefathers. You may not know, but I know . . . there were some langurs too. When taken off the boat, your fathers and langurs all looked alike. That was their condition. Now your women are on a breeding spree. For numbers to show strength in elections! Breed! Breed a lot. Who cares. But remember one thing. We made you human beings . . . my great-grandfathers . . . Get lost! Your land indeed! I'll take anything, but never say this land is yours . . .'

Then a long sigh would be addressed to us onlookers. Savages, langurs and wild peacocks. These three were brought here by our forefathers. Savages slaved in coconut plantations. Langurs made for a good tonic. Acrobatics followed peacock oil massages. And liquor with meat from Africa. Hah! Those were the days.

Valyapapan would then return to the top floor. It's been more than three decades since he took to staying behind closed doors. He comes out only on such occasions—to curse at someone.

I don't know how much truth there is in his words. Chagossians, the African natives, are relatively poor and a minority in Diego. It was poverty, I thought, that was the reason behind their increasing number of children. That there could be politics attached to it, I came to know later. Well, whatever the case of the Chagossians, Valyapapan could be right about the secret behind the many peacocks and langurs in the island, which do not have many wild animals otherwise: migration.

If you come to Garcia someday, it is quite a feast for the eyes. Scores of peacocks dancing in full plumage at the lakeside. Peacocks combing the palm groves like hens. Peacocks hopping on the verandas of every house. Langurs running across the streets of Pentasia. Langurs peeling off coconut husk for a meal. Langurs swimming through the lakes. Diego's present population is five lakhs: 28 per cent Hindus, 45 per cent Roman Catholics, 8 per cent Muslims, 12 per cent Buddhists, very few Jews, the rest Protestants, Jains and African tribes. In 1981, Diego's Senate, through an order, banned all kinds of immigration. Instead, it installed a visa system that every job-seeker from abroad has to renew once in three years.

There are records that say the first inhabitants of Diego Garcia were my forefather Hormees Avira Andrapper and family. It was the year 1713.

THE KING OF DREAMS

WHILE RETURNING HOME, I thought about Johnny's comment about me sitting on cash. Did the people in Diego still have such a misconception about the Andrapper family? Must be. How our lives are built on the illusions of others.

It was as part of a deal with the French East India Company that Hormees Avira Andrapper migrated to Diego in the early eighteenth century. Possessed of such an advantage, my family has stayed here in all prosperity since then. There had been difficulties in the beginning, of inhabiting a deserted island. But with the help of the mighty French East India Company, who could provide enough slaves, cash and other amenities, it wouldn't have been that tough.

They cultivated palm trees not only in the barren lands of Diego, but also in those of the nearby islands of Eagle, Three Brothers and Danger. Sugarcane was grown and swamps were cleared for paddy. They grew cotton, banana, yam, tuber, tapioca, tobacco and a multitude of vegetables. Within just two centuries, they raised Diego to a rich and prosperous nation. Now when you look at the streets and buildings and offices of Pentasia and Seleucia, it doesn't seem as though the changes took place within such a short span of time. It wouldn't be a surprise if some tourist wrote that this city was as old as Venice.

The French ruled Diego for two centuries. News of the freedom struggle taking place in the mainland reached us too, but did not influence us enough to make us win our freedom. The French had lost all their prowess on the waters, and the realization that they couldn't gain much by ruling Diego had prompted them to retreat.

My family had believed till the last minute that as a reward for loyally serving them for two centuries, the French would confer the power to rule over Diego Garcia to the Andrapper family. That they would be made the kings of the land. It wasn't just the Andrapper family—the whole island expected it.

My family had even started preparing for it soon after the rumours of a French exit started doing the rounds. There were minor fights over who should be the king, but finally, it was decided that it would be Valyapapan. So, when the shocking news came about Diego coming under British rule, the person who was affected the most was my Valyapapan, who had kept his crown ready. He was thirty-two then. He had just returned after higher studies in Paris. A perfect candidate in every way. But that dream never materialized. And he withdrew to the upper storey. Since then, Valyapapan has never come down, other than a few times to shout at someone. To understand the pain of losing a country, you just need to know one thing about Valyapapan: he still strictly follows the diet of Portugal's last emperor, Manual II. 'Yes, meal by meal, course by course, down to the last crumb I do follow the typical daily menu of the great Manual II. Because we two are of the same stature,' Valyapapan says once in a while, but who knows if that made him feel good or was causing him to fall apart?

The British then created a senate merely as a formality. During the first election for the chancellor's post, everyone had forced Valyapapan to contest. Victory was certain, it seems. But he turned it down, saying he couldn't abide by Britain's puppet government. He hadn't quite wanted anything short of being king. Holding close a crown that he got from the mainland, he has continued to be idle for the past thirty years or so. Can a fallen dream shatter a man so badly, however big the dream?

A GIFT

NEXT MORNING, I looked for reports of Senthil's death in the *Diego Daily*. To my surprise, nowhere in the paper was there any news of it. The *Daily* was the only newspaper in Diego. Didn't it owe the people information about what was happening in the country? Was it because there were no competitors that the paper could get away with its irresponsible policy? I called up their office and shouted at them. But it was as though such an incident had never taken place in Diego Garcia. That was their response. I was ridiculed, asked if I was drunk, and that I should endure my hangover and not take it out on journalists the next morning.

I didn't feel like giving up. After a shower, feeling fresh, I set off for Port Louis. My plan was to meet Jesintha if possible, and ask her if she'd got more details about the incident. But she was not in any of the coffee shops. I examined the spot where the shooting had taken place. It had all been cleaned up, leaving no trace or hint of such an incident. At the spot where Senthil was shot, a port worker sat having his coffee. I went and sat next to the bench for a closer look. The bench with the blood stains had been taken away. There were no signs on the ground where Senthil had fallen. As if to place an order for a coffee, I went close to the owner and asked in a whisper if he knew anything more about the previous day's incident. He stared at me suspiciously and turned to take someone's order like he knew nothing. I asked a waiter the same thing. He, too, walked away. I realized it'd be futile to stay there and so I left for City Hospital. Hoping to get more details from there, I went and met Johnny. 'Other than what you've told me, I haven't heard anything more from anyone in the hospital,' he said. 'You have probably got it wrong.'

He was doubtful, yet he eagerly joined me in checking the documents at the ICU. It was clear that his heart was set more on my family's recommendation for his promotion. I didn't bother to heed it.

The ICU yielded a bigger surprise. No one in the name of Senthil had been admitted there. With the help of one of Johnny's friends, I checked the documents again and again. Not only was Senthil's name missing in their entries, but also no one with a bullet hit had been brought to the hospital the previous evening. Next, I went through the list of people who had died in the ICU. There were three causes: two cardiac arrests, and one of old age. No corpse identified as Senthil had been brought in. The mortuary had not taken in a single body the previous day. Where had Senthil been taken to? Where did his body go?

I had seen him getting shot with my own eyes. I had seen him being moved to the ambulance-boat. Then I'd seen the dead body being taken out of the ICU and sent to the mortuary. And the Public Security had even questioned me.

'You must have hallucinated,' Johnny said, to comfort me.

'What are you saying, Johnny? Hallucinated! I told you about it yesterday, didn't I?'

'That's true. But what can I say about something that is not in the records. Anyway, why do you bother? If someone has died, his family will take care of it. Come, let's have tea.'

With all the doubts coiling up in my mind, I accompanied him to the canteen. As we had tea, Johnny kept rattling on about the advantages of getting a promotion. My mind was on Senthil. I only half heard what he said. That if he gets a promotion, he'll be included in the committee that goes abroad to recruit doctors and nurses. I heard him doubting how much good just a salary can do these days. I heard him smacking his head and railing that for a common man to build a house in Diego, he would need to pay off a loan for forty years at least. I heard him raging that even a dog wouldn't care for a normal and virtuous life.

He reminded me again while I was leaving that he wouldn't get a promotion in the next ten years without a senate-level recommendation and that he was better qualified than many of the people there.

As I was walking out of the hospital, I suddenly ran into my erstwhile smart, pretty and energetic classmate, Anita.

It had become a habit for me to match every new face I met with those of my class. For some strange reason, I had failed to do that with Senthil. But in Anita's case, I made no mistake at all. I recognized her within just three seconds of her passing by. At the same time, I registered one more thing. It was not in Class V that we two got separated, but after another seven years together, in Class XII. By then, everyone had grown much more. But I didn't remember the mature faces of anyone. My memory was marooned in the photo that I found at home. It is with the faces in that photo that I compare every face I see. But when I saw Anita, I recollected her Class X face. Her face was now more identical to that.

She couldn't identify me at all. It took a lot of effort. I realized it only then that though I could recognize myself, for someone who was meeting me after a long time, I had changed a lot.

She, too, had changed. Her vigour and smartness seemed to have withered away. The level of energy she had as a child had seemed as though it would last forever. She was exceptionally active. No event took place in school without her participation. She used to sing well, study well, elocute well. She was the school leader. There was no trace of that in the pale version of Anita standing before me. If I had seen her after another ten years, I probably wouldn't have been so surprised.

When she finally figured out who I was, she grasped my hands. 'Where have you been all this time?'

'Where were you?' I responded to her with a similar question.

'I've been here, in this City Hospital, for the past five years.'

'Are you a doctor?'

'Me? No, no, I wanted to, but my father couldn't afford it. So, after Class XII, I went to Mangalore to do pharmacy.'

'It is really sad that education in our country so expensive that going abroad to study is cheaper. How bad is the state of our country!' I sympathized with her.

'What is your state?' she asked.

'College in Thiruvananthapuram. Now, with the excuse of writing a novel, I'm doing nothing and sitting at home, like the Keralites.'

Anita introduced me to the person with her. 'This is my husband, Wilson. He works at the lab here. Did you recognize him?' She turned to her husband.

'Looks very familiar,' Wilson said while shaking hands.

'The one I talk about . . . the Andrapper kid who was in my class . . . this is him!'

'Oh, he is the one? I've heard of you. Pleased to meet you. Okay, you guys talk, I have to rush.'

I asked Anita about our other classmates. I told her about the photo I'd found in my house after all these years. She knew only about Bilal who had been studying medicine in Mangalore when she was there. He was in Australia now. For some reason, I purposefully stayed tight-lipped about Senthil and Jesintha.

We kept on talking for the sake of talking. Her excitement lasted even until we were about to take leave. She grabbed my hands again. She panicked at having nothing to give me even though this encounter was sudden. Then she dug into her purse and gave me two photographs.

'They are my kids. What else can I give you?'

Then she left. I stood there for a while holding those photos. I stood there as if I was puzzled as to what to do.

Other than meeting Jesintha a few days ago, since we had left school, I hadn't met any of my classmates, even by chance. But after the desire struck me, how fast it was happening! One by one, I'm running into them. . . Is it because we don't yearn for them strongly enough that we don't get most things?

There was a reason for thinking so after meeting Anita. She was a girl whom I'd liked in school to the extent of wanting to go to her house and asking for permission to marry her after I had grown up and was capable of making a good living. That never worked out. Somehow, I never had enough confidence to consider myself good enough to lay claim to her. While in class, she never talked more than a word or two to me. On the few occasions I tried to express my love, she avoided me tactfully. Some friends who used to tease her about me were silenced with warnings. I did not get even a slight indication of friendship or love from Anita. We were two strangers in the same class. And now? What could have been the cause of such a show of affection?

How many thoughts must pass through the minds of others of which we are unaware! If I were not to ask Anita, how different would be her response! I put her children's photos in my pocket. They lay close to my heartbeats.

PROMISE

AFTER REACHING HOME, I was in a hangover called Anita. Everything she'd ever done at school started flashing before my eyes. Anita singing, Anita delivering a speech, Anita taking the pledge in the assembly, Anita jumping up with answers in class even before the teacher completed the questions, Anita coming first in all the exams, being praised by teachers, me looking at her in awe, Anita walking up to the stage to collect prizes and returning proudly, Anita sitting with an open book in the boat after school, I ogling at her tiny breasts and chubby cheeks, doubting if there could be such a beauty anywhere else in the world . . . a lagoon of memories. I sailed through it for a long while. All that time, a nameless agony filled me. She had not flown that far and high; then why did I fail to make her mine? That was the reason for the pain.

But the agony lasted only for a short while. By then, the Senthil puzzle resurfaced and enwrapped me again. Isn't a lost friend more serious than a failed dream? And not just simply lost, but murdered, creating in its wake a plethora of mysteries.

I quickly stepped into the nooks and crannies of the case. But how do I get to know what exactly had happened? I'm not crazy enough to think that it was all an illusion. I've never experienced psychotic delusions. Even if I have, it is yet to be proven. I couldn't sit still. I left home, ignoring Momma's query of where I was off to first thing in the morning. In fact, I didn't know where I was heading. I had to go somewhere. Somewhere where I could find the truth: that was all I had in mind. I considered the various options. It was when the boat almost reached Pentasia that a face appeared in my mind. I redirected the boat to Seleucia.

I went directly to the North Seleucia Public Security Office. The investigation director, Stephen Pereira Andrapper, was a distant cousin of Papa, and an officer known for his honesty. He had played a pivotal role in solving many major cases in Diego. He had come home last month to visit Valyapapan. We had briefly chatted about Martin, his youngest son, now in Canada.

There was no one better than Stephen uncle to tell me what had actually happened. My plan was to meet him and explain the previous day's incident. I had to wait in front of the office for a long time. There was a big crowd, including weeping, wailing, raging and shouting women of all ages. When I asked someone in the crowd what was happening, his explanation was shocking. Most of the people were relatives of youth who had been forcibly taken into custody. Most of them didn't know why the arrests had been made or where they had been taken. I couldn't quite figure out what could be the crime that got so many young people arrested. But the government would always have its own justifications.

When I finally managed to get in, he received me warmly. He asked about Valyapapan and Papa and Momma. He called for coffee and inquired why I had come.

I narrated the whole sequence of events that had taken place so far. After listening to me, he confirmed that if such an incident had occurred in Diego, he would definitely be one of the people informed about it. He called two of his junior officers right then and asked if there had been any shooting reported in Port Louis recently. They were also in the dark. He also checked the secret files of the Investigation Directorate. There, too, nothing was to be found. He shrugged helplessly. 'What can I say about an incident not recorded in the case diary of a disciplined and efficient public security department?'

However, he assured me that he was now as interested in the case as I was and that he'd look into what had actually taken place. I trusted him. Because it was not the usual promise of a police officer to a common man. It was a promise one Andrapper was making to another. It was a promise that would be kept.

MISSING PERSON

I WAITED FOR three days expecting a call from Stephen Pereira Andrapper. But nothing happened. On all three days, I went to Port Louis, in the hope of meeting Jesintha. That too didn't happen. I stuck around the coffee shop for a while in the hope of some clue, some hint of suspicion. Nothing. Everyone was content with their own concerns. But what more can you expect from those who've forgotten a murder soon after it happened?

I felt my life was like a grounded boat, tied to the stake. Either I should write the novel so that I could believe that I was living through my self-expression; unfortunately, that wasn't going anywhere. Else, I should get a solid clue about the missing Senthil. Then I could find some relief in thinking that I was living for a cause. That too wasn't happening. I felt contempt for myself.

But I was not willing to give up. Determined to meet Stephen Pereira, I went to Seleucia's North Public Security Office again. It was crowded like the previous time. Superiors and juniors hurrying from one room to another with files and papers. No one even had the time to respond to my question whether Investigation Director Stephen Pereira was present.

Wasn't all that commotion taking place to ensure the efficiency of the Public Security? We ought not disturb it. So, I had to wait there for a long time. At last, my turn came. Seeing me, Stephen uncle scratched his head. '*Che*, the matter you mentioned that day, I forgot about that completely in this mess. Now what shall we do . . .?'

I was sad, angry, and fuming. Last time, I had the feeling that I was taken seriously. By now, he ought to have gathered some information. I had thought he might have forgotten to call me because of his busy schedule. Now, after I had reported such an important issue . . .

'So, you were saying . . . who is it that's missing . . .?'

'A friend of mine. He didn't go missing, he was murdered.' He understood the change of tone in my voice.

'Yes, yes. But that is something we have to prove.'

'We should prove. If you look into it, it'll be done.'

'I'll do one thing. I'll introduce one of my officers to you. You talk to him in detail. I'll follow it up then.' He rang for a peon. He mentioned some officer's name and told him to accompany me to his cabin. My only option was to follow the peon.

He took me to the office of Chief Investigator Vijay Mullikratnam. A rough guy. He looked as if he was angry at the world. He behaved as if I was a suspect. I somehow managed to explain the situation to him.

'Dude, it is very strange! First of its kind ever in Diego. By the way, how was the missing person connected to you?

'He was one of my friends.'

'How long had you known him?

'We studied together till high school.'

'What was your relationship with him in recent times?'

'We had none. We'd not met in more than a decade.'

'What was his name?'

'Senthil.'

'House?'

'Don't know. Somewhere in Peruntheruvu.'

'Occupation?'

'Don't know.'

'Address?'

'Don't know.'

'Don't know his house. Don't know his job. Don't know his address. Was not in touch with him for ten years. And you have come to complain that the guy is missing . . . Dude, do you know that someone going missing means he is not available at his address? So, if you don't know his address, on what basis are you saying that he is missing?'

'I told you, sir. He didn't go missing, he was killed.'

'Look, whether he was killed or is alive is not to be decided by you, but by the Public Security. The main issue in your story is that a person went missing after being admitted to a hospital . . . I'll ask you one thing. When someone is missing, normally who should be filing a complaint? You say you had no recent relationship with him, or his relatives?'

I had no answer. That was something I hadn't considered at all. So, it meant his family had not filed a complaint . . . Or was it not Senthil who was killed? Was Jesintha wrong in assuming the man was Senthil?

Mullikratnam seemed to understand my confusion.

'Since when is he missing according to you?'

'Sir, he didn't go missing . . .'

'Ssh . . . I told you . . . don't try to teach law to an

investigating officer. Dude, your relation with the director is limited to the home. Okay. Tell me . . .'

'The incident happened four days ago . . .'

'Listen, the Public Security at Diego Garcia has not yet received any complaint about a missing person.'

'Sir, maybe it wasn't Senthil, maybe it was someone else.'

'Dude, are you making fun of me? First you said it was Senthil. Now you are saying it may not be Senthil. Do you have any mental illness?'

'Not that, sir. Someone has been killed. And his body gone missing. My complaint is about him.'

'Don't worry, dude. You are experiencing the delusions of a teenager! It'll be all right when you get married. Anyway, since you've come here, give a written petition that your friend has gone missing. Only if you insist you want to. Then let me investigate.'

With much reluctance, I submitted a written complaint that Senthil was missing. The reason for my reluctance was that Senthil was not 'missing'.

MASTERPIECE

I WAS NOT at all satisfied with that visit. Especially the conversation with Vijay Mullikratnam. I had not gone there to complain about Senthil's disappearance. I also didn't want the 'missing' person to be Senthil. I was merely reporting an incident. One that I had witnessed. One that had not been reported by any media the next day. And my strange experiences at City Hospital when I inquired about the incident. But Mullikratnam took it all so lightly. Was his indifference natural or was it purposeful? If it was natural, didn't that mean I had failed to communicate the seriousness of the incident to him? If I couldn't convince even one person about something, how was I going to write a novel that would influence society? But if Mullikratnam's indifference was on purpose . . .? That meant the Public Security department had something to hide. Someone, if not Senthil, had been gunned down in Port Louis. And the Public Security didn't want anyone to know about it. What was the reason for it?

The more I dug, the more mysterious it became. To loosen the tangle a bit, I needed to confirm if it was indeed Senthil who was killed. And whoever it was, I needed to know why no complaint had been filed at the Public Security department about it.

I took another look at my school photo. It was to see Senthil again. However familiar we are with them, however much we may have seen them, most faces are not known to us in their details. Mostly they stay in our mind as schemas. Some special aspects. A nose. A neck. A head. A brow. Eyes. So, any one similarity can lead to mistaken identities. As I kept staring at Senthil's face in that old photo, it seemed like it was different from the face I had in mind. When I compared this face with the one I had seen outside the ICU, I felt it was indeed Senthil, and then again I thought it wasn't him. I was losing my mind.

Momma had noticed the change in me. I, who usually stayed in my room or terrace with a book, I, whom she shouted at asking if I was also planning to become like Valyapapan, had not been home in the past few days. But she didn't know where I was going or what I was up to. She knew only that I had been a bit disturbed for some days.

I was experiencing the repercussions of going out for a day and facing one incident. What would be the situation of someone who constantly interacts with society and partakes in its issues? What would be the range of his experiences? I got the sense that it was a person who goes through a lot of such experiences regularly who ought to become a novelist, and not those who writhe as a result of one experience, like me. What would be the stories they could tell you? What would be the power of their writing?

After a long time, probably for the first time since my Thiruvananthapuram days, I went out and got drunk. Seleucia had no scarcity of bars. Every jetty had a bar. And there were bars that one could step into straight from the boat.

When I returned, unusually, Papa was waiting for me.

He took me to the bar on the top floor. 'I don't want anything to drink. I had a little when I was out,' I said to him when he took out a bottle.

'I know that you have the capacity to have one more.'

Our relationship was not constrained, not like a normal father–son bond. I could say anything to him, and he never tried to impose his likes on me. Each one should decide for himself what he wants to be in life, that was his policy. Though he had not really supported my decision of going to Thiruvananthapuram to learn Malayalam, he was the only one in the family who didn't oppose it. He was never a dreamer like Valyapapan. He was studying in Paris when power changed hands in Diego. He did not regret the Andrappers not inheriting the power to rule from the French. He completed his studies and joined what could be called Diego's Reserve Bank. He held a senior position there. He was past retirement age, but the government didn't want him leave. He lived well, on a middling salary. A pure bureaucratic gentleman.

'How old are you?' he asked, offering a whisky with soda.

That was not his usual type of question. It was a toehold for some serious discussion.

'You know it better than me,' I retorted.

'I know it, but I asked to make sure you remember it. I believe that whatever be the field, one should have started work on one's masterpiece before the age of thirty. If he hasn't, that means he is not a genius. You don't have many years left to discover that, do you?'

'A rare flow of philosophy from Papa,' I teased him.

'Anyone who looks at life with a realistic eye will have a little bit of philosophy to share. You studied Malayalam for three years. What's the contribution you gave back to Malayalam? You went there to learn it. That's fine. That's what you wanted. But have you or the language got anything fruitful out of it? Okay, you said you wanted to become a novelist. An ambition of very few people. Good choice. Any father would be proud to have a gentleman-writer as their son. But you could have written in the universal language of English. You have the talent for that. It would bring you fame and prestige. But then, you said you wanted to write in Malayalam. To back it up, you cited the case of the African authors who moved to England and France, and continue to write in their mother tongue. They have only a small readership. I didn't say anything. Okay, but where is your contribution to Malayalam?'

'Papa, in a single day, one can become a ruler. A chancellor. A dacoit. A rich man. Even an accountant like you, Papa. But it is impossible to become a novelist overnight.'

'Impossible. Unless you have dedication. An extreme desire to excel in the chosen field. You don't have it. You can write in any language. If it's good, the world will find your book and read it. But it has to be written. Or else, it can't be read.

Momma said you haven't been at your desk for a week now. You are never at home. You are roaming around unnecessarily. Did you go to meet Stephen today?'

'Oh, okay. So, that is the gist of this long discourse, right? Why did I go to meet Stephen uncle? You must have got the answer from your source. Why should I give it to you?'

'Did you file any complaint with the Public Security department?'

'Yes, I did. That one of my friends has gone missing.'

'You should withdraw it tomorrow.'

'Did they get any information on him?'

'Whether they find him or not, what's your interest in it? Who is he to you? Son, complaints should always be given by those who have a claim on the missing person.'

'Papa, this is not a missing-person case as you think. It is a murder. I saw it with my own eyes. It wasn't just me, at least a hundred people were witness to it. Or can't we talk about it in this country?'

'Why don't the others open their mouth? Because it's none of their business. If you want to be a writer, become one. Remove everything else from your mind. Why should you take up unnecessary issues? What's your benefit in that?'

'But I have not committed any mistake, Papa.'

'You should never go to Public Security to get into the affairs of someone who is a stranger to you. You don't know the complications involved. We'll get dragged into a huge mess. Don't you know the rules of the land? You won't be able to even leave the country without clearing the mess.'

'That's okay. I'm not going to leave the country any time soon.'

'Says who? I've decided to send you to Canada or

Australia or Portugal. For some higher studies. You know the achievements of your classmates.'

'But Papa knows that I'm writing my novel.'

'Who said you can't do that too? But you haven't proved yet that you can earn a living just by being a writer. Not that there are no such writers. There are. Dan Brown, Roland Barthes, Paulo Coelho, Orhan Pamuk and many others. But you don't have their discipline or style or their marketing. And son, wherever you are in the world, you will be able to write what is destined to be written by you. You said the novel is about Diego. It's better to write it from outside the country than from within. Then the work will have new perspectives. New views. It'll then be known as an international novel rather than just a regional novel.'

'I know these are not your concerns. This has got to do with the complaint I've filed. Someone has fired up Papa. Or Papa is a supporter of the Public Security department. All you guys have something to hide . . .'

'No, I'm your supporter. Your victories mean a lot to me. I can't stand you losing focus. Ours is a collapsing family. In the common man's eye, we are still rich. Our fall is visible only when we compare our current assets with those before the French retreat. When we compare ourselves to the status of a newly rich man in Cornish, we are mere worms. You're the one who'll change our status, that's my dream. But now I fear for you. History proves that one who takes on others' deeds has always failed.'

I didn't want to extend the conversation further. I got up and went to my room.

However, any hope of support from either Stephen Pereira Andrapper or the Public Security died that night.

2

Thursday Market

I FELT A sort of fondness and favour towards this half-baked story that I never had for the dozens of stories I had heard before. It was not because there was something novel about the story, but there was no extravagant exaggeration stuffed in it to grab my attention. Because of that, I was curious to know what happened later.

Where could I get the rest of his life story? Whom should I approach for it? After having written the opening section so well, what fearful thing had happened to stop him? Had the police snatched him?

Had he hidden clues in the first section as to who had the rest of the manuscript? To be honest, even after reading it many times, I couldn't find any clues. In the portion that he sent, he has mentioned the names of more than twenty people, from Mohandas to Mullikratnam. How would I know who among the lot has the next part? Even if I come to know, how would I contact them from this far? I was in the dark.

That's how I presented it at the Thursday Market. This was our name for a group of close friends. From global warming to the increasing cost of cashew nuts, from Idi Amin to Iyob's books, everything comes to the table at our Thursday Market. Anil, E.A. Salim, Nibu whom we call Achachan (Grandfather), Sudhi Mashu, Pattar Biju, Saju who blogs under the name of Nattapranthan (Mad Man), and I, that's all of us. During a discussion about my new novel, I brought this topic before them, as a challenge to their investigative skills. Then everyone wanted to listen to the story. I took a printout and brought it to the assembly. Mashu read it aloud.

'A stupid guy good enough to become a novelist!' Achachan Nibu was the first to respond. No one reacted for or against it. Nibu explained his comment. 'If I was in his shoes, before approaching the police, I would have done three things. One,' he said, counting with his fingers, 'I would have caught the murder visuals with my mobile phone. Two, as any citizen journalist, I would send that video to a channel for telecast. Three, if no one was willing to show it, I'd have posted it on YouTube. Any of these actions would have naturally put the police on the defensive.'

'Nibu, that's logical when we sit here and think about it calmly,' Anil said. 'But, for these three things to happen, he should have had a mobile phone with camera. He should also have been aware that the police was not going to take up the case. But that's not what happened.'

'From what we know, he belongs to an extremely rich family in the country. A leaner elephant is also an elephant. So, let's leave the camera phone part,' E.M. Salim said. 'But I agree with what Anil said next. He couldn't have thought of such a thing then.'

'He had another option,' Nattapranthan said. 'He could have blogged about what happened. Then, the people who had witnessed or heard of the event would have posted comments, and perhaps helped him out. Why didn't he do that?'

'We are now debating how he should have reacted to a particular incident in his life,' I interfered. 'That's not my point. How can we get the rest of the story? Which character do you think has possession of it? What's the hidden clue, and where is it?'

The assembly calmed down for a while. There was a shadow of inefficacy in that silence.

'Benyamin, are you taking this seriously?' Sudhi Mashu asked me after some time.

'Yes, why?'

'The novelist mentioned in this . . . what's his name? We don't know. Let's call him Mr Andrapper for now. You are going to face the same problem that he did.'

'I don't understand what you mean,' said Salim.

'Our man is working on a new novel. If in the middle of it, he goes after this story, he won't be able to complete the novel. We don't have a Papa here to give him a telling-off.'

Mashu was worried about the novel I was working on—set in the Nedumbassery airport and the lives around it. In fact, Andrapper's father's words had motivated me to get back to my novel.

'If all of you cooperate in unravelling this mystery, I can manage the novel,' I said.

'Well, we can start a blog on behalf of Andrapper and publish what we have. We might get responses,' Nattapranthan said.

'The idea is fine,' Biju said, 'but there is a catch. This was sent to Benyamin in secret. We shouldn't make it public. Not just that, the blog may not reach the person whom we want to contact. Also, we'll be in danger if the wrong person reads it. We don't know who this guy is or what else he has written.'

We were quiet. Pattar Biju was right.

'One week!' said Salim. 'This puzzle, I'm now naming it Operation Diego Garcia—we'll come up with a solution before our next Thursday Market.'

On that note, we split. About three days after that, Pattar called me. 'Benya, I see some light. Yesterday, I came across this new catalogue of Z Books in Ernakulam. Listed in it is the novel *Archipelago* by Mohandas Purameri! This Mohandas and his book might be able to help in our Operation Diego Garcia. We can contact Z and get his number.'

It was luck. Otherwise, that catalogue wouldn't have caught the attention of Biju. I immediately contacted Z Books and was put through to its editor-in-charge, Srikumar.

'There is a novel titled *Archipelago* in your catalogue. I am curious about it,' I said.

'Yes, it's one of the best among the new crop,' Srikumar said.

'This Mohandas Purameri, where is he from?'

'From a country called Diego Garcia. He's an expat. You know him?'

'I may have read his stories.'

'Yeah, they've appeared in weeklies. This novel has won a contest organized by a magazine there. You should read it. There has never been such a beautiful work in Malayalam about the islands.'

'I'll certainly read it. Can I have his number? I want to get in touch with him.'

Srikumar readily gave me the number. I hung up and started dialling the number almost simultaneously.

0123456789

When I heard the long ringtone on the other side, either because of fervour or fear, my hand started shaking.

'Is this Mohandas Purameri? The author of *Archipelago*?'

'Yes, yes. Tell me, who is this?'

'My name is Raju. I read *Archipelago*. There has never been such a beautiful work in Malayalam about the islands. Really great.'

'Oh, thank you. I've been getting many calls from the

mainland. It's three years of my hard work, and that's evident. The subcontinent has a lot of talented writers, but there's no hard work. That's the problem. Do you know how much research I did for the novel? Archaeology, psychology, quantum physics, history, sociology, anthropology, applied maths, global warming . . . I've incorporated everything. Only then will a novel become rich . . . but the young in your mainland . . .' he went on talking.

'I called to ask you about something,' I interrupted. Otherwise, he'd never stop talking.

'Is there a writer by the name of Andrapper in Diego?'

'Andrapper? A writer? Not to my knowledge, no. There's no such person.'

'I heard that you were both part of the Parana literary group.'

'Parana? Very old history. Oh, oh, oh. Him . . . Andrapper . . . Is it about him?'

'Yes, yes, the same person. Do you know him?' I was very excited.

'Is he a writer? Good joke. He's a fraud! He came to Parana just to show off. For someone like him to become a writer, it'll take more than six generations of toil and sweat.'

'Do you know where he's now?'

'Who cares about him! Spiteful guy. I'd invited him for my award ceremony. He attended for the sake of it and left quickly. Contempt, what else? I don't keep in touch with people who can't support literature or writers. Why are you looking for him?'

'It's for a friend in Thiruvananthapuram. Is there any chance of getting his number?'

'I used to have it. Let me look for it. Can you call after five minutes?'

Exactly five minutes later, I called him. He gave me a number.

'Thank you, thank you.' I was full of gratitude. I might be able to contact him before the Thursday Market.

'One more thing. Isn't Andrapper a surname? What's his full name?'

'No idea. I only know him as Andrapper.'

I tried the number many times, but to no avail. Either it was 'out of coverage area' or 'switched off'. The road of high hopes was thus closed.

When the Thursday Market convened, I shared with the others Mohandas Purameri's opinion of Andrapper. Leave it then, Mashu advised again. Let's somehow get the second chapter too, and then stop this probe, Salim said. 'His search began on Orkut. Why don't we also start from there?' Anil suggested. Everyone agreed. Without delay, led by Pattar, we moved to a computer.

A search for St. Joseph's, Seleucia, yielded an instant result. By then, eighty-eight people had joined the community. We went through the profiles of each one of them.

We looked for someone who could be identified as a novelist or be connected to the story. But we didn't find anything.

'He said he created the community, right? Look at the founder's name. That must be him,' said Mashu. It was something that hadn't struck any of us till then! We checked that too. Unfortunately, no one had taken ownership of founding the community.

'He has done everything possible to protect his identity.

There's no use searching for him,' Nibu said.

Pattar then came up with another more promising solution. 'Let's send a message with the subject "Andrapper" to all the members of the St. Joseph's community. Just this: "I've got the first part. Do you have the second? Mail me." Other than the person who has the second part, nobody will understand anything.' All of us agreed that it was a good idea.

We created a new email ID and sent messages to all the eighty-eight members. There was nothing at all for a week. We were beginning to lose hope when a reply came with an attachment: Part 2.

As he directed, I'm sending this from a temporary ID. Please don't bother me hereafter.
X

(A) (E) (K)

I WAS MOTIVATED by Papa's words. Writing is my field; therein shall lie my success. And if I don't work towards it, even if I claim to have contributed something else elsewhere, I won't be a part of history. I won't be a success in the eyes of the world. I freshened up the next morning and went back to my desk. Saluting my ancestors, who ignored distractions with a rigorous application of the mind, and reaped success, I began my day at the desk.

My desk, which had otherwise been a mess, was neat and uncluttered while I wrote: papers stacked in order, pens and pencils in their stand, the phone in a corner. Only the one pencil with which I write was kept apart. Not even a teacup. I couldn't tolerate tea stains. There were two diaries containing notes on one corner of the desk. I referred to them occasionally if required.

Every now and then, I'd take a break from the writing and walk around the room. I also stopped to observe my face in the mirror behind the desk. I'd take out a comb and fix my hair, and make sure I looked handsome and pleasant. While writing the lengthier chapters, this behaviour might be repeated many times.

I wrote my first draft on ruled paper, using a pencil—a short one as I could never stand a longish, upright pencil. I wrote only on one side of the paper, leaving the other side blank. While writing, or after, or while taking a walk later carrying what I had written, if I felt like inserting a word or a sentence in between, I'd draw an arrow mark and write (A), (E), (K), etc. Then, on the reverse side, I'd mark the same (A) or (E) and jot down the insertion. All that would be scribbled in an illegible hand that only I could read.

I made the second draft with my best handwriting. I couldn't bear even a single mistake in it. If I had to, I'd rather change the paper altogether and start all over again.

Once or twice, I tried to type directly on the computer keyboard. There were the advantages of copying, pasting and replacing words and sentences, and changing the style, alignment, etc. But whenever I tried it, a dead language came out from me. Which meant that my writing body did not react well to the machine. It was more of a habit. My mind would flow only through a pen or a pencil, and onto a paper. My words are hidden on my fingertips. The forefinger was everything; my thumb or middle finger or ring finger or little finger simply did not have the talent to deliver words.

After I think I've completed one chapter, I'd draw a rule at the bottom, leave the room and play with my old toys for a while. Or I'd go to the kitchen and cook with Momma. Or go to a friend's shop and get vocal about a recently released movie. Or take the boat and cruise fast to some place—wherever it took me.

_____

I wrote non-stop for three days. Reams of it. I didn't leave the house at all. I kept on writing—as determined and disciplined as a boy trying to come first in an exam. On the evening of the third day, as I drew a rule at the end of the thirteenth chapter, a title rose up in my mind. The title of my novel: *The Book of Forefathers*. I glowed in the reflected glory of the title. Where did it come from? What was its origin? I didn't know. *The Book of Forefathers*. *The Book of Forefathers*. I kept on repeating the title. Mohandas, this is definitely more beautiful than your *Archipelago*. It was one of those moments when I admired the talent within me. Inspired, I took the boat and travelled swiftly for a long distance. Finally, it stopped on its own at the Oothukkuli boat jetty in Cherar Peruntheruvu.

CHERAR PERUNTHERUVU

SUDDENLY, THE MYSTERY named Senthil, which lay clogged in me for three days, sprung to life. I don't know whether it was a quick burst of energy or an anonymous force that made this happen. But when I left the house, there had been no Senthil or Cherar Peruntheruvu in my mind. Whatever it was, here I was in Cherar Peruntheruvu. Now, how could I leave without inquiring about Senthil?

If someone has died, even if no one else knows about

the death, his parents must be aware of it. But why didn't they complain to the Public Security? Or didn't they know about it yet? In that case, what could I tell them? If, instead, they thought he had just gone missing, would my visit cause suspicion?

Doubts and questions are of no use. If I've to find his parents, I'll have to look for them. But where was Senthil's house? I had a slight memory of him once saying that he and Jesintha were neighbours in Cherar Peruntheruvu. But how could I find him with just that? Who knew how many Senthils there were in Tamil Colony? How would I identify this particular Senthil? But there could be only one Senthil who died recently.

Non-Tamils in Diego usually didn't venture into the Tamil stronghold. I'd been to that street once or twice before. That gave me some familiarity. Everything about the street had a Tamil touch. There was a huge board, Oothukkuli Padakukuzhaam, right at the jetty. The radios played loud songs, and uttapam stalls were all around. 'Dey' and 'poda' greetings abounded, along with provocative stares of young men. In short, it resembled a movie set. The area evoked artificiality even at first sight.

There was a history to the street's name, Cherar Peruntheruvu. The Tamils there believed that it was the Sangam period Cherar king Velkezhukuttavan who was the first to set foot in Diego and establish a kingdom. He earned the title Kadalpurakottiya as an honour for finding Diego. Before the advent of the Portuguese, the region was called Ilam Cherarnadu. They also believed that Velkezhukuttavan's elder son, Irumporai, was the first king of this land. The natives say the place is mentioned in Paranar's *Anchampathu* and Ottakoothar's *Takkayakapparani*. It has long been the Tamils' emotional plea to reinstate the old name of Ilam Cherarnadu instead of the French name Diego Garcia. They put forth this demand during every Senate election.

———

I stepped into a tea shop at the corner of the street. I asked the old man at the counter if anyone had recently died in the area.

'Ayya . . . those who are born have to die someday.' The gaffer got excited. 'Four last week. Our Kuppuswami had been ill for long. Good that he died. Then our Murukappan. It was some liver disease. It's only good for us if we don't drink too much. Then there was one teenager in the next street. Don't know his name.'

Diego's Tamils talk a mix of Malayalam and Tamil. They can easily understand Malayalam. That was a blessing for me. 'Was his name Senthil?' I asked.

'Senthil, Kinthil—who knows! If death happens at a young age, what can we do? One hears he was well educated. Then there was Selva. Our Kolanji's wife. Suicide. Nobody knows the reason. Only the smart ones can know a woman's mind. By the way, why are you asking?'

'It's my friend who died. Need to go to his house. That's why I came. Where is his house?'

'Oh lord, his Appa's and Amma's tears have still not dried up. The fourth street from here, where the Cheramannan Kuravai Koothu used to be held. And the eighth lane from there. There is a statue of Periyar there. Ask someone there. It was there that Selva . . .'

Following his directions, I walked through the Kuravai Koothu street, thinking about the last time I'd been at Cherar

Peruntheruvu. The well-known Tamil writer Charu Nivedita had been with me.

Kuravai Koothu and Vadakkirikkal are the two major festivals of the Tamil here. Both are related to the Sangam period, say historians. If a king or warrior kills his opponent in the battlefield, they quit fighting and start dancing. That's Kuravai Koothu. Its variant Thunangai Koothu is also popular here, with women too participating in it. When Adu Kottu Pattu Cheralathan, the heir of Vel Kezhu Kuttavan, who is mentioned in the sixth book of the Ettuthokai anthology of Sangam poems, visited Ilam Cherarnadu to feast with his brother Irumporai, he came to know of his army's victory over the Ay kings. He celebrated it by dancing on these streets, and Kuravai Koothu is a reminder of that, according to legend. Charu Nivedita had come to Diego to see the original dance form, which had become extinct in Tamil Nadu. I got to know him through some common friends in Thiruvananthapuram.

Vadakkirikkal is a week-long mourning. Warriors consider it despicable to be wounded on the back. If it happens to someone, he has to observe a fast, holding an open sword, facing the west. On the seventh day, he would fall on the sword. The festival laments the suicide of Uthiyan Cheralathan, who was wounded on his back during the Venni battle with Karingala Cholan. The fast honouring his memory extends to seven days. It is said that till recently, people would leap on the sword and die, or injure themselves with it. After the British came to Diego, they banned the festival through a decree. That led to huge riots in Diego during the late 1970s. The government was persuaded to allow the festival but without the ritual suicide. All under the watchful eyes of the Public Security. During

Charu Nivedita's visit, he had spoken to some elders who had memories of someone or the other from their families having died by the sword.

Many of the customs that are extinct in our native mainland still live on among the migrants. To see the soul of our ancient culture, one would have to go to Diego, Sri Lanka, Malaysia or Singapore, Charu Nivedita later wrote in *Kalachuvadu*.

A chap, who was chewing paan standing beside Periyar's statue, helped me find Senthil's house.

ANPU

SENTHIL'S HOUSE HAD an extended porch. It was bigger than what I'd expected, and had been smartened up recently. Two or three elders were sitting outside, chatting. I walked towards them. Seeing a stranger, they paused in their conversation and looked at me. I recognized one of them as Senthil's Appa. It was only because of the similarity in their faces. Though dead, the face I saw in the hospital had strongly resembled the one before me.

'Senthil's Appa . . .?' I grasped his hand and asked.

'No, his Chittappa. Who are you? Haven't seen you before.' He got up slowly.

'I was his friend. I came to know about this just recently.'

'I see. You were working together . . .'

'No, we studied together at St. Joseph's.'

'Oh, okay. That was a long time ago. He had finished studies, got a nice job and was happy. Hah. Everything is god's will.' He sighed. 'Anybody inside. . .? Senthil's friend has come . . .'

He pulled up a chair for me. I sat. He inquired about me—name, place, studies and job. Except my Andrapper connection, I told him everything.

A few minutes later, someone older than I'd expected stepped out of the house. I was sure it was Senthil's Appa.

Seeing him, I got up. He stared at my face. I felt a strange fear. Didn't you just stand there when my son got shot? When the Public Security came, didn't you evade being a witness? Isn't that why they are now giving excuses for not finding his killers? Why did you come here? Aren't you one of them? Many such questions would arise, I feared. I felt an urge to scoot off before that happened.

He held my shoulder and started crying. 'Left us ... he left us all ... without saying a word ... he left ...'

I tried to hold him close and comfort him. He stood weeping on my shoulder as though he had found a refuge.

However, he quickly composed himself and wiped away his tears. He then addressed the people sitting around: 'Don't you know him? He is our Andrapper's child. Was my son's best friend. They were together in school. Don't you know? Senthil always used to talk about him.'

When he mentioned the Andrapper name, the group's suspicious looks gave way to that of respect.

Senthil's father turned towards the house. 'Can't you see that Andrapper's child has come? Get him something to drink!'

'No, it's fine.' I tried to stop him. But he went inside. I walked back to the others.

'You know Senthil?' one of them said. 'He was well educated. Soon after Plus Two, he went to Madras. Studied there for five years. Came back and got a job immediately. You know, right? At the Accountant General's office. His marriage had been arranged. Should have taken place in two months. Who thought it will all end up like this!'

So, all of them had come to know of everything. I, with all those unnecessary doubts stuffed in my head, had walked up and down to the Public Security department. What a blunder! I should have come here straight.

'Any idea what actually happened?' I asked.

'It was a cardiac arrest.'

'What?' I got up in shock.

'Yeah. It was a cardiac arrest. He'd left in the morning for work. Couldn't make it to the office—he died on the boat. Then, just as a formality, the body was taken to the hospital. That's all.'

'Who said this?'

'Who said, as in . . .?' They looked at each other for a minute, unable to comprehend my question.

I quickly realized my folly. Before they could ask or I could say anything more, fortunately, a girl walked into the scene with a tumbler and a jar of water.

They turned to her. I did too. She was so beautiful that I couldn't turn my eyes away. My mind briefly lost its poise. She poured some water into the tumbler and gave it to me.

'Aren't you my brother's friend? I know you. Do you recognize me?' she asked, with a smile loaded with sadness.

'No.'

'I was also there in St. Joseph's. Senthil's sister. Anpu.'

Yes. Anpu. Anpu. Anpu. Her name and face rushed to my memory. A name and face that shouldn't have been forgotten, but had been forgotten. She was our junior in school and was beautiful even back then. Senthil, Anpu and Jesintha used to come together to school. During lunch, she would come to our classroom and share the food from Senthil's plate. There was an intensity to the brother–sister relationship. To see her, the boys would scramble around the classroom during lunch. And here I was, not being able to identify her!

My mind was stirred up by what I had just heard. Cardiac arrest! What an idiotic tale! Who made them believe that? Haven't any of them heard that Senthil was shot? I finished the water that Anpu gave in one gulp.

'More?'

'Um.'

She poured another glass of water. I finished that too at one go.

'More?'

'Um.'

I drank that too in a gulp.

'More?'

'Um.'

She stared at me in disbelief. As if I had come from a place without water.

'More?'

'No, thanks.' I handed over the tumbler. She went back inside. I wanted to see Senthil's Amma. But she never came out. I sat there for some more time.

The rest of their discussion was about the chances of getting a heart attack at such a young age. I didn't have anything to contribute to it. After a while, I got up to leave.

Senthil's Chittappa looked inside the house and shouted, 'Anpu! Senthil's friend is leaving.' She came out running. I said bye to her.

She accompanied me to the end of the street. We didn't utter a word to each other. Just before parting, I said we'll meet again later, and left.

Yeah, left. It was one kind of leaving. I don't remember

getting into the boat and reaching home. My mind was completely muddled. I felt a strange fear. I latched the door to my room and went to bed. For the next four days, I had high fever.

WEDDING CASSETTE

MOMMA DIDN'T LET me go out for two days after I recovered from the fever. 'I told him not to sit idle in the house. My mistake. And so he goes roaming around east and west. That too in the damn sea breeze. As Papa says, show some responsibility and write something.' Momma was all over me.

I did try. To be responsible. To be a writer. To sit tight and write. But I did not succeed much. The enigma of Senthil had wrapped itself around my mind like a viper, making it impossible for me to think about anything else. Cardiac arrest! The relatives of someone who had been shot dead in public were made to believe that he had died of a heart attack. How could I tell them the fact? Even if I tried, would they believe it? What proof did I have to present to them? Nothing, not a single thing.

I was going crazy sitting in the closed room. I went out for a walk along the lakeside.

Children were playing cricket in a field nearby. Diego's new generation had turned to cricket, following the changes in the mainland. During my childhood, India, Pakistan and Sri Lanka were winning world cups. Back then, when the new migrants from the mainland ardently watched cricket, all our games were carried out in water. In fact, Diego's national game was water polo. We were into swimming, rowing, water volleyball, diving and bellyflopping. Today's children had come out of the water, to the ground. I stood there for a while watching them play.

They were playing with a bat they'd made out of wood, and a rubber ball. Three not-so-straight branches had been stripped to make the stumps. A game that was played at the international level—with the players ensconced in protective guards—was being played fearlessly by the children. Their enthusiasm bowled me over. How sincerely they enjoyed the game! The most surprising aspect was that there was no umpire to control their game. The players were themselves the observers. The non-striker called the no-ball. The bowler decided if the batsman was out LBW or not. He even consulted with the batsman. Most of the decisions were made without a fuss. If it was a crucial call—a run-out or a catch or a stumping—they would discuss among themselves to reach a decision. The player who was given out accepted the outcome without getting upset. I was amazed by the honesty in their play. I felt contempt for the professionals and their games.

When I got back home in the evening, Chettan, his wife and Momma were watching a wedding cassette. It had been sent from the mainland. My Chettathi was from the mainland. It was the wedding of one of her relatives. 'If you aren't seized by the spirit of writing, come and sit with us. Let's see if we can find a girl for you,' Chettathi called out.

There's nothing more boring than watching an unknown person's wedding cassette. But my Chettathi was obsessed with it. She could then pick up fashion trends in the mainland. And search for a prospective bride for her brother-in-law. Reminisce about relatives and friends. She found all this useful.

I wasn't at all entertained by the cassette, and I sat there with them, flipping through the newspaper. In between, she hollered, 'Hey, look, that's a nice girl!' By the time I turned my head, the scene was over. She then rewound it for me. True, it was a pretty face. The girl was there only for a flash, so Chettathi pressed the rewind button once again. She rewound it a little too much. A face appeared out of the blue. 'Stop, stop there!' I jumped up.

'Um. Why, have you found another interesting one?' Chettathi smiled. She pressed the pause button. I moved closer to the TV. Yes, no doubt, it was her.

'Isn't that Jyoti?'

Chettan was three years older than me. He knew most of the people in my class. He'd noticed her too.

'Yeah, it's Jyoti.'

'You know where she is now? I asked him.

'The cassette shows she's in the mainland.'

'No, where exactly is she? And what's she doing now?'

'No idea. Must have married someone in the mainland and got settled there. Has anyone who went there come back? That is, other than you?'

Chettathi had moved on to watching the next scenes in the cassette.

'I need the phone number of the house where this wedding took place. I need to find Jyoti at any cost,' I said.

'Da, she is already married. See the mark on her forehead. You go for the girl I showed you. I've known her since she was a child. She has completed her graduation now.'

'Please, I'll think of the alliances later. Give me the number.'

She called up someone or the other and managed to get me the number. 0091 477 2261489. I called the very next day. A guy named Salu took the call. I asked for Dr Jyoti. He didn't know anyone by that name. I asked him to watch the cassette and identify the girl. I repeated many times the part where she was appearing in the cassette and gave all the possible details I could.

Salu was a responsible chap. He called me back in three days. He said it was not Dr Jyoti, but Jyoti Prasad and that she was his neighbour who now worked in Alleppey as a clerk in the railways. I thanked him.

I felt sad. The difference between what we expect and what actually happens . . . Anita and Jyoti were not only the best in class, but also in the whole of the school. Within the range of dreams we were capable of at that time, we expected the two of them to become doctors. Neither of them did. That was not the problem. They were not meant to be a pharmacist or a railway clerk. They could have led better lives and got great jobs. They must have their own reasons to explain why their lives had deviated from our expectations. But I was annoyed with them. They failed my dreams of their lives.

The next morning, I got a call. As I was in the bathroom, Papa took it.

REJECTED

WHEN I CAME out of the bathroom, Papa called me to his bedroom. He was getting ready to leave for work.

'Papa, who was on the phone?'

'Did you do the thing I'd asked you to?'

'What thing?'

'Don't remember, do you? Poor memory is not good at your age. Especially for a novelist, who has to remember a lot of things in order, and on time.'

'Papa, please don't start lecturing in the morning. Just tell me.'

'What happened to the withdrawal of that case?'

'Oh, that . . . I swear I forgot about it.'

'I told you to do it ten days ago. What were you doing till now?'

'For the first three days, I followed your advice—to write laboriously. The next four days I was labouring under a fever. And for the last three days, I've been in labour, waiting for the details of a classmate.'

'That means you've wasted two-thirds of your life. I'll say you lived only on the first three days.'

'Yeah, that's fine. I'm getting to know a lot of people who are not even able to live those three days for themselves. Tell me who called . . .'

'It was from the Public Security department. Mr Vijay Mullikratnam. He has asked you to visit him this morning.'

'For what?'

'That I didn't ask. Go—that's fine. But by the time you're back, the case shouldn't exist, okay? I'll be calling Stephen in the evening. Your papers for Australia are being processed, you know that, right? They'll be ready any time.'

Without much delay, I went to the North Public Security office. It seemed as if Vijay Mullikratnam was waiting for me. As soon as I reached, he called me in. 'Dude, how punctual you are! Within an hour of calling you, you are here. Good. Youngsters should be like this. I like it. Dude, if Chief Investigator Vijay Mullikratnam takes over something, that will be promptly done. You can ask anyone in the department. I called you here to prove that in person.'

'Not sure I understand, sir . . .'

'I conducted a thorough investigation about the case we discussed. I've been on it for the past ten days. I've studied it from all angles. And I've found him. Dude, your complaint was right. Senthil had gone missing. But it's not what you think, there is nothing suspicious about it. Unfortunately, he experienced pain in the heart while he was on a boat. The boat driver took him to the hospital. Bad luck. They couldn't save him. Because nobody knew about his whereabouts, he lay in the mortuary for two days. That's why he was missing. That's all. But good, dude, it's nice you were concerned for your friend. You were anxious about him going missing. These days it's difficult to find people like you. Really, I appreciate what you did.'

'I've been to Senthil's house,' I said casually.

'Oh, I see. But that day you said you didn't know where he lived.'

'We don't need great investigative skills to find a house in this small island, sir.'

For a minute, Vijay Mullikratnam was taken aback. 'That's true . . . It doesn't need investigative skills to find Senthil's house, just a wagging tongue. But for an investigator, finding Senthil is not the only issue. Or is it? No. I found the boat in which he had the heart attack. I found its driver. Went to hospital. Met the doctor who attended him. Met his parents. Found out that everything is correct and in order. Dude, it was only after that that I decided to close the case.'

'Sir . . . what? Are you closing the case?'

'Yes. It was the duty of the department to call you here and inform you about it. We follow strict discipline in every case. This morning, I talked to your Dad. He was depressed. I know him personally. . . Anyhow, that's over. I hear you are going abroad for some higher studies. Good, you can travel anywhere. The department won't have any objection to that. Dude, I wish you every success.'

I left the place without a word. I wasn't too disappointed with such a response. I'd seen it coming.

DA VINCI

IN FRONT OF the Public Security office, as I was stepping out, a young man ran up to me from the verandah, calling, 'Eda, Pachu!'

To be honest, I panicked. A chill went up my spine: an abnormal fear. It was after a long time that someone was calling me by the name which had once irritated and later amused me. Pachu had been my nickname in school, so I was sure it was an old friend.

'Don't you recognize me?'

I'd been staring at him. It took some time to identify him. 'Vinod!'

'No, da Vinci.'

We laughed.

'Why are you here?' I asked.

'And you?'

'The Inspector Director here is a relative, so I came to meet him.'

'Okay. I'm lucky to see you. I need your help.'

'What's the issue?' I asked hesitantly, wondering if I'd invited trouble.

'For the past twenty-two days, I've been walking up and down here. Just to get something done. Do you know that I've rented a boat and run it as a taxi?'

'What happened to your painting?'

'What can painting do when I'm struggling to make a living! When I don't get boat rides, I go paint boards. That's the art world of your own da Vinci. Let it be. You listen to this. I'd taken my boat to Pentasia one day. Then another boat came and collided with mine near the jetty. A private boat. The mother of some big shot in the Senate was in it. My boat had been stationary, it was the other boat that came and hit it. Now if you've heard the hullabaloo, you'll think I was the one responsible. Let it be. My boat suffered major damage. And theirs sustained just minor scratches. That's all. Ideally, I should have filed a case with the Public Security. When I said that, the old girl said it would eat up a lot of time, so she'd rather pay the repair charges directly to me. I thought that was fine, although there would be a hundred formalities like insurance papers, inspection, etc. that would take up at least two days. The woman opened her purse and gave me some Diego francs. She didn't even count them. So, I let it go at that, thinking she was a good soul. My bad time starts then. I went to repair the boat and then I realized that the currency notes were a first-class fake! The mechanics straight away called the Public Security. Who will believe my story? I was inside for three days, then I got bail. Since then, I've been walking in and out of here. Now they hold me responsible for all the fake notes in Diego. As if that isn't enough, the woman filed a hit-and-run case! And yet another case from the Public Security because I hadn't notified the accident. I'm innocent, I swear I'm innocent. But I have been trapped. Please help me out in some way. My family depends on me and the boat.'

He was on the verge of crying. I felt helpless.

'What can I do here?'

'Anything at all that you can, please. Don't you believe me? I'm not the kind who'll get into a fake-currency racket. If you visit my house, you'll know my situation. If I had really made the deals that I've been accused of by the Public Security, I wouldn't have been driving around the lake in an old Sparrow owned by Samudra. At the very least, I'd have gone with a stylish, limited-edition Yamaha or a Honda like you guys. Who will want to live a sorry life if they have the money?'

I couldn't ignore his words. I took him to ID Stephen Pereira Andrapper's room and described his sorry situation. Stephen uncle sat there staring at me. Then he asked Vinod to wait outside. He made me sit, then he stood up, stretched out his hand and whacked me on the head. I felt as if my ear had flown off.

'Think of it as your Papa hitting you. If I wouldn't do it now, I'll later get shouted at by your Papa. Have you adopted all your friends? Didn't I just put an end to one issue? But before leaving the building, you've come up with another one. What do you think, that this is an office that takes your recommendations? This is not the princely state of the Andrappers. This is a British colony. Every citizen is bound to obey the rules. Whoever commits a crime will have to be punished. And will be punished. Are you endorsing a third-rate criminal who has taken up the fake-currency business? Do you know against whom he is placing the charges? The Under Secretary's Mother. Do you know how many years he'll be in jail for the charges against him? And for your kind information, he's on bail now not because we think he's innocent, it's because we need to know the people he is in contact with. To find out about all those who are involved in the fake-currency racket. And you come with your recommendation! It's good that you came to me. Leave now! And never ever enter this building to see me.'

I bowed out. Vinod was nowhere around. I thanked my luck and left the place quickly.

MARIAM CHURCH

A HALF-HOUR BOAT ride from Venecia, past the Balton Strait, and you'll reach Diego's northern border of Bodom, a small island. Other than a British military camp and two or three recently built resorts, there are no permanent residents. But in the middle of vast palm groves, there is an ancient church. It was abandoned for a long time till its revival a few decades ago. It's called the Mariam Church. It lies closed most of the year, but wakes up to major celebrations from 1 to 5 October. There's a large crowd on those days. All of Diego's hawkers gather there. Diego's transport department runs special boat services to Bodom. It's the harvest season for taxi boats and smaller vessels. More than a festival, it's a great shopping carnival. There was a time when people used to buy their year's stock of household goods at the Mariam Church festival—from cooking utensils to garments, crockery, kitchen implements, sesame and jaggery. But after the new shopping complexes came up in Diego, the local fair lost its sheen. It used to be a remarkable sight, with Diego's wealthy, their wallets stuffed with francs, moving from one salesman to another. Now it had shrunk to a poor man's parade.

But these days, a lot of foreigners come for the festival.

There are a number of churches for Jesus's mother, Mariam. There are many for Magdalena Mariam too. However, this particular church doesn't stand for either of them, but for a third Mariam.

Here is the myth and the faith.

Once upon a time, the Kerala region was ruled by a king called Thoma. A Hindu prince fell in love with his only daughter, Maria. When the prince approached with a marriage proposal, King Thoma asked him to convert to

Christianity. So, the prince became a Christian and married Maria. After the time of King Thoma, the prince became the king. Meanwhile, in his own province, a minister named Paliathachan had taken over the throne. He blackmailed the prince into renouncing Christianity to get back his kingdom. But when he returned, Paliathachan and his cronies arrested and exiled him to Ceylon. The abandoned Maria pleaded with Paliathachan to send her to her husband in Ceylon. However, he wanted her to renounce Christianity in exchange. But Maria was not willing to let go of the faith of her ancestors. In a fit of rage, Paliathachan sent her in exile to Bodom. With just a few helpers, Maria spent years and years on this island, praying to be united with her husband. Meanwhile, in Ceylon, the prince regretted his decision to leave Christianity and his beloved wife. Determined to be with Maria again, he changed his appearance and set sail to the Chera region. And believe it or not, struck by a huge wave while at sea, he ended up in Bodom. It is said that this church was built during her time in Bodom.

Mariam Church is known for the special prayers for husbands who were away; the belief was that the prayers would come true. All of Diego's married women are the devotees of Mariam Church. They believe that all their husbands' achievements are the result of their prayers. My sister-in-law is one of them. There is a mass at the church on the eighth of every month. Whatever happens, she finds time to attend it. She'll start the arrangements a week in advance. And usually, via my brother, the responsibility would land on my shoulders. I'd take her there, but I never ever entered the church. I'd roam around outside till she finished her prayers. Or would stay in the boat with a book.

On that day too, I was whiling away my time in the church

premises, when a department boat arrived. It parked in the jetty. The crowd started to flow to the land. I saw a flash of Anita's face among them. I felt a tremble. My hand swiftly moved to my wallet in which I had the photo of her children.

I rushed towards her. She was surprised.

'You, here?'

'Why? In a world full of believers, can't I be a believer too?'

'It's not that. Only that it's a strange coincidence to see you here.'

'I come here most months. Not for the mass but as a chauffeur. With my sister-in-law. It was a coincidence when we ran into each other the last time. This is another coincidence. The next one will be the next time we meet. Life is a grand total of coincidences.'

'OK, OK. Let me get into the church,' she said, laughing.

'This is . . .?' I asked, pointing to the woman with her.

'Ayyo, I forgot to introduce her. Sorry. This is my friend Melvin. She is a nurse at City Hospital, at the Accident and Emergency department,' she said and entered the church.

There was a fire in my belly. At the Accident and Emergency department in City Hospital! This was a good route to probe into Senthil's death. I had to know for sure. Even if the whole world told me that Senthil had had a heart attack, how could I believe it? I decided to wait till they came out.

JEALOUSY

AFTER THE MASS, when my Chettathi, Anita and Melvin came out, I was surprised to see them together. I didn't expect them to know each other. I came to know only later that it was a quick acquaintance formed while sitting near each other at the mass. Chettathi was good at that, too. Typical of women at home. Nobody is spared without being asked their name and whereabouts. Chettathi and Anita were surprised that all three of us knew each other.

Though Anita initially declined Chettathi's offer to drop her, she succumbed to the repeated pleas and got into my boat. During the journey, I purposefully brought up the topic about our class. My intention was to find out if she knew about Senthil. But she didn't utter a word about him. She asked if I had found any more of our classmates. 'Oh, I forgot to tell you. A few days ago, we were watching a wedding cassette from Kerala, and there I saw Jyoti, wearing a silk sari and all.' Before I could finish what I had to say, Chettathi interrupted. 'Listen, Anita, it seems he had a crush on that girl. He kept calling the mainland for three days without a break to find out her details. You should have seen his despair when he came to know she was already married,' she broke into laughter.

'My Chettathi is crazy,' I said. 'Alexy is in Seychelles. Bilal is in Australia, you told me that, right? Do you remember our da Vinci Vinod? He is running a taxi boat now. I met him yesterday.'

I made it a point not to talk about Senthil or Jesintha. Not getting any reaction from Anita, I turned to look at her face. She had her eyes fixed on me. I saw a shadow of jealousy on her face. It seemed as though she'd been struck by my Chettathi's words. To change the topic, I turned my attention to Melvin.

Melvin appeared somewhat reserved. She limited herself to just replying to my queries. She was one of the recent recruits from Kerala. The ministry had allotted some of them a villa close to Anita's house. She opened up a bit when I asked her about her job at the Accident and Emergency section.

'It's a sad place. One is shocked to see that there are so many patients in such a small place. The same with accidents. Stand there for a while and we know how lucky we all are.'

'I'm planning to do a study on accidents in Diego. Just out of curiosity. Can you help me out with some details?' I had an inspired moment.

'You'll get all that you need if you ask any office staff. They have full records in their system.'

'I don't need official records. What I want to know is about the experiences of people working there. How do you face the various patients and accidents and experiences? Do you think you can tell me about that?'

'Why not? There are people in my villa who have been working here for years. They will have lots to say.'

'Anita, please. You should help me with this. I want to meet them one day.'

'That's fine. You let me know.'

After dropping Chettathi home, I drove Anita and Melvin to their bay. From there, Anita pointed out her house to me and invited me to drop in. I promised her that I'd visit someday soon. She told me to chuck the formality and to come for sure. 'I'll come. I'll have to come,' I said while leaving. She might have misunderstood it, as she could not have got what I actually meant.

SCRAPBOOK

AFTER A LONG while, I logged into my Orkut account. There were four friends' 'requests' pending. The first was from one Sajeesh, who had been with me at MG College, Thiruvananthapuram. He was now working with a newspaper. Two were juniors from school. They were running a computer shop somewhere in Diego. The fourth was a request from my classmate, Rahim. There was a sudden joy seeing him after ages, although on the computer screen. At last, other than Alexy, someone had come searching for me. I went through his profile. He was working as an engineer at a construction company in South Korea.

Our class. Twenty students. Since I began the search, I'd found seven of them: Alexy, Jesintha, Senthil, Anita, Vinod, Jyoti, and now, Rahim. Eight including me. Anita said Bilal was in Australia. If I took that on faith, he'd be the ninth one. Though he had left in Class V! There were still ten left. Hidden in unknown corners of the world in unknown forms: Babu, Supriya, Leena, Seyfu, Daniel D'Silva, Little Anita and four others whose names I couldn't recollect. I might see all of them someday, somewhere. Or at least come to know where they were.

I opened my Orkut scrapbook. Many people from various walks of life had posted greetings. I saw many faces there that I hadn't seen for years. Alexy and Rahim had each commented once. Alexy's was just a casual post. In the first few days, he had written regularly. About friends. About class. With queries about Diego. And I had replied with enthusiasm. Then it slowed down. As if there was nothing more left to say, and I realized that ten years of life could be written in just ten lines. Then, once in a while, a random comment. That's it. Alexy and I had reached that stage.

Rahim's comment had greetings as well as inquiries about me. I replied. Two lines about my life. The happy news of meeting Anita, Jesintha and Vinod. The tragedy of Senthil's death. That was the content of my response.

He was online, so we began to chat. It was shocking. He

didn't ask about anyone whom I'd mentioned in my post. 'Do you remember that chick?' he asked, about Anpu.

I wasn't shocked or surprised that he remembered Anpu when I spoke about Senthil. People recollect the past in different ways. But not a single word about the deceased Senthil; no queries about any of our classmates; he had gone straight to Anpu!

I wrote a brief reply that I had met her a few days ago.

He grilled me about Anpu. Many of his questions were beyond that of casual interest in a classmate's sister. Not only that, I didn't know why he was asking all these questions during our first conversation in more than a decade.

Then he moved on from Anpu to the rest of the girls in our class. Anita, Leena, Supriya, Jyoti . . . All his comments were about their figure. It was annoying. Luckily, before he could bug me with further queries, he went offline. But just before that, Rahim said something useful. That Bilal is in Diego on a visit; he also gave me his phone number. I called Bilal without delay. Bilal himself answered. It took a while for him to identify me. Understandable—ten years is a long time. But even after he recognized me, Bilal's response was cold. I thought he'd be excited to hear from an old classmate. Instead, when I suggested we meet before he returned to Australia, he was noncommittal. He said something vague about next week, if he was free. Though I was upset by his response, I tried to recoup by telling him about the Orkut community I had started, and how I'd found Alexy and Rahim there. He said he wasn't interested in such things. I didn't give up. I said I met Anita, Jyoti and Jesintha. Oh, okay, good, was his reply. As my last shot, I told him of Senthil's demise. That's sad, what was the disease that caused it, he asked. I panicked for a moment. Heart attack, I replied. He ridiculed the sorry state of third-world citizens who hogged without any concern for their health. After that I just didn't wish to drag on the conversation.

Changing times and changed circumstances result in new relationships. New friendships are made, and old ones alienated. They wither away. That was how I explained away Bilal's response. I was content with my explanation. Until some days later, when I got a mail from Paris.

GIFT

THE NEXT DAY, I woke up with the plan to meet Anita and Melvin. I called Anita in the morning to fix up a time, but she didn't pick up her phone. I decided to try her number after a while, and entered the bathroom for a shower when Momma yelled from outside that I had a visitor.

Who could have come to visit me so early in the morning? Momma said it was a visitor, but nothing about whether it was a man or a woman. Who could it be? I was sure it was someone Momma hadn't seen before. A row of faces flashed past me of all the people who could visit me and whom I wanted to meet someday. Among them were Anita, Anpu, Leena and Jyoti. And Vijay Mullikratnam, Vinod and Jesintha. Also Alexy, Bilal and Rahim. Senthil's Appa and Amma, and even Senthil's murderer, who could have come to confess to me. When I finally went downstairs, it was none of them—it was Johnny. I hadn't expected to see him, so I was surprised. Johnny gave me a hug. 'I'd been planning for days to come and meet you. Sorry that it took so much time.' He then stepped out to go back to the boat, and returned carrying a wrapped gift. 'Something small from me. I know it's nothing for you. But just for my pleasure.'

I didn't understand what was going on.

'I knew it,' he continued, 'if I tell you something, it will be done. Do you know how many people in the department I'd approached to get it done? How many people I'd paid? Nobody did a thing. It was my luck to see you there. I knew the influence the Andrappers still have in the government. A hundred thanks to your kind heart. I got my promotion papers last week.'

Now I understood what it was about. But Johnny had mistakenly assumed that his promotion was the result of my recommendation. I let it be. I needed to get certain things done by him. It was a mystery as to how he got a promotion when he wasn't in line for it. Who was the unknown god who, in my name, had helped him?

'Johnny, can you help me with something?'

'What kind of a question is that? Who else am I going to help? What do you want, tell me.'

'The incident I told you that day, the murder? We need to look again to see if we can get any details of it in the medical records.'

'You haven't let go of that?'

'Things are getting more complicated. I can't let it be, Johnny. You know, the Public Security is saying that his death was due to a cardiac arrest?'

'Oh, I see. By the way, I had inquired in the department on why it was missing in the medical records. They explained that it was a clerical error.'

'What have they recorded as the cause of death?'

'I didn't notice that. I'll have to check.'

'Then we should check it today.'

'Why? If the Public Security says the cause of death is cardiac arrest, the medical records will show the same. No doubt about that.'

'I know. But still, we should check. I need some more information.'

After finishing the coffee that Momma had brought, I accompanied Johnny to the hospital. It was clear to me that he wasn't keen on it. He kept making excuses to avoid me but I was shamelessly stubborn. I made him check each and every record in the office computer of Accident and Emergency. There were no records of Senthil anywhere. Johnny was surprised by their absence. Suddenly, another idea struck me. I asked him to check Senthil's name not just in City Hospital records, but also in all other hospital lists of Diego. That worked. After a lengthy search, Senthil's file appeared on the screen. As we had anticipated, his death was recorded as a cardiac arrest. According to the file, Senthil was not admitted at City Hospital, but at Pentasia North Health Centre. Even the mortuary in which his body had been kept was mentioned as being of that centre. That meant Senthil's body was never brought to City Hospital. I was shocked. But these were not the important details I wanted. I was looking for the names and details of the doctors and nurses who were on duty that day at City Hospital's Accident and Emergency department. I got them. That was all I wanted.

On my way out, Johnny accompanied me till the verandah. 'What's your plan now?'

'I need to find these people. To know where Senthil was actually admitted.'

He was quiet for a minute. Then he said, 'I don't know if I can advise an Andrapper. But that's not the matter. As far as I've understood, some big shots are involved in this case.

Otherwise, it wouldn't have turned out like this. My advice is that you let it go.'

'That means at least you admit that Senthil's death was a murder, right?'

'My question is how does it benefit you and me to get involved in this?'

'Benefit? There's no benefit. I just want to know the truth.'

'What'll you do with the truth? Cook and eat it?'

'At least to convince myself that what I'd witnessed was the truth . . .'

'I don't want to argue with you. If this is of any use at all to either of us, I'll help you! But if it isn't, please let me go. Even if I got a promotion because of you, please don't bother me again.'

'No, I won't bother you.'

Once I was outside the hospital, I took out my notes. The details of the staff of Pentasia North Health Centre were of no use now. Those whom I needed to meet were the staff of Accident and Emergency. There were more than twenty nurses. Anita or Melvin would know at least one of them. I called Anita.

FEAST

AS WE HAD previously arranged, I reached Anita's place the next morning. On hearing the boat, Anita ran up to the jetty. Her house was really close to the bay. She took me inside, holding my hands. I'd never got such a warm and joyous reception from anyone before. I'd heard stories from my grandmother about that kind of welcome at our relatives' houses in Alappuzha. These days, greetings are hollow smiles with eyes still glued to the television.

I met the children whom she had showed me in the photograph, and her maid. Wilson had left for work. Since I had expected to find the children at home, I'd stopped at a toy store to buy a spiderman and barbie, and some chocolates. The children were delighted. Though Anita scolded me about the gifts, her face said they made her happy too. I was rarely good at such small courtesies, so I felt proud at having got it right this time.

Anita had prepared a big feast to welcome me: boiled *appam*, fried banana, half-boiled egg, puffed rice, *kuzhalappam*, jackfruit chips, biscuits and coffee. There was food enough to feed some ten men. Yet she said, 'When you called me yesterday, I was at work and so I couldn't make anything after coming home.'

I ate as much as I could. I even asked for a second cup of coffee. I chatted with the children as I ate. They behaved as if they had known me for a long time. They climbed all over me and their mischief continued despite Anita's chiding. They took my mobile. My boat's key. Took off my sunglasses. And my wallet. They were surprised to see their photo in it. Anita, too.

'You still have it?' Anita asked. 'I just gave the photo to you in the joy of seeing you . . .'

'This is the best gift I've ever got on this island. You think I'll throw it away?'

Though she didn't say anything in response, I saw another glint of delight in her eyes.

After the feast, we left the children with the maid, and went to Melvin's house. It was more of a palace than a house. I was wondering who had built such a big house in that area. Over twenty hospital staffers lived there on rent. But to whom could the owner have rented it if he hadn't got such a group of tenants?

'What is your investigation about?' Anita asked while we were waiting for Melvin.

'It's about accidental deaths in Diego. About how many people die in boat accidents, fire accidents, falling from heights, electrical accidents . . . the total toll, how they die—such details.'

'Shouldn't you get that from the Public Security office? What will you get from these nurses?'

'If I wanted only statistics, the Public Security would have been a better option. But what I really want is the experience of the people who directly interact with the accident victims. Doctors, nurses, those in ambulance-boats, yes, even the public security officers . . .'

'Are you mad? Instead of getting married and having a peaceful life with your wife and kids . . .'

'That's true. But what to do? The one whom I wanted to marry is now the wife of someone else. So, I'm not considering marriage now.'

'Eh, who is that, the unlucky girl who didn't get you?'

'Whoever it was, is gone. What's the point of going over it now?'

'You should try again. If she knows about you, she might leave her husband and come to you.'

'If someone calls you like that, will you go?' I was expecting an answer from Anita but Melvin's entry into the room cut short the conversation.

It was well near noon, but Melvin looked like she had just got up. She confirmed it, saying, 'I'd dozed off.' The queue of residents that followed her down the stairs showed that it wasn't just her, the rest of them, too, had got up just then.

'Are we a little early?' I asked.

'This is our routine. If you hadn't come, we may have slept till noon. Sometimes we wake up only around evening. I'll make some coffee for us.'

'Ayyo, no way. I already had a big feast,' I stopped her.

'He's kidding, Melvin. It's his first visit, but I couldn't make him anything. I was on duty yesterday,' Anita whined.

Meanwhile, another resident joined us.

'This is Mercy. She's from Kollam. Been here for years. Will be of use to Anita-chechi's friend,' Melvin introduced her to us. She gave us a sleepy smile and sat near Melvin.

'We need coffee for sure.' Melvin left us with Mercy and went inside.

'What's the investigation about?' Mercy asked.

I repeated my explanation to her, line by line.

Mercy recalled a boat accident that had killed more than sixty-four people and a fire at a four-storey building that had taken the lives of thirty-three Tamil workers. She condemned the incompetence of the Accident and Emergency department that could not handle even small situations like these.

By then, Melvin came back with the coffee. I casually asked her about random things. As someone new on the staff, she wasn't aware of many things. I asked her to share a moving experience related to accident deaths. She narrated how once, in her hometown, she had to nurse a friend who had jumped in front of a train, and how another girl—a bus accident victim—had jumped up from the hospital bed saying she was fine and then fell dead.

While we were talking, two more women came down the stairs. Jaya and Sudha. Mercy introduced them. They pitched in with their anecdotes when they figured out we were talking about accidents. I didn't have to repeat my lies. While talking about deaths caused by accidents, Jaya raised an important point. In Diego, a land of water, incidents related to water were very few. So were boat accidents. Most of the deaths were due to electrocutions or fire accidents.

'It's surprising,' Anita said. 'In this land of water, more deaths are caused by fire, which can be doused with water. Eda, this is another topic you can explore. By the way, what's the scene with murders?'

I was relieved that the conversation had taken this turn without my intervention.

'No clue. Very few cases come to our hospital.'

'You probably pay special attention to such a case even on a hectic day?' I said.

'No other choice. There have been cases of a wife set on fire with diesel, or some stabbing cases,' Jaya said.

'Does anyone remember if a man was brought there last month or so after being gunned down?'

Everyone fell silent. The conversation came to a halt. I noticed their faces turning pale. Anita, too, looked at me as if at a stranger.

'We don't know. We haven't heard of any such incident,' Jaya said hastily.

'None of you?' I asked, with the sharpness of an investigative officer, scanning their faces one after another.

'No.' Jaya was adamant.

'Let's leave,' Anita said, not willing to prolong the conversation.

'Sure. Thank you, everyone, for all the stories. When I publish my report, I'll acknowledge all of you, okay?'

'Oh, that is fine,' Melvin said.

We said bye and left.

Anita accompanied me to the jetty. We were silent as if there was nothing in particular to talk about.

'Thanks for making it possible for me to talk to them,' I said, getting into the boat.

Her reply was a question. 'Were you lying to me about being jobless?

'Job? Me?' My eyes popped out.

'Tell me the truth. Aren't you an investigative officer at the Public Security department?

'I'm not cunning enough for that, Anita.' I chuckled. 'Do you know who was the one who died that day? Our Senthil. The Senthil in our class.'

I revved up the boat as she stood startled.

3

Interpol

I CONVENED THE Thursday Market on Tuesday. Since it was an unusual occurrence, the others could only assume it was about some urgent matter. I'd not told anyone about getting the second segment of Andrapper's novel. Not even Biju. On hearing about it, everyone got excited. Mashu would believe in its existence only after seeing the copy. And Salim, only after reading it.

'Let's do an opinion poll,' I said after everyone had read it. 'Should we bother looking for the rest of the manuscript? That's the first question.'

'No, we shouldn't.' As usual, Nibu started off. We should, unless it affects my writing in any way, said Mashu. Since it is from an unknown geography, we should at least try to know about it, said Anil. Let others decide, but if there has to be a deciding vote, he'd vote to continue the search, said Nattapranthan. Biju said he would decide after getting to know how this would be of use to Benya.

'If it's a story that he has only heard of, a writer can use his imagination and make it a novel. But this one has already been written. One can't add much to it. At best, Benya can play the role of an editor. That's why we shouldn't put in too much effort,' said Salim.

'Nibu, why do you say no?' I asked.

'Look, if he wanted to, he could have pursued the culprit in a more focused manner. But he is fooling around, unsure whether he wants to be a writer or if he wants to follow up on

99

Senthil's death. What'll we gain by tracking the meaningless life of such a person?'

'He was trying to find out something, and life has taken him on such an unanticipated detour. That's what is drawing me to his story,' I said. 'We should not bother about whether Senthil's murderer is found or not, and whether the writer's method is appropriate. What's the route he has taken? Where did he reach? Shouldn't we only be concerned about that? And don't fret about my writing. My *Nedumbassery* is coming along well.'

'So the majority is for going ahead with this,' said Anil. 'Now how do we get hold of the next bit?'

'Before we get going, we should sort out the facts we've got. That'll make it easy,' said Mashu.

'The maths teacher's shortcut,' quipped Nattapranthan.

'The gentleman's name?' Biju made a questionnaire.

'Andrapper,' Salim said.

'No, let's now call him Pachu Andrapper. That was his nickname in school,' Anil said.

'OK. Place?'

'The land of peacocks and langurs, Diego Garcia.'

'Any other details?'

'He's unmarried. Can't be that old,' said Nibu.

'Title of the book he's writing?' Nattapranthan reminded us.

'*The Book of Forefathers*.'

'Anything else?'

'Who are the main characters in the second segment?' Mashu asked and proceeded to answer the question: 'Anpu, Appa, Jyoti, Salu, da Vinci Vinod, Anita, Melvin, Rahim, Bilal and some nurses.'

'All right, now comes the difficult part. Who among these

people will have the third segment? How will it come to us?' asked Biju.

'Through the same source: St. Joseph's, Seleucia.' Nibu Achachan gave us the easy way out.

'We might get twice lucky, but there won't be a mail,' said Salim.

'How about a third time?' Nattapranthan came up with the idea: 'There is a pervert among them. What was his name? Yes, Rahim. Let's email him, posing as a woman. He'll fall for it.'

There was a round of clapping.

'Fine, let's find his address.'

We gathered around the computer and did a quick search for a Rahim from St. Joseph's, Seleucia. We drafted a letter and were about to send it to him when Mashu came up with another idea. 'Let's send it in Anpu's name. He'll be more responsive if it's from her. Let's write that it's about Senthil's death, and ask him if he has the number or email ID of his classmate, Pachu.'

We all agreed to that. Soon an email ID was created in Anpu's name: anpudg@gmail.com.

'What's the "dg" for?' I was confused.

'Diego Garcia,' said Nattapranthan.

'Oh, Baldy, your intelligence is awesome,' Nibu planted a kiss on Nattapranthan's bare head.

'We are committing a cybercrime using my computer. If I get caught, I'll tell on all of you,' I threatened.

'See how scared the novelist is!' Biju said. 'And he is the one out to catch a criminal!'

'I've already made it clear that I've no interest in finding the criminal,' I said, raising my hand.

'No? Now be truthful. How many of us don't care about finding him? Raise your hands,' Biju said.

I was the only one to raise my hand.

'You guys want Andrapper to find Senthil's murderer?' I asked.

'Yes,' said Nibu. 'What's the point of shadowing his path otherwise? I believe that Andrapper will find out in the end.'

'Let's hope he does,' Mashu said.

After sending the mail to Rahim, the assembly wrapped up that meeting.

As if he was addicted to the computer and spent the whole day at it, Rahim's reply came within half an hour. It was filled with the sorrow of losing Senthil. And concerns about Anpu. Just a few lines towards the end: 'Was Pachu asking about Senthil? If so, I've no clue at all. Never trust him in any way. He has bad-mouthed you in the past. He was always good at seducing girls.' And more such advice.

I burst into laughter. Anyway, I decided not to let him be. I sent another provocative and flirty mail. 'I know Bilal is in Australia. Is there a way of getting his contact details?' I added as a postscript. His reply came in ten minutes. His tone had changed. There was visible desperation in his queries about Anpu. 'Please give me your mobile number. Let's chat more often. Let's make sure we meet', etc. He'd however included some details that I needed: Bilal had left Australia some time back. Rahim had no clue where he was now, but he sent me his email ID.

I emailed Bilal the same night, before going to sleep: 'I'm a publisher and am trying to find out about a novel written by Pachu Andrapper. If he is currently in Australia, please let me know how to get in touch with him.'

Next morning, as soon as I woke up, I ran to the computer. There were at least ten emails from Rahim. His queries ranged from what's for breakfast to what colour nightie I had worn last night! But there was no email from Bilal. After two days, I sent a reminder. That got me a reply. Bilal said he had left Australia for France. Till recently, he had been in touch with Andrapper, who had even decided on the date he'd reach Paris. But there was no news after that. Emails to him bounced back.

This was crucial information. But when I sent him a few more emails with the hope of getting to know more, there was no reply. I told him that I was supposed to collect the portion of the novel Andrapper had given him. He didn't respond to that either. That door seemed shut.

The Thursday Market convened twice. Many discussions took place, many ideas came up, many possibilities were debated, but we were unable to reach a conclusion. The only thing we agreed on was to try the St. Joseph's route again, and I did, but to no result.

One day, we were going to a movie in Anil's 1980s' Ambassador which we called Cultural Ambulance. It ferried ailing culture vultures every day, as Anil often said, so what else could its name be? An idea suddenly struck Nattapranthan's bald head. 'Turn the car back! I've a hunch about Operation Diego Garcia. If I'm right, then the person I've identified will have the next segment of the novel.' In response to our flurry of questions, he wanted us to turn around and go to my house to look up the printout of the second part of the novel. 'If you don't get it right, then we'll tattoo your head and march you on the street,' threatened Nibu. So we ditched our movie plan and went to my house. On the way, we tried to identify the one who would have the rest of the manuscript. Nattapranthan rejected each and every choice of ours.

At my place, while riffling through the printout, he asked, 'Did any of you see a Salu in this story?'

'I remember a Salu,' Salim said. 'He was the one helping Andrapper find his classmate, Jyoti.'

'Isn't that his role in this story?' Nattapranthan asked emphatically. When we nodded in agreement, he asked, 'Then why has Andrapper mentioned his phone number? What's the purpose of that number?'

That question stumped us. It's true. If that was not a clear clue, nothing else could be. We celebrated the breakthrough and called that number immediately.

It was a house in Alappuzha. An old lady who picked up the phone said Salu was not home yet. We asked her for his mobile number. 'Ayyo dear, there is no electricity here, please call later,' she said and hung up. We couldn't bear to wait till the next morning, as Salu was the only option left. The next day, early morning, I called him and introduced myself as a publisher. I had to sweat a lot to make him understand whom I was talking about. It was only when I said Diego Garcia that Salu finally figured it out.

'Oh, Chuang Tzu! We were friends, thanks to Orkut,' he said.

'Why Chuang Tzu?'

'That's what I used to call him!'

His replies to my questions were evasive and vague. When I asked if Chuang Tzu had sent anything to him, he pleaded ignorance and disconnected the call.

I wasn't convinced. It felt like he was trying to hide something. I called Salim and gave him an update. Let's go to his house and meet him, he suggested. If he doesn't answer the phone, how will we find the place, I said in hesitation. 'We'll go to every house in Alappuzha and see if there is a Salu,' he said. The enthusiasm to get things done even if it meant any corner of the world—that's what I liked about Salim.

So, without taking others from the Thursday Market, we left for Alappuzha soon after. At that point of time, I had no clue how to find Salu or to find out if he had the third portion of the novel. When we were close to town, Salim called Salu's house and got his mobile number. Then Salim called Salu and told him that Jyoti who worked in the railways gave us the number and that we had a packet to be delivered to her house. Was it possible to come to town and collect it, Salim asked. The ruse worked. 'I'll be there in half an hour, in front of the bus stand,' Salu said.

'We'll be in a silver Innova, this is its number . . .' Salim told him. 'How will we find you?'

'I've a black Splendour bike. I'll call if I can't find you.'

We had to wait for only about ten minutes for Salu to find our car.

'I'm Salim, and this is Priyanandan, my friend,' Salim introduced us.

'The film guy Priyanandan?' he asked.

'No,' I smiled.

'Get in, we'll be back in a jiffy,' Salim invited him to the car.

'My bike.' Salu hesitated.

'Leave it here, we'll drop you back.' Then Salim addressed Salu with theatrical seriousness. 'Salu, we are from the Interpol office in Thiruvananthapuram. You are in our custody now. I need clear answers from you to our questions.'

'Oh, I see, okay, ask me your questions,' he said calmly, without any panic. I figured it would be difficult to dupe him.

'Who is this Chuang Tzu?' Salim asked.

'A Chinese philosopher. Why do you ask?'

'What's his connection to Andrapper?'

'Which Andrapper, sir?'

'The one at Diego Garcia.'

'I also got a call last week asking about this guy. Was it you, sir? It's his Orkut profile name. Chuang Tzu.'

'How did you meet him?'

'He first called me to ask about the Jyoti you mentioned. Then we became friends on Orkut. He called me regularly after that. And we had met once.'

'You met Andrapper?' I abruptly broke my silence. Andrapper had been just a name so far, and here, next to me, was someone who had actually met him. Andrapper, my dear anonymous writer. I felt a strange sense of joy. I touched him casually. It was like touching Andrapper.

'Where did you meet him? Salim asked.

'One night he came to Alappuzha, without any notice,' Salu said. 'He said he was returning from a relative's place. We went to Jyoti-chechi's house the same night. From there he took a bus to Ernakulam.'

'Who was he going to meet?'

'He didn't tell me.'

'You've not been in touch after that?'

'No. There was no reply to my messages on Orkut. Then I moved from Orkut to Facebook, and that relationship ended.'

'Everything you've said is true?'

'Yes, sir, absolutely true. Sir, what's the issue?'

'We suspect that he is an international criminal. We are trying to locate where he is now. Can you help us with that?'

'Sure. What can I do for you?'

'Let's go to your house now. We'll stay in the car. You go inside and get us the stuff he left with you. Can you do that?'

'Stuff? What is that, sir?'

'His notes. He titled it *The Book of Forefathers*. We've got the rest of the content, that's how we came to know about the portion that's with you.'

There was no defiance in his tone when he said, 'Okay, I'll give it to you.'

I was overjoyed. 'You actually have it with you?'

'Yeah. Must have been with me for around six months. Came by post,' he said.

Around the same time I got the first part, I calculated. So, everyone was sent their portion at the same time. Some got it by email and some by post.

'Why didn't you give it to anyone till now?'

'He had specially instructed that I should give it only to someone responsible. I guess you guys fit the bill.'

He directed us to his house. When we reached, he pointed out Jyoti-chchi's house. I wanted to meet her and ask about Andrapper, but Salu said she was in Ernakulam for some medical treatment. 'Now that we know the house, we can come later,' Salim said. Meanwhile, Salu went inside his house and came out with the envelope. I grabbed it from him eagerly.

Salu M. Philip
Vettikkoottathil Veedu
Alappuzha

I wanted to open it and read it right then. But I resisted till we dropped Salu back at the bus stand for his bike.

'Okay, if we need any more help, we'll call you,' Salim said with a straight face when we reached the bus stand.

'Interpol's Thiruvananthapuram office, right?' he asked.

'Yes,' I said.

'When did Benyamin sir join Interpol?' his question came as a jolt.

'Benyamin? Who is that?' I tried to salvage the mission.

'Huh, don't try to fool me, sir. I recognized you the moment

we met. I've seen a photograph of you. I was waiting to see
how long this Interpol game would go on for. When you're
playing a prank, I felt I should return the favour. It was
Chuang Tzu who told me about your book. We discussed it
quite a lot. Both of us liked the book. In his covering letter
sent with this packet, Chuang Tzu wrote that he bought your
book from a stall in Ernakulam, and that someday, you'll end
up buying his book from Ernakulam. And that I shouldn't
give these papers to anyone other than you. I suspected the
last call was also from you. But then I was guarded just so
that I could make sure it was you.'

I was left speechless. My head stooped in shame. But Salim
was more embarrassed.

Salu bid us goodbye, requesting us to tell him if we
happened to meet Andrapper. The two of us were so mortified
that we kept quiet throughout the drive. After a while, I
opened the envelope and started reading—the third part of
Chuang Tzu Andrapper's life story.

A RAINY MORNING

DAWN REVEALED A rainy day. Diego had no distinct seasons.
It could be warm or cold or stormy or wet at any time of the
year. Things could change any time. Tropical depressions made
the weather unpredictable. Diego's sky could gift a shower
any month of the year. This was one such unexpected shower.

Though I felt like writing something in the comfort of
the rain, the body was too lazy to get up. Only someone
who can tame the needs of the body to the aims of the mind
can become a good writer—true not just for a writer, but to
achieve success in any profession. I tried to make myself get

up. I scolded myself. But I failed. My body rejected all the demands of my mind. A lazy body is like a curled-up old dog. When I say I loafed around till noon, you'll get the idea—how demanding my body was.

I heard the doorbell ring, but didn't care to get up. I turned the other side, ignoring it. It was only when Momma screamed from the stairs, 'Eda, you've two visitors!' that I scrambled to get up. 'For me? In this rain? Who could they be?' This time, I didn't guess. I washed my face and went downstairs.

Melvin! And Sudha, whom I'd met earlier.

I was amazed. 'Come, come in. A surprise visit? In this rain?'

'It's nothing. We were just passing by. So we thought we'd drop in on you. That's all.'

By then, Chettathi joined us. I said, 'Chettathi, look who's here. You met at Mariam Church, she was with my classmate Anita. We gave them a lift, if you remember.'

When Chettathi recognized Melvin, she embraced her as though they were long-lost friends. 'Oh yes, now I remember. Melvin, right?' Then she held Melvin's hand and made her sit on the sofa, next to Momma.

'Momma, I was talking about this pretty girl that day. Momma's son is not bad, huh? See, with one meeting, he's made her come to our house. If you want, we can even consider this a formal engagement ceremony and take things forward. What do you say?' Chettathi laughed aloud, amused by her own comment, while Melvin and I felt uncomfortable.

'Ayyo! Sudha-chechi said she wanted to meet Anita-chechi's friend,' an embarrassed Melvin explained to Momma.

'Meet me? Sudha-chechi . . . what's the matter?' I asked.

When Sudha did not say anything, Chettathi quickly figured out the situation. 'Come, Momma, let's prepare lunch. Let them sit and talk,' she said.

'No, no, we won't be staying for lunch,' Melvin hurriedly told Momma.

'Why, dear? You think I don't approve of your visit?' Momma said, unusually teasing. 'My only worry is what will someone who sleeps till noon do with a pretty wife like you?'

Everyone laughed. But Melvin seemed on the verge of tears. Often, our actions are interpreted in ways that we would never even have thought of. When that happens, what else can you do but become helpless, like Melvin?

Chettathi took Momma inside.

I was contrite. 'Melvin, I am sorry. I apologize for the misunderstanding. It's a problem with the Andrapper house.'

'That's okay. They were not abusing me,' said a conciliated Melvin.

'Why did you want to see me?' I asked Sudha.

She continued to be silent. Then she gathered herself and said, 'For the past few days, I have been thinking of the case that Anita's friend mentioned.'

'What case?'

'That murder. What I told you then was a lie. Actually, I was present when the case was being attended to.'

I stared at her in disbelief.

'I attended to the man's case. He had died before he reached the hospital. We didn't have much to do other than filling the forms for the mortuary. I did that. I don't know the rest. I was scared to admit it last time. But then I couldn't sleep in peace. I don't know if it's right in terms of medical ethics and the law here. I wanted to tell you. That's why I've dragged Melvin here and come to see you.'

Sudha said all this in one breath. The pressure that had been caused by the cover-up was pretty evident.

'Are you sure he was shot?'

'Yes, the doctor identified the wound. We recovered two bullets.'

'Was that what you entered in the medical file?'

'Yes. I saw what the doctor noted down.'

'Then how come the case is missing from the hospital files?'

'That I don't know. Only they can answer that.'

'Who was the doctor in charge?'

Sudha paused and then said, 'Doctor Iqbal.'

'We heard of it from Sudha-chechi. When we came to know that there was some mystery about this case, we kept quiet. Why would we get ourselves into trouble? That's why we denied knowing anything. Sorry,' Melvin said.

'You haven't done anything wrong! Even the Public Security is trying to erase this case. I just casually asked about it that day.'

'Who told you about this?' Melvin whispered as if we were discussing a secret.

'I was witness to it.'

'Witness?'

'Yeah, I was present when the incident took place. I even came to City Hospital. But after that, the case totally vanished. I was curious about it. Also, the guy who died was an old classmate of mine.'

The conversation ended there.

Momma had made meatball pasta for them. A special dish for our guests. Melvin tried to slip away, but Momma was adamant. I hadn't seen her so affectionately insistent. It looked like she believed Chettathi's every word. Momma had accepted Melvin as my girl!

MASS AMNESIA

MY BOAT STOPPED in front of City Hospital. Sudha's account had energized me. Things were falling into place, I felt. When one makes multiple attempts to hit a target, at least one has to succeed. One person finally agreed that I wasn't hallucinating about Senthil getting shot. And it wasn't just any person but the nurse who had attended his case. What better proof could one want! Mr Vijay Mullikratnam, I'll prove you wrong. I'll go to any extent to do that. The next step was Dr Iqbal, the doctor who had attended to Senthil along with Sudha.

I headed straight to Emergency. Someone there told me Dr Iqbal was in the outpatient ward. I roamed around for an hour before going to his room. Patients, their relatives, scurrying nurses, attendants, trollies, drip stands, wheelchairs, plastered legs, wrapped-up bellies, vomiting, Band-Aids—the verandah was overflowing. I waded through it to the doctor's room. Though it was past noon, there was a crowd outside his room. I went and sat with the patients.

An overweight nurse mistook me for a medical representative. 'No time to spare for you today. Come on Tuesday.'

'This is a personal visit.'

'If it's personal, then meet him at his house.' She turned her back like an angry elephant and marched inside.

I wondered what makes some nurses so grumpy once they get into their uniforms. When she came out to call the next patient, she saw me again. 'Haven't you left yet? Whatever you say, don't think I'll let anyone inside without an admission card!'

Patients were looking at me with some sympathy mixed with a degree of contempt.

'Sister, please. I request you to help me. It'll be more crowded at his house. That's why I'm here. I'll take just five minutes of his time.'

She faltered at my pleading. 'Hmm . . . Haven't you seen the number of patients waiting? If there is time in between, I'll call you. Don't disturb me till then, okay?'

'Yeah, okay.'

I walked past the partition and sat in the verandah. The flow of patients to the room was slow. The doctor took a minimum of fifteen minutes on each of them. If this continued, I wouldn't be able to meet him for another three hours.

While I was sitting there, I noticed one of the patients—an African—looking at me often. It was as if he had something to tell me. There was a friendliness to him, but I couldn't place him. After some time, he came up to me and asked, 'Aren't you Andrapper?' When I nodded, he continued. 'We were together at St. Joseph's. I'm Mohammad Mustafa.' Suddenly, as if a blanket had been whipped off my memory, a number of images came to mind. The guy who stood next to me in our fifth standard photo. Mohammad Mustafa. The one who, during a fight in sixth standard, stabbed a compass into Seyfu's chest. Mohammad Mustafa. One who could never get his shirt buttoned straight. Mohammad Mustafa. He who used to pronounce 'helicopter' as 'helicottepar' and 'bucket' as 'buttekk', and 'Adis Ababa' as 'Acid Ababa'. Mohammad Mustafa. The victim of our group song, 'Yellow, yellow, dirty fellow sitting on a buffalo'. The curly-haired Mohammad Mustafa!

'Why are you here?' I asked.

'Hey, man, why am I at the hospital? To get a shave!' He laughed with impish glee, revealing his gums. I joined him, a bit shamefaced.

'I come at least twice a month to meet this doctor. I've a horrible disease: sickle-cell anaemia. I have terrible body pain and have to take medication. Some doctors don't prescribe the required dose. But this man is different. Just give him a little extra and he'll recommend any dose. I tried ganja, but it wasn't strong enough to numb the pain. Morphine is better. I can ignore the pain and swim in that high. That swimming has become my fate.'

Sickle-cell disease. Pain. Morphine. Fate. I couldn't comprehend it fully. Before I could ask anything, the fat nurse called out his name. As patients leave the doctor's room through another door, I couldn't meet him later. I continued to wait but not for long. When the nurse called out a number and couldn't find the patient, she gestured to me to go in. I said an extravagantly humble thanks, to which she responded with a stingy smile.

Inside was a fair, handsome man. The prayer bump on his forehead was prominent. Then the hairy ears, the cute bald head and the long nose.

He welcomed me, pointing at his watch. 'It's time for me to pray. The only routine I manage to keep among the vast number of things I don't.'

'I won't disturb you. I just wanted to check on something small and I'm out.'

He smiled gently. 'Tell me.'

'I'll come straight to the point. I'm doing a thesis. "Island: Its Lives and Minds", that's the subject.'

'Very interesting. What do you mean by it?'

'What are the difference between people who live on islands and those on the mainland? Do the limitations of an island change a person? Does his perspective become restricted? Is a person's level of tolerance related to the vastness of nature? How does living on an island shape one's mind? These are the avenues I'm pursuing.'

'Nice and distinctive topic. All the best. As far as I know, being on an island does affect our viewpoint. We don't take the long view, we see only short distances. So, myopia is very common. It's yet to be studied how myopia influences a man's intellectual insight and creativity. If you explore that, it'll be a success.'

'Are there any diseases specific to our island?'

'Some skin diseases due to the constant contact with sea breeze . . .'

'Sir, what's this sickle-cell disease?'

'Oh right, there's that. It's a hereditary disease, which we can say is the result of the social restrictions on the island. A rare disorder of red-blood corpuscles that causes extreme pain in the joints. It is mostly found in communities that marry only among themselves. Here it's prominent among the Chagos. It's because of the island's boundaries forcing them to marry only among themselves. That's why now our government is promoting marriages with outsiders.'

'Why do they ask for morphine, sir?' I asked, thinking about Mohammad Mustafa.

'There is no cure for that disease. One has to writhe in pain one's entire life. The affected use morphine or any such drug to forget the pain. No other way to live.'

'Sir, now to the third part of the thesis, "Islands: Accidents and Murders". Doctor, you must remember that last month, a young man was bought here with gunshot wounds.' I dived into my topic of interest.

'Gunshot wounds? Don't remember!'

'But I remember you handling it. You were in the Emergency and attended to the case.'

The expression on his face changed suddenly. And as if to hide it, he sat kneading his forehead. 'In OP, Emergency and at my house, I attend around a thousand cases a month. I don't have such a sharp memory as you young men.'

'That may be true, doctor. When the job is just a duty, it's normal that we don't remember everything about it. But the exceptional cases, —those we don't forget. I think this is one of them.'

'It is the person himself who has to decide what to remember and what to forget, others can't do it for him. What is important for you may not be relevant for me. I, too, have the freedom to remember and forget, right?'

'Of course! But if everyone forgets something that everyone is supposed to remember, then we should assume we have a problem. Don't you agree, sir? Like short sight, a disease called short memory. Is it because we live on an island? Have you ever felt so, doctor?'

His face had turned dark.

'My duty is to prescribe the right treatment to my patients. I'm doing that. The rest is beyond me. I don't think I can help you in any way. It's also getting late,' he looked at his watch again.

'I'll come again, doctor. Perhaps you'll have a better recollection of what happened, then.'

'There is no medical book that says we can recollect events about which we've absolutely no clue. So another visit will be useless,' he said as if it was the last word on the subject.

I left without thanking him. Gratitude is for people who deserve it.

THE ROOM OF FOREFATHERS

SOMETIMES, IT'S LIKE that. From the hotbed of experiences, I return to the writing desk. It could be that writers become weakened by the very intensity of their experiences. Like diseases, weaknesses, too, are in our blood. There could be rare instances of writers flexing their muscle, but is there any writer around known for his fitness and strength?

It was one of those days for me. By evening, after returning from the hospital, the spirit of the written word had infected me. A spirit that affects one all of a sudden, without any external stimulus. Under that influence, I wrote a lot, and almost without any breaks. As I was writing, I felt the need for some reference books on Diego. I knew that the best place to get them would not be any library in Diego, but a room on the second floor of my house. We used to call it the Room of Forefathers. It was in that closed room that every historical record of the Andrapper family was kept. Many years ago, I'd gone into the room a few times with Valyappachan. I could only recall the smell of old books on the shelves, and the darkness. I wanted to enter the room again. The key was with Valyapapan. I went upstairs. Valyapapan was seated near the window, an open book on his lap, his eyes fixed on the lake, lost in some thought. When he turned to me, I made my request.

'It's not a room that anyone can enter casually. Our ancestors made some rules and regulations for it. Every senior member in the Andrapper family should be in the know about the entry, the person who wants to enter should record his name and signature in the register, and the room can be opened only in the presence of two witnesses. They should certify that nothing was taken out of the room. Even now, these rules are mandatory for everyone.'

'Valyapapan, all these rules were made when there was a lot of wealth and power. To stop people stealing stuff. What's there to steal now? Give me that key. I need to refer to some books,' I said lightly.

'It's not a storehouse for wealth and treasures. It's the Room of Forefathers. It stores the memories of the many generations that lived before us. It's a holy place. Only those who know the value of it can be allowed to enter.' Valyapapan became more serious.

'I promise that I won't do anything harmful to its sanctity.' I became humble.

'Okay. This is the first and last time. Never ask for it again. One more thing. Every rule has to be followed. Just that we don't have any witnesses. Instead, let your conscience be the guard.' Valyapapan handed over the key.

I couldn't ignore those words. I wrote and signed my name in the register outside the room before opening the door. The scent of oldness wafted into my nose. I remembered the day I had held Valyappachan's hand and stepped into the room. Now, when I stepped inside, I sensed the gravity of Valyapapan's words. It was not just an ordinary room— generations were stacked in those shelves.

To one side was a pile of old records, in palm-leaf manuscripts and leather sheets. Another side had books, files and documents in paper. In exactly the middle of the room was a huge almirah, its racks labelled with the name of each forefather—it resembled a family cemetery. Hormis Avira Andrapper was at the extreme bottom. Above him were twelve ancestors: Philip Avira Andrapper, Antony Avira Andrapper,

Joseph Andrapper, Stephen Andrapper, John Andrapper, Andrew Andrapper, Mathew Andrapper, Stanley Andrapper, Samuel Andrapper, Felix Andrapper, and at the very top, my Valyappachan, Rostin Andrapper.

For the generations to follow, there were empty racks waiting. From the next generation, Valyapapan Joseph Andrapper, from mine, my brother Jeff Andrapper because Valyapapan didn't have any sons. I was not fortunate enough to be in the series. Only the firstborns of each generation were entitled to the glory.

I was curious to know what was inside the racks. I touched the handle of the almirah with great care when suddenly I heard the door bang. It was Valyapapan.

'You said you only wanted books. There are no books in the almirah. Don't take advantage of my affection for you.'

'Valyapapan, it's just out of curiosity. I've been staying in this house for all these years and if I haven't seen this place, how can I be proud of being an Andrapper?'

'If you're interested, there is no harm in seeing it. But you ought to be reverential.' He pulled open a rack for me. 'In the memory of our forefathers, we keep three things in these racks. One, the portrait of the forefather, drawn by the best artist available in Diego at the time. Two, his most favourite object. Some choose the object when they're alive. When I die, you should keep the crown in this room. That meaningless crown symbolizes my life.'

What would Jeff choose to be kept in this room? It would be his favourite laptop, what else? What would I choose if I get a chance? The novel which is to be written!

'The third item is the most important thing,' Valyapapan said. 'It's called the *hasta phalakam*.'

'Hasta phalakam? What's that?' I was eager to know.

From the rack, Valyapapan pulled out a small wooden casket. Its lid was sealed with wax.

'This is the hasta phalakam box. It is believed that this was the idea of Hormis Avira Andrapper, who was extremely intelligent, a visionary. He must have envisioned every generation that would follow him. That each one of them should leave a distinct mark on this earth. That's why he introduced this hasta phalakam box as a mandatory custom in the Andrapper family. Only someone who could see ahead in time could have come up with such an idea. Those who think only of the contemporary world can't grasp his logic.'

Valyapapan softly scraped away the wax seal. Then he opened the lid and held the box up to the light. Inside was a clay plate with someone's hand impression. There was blue paint on it. The colour highlighted the lines, crests and troughs clearly.

'This is the right-hand impression of our forefather John Andrapper,' Valyapapan said, pointing at the name on the label of the rack we had opened. 'Look at this. This is the hand that guided this family for a long time.'

I took the box from him with both hands. Then, as if it was a baby, I kept it close to my chest and looked at it for a long while. A hand impression made centuries ago. The lines of time lay deep in it. A smart person could not only read these lines to decode his life, but also the times. Who could arrange a better memory for tomorrow!

'Tell me everything about the hasta phalakam,' I said.

'It is brought in on the day the head of the family dies. The box is filled with the best soil available in Diego, mixed with clean sand and glue in a particular proportion. The hand of the dead father is then imprinted on it. He leaves the world after gifting this to time. Once the clay dries up, it gets coated with blue paint, to make the impressions sharper.'

I looked at it for some more time before returning the box. Valyapapan closed the lid, resealed it with wax and put it back on the rack. Then he pulled out another box. It contained a pure-white porcelain bowl with drawings in gold on the rim. Probably a Chinese bowl. That must have been the favourite object of John Andrapper.

Valyapapan then showed me a framed picture. In typical Portuguese attire of the era, my ancestor John Andrapper solemnly looked at me.

'The Room of Forefathers is not a museum. It's the life of our family,' Valyapapan said, closing the almirah. 'Don't go around telling people about this. We should maintain the privacy of the family.'

In front of the almirah that contained generations within it, I stood a long time, with folded hands.

KANYABHOGASOOKTHAM

VALYAPAPAN WENT BACK to his recliner. Among the books and documents in the room, I began to search for references to Diego. It was a more massive and significant collection than I had imagined. Some I opened and read, for fun.

The first one I stumbled upon was a deal struck by the French government and Diego on the official language:

Le français restera langue officielle des Dego Garcia aussi longtemps que les représentants élus de la population n'auront pas pris une décision différente.

(The French language shall remain the official language
of Diego Garcia as long as the elected representatives of
the people shall not decide otherwise.)

Article XXVXI of Traite de Cession

It was in violation of this deal that the British authorities,
in 1975, through a decree, declared English as the official
tongue. How many similar violations have there been! The
history of them is called Diego!

Another file I saw had a crucial order of authority that the
French East India Company handed over to the Andrapper
family. Its loose English translation is:

The Andrapper Family, of Portuguese lineage from
Andrew Pereira, now headed by Hormis Avira Andrapper,
will be the de facto owners of Diego Garcia and the rest
of the Chagos Archipelago such as Peros Banhos, the
Salomon Islands, the Three Brothers (Islands), the Egmont
Islands and the Great Chagos Bank.

Diego Garcia and the Chagos Archipelago will be ruled
and administered by the Andrapper family, but the land
will remain and serve as a coiling station for French ships
at the Indian Ocean. The French East India Company does
not have any plan to develop the land as a French Colony.

The family will have all the de facto authority to rule the
Inhabitants, Migrants, Workers and Slaves. All the income
from the land, plantations, industries and the atoll will
go to the family, and no tax will be paid to the French
East India Company.

This is a mutual agreement made between the Andrapper Family and the French East India Company.

Article XXVII of Traite de Cession

There were also a lot of rare books. Thomas Stephen's *History of Christ*, Abraham Rogers's translation of Bharthrihari, Fr. Roths's Sanskrit grammar, and Fr. Zha Kalmethy's translation of the four Vedas were among them. In the same shelf were Benjamin Bailey's short essay *Madyanirodhini*, Raja Ram Mohan Roy's interpretation of the Upanishads, and King Bhoga's *Samarangana Sutradhara*. Then there was a translation of the book *The story of Phulmani and Karuna*, written by Catherine Hana Mullens, alongside *Interesting Tales by an Outsider for India's Women*.

Who among my ancestors had been such a lover of books? A man interested in collecting books? It could not have been Valyappachan Rostin Andrapper. There was no proof of his interest in literature. It must have been someone before him. Felix Andrapper? Samuel Andrapper? Stanley Andrapper? Whoever it was, it must be from him that I got my love for books. The stories he had wanted to write might finally be written by me. These desires never die. They get transferred, through one's genes, down through generations, till they manifest at some point.

I also found valuable documents of Diego Garcia's history from the Room of Forefathers. A logbook titled *A French Ship's Journey to India—1642* was the most remarkable of them.

To the east of Venecia's St. Raphael Airport lies a small village called Sanchi. Most of its inhabitants are Buddhist refugees from Sri Lanka. A bodhi tree with large, spreading branches is the landmark of Sanchi. Believers claim the tree is over two thousand years old. According to the Buddhists in Diego, Mahendra and Sanghamitra, who left the subcontinent to spread the religion in Sri Lanka, lost their way and first landed in Diego. They were said to have planted a branch of the bodhi tree here, and another one in Sri Lanka. As they were from a place called Sanchi, this region also came to be called under the same name, according to legend.

The Buddhists of Diego rely on this logbook as evidence to prove that they were the first inhabitants of the island. It was because of this book that they enjoyed special status and Senate positions.

I flipped through the pages with interest. It was a travelogue by Vice Admiral Theogin, captain of the French war vessel *La Favorite* that had been to many countries. The voyage began at Le Havre in France and continued to various ports such as Rabath, Banchu, Seytna and Tholanaro, before the ship went to Goa. It finally anchored at Diego's eastern side in May 1642. Theogin refers to Sanchi as Seynchi.

He mentions visiting the eastern islands of Seynchi, home of the ruler of the Garcia Islands, Maharaja Veeravardhanan. He spoke fluently the Buddhists' language of Pali, and most people in the region followed Buddhism. There was a beautiful monastery built on a cliff facing the sea. The king told Theogin that he had not allowed the Portuguese to step on to his soil and that he wished to be a French ally. He angrily asked Theogin why the French kings were not trying to defeat the evil Portuguese at sea.

Nowhere in our history had a King Veeravardhanan ruled Diego. But Theogin's logs clearly record a meeting with a ruler of that name. Is he saying that that ruler belonged to the Andrapper lineage?

Before I left the room, I stood before the forefathers' almirah once again. I felt intensely curious about the favourite objects of each one of them. I knew I was breaking Valyapapan's trust and the Andrapper family rules, but I couldn't resist the temptation.

I peeped out of the door to see if Valyapapan was standing guard somewhere. He had dozed off on his recliner. I could open the racks in peace. I went back into the room, slowly opened the topmost rack, which belonged to my Valyappachan Rostin Andrapper, and took out the box with his favourite object. There was an ashtray made of glass, and a set of pipes. I remembered that he was a chain-smoker. What else could be his favourite objects but an ashtray and pipes!

The next one was that of Felix Andrapper's. His favourite was a nutcracker, which had intricate woodwork and gold enamel work. I wondered about an epoch when a nutcracker could be considered the most interesting artefact.

Then came Samuel Andrapper's rack. It had an elephant tusk with goldwork and a long gold chain.

Stanley Andrapper's box contained the best of surprises. It had a book, yellow with age, with torn edges and pages almost eaten up by silverfish. I eagerly flipped through it. There were just twelve pages to it. In a Malayalam so ancient that I read the title with great difficulty: *Kanyabhogasooktham*.

I was extremely eager to know its contents. But then I heard Valyapapan yelling, 'Aren't you done with your search? Stop it for now. Continue later.' I quickly closed the almirah, but I didn't feel like parting with the book. I was dying to read it. I hid it from Valyapapan by inserting it into the French travelogue, and briskly walked back to my room.

Once inside, I latched the door. I tried to read the text. It was hard work.

Author: Ittooppa Paili Avarkal. Not for sale. Printed at
Madirasi Press.

The first page had these details, apart from the title. My
curiosity grew manifold as it was written by a Christian, when
usually these kind of books bore the name of sages.

Unlike the title *Kanyabhogasooktham*, or the Rules of
Virgin Pleasure, which hinted that it was for those who
wanted to enjoy women, the book was actually for women
who wanted to be enjoyed, according to the foreword. 'This
is a concise version of the archaic work written on palm
leaves by my legendary ancestor Itti Korata, keeping in mind
those chaste women who want to make love before they get
married. We express our gratitude to the Christian missionary
who helped us in bringing it out.'

There was no mention of the name of the missionary. No
clue of the year of publication. The foreword said that the idea
of publishing the book was inspired by *Samkshepavedartham*,
another book printed by the Madirasi Press. So, it could be
assumed that this came out during the late 1700s or early
1800s. Very interesting things were mentioned in the book;
although half of it was lost to silverfish and fungus, I soldiered
on. The crux of the book was on how to choose a man if an
unmarried and healthy woman wanted to have sex. It was
advised right at the start that only if the woman could not
control her feelings through prayers, fasting, fantasizing, self-
stimulation, hard work and spirituality—only then should
she invite a man to her bed. If the act could give the woman
feelings of regret, sin, self-despair, abstinence or depression,
she should preferably wait till she gets a husband.

Don't choose men younger or of the same age, was the
first instruction. The reason given was that these men are

impatient, impulsive and ignorant of the subtleties of sex. They are incapable of satisfying women; instead, they will focus on their own pleasure. Their haste and inexperience will hurt you beyond limits. No pleasure, but only pain can come from them.

Don't chose old and unmarried men—they have wrong notions about sex and lack confidence. You cannot get what you expect from them. Sex with them will make you depressed and averse to it.

Middle-aged married men are the best. More than looking for their pleasure, they will seek yours. Their knowledge will help avoid pain. Their patience will make you happy. Their experience will protect you from getting pregnant.

But beware of men with more than four children: they lack control. Beware of those with children in quick succession: they are easily satisfied. Beware of the fat ones: they are lazy. Beware of men who fight with their wives: they will be dishonest. Beware of junkies: they are irritating. It was a long list. My favourite among them was: Beware of scholars, lawyers and artists—they are crazy sex freaks, but incapable of 'doing anything'.

I wanted to read the entire book without skipping a word. But Chettathi came to my room to ask for something. I had to quickly hide the book under the tablecloth. I couldn't get back to it for the rest of the day.

That night, for no reason, my mind was awash with memories of Anpu. Senthil's sister, Anpu.

CARDIAC ARREST

I stayed in bed longer than usual, unable to free myself from the previous night's dreams. Usually, dreams fade away by the next morning. But those particular dreams remained vivid in my memory. I began to doubt as to which version of me was more real: the person in my dream, or the person in reality. For me, both are experiences—dream and reality. The mind engages with both with the same intensity. How can we say which is true and which is fake? And sometimes, we do wish for dreams to continue into life and life to continue into dreams. I tried to fulfil the wish by daydreaming. But that didn't help much. I had to meet Anpu to gain some control over my dreams. I freshened up and left for Cherar Peruntheruvu.

Senthil's house was dead silent after all the hullabaloo of after-death ceremonies. The only reminder of a death was a small pandal stretching out of the house. When I rang the bell, Senthil's father opened the door. He was surprised to see me. '*Kanna*, you are here so early in the morning.' He stepped on to the verandah, hugged me and took me inside.

'I had to come this way for something, so I thought of popping in for a short while.'

'Good, good, I'm glad to see you. Nobody visits us. Only you two classmates come. The house has gone silent. Anpu, look who is here!'

Anpu came into the hall. Either she had woken up late or gone back to bed after getting up. She looked drowsy as she bundled up her hair. But it only added to her beauty. Truly beautiful girls look even better unadorned. I felt lucky to have seen Anpu in such a state.

'What news?' she asked me with a smile tinged with sorrow.

'Nothing. I'm fine.'

Thus ended the conversation. It was like none of us had anything to say. We were each of us lonely in our own tent of memories. Why did I rush here? Yeah, to see Anpu, but I also had some questions in mind about Senthil. However, at that point I couldn't recall any of them. 'I dropped in while passing by. See you later,' I said, getting up.

'I'll make some coffee,' Anpu said.

'No. It's fine.'

'*Ennada*, kanna, why are you in such a hurry? Anpu, go and get him coffee.' Senthil's father did not want me to leave. I sat again, humbled by the affection.

Anpu went inside.

We returned to silence.

'Can someone have a cardiac arrest at his age?' he asked me suddenly.

I was shocked. 'Any age . . .' My hands were shaking as I said that.

'When a cardiac arrest happens, won't the person feel something, anything, before that? No pain, nothing?' he asked.

'Yes, there will be pain.'

'When?' He would not let go.

'Don't know for sure. But I've heard that for some the pain could start a few hours before the actual event.' I was squirming in my chair by then.

'He must have kept quiet, right? Stupid guy.'

I almost got up to rush to him and scream, 'No, no! He did not die of a cardiac arrest!' But Anpu was already at the door with coffee. I reached out and drank it greedily.

Later, I realized it must have been weird. What would Anpu have thought of me? The first time I had come, I snatched the glass of water. The second time, the coffee. Would she think of me as a glutton? By the time I finished the coffee, it was pouring cats and dogs. I stepped out to the verandah,

I couldn't have run to the jetty without an umbrella. I just needed to get to the boat, where there was a raincoat.

'Anpu, please do me a favour. Give me an umbrella. I need it to get to the jetty.'

'Let the rain stop, kanna. You wait,' said Senthil's father.

'No, Appa, I'm in a hurry.'

'Okay, Anpu, drop him at the jetty.'

Anpu came with two umbrellas. We walked into the rain. She repeated what her father had said. 'Anna had lots of friends, but none of them comes here now. Only you two come.' It seemed as though she was crying.

'Appa said the same. Who's the other visitor?' I asked.

'Akka. Jesintha.'

'Who?'

'Don't you know Jesintha? She was in your class. Earlier, we lived on the same street. Now Akka's family stays at Cornish.'

'You mean Jesintha came here to see you?' I found it hard to believe.

'Yes, she was here even a few days ago. After Anna's death, she's been coming quite often. When she sees me, she starts crying. The two of them were friends since childhood.'

'Yeah, yeah . . .' I began to shiver in the rain. 'You have her number?'

'Yes.' She knew it by heart. '9876543210.'

I saved it on my phone and told her, 'I need to meet you alone someday. When you come to Seleucia, call me for sure. Wherever I am, I'll come and meet you. This is my phone number.' I gave back the umbrella after stepping into the boat.

'Sure, I'll call. Please come this way again. Appa likes you a lot.'

'I'll come.'

She waved at me.

After the boat was on its way, I took out my phone and called Jesintha's number. Instead of a normal ringtone, I heard a new Tamil song.

DECEIT

JESINTHA TALKED AS if we had met just the previous day. I thought she might panic on getting a call from me, and that she'd disconnect it. But she made small talk, told me some of the gossip going around the port, and asked about my writing.

'I need to meet you urgently,' I said in a heavy tone.

'Why not? Tomorrow morning, if it's not raining, shall we meet at the same place? Or any other coffee shop of your preference. Or do you want to meet today?

'No, tomorrow is fine.' I hung up. I had been hoping that she would try to evade me and I could trap her, but she disappointed me. Where is the thrill for an investigating officer if the suspect comes to his office and surrenders! Still, I dreamt all night about grilling Jesintha.

It didn't rain the next day. I went early to Port Louis and sat at my favourite table.

For a moment, I got it wrong, with the thought that it was my first visit since the shooting, till I remembered that I'd come again the next day. On seeing me, the coffee shop owner came to chat. 'It's been a long time. You've not been around?'

'I'd gone to the mainland.'

'Oh, did you?' He was curious. 'You go there often?'

'Yeah, I went to college on the mainland.'

'What's this mainland like? Is it bigger than our Diego?

How's the weather? Does it have more water than Diego? Is it true that there are lots of trees there?' A barrage of questions.

'One has to experience the mainland, one can't describe it.'

'Oh, is that so? I've never been anywhere other than this island,' he said a little sadly. 'My fate is to see nothing, know nothing, and die in this coffee shop.'

Jesintha arrived.

'Hello, why did you want to meet me all of a sudden?' She pulled up a chair and sat facing me.

'That's easy to figure out.'

'When I got some free time yesterday, I guessed a lot of possibilities—from a crush you suddenly felt on me to a financial emergency. Now tell me which one it is.'

The shop owner served us the coffee. 'The next time you go to the mainland, please let me know. I'll also come. I want to see the world,' he said to me.

'Did you go to Senthil's house a few days ago?' I asked Jesintha.

'So, that's the matter. I was wondering where you got my number from. Anpu gave it to you, didn't she?'

'Why? Shouldn't she have given it to me?'

'Why are you like this? All your negative questions! It's boring, okay. You are like a girl sulking!'

I sat quietly for a while.

'How can you fool those nice people?' I asked.

'Fool them? I don't understand.' Her face had turned dark.

'How can you pretend in front of them when you know what had actually happened?'

'Oh, I see. Let me ask the same question to you. You've also been to that house a couple of times. Why didn't you tell them everything?'

I was silent.

'They're yet to come to terms with the shock of the death. They console themselves, calling it fate. In the midst of all that, should I go and tell them that their son was murdered?' Her voice got louder.

'Shh. Shh. Softly. Keep it between us.'

'Why softly? Everyone in this area knows that someone was shot dead here. But the Public Security has another story. What can we do?'

'Don't you know how it happened?' I asked in a sceptical tone.

'I know as much as you know. Probably less. That day, you were in a better position to see it happening. I was facing the opposite side.'

'I can't believe it! You just stood there watching a classmate and a neighbour dying in front of you. When the Public Security came to question us, you stopped me from giving an account of what had happened. You're lying to me. You know everything.'

'Who am I to know everything? God? Yes, it's true, Senthil was my classmate and my neighbour. But when he got shot that day, do you know how many years it had been since I'd seen him last? After seventh standard at St. Joseph's, I left for Sri Lanka. You know that. I hadn't seen him since. You calculate how many years it has been! I grew up. He also grew up. I don't know what he had become in those years we didn't meet. I don't know what excellence he had achieved to get shot dead on the street. Though I recognized him when I saw him, my intuition told me to be cautious. It's an ability only women have. A protection that saves us from landing in trouble. We are cautious about everything. You guys don't understand it. It's thanks to that same intuition I stopped you from being a witness. I was right, wasn't I? Look at the Public

Security's reaction! They have destroyed the entire case. For whose sake? I don't know. But they have done it for someone. If you had given a witness statement, I'm not sure you'd have been sitting here in front of me now.'

I had nothing to say. No argument.

'It's my policy to take care of myself before poking my nose into another's business. You can call it selfishness. I don't mind. But that's how it works in this world. I want to enjoy my life. This policy has taken me from a shack at Cherar Peruntheruvu to a flat at Cornish. If I knew anything related to Senthil's death, and if I had something to hide, like you suspect, why would I have told you that it was Senthil? You would have never come to know. Right? Do you know that the day after the incident, I went to his house. I thought the body must have been sent home. I'd gone to attend his funeral. But when I went there, his family had no clue that he was dead. How could I have told them what I saw? It was awful! And when I went the next time, they all believed that Senthil had died of a heart attack. I kept thinking of telling Anpu the truth every time I visited. But I couldn't. If you see that as deceit, I've nothing to say.'

I sat unable to look at her face, toying with the empty cup.

'I'm already late for office. Call me when you want to meet again. I'll always be available at this number. See you.' She slipped on her shades and left.

Smart girl, I told myself. Whether you are right or wrong, you've succeeded in convincing me. That's smartness. This world is for people like you. It's not surprising that you have a fancy flat at Cornish while I continue to stay at the house of my ancestors.

REALIZATION

I REACHED HOME to find the family in the midst of celebrations. Momma came and hugged me as soon as she saw me. Lucky you, said Chettathi. Papa, oddly, was sipping his drink in the front room. Some great moment of glory—but I had no clue what it was. I stood there like a fool till Papa offered me a drink. I declined because I was afraid that there had been some progress in Momma's and Chettathi's interest in Melvin. But fortunately, that was not the matter.

'The visa papers are ready for your Australia trip,' Papa said, patting my shoulder. A shiver passed through my spine. 'It's just formalities left now. Go to the embassy for a formal interview, and get the visa stamped on your passport. That's all.'

I made no reply. Actually, there should have been a tirade of words from me. But the turn of events had left me speechless. Papa had mentioned it to me only once or twice. I had not realized how serious he was about it. I got up silently and went to my room.

After a while, Papa came to my room. I turned my back, facing the other side.

'You were always like this when you were sulking. How true it is that habits don't change however much a man grows up!' Papa said, sitting on my bed.

I dragged the blanket over my face. After I did it, I realized that it was another feature of my childhood tantrums.

'After a certain age, we should consciously rid ourselves of some habits,' Papa said. 'Especially if that helps us, the family and society.'

'I don't want to listen to old philosophy. I am being kicked out of this house and deported from this island. Isn't that what all of you want?'

'Don't act like a fourth-rate dramatist. I expect a better response from you. It's for your future, a bright future. Don't you have a dream? The dream of writing a great Malayalam novel. A novel that will be read by the world. To realize that dream, you've to sacrifice some things. All great deeds demand that. Has anyone conquered the Himalayas walking on a red carpet? Anyone?'

'If I go away from here, will talent flow into me? Will words fly towards me?' I asked, fuming.

'I'm not saying that. But your perspective will expand. Your visions will widen. Every great writer in the world has written their great works after leaving their hometown. I'll tell you of my experience too. The person I was before Paris, was transformed after my time in the city. Our small dreams grow into big ones. That's probably the only advantage of an expatriate life. Consider your case. Did you give any thought to becoming a novelist before you went to the mainland? I don't think so. Life there altered your dreams. Changed your aims. *That's* what I'm saying. It'll add new depths to your novel. Those that you wouldn't even be able to think of now. If you stay back, your life will fade into anonymity. You're old enough to think for yourself. My advice will only irritate you, so I'm leaving. You have one night to make a decision. A night to choose who you want to be. All those who became nothing in life would have also had a similar night. They must have spent the rest of their lives regretting the decision they took on that crucial night. There is nothing worse in this earth than a life filled with self-contempt. All those who succeeded in this world have also had a similar night. Remember that.'

Papa's words echoed in my mind long after he left. Why was I keen on staying back? Of what use was it to me? What misfortune could befall me if I leave Diego? What would I gain? How did my family benefit from deporting me? But wasn't that a figment of my imagination? An argument to fight a decision taken without my approval. What else could it be? Nothing remained on this island to hold me back. For a man of my age, it should have been a binding love affair that was keeping me back. But there was no such affair. What else? Attachment to the family? No. Friends from whom I couldn't part? No. Fun gatherings? No. Convivial evenings? No. What else? Perhaps the only reason to stay back was the mystery of Senthil's death. The curiosity to know the answers and to chase after them. But wasn't it childish to say I'll be satisfied only if I can find out the motives and the people responsible for his death and its cover-up, like in a detective novel? Suppose I find out someday, can I even raise a finger against them? What support will the law and the government give me? Nothing. There was a community of people immersed in fraud and forgery. They were beyond all law. Their rules were not ours. I wouldn't be able to do anything against them. Senthil's death was a murder, but it had not been committed by gangsters or militants or underworld goons. It had been perpetrated by people ensconced within the walls of our legal system. I cannot do a thing. Finding them could be the gravest mistake to make. To realize that it was a mistake was the real worth of that restless night.

I decided: Tomorrow, I'll go to the Australian Embassy and get my visa done.

PAPERS

IT IS NOT dreams or choices that decide the fate of a man, but his circumstances. Or else, how could my boat ride to the Australian Embassy end up at the Oothukkuli jetty near Cherar Peruntheruvu?

When I got ready in the morning and said I was leaving for the embassy, everyone's jaws dropped.

Papa couldn't believe my overnight transformation. He congratulated me. 'Now, I'm convinced that you are good at taking the right decisions. You'll succeed. Wherever you go, you won't figure in the list of losers.'

The appointment was at 10.30 a.m. 'No big deal. They won't ask anything that you can't answer. I've arranged for everything. This house is waiting for some good news.'

I was halfway to the embassy when the call came.

It was Anpu. 'I need to meet you urgently.'

'Why, Anpu? What news?'

'I'll tell you when you come. Will you come?'

'Is it that urgent?'

'A bit.'

'Okay, I'll be there.'

Anpu needed me. I turned the boat to Cherar Peruntheruvu.

When I reached Senthil's house, Anpu and her father were at the door waiting for me. Seeing that, I became more anxious. 'What happened, Anpu?'

'Two men came from Senthil's office. They brought a lot of papers and asked me to sign them. They'll come later today to pick them up.'

'Appa has some doubts. So, he told them that he needs to show the papers to someone before signing them,' said Anpu.

'Not just someone, kanna. Someone whom I can trust.

There is no one in this street like that. I don't even like my relatives. Illiterate morons. That's why I made Anpu call you.'

I went through the papers. Some relieving orders from Senthil's office. Two or three documents from the Public Security. Death certificate from the hospital. And a notary declaration saying there was no suspicion of anything out of the ordinary in Senthil's death.

'Who brought all these?'

'I don't know. When I asked, they said they were from Senthil's office. Is there any problem?'

'No, nothing. I was just asking.'

'Then shall I sign them?'

I hesitated for a moment. There was something dodgy going on. How smartly they were plugging the loopholes. The family is the last voice left, and they want to silence it too. These papers would do that. But what reason could I give to stop them from signing?

'Appa, I'm happy that you trust me and have asked me to verify these papers. But I don't have the expertise. However, I can help you out. Please give me two days. I'll show these to someone and return them to you.'

'They said they would come today,' Anpu said.

'I'll tell them to come after two days, right, kanna?' her father intervened.

'Yes. Please also get the details of who they are.'

'Okay, kanna.'

'I'm leaving then,' I said, folding the papers.

'Ayyo no, please have some coffee.' Anpu stopped me.

'No. I had coffee before I left home.'

'That's okay. You can also have the coffee I make.' She ran into the kitchen.

I couldn't resist the offer. I waited for her to return.

Senthil's mother brought the coffee. I had nothing to say to her. Her face was still damp with tears. I knew that it would only get worse if I asked anything. As I feared, tears flowed down her cheeks soon enough. She wiped them with her sari and went back inside.

4

Archipelago

SITTING IN SALIM'S vehicle, I enthusiastically called the Thursday Market and announced the adventurous Interpol heroism which got us the third part of *The Book of Forefathers*. How? How? Each member of the assembly was eager to know. I mollified them with the promise of a detailed account when we met.

I read the text twice before I reached home, watching out for the hint of a phone number or an email ID or a postal address. The secret message had been deciphered by others the last time, and I was keen to crack it myself this time. How can I not have an investigative mind; after all, I am a writer! It is to me that Andrapper had sent his autobiography. Wouldn't I have had to find out these details on my own if there had been no Thursday Market? How would I have done it then? These thoughts were driving my search. But it was a tough nut to crack! There were no hints this time, or I couldn't find any. I'd have to rely again on the Thursday Market.

By the time we reached, each and every one of them had caught the Cultural Ambulance and gathered at my house. Hearing Salim's vehicle, Nibu rushed out to me, grabbed the papers and ran inside. 'See, the one who did not want to waste time on this now wants to read it first,' quipped Biju. 'Then Biju can read it the last,' replied Anil. 'I'll be the first,' Nibu insisted. Then, following a consensus, Nibu handed the text to Mashu who read it aloud. After that, Salim recounted the heroic tale of how we got hold of the papers. Towards the end, all of them laughed their guts out at Salu's antics. They also had fun at the expense of 'Interpol Benyamin'.

'The devil's arrived, now get ready to tackle it,' declared Biju. But nobody could find anything in the text. They had drawn a blank, as I had.

To break the silence, Mashu, like in the past, took out the checklist. 'Author's name?'

'Since his brother's name is Jeff, he could be Steve,' guessed Anil.

'Could be Jeff and Jerry too,' Biju said.

'What's wrong with Jeff and Justin?' was Nibu's contention.

'His current name is P.C. Andrapper!' announced Baldy.

'PC?' asked Salim.

'Pachu Chuang Tzu Andrapper.'

'Who are the fresh faces introduced in this segment?'

'Only Dr Iqbal. The rest are all reappearances.'

'Then he is our leading man. Let's think about how we can find him,' Nibu said.

'That'll never happen. In the story, Andrapper has shown contempt for him. Dr Iqbal is not the one,' Salim said.

'Who's the one then?' Nibu got angry.

'Find out!'

'What's this, an Agatha Christie novel, to go on looking for clues?'

'Whether it's a detective story or not, we'll have to find out,' Mashu said. 'Let's take it as a challenge. For now, let's take the Cultural Ambulance and return to our homes instead of wasting time daydreaming. All of you mull over it. Next Thursday, come with your heads filled with your guesses, queries and findings. Benyamin will scan these pages and send them to all of us tomorrow. Okay?'

We all agreed with Mashu. After drinking the coffee made by my wife, all of them left, winding up the assembly.

———

Next Thursday, we gathered earlier than usual. Mashu called us to order: 'All right, like I said last week, let's get to know the Agatha Christie and Sherlock Holmes in each of you!'

We looked at each other to see who'll go first.

'Let our author begin,' Biju suggested.

'I went through the three parts in detail,' I said. 'I can't find anything new. Pass!'

'I took the same old route: Orkut,' Anil said. 'I found Chuang Tzu's profile. There's no photo of him, just that of a flower. The posts are restricted from public view. Locked. I sent a message, but haven't got a reply yet.'

'I read *Kanyabhogasooktham* four times. And forwarded it to four girls,' said Nattapranthan. 'I've sent a scrap to Chuang Tzu asking for its full version. While doing that I found a profile of Melvin—his probable girlfriend—and sent a friend request. She hasn't accepted it. If she likes my bald head, we are saved.'

'I did a more practical thing,' Salim said. 'I got in touch with Charu Nivedita. According to Andrapper, Charu has been to Diego. He remembers meeting Andrapper and being hosted by the family. Charu said the Andrapper house was one of the biggest there. He also gave me the number of one Shivasankar, who writes scripts for Tamil serials from Diego. I called him and he gave me some good news. Apparently, some days ago, he met our Andrapper on the streets. He even chatted with him. Shivasankar has promised to ask around about him and update us. That means Andrapper is within our arm's reach!'

When Salim stopped, we all clapped. There was no way Salim's effort could have gone unrecognized.

'Nobody has heard what I did,' Biju said, peeping from behind Nattapranthan.

'Ayyo da, we forgot about Pattar,' Anil said. 'Okay, let's hear your findings.'

'I mailed Rahim and Bilal. Both of them replied. Rahim says Andrapper has changed drastically. During their schooldays, they spoke about girls a lot. But Andrapper has now become a serious person. He even emailed Bilal disapproving of Rahim's behaviour. He claimed that Rahim hadn't changed while he himself had become an angel. Rahim wrote that he knows nothing about Andrapper and does not wish to answer anything about him.

'According to Bilal, they all thought Andrapper would grow up to be the most successful among them—a business magnate or a minister or a chancellor. However, while the rest of the classmates have all settled down with jobs, Andrapper, even at twenty-eight, is jobless and roaming around aimless. Rahim had invited him to France many times but he didn't go. According to Rahim, Andrapper likes to be bone idle. He doesn't know where Andrapper is now. Either he must have gone mad like his grandfather or must have committed suicide.

'This is what the two have to say about Andrapper,' Biju concluded.

There was a minute's silence. Could Bilal's words be true? Were we searching for a story that ends in lunacy or suicide? If so, what was the point of the quest?

'I've another bit of significant information,' Biju said. We turned to him anxiously. 'From now on, we don't have to call him Pachu Andrapper or Chuang Tzu Andrapper or P.C. Andrapper. His real name is Christy. Christy Andrapper.'

'Christy Andrapper . . . How do you know?' I asked.

'Very easy. It was in Bilal's mail.'

'For this precious information, here's a kiss from me.' Baldy kissed Biju.

'All these details are useful. They'll help us get closer to him. But none of your observations tell us how to locate the next segment,' I said.

'Benyamin, there is one thing going for us. He doesn't want to hide the remaining sections of the manuscript from us, he definitely wants us to get them. That means we don't have to think too hard. The route is likely to be easier than we expect. I'm sure about it. Let's wait,' Mashu said.

'When we don't have the answers, everyone tends to reach this conclusion: Wait for the next part.' Nibu was annoyed. 'If we have failed to crack the puzzles conjured up by the ordinary brain of Andrapper, we should admit it, and not come up with stupid excuses.'

'Let's not bicker over this,' Mashu said soothingly.

'We are still waiting for some replies. From Shivasankar. From Melvin. Maybe even from Chuang Tzu. Those are bound to be of some help to us. If anyone identifies a clue in the text or gets a promising response we can meet, or let's wait until next Thursday,' Anil said.

The Cultural Ambulance ferried them away. To be honest, I felt let down. I had expected these daredevils to come up with something. That has not happened. I have to wait. It would be great if Shivasankar decided to visit the Andrapper house. If Melvin accepted Baldy's 'friend' request, then, as he said, the next part was likely to be with her. But why was I waiting for Baldy to get a response, why couldn't I send her a message? He must have mentioned my name to her. It was better to get in touch directly. I logged on to

Orkut, found Chuang Tzu, and via him, reached Melvin. I was stunned to see her profile photo. If it wasn't some film star's picture, then she was really pretty. I felt envious of Christy Andrapper. Now I was less bothered about gathering information about him, I just wanted to be her friend. I quickly send her a friend request.

Days passed. I didn't get to hear from her. Nobody got any replies. Salim called Shivasankar one more time. He got the depressing news that not even Andrapper's relatives knew about his whereabouts. So, that route was closed. More days passed. We held a couple more Thursday Assemblies. Nobody managed to get anything. The investigation had come to a dead end. I returned to writing my novel, *Nedumbassery*, which had been delayed for a while. But even after spending hours at it, I couldn't write a single satisfactory line. My mind was full of Christy Andrapper. His life and *The Book of Forefathers*. I understood that I'd be restless till I get the rest of the parts. I read the portions I had again and again, a thousand times, with the hope of finding hidden clues. Nothing. I was afraid that Mashu's prediction was coming true. Was the ghost of Andrapper eating up my *Nedumbassery*? Was it going to disturb my otherwise disciplined literary life? No, no. I tried to compose myself. But my fear was becoming a reality. My writing came to a stop. My novel came to a stop.

It was then that I fell sick. I had to spend almost a month at a hospital in Ernakulam. One day, a friend, Ajay, who came to visit me brought a stack of books. In it was *Archipelago* by Mohandas Purameri. A book about Diego Garcia. A book that I started to read despite the high fever. There was a preface by its editor, Srikumar, about the novel and its publication. It also described his trip to Diego to collect an award for the novel, and about meeting a couple of expat authors there, including Mohandas Purameri. He expressed his hope that some of their works would find their way to his publishing house Z Books, and for diaspora literature in Malayalam to scale new heights. I felt a shiver of excitement. Srikumar had been to Diego. He had met writers there, and talked about their work. It was possible that Christy had been one among them. Wouldn't they have talked about his novel? Was it possible he had handed over a portion to Srikumar? I was restless with queries. I had to call Srikumar.

When I got through to him, I began by asking about *Archipelago*. Like the previous time, Srikumar championed it passionately. I asked him about his Diego experience.

'I'd gone along with our Perumbadavam sir,' Srikumar said. 'I met Mohan Das there.'

'You say in your foreword that you met other writers too?'

'Yes. I am going to publish two of them soon.'

'Did you meet someone called Christy Andrapper?' My voice trembled in anticipation.

'Christy Andrapper? How do you know him?'

'We are Orkut friends.'

'Oh, I see. Any idea where he is now?' Srikumar asked.

That was a let-down. 'I called you to ask the same,' I said.

'How I met him is an interesting story,' Srikumar said. 'I had gone to a bar in Diego. It was a barmaid there who told me about him and his book. And I tracked him down at the award function for *Archipelago*. When I asked him about the novel, he was taken aback. He gave me the publishing rights for his work.'

'Did he send you his novel?'

'What did you say was your name?'

'I am Benyamin.'

'Oh, Benyamin? Where are you calling from?' Srikumar got excited.

I narrated my hospital story to him.

'He didn't give the whole thing, Benyamin. He sent me one part of it, for me to read. He said the novel is with you for editing, and when you ask, I should send the portion I have to you.'

'You still have it with you, right?'

'Oh, I'll have to check. There are hundreds of manuscripts here in this office.'

'Please find it for me.'

'Yes, I will,' Srikumar promised.

I was nearly jumping with joy. The next section was finally on its way to me.

'Has Andrapper been in touch with you after that meeting?'

'We met one more time. Quite unexpectedly, when he had come to Ernakulam. He had come to attend a friend's funeral. We went there together. I had to leave soon. He was supposed to give me a call afterwards. Never did. Then there was no news of him. And I forgot about it. It's when you called that it all came back to me.'

'How can I get the papers?'

'I'll drop them off.'

One evening a few days later, Srikumar, along with the poet V.M. Girija, visited me at the hospital. He had with him the envelope with the papers. I literally grabbed it from him. I could barely lend an ear to Srikumar's inquiries about my health. My mind was wholly focused on *The Book of Forefathers*. As soon as Srikumar left, I started reading.

PARALLEL COUNTRY

FOR THE NEXT two days, I couldn't think about the papers the Public Security officers had given Anpu to sign. I was being scolded, sometimes almost shouted at, by one family member after another. The one who dampened our hopes, the one who screwed up his future, the one who is defiant, useless and hopeless, and other similar curses were showered on me. They seemed to believe that going to Australia was akin to going to heaven.

What surprised me more was that even when I'd chosen to study at Thiruvananthapuram, there had been no such ruckus. Usually, students from Diego go to Bangalore, Pune or Mangalore for higher studies. The richer lot chooses Cape Town or Port Elizabeth in South Africa. Or Lisbon in Portugal. Or they go to France or England. The family had decided to send me to France. But I was firm in my choice of Thiruvananthapuram. Since then, all my faults and follies and my joblessness had been blamed on that choice.

Papa and Momma were getting more anxious about my ability to achieve success in life as I grew older. But I could interpret their reaction only as a conspiracy to create a dreadful atmosphere in the house and push me out of it. For, I couldn't consider the possibility of moving out of the house or the island. I had things to do. I had to stay back till I'd accomplished them. So I faced everything with absolute silence. It went on until the night when Papa got more drunk than usual, stood in the courtyard and trumpeted: 'He has decided to destroy his life. No one should try to stop him from that. A man's fate is not decided by God. He chooses it himself. Let him be.' Momma carried on with her muttering and tears till noon the next day, but that too stopped.

Once calm returned, I thought of Anpu's papers. I took a look at them again. Even a blind person could have sensed that there was something fraudulent in it had he known that Senthil was killed; otherwise, they were like any other government papers. How was I going to stop Anpu's father from signing these at least for a short while? I decided to rely on measures such as not talking to him, not visiting him and not answering the phone if he called.

My probe into Senthil's murder had come almost to a standstill. There had been no progress in my writing either. I couldn't concentrate on anything. My thoughts were scattered. I couldn't pummel and shape them into orderly structures of words. And there was nothing else to do. If I stayed home, Momma's worries and complaints followed me around. I'd get ready in the morning and leave the house to wander around the streets of Pentasia or Seleucia. Those wanderings revised my opinion that I knew all the streets and bylanes of this small island where I had grown up. Exploring became fun. I found alternative routes and shortcuts to reach various familiar destinations and shops. I saw for the first time the Liberty Beach, where only the British had been allowed entry in the past, the Jew Street of the French times, the Dhivehi Language Institute and the British military camp. I got to know my island better.

It was amazing how Garcia had evolved in the last decade. During my high-school days, the roads of Diego had looked like the roads of an average village. Over the years, many rural locales had become urban. They now had skyscrapers, and each building had spacious boat-parking facilities, wide waterways leading to them, etc. I got lost at many places. I didn't belong there, I felt a kind of strangeness. Places affordable only to the new rich were gaining prominence in Diego.

One day, while walking through one such crowded street of Seleucia's Du Norde, I heard someone call out my name. I turned around to see someone clapping his hands in a nearby juice shop. At first, I doubted if it was for me, and then I went close.

'Don't you recognize me? I'm Babu. We studied together.'

'Babu! Why are you here?'

'Here? This is my shop.'

'Oh, I see. But I haven't seen you before . . .'

'You'll see me only if you come this way. Well, why would you rich guys come this way? This is a fake goods market for the poorer lot.'

'How is your business?

'It's okay. What will you have? Mango, musambi, grapes, pineapple, kiwi?'

'Thank you. I don't want anything.'

'Oh, don't act pricey. Come, sit . . . Hey, man, make a special mango juice for him. By the way, I forgot to ask. What do you do now?'

'I'm a novelist.'

'Novelist? You still have the old craziness, huh?'

'Some craziness is not to be junked.'

'You still have the stamp collection?'

That reminded me of the hobby I'd once had. I had a huge collection. Almost three-fourths of it was Babu's contribution. He made me pay for it. Bugger. It had taken me a long time to figure out that all his stamps were fake. That they were pictures cut out from foreign magazines. I was such an idiot.

'You fooled me with those duplicate stamps,' I said.

'True. I was thinking the same! You were my first victim. Not because you were a simpleton but because you were the richest in our group. Now I fool the richest people in the world. Not with this juice business, okay? There is no fraud in that. But this is just a side business. The real deal is somewhere else.'

'What's that?'

'Don't ask. I've done all the fraud and forgery possible in the world. Fake phone-recharge coupon, fake channel recharge, resale of cable TV, duplicate computer programmes, movie piracy, music piracy, blue film business . . . Then at a slightly higher level, duplicate ID cards, passports, ATM cards, that's another section altogether . . . There is nothing I don't do.'

'You've become a god of fraud! Don't you know all this is illegal?'

'Illegal! What's legal? Whose law made by whom? The law for the rich to become richer, what else? Do you know how many cheap services are sold for big money with government help? Can any poor man afford to pay the price they ask? No. That means none of the facilities will reach poor people . . . We don't want to rot and die without knowing and enjoying these things. So, we snatch them for ourselves using all possible tricks. Why do telephone companies need such huge profit margins every year? Nothing will happen if it dips a bit. So I sell fake recharge coupons. What do TV companies think? That we poor shouldn't watch the major channels? So I sell duplicate cards. When they think we don't have to update our computers or learn new techniques, we make sure we do. So pirated programmes are sold. Don't these film stars take crores to preach against pirated cassettes? Why should we go to theatres, pay through our nose and make them richer? Damn them. I'll sell duplicates. The rich can buy the original and watch. Nobody in the world should live on a poor man's money. You come with me . . .' He took me to a nearby shop. It had an extensive collection of vintage goods. 'This is also mine.'

I walked around, looking at the artefacts, wondering how he had got so many antique items in Diego.

'How old do you think this is?' he asked me, showing me a wooden sculpture of the Buddha.

'Some forty years? Sixty? Hundred?'

'Around eighty years old. You want this?'

'How much is it for?'

'Eight hundred francs.'

'That's a good deal.'

He laughed. 'No, you are a dumbo. I'd fooled you when we were children. Enough of that,' he said, taking my hand and stepping out of the shop. 'Actually, that is just three days old. After it is made, it's dipped in mud, scratched with sandpaper, etc. Anyone will easily think it's a hundred years old. More than enough to dupe fools like you. They will grab it and proudly exhibit it in their living room. Nothing feels better than fooling a rich man who brags.'

He laughed again.

When a nation conspires to loot its poor people, they, in turn, defy it with parallel nations, like this business in fakes.

The juice that Babu served me was too sweet.

SPUTUM

I LOGGED ON to the Internet after a long time. There were invites to join some four or five amusing Orkut groups. One was a group of people with names starting with C. Another for lovers of pink. A 'lazy lot' group. A left-handers' group. One for stamp collectors. Another for people who like the game *ituly*. One for those who puke after drinking. Strange are the ways that people find to connect with each other.

There were also two 'friend' requests. One was from an old associate. The other from Melvin. I was pleasantly surprised. After her visit to my house, I wasn't sure if she'd ever want to see me again. She wrote: Hi, haven't seen you around. Have you forgotten us?

I added her as a friend, and replied: How can I? I'll drop in sometime. I've been a bit busy.

There were four, five other scraps. Random greetings that didn't deserve a reply. But one of them was from Bilal: 'I've sent a mail. Make sure you read it.' I wasn't too pleased to see it. When he had come to Diego, I'd tried to meet him. His response had been disheartening. Even the mention of Senthil's death was turned into a joke. Why this mail now? I opened it half-heartedly.

Christy, I ignored your calls and gave you the cold shoulder because of a misunderstanding. If an old friend or a relative who hadn't been keeping touch makes a call to an expat in town, it is because he is a salesman of insurance or mutual funds. This has been proved right a hundred out of hundred times. I've been proved wrong only in your case. I initially thought that you were calling me to trap me in some such venture. It was later that Rahim said you weren't involved in any fraud, and that you were actually a writer. I'm sorry. We'll meet next time I come. Oh, I didn't tell you—I've left Australia for France. Higher studies. Let me tell you, you should say goodbye to your novelist ambitions and come to France and study some more. This is a good time for that. I am pursuing my education here with the money I made working for those four or five years in Australia. In your case, I know money won't be an issue. France was my dream, that's why I came here. If you are coming, please let me know. I'll arrange everything. Stop loafing around. Get serious.

Another bit of news—the Sri Lankan in our class, Jesintha, I met her in Paris out of the blue. She was with a foreigner. Perhaps her husband. I was standing in a queue at the Louvre. Though I went and talked to her, she couldn't recognize me. Or maybe she was pretending she couldn't. You mentioned that you meet her often. Is that true? Then please find out if it was indeed her that day. Do reply. Apologies again for the misunderstanding.

Bilal

Jesintha. In Paris? Could be true. She had chosen to enjoy life. She could do anything. Go anywhere. Maybe that's how she made a living. No one can become so prosperous in such a short time. It's shameful to ask about that. So I decided not to go to Port Louis in the near future. If I met her, I'd end up asking her. That's the kind of person I am. But it's human nature to contradict one's own decisions. I said to myself, I don't have to see Jesintha, but I have to go to Port Louis. I have to go there, sit in that chair, have coffee. But if I saw her, I'd feel compelled to ask about Paris, so I controlled myself for two days. On day three, I went to Port Louis.

I parked my boat at the private jetty and was walking past St. Martin Church on my way to Port Louis when someone stopped me.

'Don't you know me?'

I couldn't place him.

'Shivasankar. Tamil writer. Remember, we were together at the Parana literary group?'

'Oh, yes, sorry, now I remember. Where are you now? And how is the writing?

'I wrote two novels. Neither did well. Now I'm into scripts. I write television serials for two channels in Madras. Anyway, did you hear about Mohandas? The Malayali. He's won the prize for the best novel of the year given by *Pentasia This Month*. I, too, had submitted my work but got nothing. There are huge celebrations for him all over the place. A magazine has published four full pages about him and his novel.'

Shivasankar gave me his number before he parted. 'We should meet again, call me soon.'

He left me crushed. Mohandas! An award for his novel! That too for the first Malayalam novel from Diego! I, too, had plans to make a submission. As my work drags on and stretches into infinity, a guy who had started his writing career with me bags the award. When he had mentioned it to me, I didn't take it seriously. I thought I had more talent and scholarship than he had. But my writing hadn't achieved much. I had filled my head with unnecessary issues and killed my days of productivity. Nobody was going to ask me why I hadn't probed the reasons behind Senthil's murder. But at least my father would ask me what I'd achieved with my literary life, what I'd contributed to Malayalam literature.

I headed straight to a bar in Seleucia and drank heavily. Danced with the bar girls. Bragged that I was Andrapper and that I was working on a novel, a masterpiece about Diego's history. I thumped my chest and declared the novel would win the Booker or the Pulitzer, not some puny local award. I think I even made a bar girl sit with me and narrated the novel. I made her hold my hand, kiss it and say, 'These are not man's fingers, but God's fingers.' And throughout the escapade, I was burning with envy for Mohandas. I tried to mollify myself with arguments that there would be other opportunities to win awards, that awards were not the last word on anything, that the greatest works never received awards.

However, I could not convince myself. If I could have got hold of Mohan then, I would have drowned him in the sea. I felt such wrath! Then, when I was about to pass out, I called Mohan. I wanted to curse him, but I showered him with hollow praise. I told him that he had made the Malayalis of Diego proud, that he should write more, and that I was especially proud of him.

Mohandas invited me to the award ceremony the next week. I promised that I'd be in the front row. I kept on talking. I made compliments that, in recollection, make me cringe. I finally disconnected the phone and spat. All my fury was packed in the sputum.

ANDRAPPER

MY NOVEL HAD come to a halt. So had the investigation into Senthil's murder. Questions about the future led me to research the Andrapper family's history. For that I went to the forefathers' vault, sometimes with the permission of Valyapapan, sometimes without his knowledge. I spent hours and days there. I dived into the relics of Andrapper history. I dug out letters written during various periods, government records, travelogues, citations, business deals and memoirs. I studied them in detail. The family history I deciphered from them could be summarized as follows.

Among the crew of the renowned explorer Vasco da Gama, the man who had changed the history of the Indian subcontinent, was a common Portuguese sailor named

Andrew Pereira. It is said that Andrew Pereira found Kerala to be a dreamland, and it took him only a few days to learn to speak Malayalam. He thus became the first European to master the language.

For the same reason, Andrew Pereira was also part of the crew of Pedro Álvares Cabral, who came to the mainland after da Gama. It was on that trip that Andrew became an influential person in the land. He was designated by Cabral to accept the reception and gifts from the then Kochi ruler Unnirama Varma Koyithamburan. His knowledge of Malayalam so impressed the king that Andrew not only won his heart, but also his permission for Portuguese shops to be set up for business. He became the chief of trade henceforth.

On Vasco da Gama's next voyage to Kochi, Andrew was accompanied by his wife Diarus Katrina and son Diego Pereira. As soon as he landed, he met Unnirama Varma Koyithamburan and conveyed his wish to settle in this beautiful land with his family. The king was facing troubles from his local rival, the Samoothiris, and hence was more than pleased to welcome a Portuguese commander. He endowed a grandiose house in Kochi and some plots around it to the Pereira family.

After that, Andrew Pereira acted as a mediator and translator in all the trade deals between the king and the Portuguese. Meanwhile, the king wished to train his army in western-style warfare. So, Pereira took over the additional responsibility of training the Nair infantry. Within days, he became closer to the king and won the respect of the Nair brigade. He never abandoned the spices of Kochi and life in Kerala. The descendants of Andrew Pereira—the one who came from Portugal's Lisbon to win the heart of the king and of the natives of Kochi, to live and die there—constituted the Andrapper dynasty.

The history doesn't end there. In 1545, Andrew's son Diego Pereira was instated as a chieftain by the Kochi king. The Andrappers were the only family with foreign origins among the seventy-two families who held the same honour. On the mainland, the glory of the Andrapper family flourished for some two hundred years, till 1754, when King Marthanda Varma attacked the region and merged it with Travancore. But our great grandfather Hormis Avira Andrapper had reached Diego Garcia before that.

In the 1660s, the mainland saw the Dutch gaining supremacy, and the Portuguese losing it. One 8 January 1663, the Dutch army conquered the Kochi Fort. With that, all the possessions in the name of the Portuguese king changed hands to the Dutch. The waning of his dynasty and its fading relations with its roots resulted in Mathew Andrapper dying of a broken heart. For the Andrapper family in the mainland, it was the dusk of glory. But in Diego, it was a dawn.

Mathew Andrapper's fifth son Hormis Avira Andrapper was capable of rising from the ashes. Not willing to submit to the Dutch, he shifted to Pondicherry with his family, and engaged in farming and trade. He did well. The founder of modern Pondicherry was this great-grandfather of mine: Hormis Avira Andrapper. But the history books in the mainland assign credit to the French. Not much later, in 1674, the French East India Company reached Pondicherry. Its first governor general, Francis Martin, struck a deal with Hormis Andrapper: that the French East India Company would take over trade in Pondicherry in return for a country for him to rule, a country named Diego. He would have full freedom to till the land and do business there. The entire power over Diego would be in his hands. In return, the French would be able to halt and fuel their ships in Diego.

Actually, it was a great test. To give up the growing business and the yielding land, and leave for an unknown place. Like an aimless voyage in search of treasure. Like trading a completed poem for a blank sheet of paper. But if it turned out to be successful, Hormis Avira Andrapper would own a country! He would have total control over it. He bravely took the chance. He was the grandson of Andrew Pereira, who had made journeys into the unknown; he was my great-great-grandfather who would be filling the blank sheet with words a long time later.

He ceded Pondicherry and accepted Diego. That's how Hormis Andrapper, with his family, thousands of slaves and servants, and with machinery, boats and vessels landed in Diego.

It is in the memory of this that the Arch of Diego was erected on the north bank of Seleucia. My great-grandfather's name is clearly chiselled on it. Not just that, his body lies buried in Diego's main Catholic church of St. Antony's.

The rest of the history is known by heart to every soul in Diego. It was not only a history of growth and development, but also a history of broken bonds.

Unfortunately, the French East India Company was dissolved in 1769 and taken over by the French government. After that, the French converted Diego from a stoppage point for ships passing by to a full-fledged naval base. They had bigger ambitions in the Indian Ocean. Diego was an excellent base to lead them to success. Though their initial attempt to conquer Madagascar was a failure, their invasion of Mauritius also happened via Diego. Throughout, the Andrappers were loyal servants to the French. Without contesting or combating the French, the Andrappers hung on as backwater monarchs. It must be because of that that

Valyapapan couldn't take the French treachery. They had dismissed many years of loyalty.

I went to Valyapapan's room. He was snoozing on the recliner. The crown he had got from Hyderabad was there next to him.

RAJANBABU

I REACHED EARLY to grab a front-row seat at the award ceremony for Mohandas. Many authors from various language backgrounds were present. Malayalam was represented by Perumbadavam, and Tamil by Thoppil Mohammad Meeran. Romesh Gunesekera from Sri Lanka and Richard Kunsman from South Africa were among the dignitaries.

I felt jealous. I hadn't thought *Pentasia This Month* could organize such a brilliant function, else I would have made the effort to submit a novel to the contest.

Mohan introduced himself to every guest writer present. I, too, wanted to acquaint myself with them. But who was I? How could I present myself? As someone who was working on a novel? They were all famous. People swimming fluidly in words. If they heard of the difficulty I experienced in writing my novel, they might laugh at me. I made space for myself in a corner.

Seeing me, Mohan came over and gave a hug.

'I'm happy you've come. I invited everyone in the Parana group. Nobody has turned up. Jealous, what else! None of them thought I'll win this award.'

He kept talking—about the Parana group's contribution to the award, how his literary life grew, and how much effort he had put in. He was proud of himself. I listened to him and showered him with compliments. His hard work and dedication to writing deserved to be appreciated, howsoever reluctant I was. His discipline versus my laziness. But I didn't like acknowledging my weakness. I liked to consider myself perfect on all counts. I told myself, Mohan, none of your great prizes can destroy my ego. I'll always be above awards. Till I die. Even after death . . .

When he started talking about *Archipelago*, I twitched. I shook a bit. Oh God . . . Had he written the story that I had left incomplete? He had stolen my title . . . and perhaps the story too . . . That terrified me more than my not completing the novel or losing an award. If that was the case, then what was the point of my novel? Even if the words were entirely different, the plot might be the same. But who would believe me? People will believe the one who finished writing it first, and won an award.

As soon as he finished his first sentence about his novel, I excused myself and walked towards the exit. No, ran, to be precise. I could not stand it. It was enough to stop my heart. I could not bear to hear that my novel had come out from another's pen.

As I imagined Mohandas standing perplexed at my sudden exit, I ran into Rajanbabu climbing the stairs of the hall.

Rajanbabu! The most reputed journalist in Diego. The editor of *Diego Daily* for the past twenty-five years and the special head of the Malayalam section. He also headed more than seven Malayali associations in Diego, and was the managing partner of over forty-five institutions. It was said that his proximity to the people in power had aided his growth. Whatever be the truth of that, his name topped the list of media persons in Diego. He had strong links with the British authorities as well as the big shots in the Senate. His followers said that whenever there was a problem, he came to the rescue. He used his contacts to effect solutions.

Rajanbabu had been the chief guest of that year's Parana Literary Summit. He spent a lot of time with us discussing literature and listening to our stories. He left only after promising support to such a distinguished group. I had been instrumental in inviting him to the summit. (I had used the Andrapper family connections.) But after the group disintegrated, I stopped meeting him. I tended to avoid him if we both happened to be at the same conference. But now, I couldn't get away. He had already seen me.

He was in a hurry. Haste was his signature. But even in the midst of his rush, he spotted me.

'Aha . . . you? It's been a very long time.' He stopped me, grabbing my hands.

I was surprised that a celebrity of his calibre remembered and recognized me.

'At that Parana Summit, I felt you were the most talented. Did you stop writing? I thought you'd have participated in this contest.'

I couldn't respond to his comments and questions.

'I saw a great writer in you. I hoped that you would groom that talent. But for you kids, it must have been just a joke.'

'No, writing is not a joke for me, sir. I will write a beautiful novel about Diego. One which Diego can be proud of. It's in me—half on paper, and the rest in my mind. Whatever happens, I'll complete it. Nothing can stop that—be it another novel by anybody or another award for anybody or another incident. If my novel doesn't exist, I won't exist.' I sounded mad.

For a while, he stared at me. 'Good. This is the confidence I was looking for from young men like you. Once you complete it, please come and show it to me. I wish to serialize it in my weekly.'

'Certainly, sir. But before that, I need to see you once. I have something urgent to discuss with you.'

'You are most welcome to drop in. Just give me a call before coming.'

He walked inside in a hurry.

My thoughts were on Senthil.

PUBLISHER

I WANTED TO leave quickly. But there were a lot of acquaintances, colleagues in literature, all equally sad. Some who couldn't send a novel to the contest. Some who hadn't won the contest. But none talked about the contest or Mohandas. The discussions ranged from Ben Okri, Leela Soma and Kaavya Viswanathan to activism and blogging, and the Paris Poetry Festival and the Man Booker Prize. I joined them. I wanted to uproot any thoughts about Mohan and his novel from my mind. Else, they would lie there undigested and eat me up.

We were standing in groups and chatting when someone pointed out that somebody was calling out my name.

'I'm Srikumar, from Kochi. I've come with Perumbadavam sir.'

Hearing 'Kochi', our eyes widened. Any place name in the mainland and the presence of anyone from there, widened our eyes. We welcomed him, heartily shaking hands.

'Can I talk to you alone for a minute?' he asked me.

'Of course.'

We moved away a bit.

'I'm the editor-in-charge of Z Books, which is a medium-sized publishing house in Ernakulam. I usually attend all the book festivals. I know I can find interesting writers at these gatherings. Rarely have I got it wrong. Rather than publishing the second-rate stories of celebrated writers, I like to go with the first work of fresh, raw talent. If the writer is talented, it's visible in their debut. It may go unnoticed, and the print run and sales may be low, but it will stand out from the rest. I was sure I could find such a person here too.' He kept talking. 'More than works that win awards, I like the manuscripts which get rejected. Most of the time, those are better than the one that won. I met a couple of people yesterday. To be honest, it sounded as though their work might be better than Mohan's *Archipelago*. Awards are won by compromised works that accede to the status quo, which won't annoy anyone. Such works don't interest me. And yesterday, I happened to hear about your new novel. I liked what I heard. I've been looking for you since then. If we hadn't met here, I would have found your house and come there. I am that intrigued! Please publish your work with me.'

More than the sudden offer, it astonished me that he had come to hear about the story of the novel.

'Who told you that I was working on a novel?'

'That was what I meant by unexpected. I now feel like I came to Diego only to meet you.'

'Tell me who told you?'

'What does it matter? Won't you please agree to publish your novel with me? I don't promise you awards or reviews by famous critics or a high print run. But I can find you the best readers. You've to trust me on that.'

'It's not a matter of trust. I haven't even finished half the novel. I've no clue when I'll complete it or how it will end. How can you commit to publish such a novel?'

'I was excited the moment I heard the story. I've been restless till this moment—about meeting you. It's fantastic. There has never been such a work in Malayalam, for sure.'

'You are dodging my question again. I've not told anyone about my novel. How did you come to hear about it? Did my father tell you? Or Rajanbabu sir?'

'I don't wish our discussion to become an argument that leads nowhere. I'm not one of those publishers with bags full of cash who keep producing books like piglets. I publish just ten to fifteen books a year. Books that will become part of history or create a new path. That's my dream. It is my insatiable desire for books and reading that keeps me in publishing. It is that person in me who doesn't want to miss your work in any way.'

'But there is no surety that I'll complete the novel.' I tried to dissuade him again.

'That's okay. I'll wait till it is complete. I won't call up and pester you like other publishers. I have the sense to know that all great works are born after great struggle. I'll give you the time to go through that great struggle. So, are we in an agreement?'

'We don't need an agreement. If I ever finish writing the novel, you'll be its publisher. This is the word of a writer.'

Thus, I gave the rights to publish an unwritten book to editor Srikumar of Z Books, Ernakulam. But how he came to know the plot of my novel remained a riddle.

MELVIN

ORKUT BECAME AN obsession with me after Melvin's scraps started appearing regularly.

Scraps, comments on my photos, invites to communities, messages . . . as Melvin's visits increased, I gradually became addicted. I used to be aloof about the discussions and comments on various social networks until then. Even if I had a different opinion on some topics, I never got involved in any discussions. Melvin broke the mould.

With that, my writing almost stopped. The anxiety about Senthil disappeared. Anpu called twice from her mobile phone, but I didn't bother to pick up. It was as if I was in a trance. I was on the Internet all the time. Checking every hour for a scrap; responding if there was one, upset if there was none.

There was nothing much in the scraps. Random queries. Casual hellos. Routine greetings. That was all. Still I waited for her response.

When she started sending scraps about Senthil's death, I made the scrapbook private, and requested her not to mention anything in public. She wrote a long mail of apology the very next day. On reading it, I wanted to see her. I didn't inform Anita. I just directly went to the palace-like hostel where she stayed. I'd decided to go to the hospital if she wasn't home. Sometimes, it seems like the world works the way we want it to.

When I reached, there was only Melvin at home. The rest of the nurses were away at the hospital. She didn't panic on seeing me. She received me happily. We had cardamom tea and talked for a long time. There was no hurry to pack me off.

I'm usually not a talker, but a listener. I had the same impression about Melvin. When two such people meet, the conversation ends after a few greetings and then they try to move away from each other. But it seemed that when she was left to be herself, Melvin was quite a talker.

'The dreams we have become real some time later, don't they?' Melvin asked out of the blue.

'Why the doubt? That has been the belief of man for a long time. But it rarely happens. It is a coincidence if dreams and reality match.'

'I don't know if you'll believe me. I dreamt last night that Anita-chechi's friend would visit today.'

'Who, me?'

'Hm.'

'Really?'

'I swear in the name of Mariam.'

'Was it daydreaming or . . .?'

'It was a dream.'

My phone rang. It was Anpu. I hesitated about whether to answer. I was sure it was to ask about the papers. What could I say? I didn't take the call. The phone rang for a while before coming to a stop.

'Who was it?'

'A friend.'

'Did he also dream that Anita-chechi's friend would come there?'

We laughed.

'Not just today, that would be a dream that comes to her every night. It was Anpu, sister of Senthil,' I said when the laughter ended.

'Oh, I see. What's the matter?'

'Senthil's office had sent some papers to be signed. She wants my advice on that.'

'What are you planning to do about it?'

'Nothing. I had gone to see Dr Iqbal. He said he had not attended such a case. Without a witness, I can't do anything.'

'If I'm sufficient as a witness, I'll come.'

'But you are not a witness. The Public Security won't accept your account. Will Sudha-chechi come?'

'I don't think so. She is scared. The hospital records are supposed to be confidential. It was because I compelled her that she talked to you. Tell me, was there anyone else at the scene?'

'When the incident happened, I was with my friend Jesintha. But she is a pragmatic person, she will not put herself at risk. She won't come forward. I don't know any of the others who were there.'

'Try to remember. Some face might surface. In cases like this, it is usually the public who bravely come forward.'

I stood up to leave. Melvin accompanied me to the gate.

'I have noon shift, otherwise I'd have come with you to Pentasia.'

'Why? Did the dream last night have such a climax?' I quipped.

'Oh, you are still at it! Well, it had a better ending.'

'Really, what was that?'

'I'll tell you later.' A blush spread on her face.

We parted smiling. But Melvin could never share the dream's ending.

COFFEE SHOP

TILL MELVIN SUGGESTED it, the possibility never occurred to me. I had been tracking Senthil's death through government records. I didn't give a thought about the living records—the eyewitnesses. There were some ten or twenty people present when the incident took place. About a hundred people must have seen Senthil lying dead. Won't at least one of them be brave enough to admit he had seen it? Won't at least one of them be uneasy, like me? Actually, I should have started my inquiry with the witnesses. This is the difference between an investigative officer and an imaginative writer. Even a common man would have approached the case with more discipline and order, and may even have cracked it by now. I had just wasted time going round and round, to no avail.

The fact was that I didn't remember the face of anyone who was present at the time of the incident. Who else was there other than Jesintha and I? Searching for a third face, I spent three days picking my brain. Suddenly, I remembered one person: the coffee shop owner. Damn, how did I miss such an obvious thing! He had feigned ignorance when I'd asked him earlier. But this time, I decided not to let him slip away. I rushed to the place immediately. I hurried thinking I must reach there before he disappears. I didn't want to miss him because of a momentary delay. I ran to the coffee shop, leaving my boat at the bay.

Luckily for me, he was there, seated on a tall chair. I was relieved. I slowed down and went to my usual table. He raised his hand seeing me. I signalled him to join me.

'I'm going to the mainland, do you want to accompany me?' I threw a bait.

'Oh, really? When?'

'Next week.'

'I'm also coming! I'm also coming. I need to see the mainland. There is no point to a life if you don't visit the mainland at least once. What do I need to do?'

'Nothing. You just need a clearance from the Public Security department. You've been in Diego for how many generations?'

'Ah, who knows. I know that I was born here. That's all.'

'Where is your family from, originally?'

'I don't know.'

'Do you know your great-grandfather's name?'

'Great-grandfather's name . . . I don't remember. Why are you asking these questions? Is it that difficult to go to the mainland?'

'If you have been here for less than four generations, you can get PIO status. But don't worry. You have a passport, right?'

'Yes. I got it five years ago, in the hope of visiting the mainland someday.'

'Then let's arrange for the visa. It'll take only three days, and costs just ten dollars. And then the packing. That's all. The Public Security is a hurdle. How will we get the clearance?'

'I've no idea, sir . . .'

'I'll take care of it. You'll have to come with me to the Public Security office.'

'Oh, I'll come. I'll come wherever you want me to. I need to see the mainland somehow. Oye, Majid, we are going to shut the shop for a week. I'm going to the mainland. Make a super special coffee for sir . . .'

'Sit down, let me tell you something.' I slowly eased him on to a chair. 'When we go to the Public Security, we need to talk about one more thing.'

'What?'

I moved closer to him.

'About the shooting that took place that day.'

'What shooting? Here? I don't know about any shooting . . .' He got up in panic. 'Nothing of that sort has ever taken place in my coffee shop.'

'Who ordered you to say so?' I stiffened my voice as much as I could. 'Look, I now work at the Investigation Directorate. I'm in charge of the case now. Don't lie to me.'

'Yeah right, an investigating officer! You think I'll get scared hearing that? Better don't go around saying that, you'll be the first to get into trouble.'

That shook me. 'How will I be in trouble?'

He came close to me. Stared at me. 'Like me, you are also an eyewitness. It doesn't take much time for a witness to be called an accused. So, let it go. Let's stick to talking about the mainland.'

I finished my coffee and got up. There was no point in lingering. We had nothing more to say to each other. He had made it clear that he was not willing to cooperate with me.

I walked slowly to the jetty. I had been so excited before meeting him, and confident that everything would fall in place. I had even dreamt of going to Vijay Mullikratnam and challenging him: Look, here's the second witness. Now can you tell me that no shooting happened?

But man is a coward. If something costs him even a scratch, he won't stand up for it. Why should I put my life on the line for the sake of someone else? What will I get out of it? What have I to do with him?

I reached the jetty and was about to get on to the boat when someone tapped on my shoulder. It was the waiter at the coffee shop. 'I'll come with you, wherever you want. I was also a witness to the incident.'

THE OUTSIDER

I DIDN'T HAVE anyone other than Melvin with whom to share the happy news. So I called her immediately. She, too, was excited by the turn of events.

'See, this is why you should sometimes ask women for their opinion!'

'Oh yes, I agree.'

'When are you going to the Public Security?'

'Before he changes his mind. Not to the Public Security though, but the *Diego Daily*. I need to get a story done by Rajanbabu sir.'

'Can I come? I'm off hospital duty tomorrow.'

'Why are you interested in visiting a newspaper office?'

'It's not that, I wanted to meet . . .'

'The guy? I'll take you to the coffee shop one day.'

'Not him, Anita-chechi's friend.'

'Me? Didn't we meet yesterday? Anything urgent?'

'Mm . . . I was thinking of going home next week. I might get leave. Before that, I wanted to tell you something.'

'Let me put an end to this case. Then I'll come and meet you.'

'So you won't come tomorrow?'

'Tomorrow? I'll try to drop by in the evening.'

'I'll wait. Please come.'

———

The coffee shop was open in the morning and then only in the evening. My fellow witness came to the jetty soon after the shop closed for the morning. Though I regularly saw him at the coffee shop, I didn't know his name. It was during this trip to the *Diego Daily*'s office that I got properly acquainted with him.

Sadur Abdul Majid lived in the nearby island of Hamla with his wife and three children. He moved to Diego from Pondicherry twenty years ago, at the age of eighteen.

He had been working at the same coffee shop for the last eight years.

'Do you know who I am?' I asked him.

'I don't want to know. I've seen you at the coffee shop, that's good enough.'

'Then how did you have the courage to come with me?'

'I saw something and just have to tell that to a Public Security officer. Why do I need courage to admit that I saw something?'

'Then why didn't you admit it when the Public Security asked?'

'The owner wouldn't let me. He always says it is his shop, his rules. What right did I have . . . That bastard.'

'Is there such an issue here in Diego?'

'Very much so . . . you don't know. It's an issue faced by us poor people. And I've been here for decades. Imagine the plight of the new immigrants. "What are you doing here? Why are you here?" I'm fed up of these questions that make me feel like a suspect.'

'You are from this place! Why would anyone ask you such things?'

'There is an invisible wall between people like you and the migrants. If you breach that wall and come this side, then you'll understand our situation. Nobody will come to your side and tell you.'

I was reminded of my life in Thiruvananthapuram. I had faced a similar experience. There, I had been a migrant for three years there. A migrant who had come to share and also loot all that the natives had kept for their own enjoyment. As a migrant, I was treated as a person not entitled to any benefits or fruits of the country's progress. I had to make sure I followed the rules there, not make any trouble, not try to grab authority, show muscle power or gain fame, make no attempt to love their women or enter their family—I was to remain an alien. It hurt when the people of Kerala meted out such treatment to me. Despite my experience, I had failed to see that in my own land, another set of people faced the same hostility from my fellow citizens. We always care only for ourselves. Others are our enemies. Was it the same across the world?

'Let it be, sir. That is how it is. Tell me, what's your relationship with Senthil?' Majid asked.

'Senthil? You know him?'

'Yeah, quite well. He was also a regular at the coffee shop. Not just that, he travelled to Pondicherry once a month. I gave him things to hand over to my parents. He's been at my house in the mainland many times.'

'What was he doing in Pondicherry?'

'Don't know. Must be some office work. But he used to go there pretty regularly. That's all I know. Are you his friend?'

'We studied in the same class in school. But on the day of the incident I was seeing him after a long, long time. I've been pursuing it since then, but it has reached nowhere. I should have come to you before.'

'Where are we going now? Doesn't look like the Public Security department.'

'We aren't going to the Public Security office, but to the *Diego Daily*. It's a newspaper. They might be able to help us, that is, if they want to.'

'I doubt it, sir. A lot of journalists came to the coffee shop and asked questions. Nothing happened. Nothing.' Majid dismissed them with contempt.

'The media had come there to report?' That was news to me.

'Yeah, they had come. Lots of questions. They heard our

answers and left. But nothing got printed. The poor man's issues don't get printed in this stupid place.'

'This won't be like that, Majid. I know someone very well. He could turn it into big news.'

'Okay, let's see,' he said in a tone of challenge.

When we reached, Rajanbabu sir was away on lunch break. 'Please sit, he'll be back soon,' said the receptionist.

He was back within ten minutes. 'Hello, Junior Andrapper, how come you are here? Is your novel complete?' he asked, enveloping me in a warm embrace.

'No, sir, but I will finish it soon. I've come on another matter.'

'Come, let's go to my cabin.'

I introduced Majid to him as we walked in.

'You chose a good time to come. I'll get busy with the desk in a while. Tell me, what's the matter?'

I narrated my story to him—from the shooting at the coffee shop to meeting Majid. The only two characters I avoided mentioning were Sudha-chechi and Melvin. Majid added some details to my story, saying that media reporters failed to report the story.

Rajanbabu sir listened to the whole story patiently, with folded hands. After we finished, he pulled out a bunch of papers from his drawer and placed them before me. A detailed report on Senthil's death! I glanced through it. Needless to say, it followed the point of view of the Public Security. The facts were presented in an orderly manner to support their arguments. The quotes of the boat driver who carried Senthil, the doctor's death certificate, investigative outputs from officer Vijay Mullikratnam, etc. The last piece of paper really shook me. It was an affidavit from Senthil's father, certifying a natural cause of death.

Careful not to show the effect the papers had on me, I returned the lot to him.

'I'm one of those who believes journalists shouldn't get emotionally taken in by news. It's natural to have doubts about a death when it's your friend's or acquaintance's. But the duty of the journalist is to find out the truth. To do that, we approach various people and clear our doubts. We ask questions. Conduct an investigation. Our reporter followed the same procedure in your coffee shop, too. But every finding doesn't have to get printed. We publish only unbiased information. When the Public Security office presents such clear evidence, then we have to believe their version—that there was nothing suspicious about Senthil's death.'

'Even after listening to us, do you honestly think the Public Security's version is the right one?'

He fumbled for a minute.

'Journalism is not about my personal beliefs. I'm only a part of a big system. The decision of that system is more important.'

'Okay, sir. I have one question before we leave. I know that journalists don't follow up on natural deaths. How did Senthil's case come to your attention?'

As an answer to that, Rajanbabu sir took another sheet of paper from his drawer and showed it to me. It was a fax message making the accusation—that Senthil's death was a murder. It demanded a probe into the issue to expose the truth. It was from a group called Uthiyan Cheral Tamil Kazhagam.

I was hearing of the group for the first time.

I was about to ask Rajanbabu sir about it, when he got a call.

'Oh my God!' He jumped out of his seat.

'What happened, sir?'

'The chancellor has passed away!'

'Oh, so what!' Majid wasn't concerned.

'When?' I asked.

'Just now, the news came just two minutes ago.' Rajanbabu rushed out of the cabin.

I understood no more help could be expected from the *Diego Daily* office. I left the office with Majid.

Philip Gunawardhane! The chancellor of Diego Garcia. He was of Sri Lankan origin and a Catholic. These twin advantages had worked in his favour and that of the Diego Republican Party's in every election. Negating all other socio-religious equations, Lankans who make up nearly 30 per cent of the population, and Catholics who add up to 45 per cent were behind Philip Gunawardhane. Even Malayalis, who were greater in number, could not affect his chances. He had started his political life from the lowly post of municipal councillor. Then senator, vice chancellor, and for the last five years, chancellor. I'd seen him in person at one or two functions some years back. He appeared to be in his prime. In recent years, on television, he never looked less than hale and hearty. So his demise was unexpected.

I felt no misery on hearing that the ruler of my land is no more. Not that I had any enmity towards him, but it was a fact that commoners like Majid felt no attachment towards him, as was evident from Majid's nonchalant reaction to the chancellor's death. I've never seen him mingling with the public. His election campaigns were rather formal. But even so, he was bestowed with the opportunity to win and rule, purely based on his religion and origin.

In short, the days of solidarity had ended—that's it.

On our way back, I worried about the mysterious Uthiyan Cheral Tamil Kazhagam. 'What is it?' I asked Majid.

'Who knows? There are a total of twenty Tamil associations in Diego. Must be one of them.'

I'd never heard of them. Twenty associations and one Majid. Another door has been thrown open for investigation.

THE LITTLE EMPEROR

AFTER LEAVING MAJID at Port Louis, I reached home and found Valyapapan sitting in the courtyard, miraculously alert and fresh, after a long time. I'd never seen such energy, enthusiasm and grace on his face as on that day.

'Where were you? I've been waiting for a long time.' He stood up when he saw me.

'What happened, Valyapapan?'

'Didn't you hear about Guna? Come, let's pay him a visit . . .'

I was surprised. Valyapapan, who doesn't bother attending the funerals of relatives, wanted to go to the chancellor's? Anyway, I didn't ask any questions. He was coming out after a long time. I thought, let him get some fresh air. Let that help him get out of his foggy dreamland.

We left by boat.

———

Francis House was the official residence of the chancellor. It was the holiday home of Pondicherry's first French governor general, Francis Martin, and later came to be known by his name.

When we parked the boat in front of it, some Public Security officials stopped us, but then a senior guy recognized

Valyapapan and accompanied us to the house. I went up
with them as far as the portico of Francis House. It was only
then that I understood the high regard in which Valyapapan
was held by the senators and officials. They respected and
admired him as if he was a senior head of state. A circle of
them escorted him. The respect seemed to be borne out of the
thought of protecting themselves, if, even by one-hundredth
of a chance, he became the ruler of Diego. Becoming a
government official involves having a peculiar mindset and
training. Everyone cannot be one. I wasn't keen on becoming
a part of their act, so I moved back and sat on a bench in
the middle of the lawn.

It was fun watching the proceedings from there. The Public
Security officials and senators darted in and out of the house.
Nobody bore any signs of the grief or trauma of a death; their
concern was more about executing their duties. The aim was
to gain the appreciation of their superior officers and perhaps
a promotion. That was the only burden that VIP deaths inflict
on the living lot, I thought.

After a while, many of the personal staff of ministers came
and sat on the benches next to me. Though I couldn't make
out their conversation, it had the cheer and jeer of palace
gossip. A couple of times, the Public Security officers requested
them not to create a security issue by gathering and talking,
but none of them paid any heed. They continued with their
discussions. Throughout, a fat guy in that group kept turning
back and staring at me. Either he was wondering who I was,
or we must have met before, that's what I deduced. Then, he
stood up, walked up to me, and called my name to check he'd
got the right person.

'Do you recognize me?'

'No . . .'

'Try again . . . see if you can place this face in any of your memories.'

I tried hard, to no avail.

'Little Emperor, it's me!'

Daniel D'Silva! Yes, it was him. The front bencher in Division A. The boy with a bass voice, because of which we'd predicted for him the career of a radio jockey. He was the only one who used to mock me by calling me 'Little Emperor'.

'Da, you've become too fat to be recognized! What do you eat so much of?'

'This belongs to the fisheries department. So, the size is here to stay.'

'But this is a bit too much. I couldn't recognize you at all!'

'What do you do now?'

'Me . . . well, I'm yet to find a job.'

It's after I said this that I realized that I had begun saying this only recently. To be precise, after attending Mohan's award function. Till then, I used to introduce myself as a writer. It seemed I had lost confidence.

'Even now? Seriously?'

'Yeah, but I'm looking.'

'That's sad. The grandson of someone who should have been ruling a country is now hunting for jobs in the same country. There's scope for a news feature.'

'I'm thinking of writing it myself,' I joked.

'You know, I used to call you "Little Emperor" not to pull your leg. I was jealous. If I were in your place, I would have stepped into politics right then. I'd have played the sympathy card in the election. And would have become at least a deputy minister by now. You still have time. The hook should be "scion of a great family that's relinquished its power to the people"—you can reach the skies. If you're interested, tell me. I'll work with you.'

'I'll think about it.'

'Don't take it lightly. I'm serious. I'm fed up of these frauds. I'm sure you're better than them. If I'm with you, I can eat my meal without a guilty conscience. I can tolerate everything else, but these buggers have an itch every fucking evening! I have to then find girls. Do you know how this eighty-two-year-old died? From an overdose of Viagra!'

We saw Valyapapan stepping out.

'Isn't that your emperor? he asked me softly.

'Yeah, see you then.'

'Give me your number. Let's catch up soon. We need just the Andrapper name in order to do well. You don't know its value in Diego, but I know. Especially at a time when democracy has become rotten.'

I bid him farewell and helped Valyapapan climb down the stairs. While in the boat, my thoughts were devoted not to Daniel D'Silva's words, but his voice. The voice that we once thought was deep enough to make him a radio jockey. I didn't notice anything special about it now. His was now just an ordinary voice. The wonders of childhood are often an exaggeration of our ignorance.

POWER

'THIS IS A death I was waiting to hear about.'

When we had been on the water for a while, Valyapapan said that as if to himself. In the rumble of the boat, I couldn't hear his words clearly. Did he really say that? I looked at his face doubtfully. But I didn't have to ask. Valyapapan's mind was then like a red-hot boiler with thoughts simmering; it had to spill out words somewhere.

For the first time, Valyapapan opened up to me.

'I was afraid my time would come to an end before I heard about this death. Now I'm relieved. I got the news, and I saw the dead man in person. Now I can die peacefully. Philip Gunavardhane. You should have seen him lying dead. The craving for power was etched on his face.

'I know it's cruel to celebrate someone's death. But sometimes, it can be justified. Son, it's not the outrage at someone who took away my fortunes, or jealousy, it is the fury of being stabbed in the back. However much I tried, I couldn't wipe out that feeling. Even if it was only enacted within my mind, I spat on his face before I left the place.

'You might think that it's the sorrow of not becoming Diego's ruler that chained me within a room. That it's the madness of a man who has lost power . . . Not at all. I never wished for power. If I had, I could have easily become the chancellor of this country. But that was not what I wanted. This land, by all means, belonged to us. Nobody presented it to us for free. We won it as part of a big business deal. I now bear the shame and burden of losing it. Haven't you wondered why, I, like a joker, follow the daily menu of King Manuel II? Like me, he was also fated to hand over his powers. My parody is a reminder of that. A mocking reminder.

'Can you imagine where my place is in the Andrapper family history? Maybe, this generation will understand me and accept my circumstances. But at a time when I become just a name, when future generations see me in the legendary list that starts with Andrew Pereira, they will feel scorn. They will enter the Room of the Forefathers and read my name with contempt. Joseph Andrapper—the man who squandered the family dominions once and forever! The man who wasted the fortunes of future generations. Mr Joseph Andrapper, what did you do to enable us to reclaim those powers? I sometimes feel a thousand generations rising in front of me with that question. Some days, even your silence feels to me like an accusation. Every time you climb upstairs, I get scared. I fear that you're coming to ask me that question.

'Not just me, all kings and patriarchs who had to sacrifice power will be seen in this light by future generations. Though the history books and the public will praise us as libertarians and messiahs of democracy, there is nothing more terrible that can happen to anyone than getting booted out of power. History could list many reasons for that loss, but the new generations will blame only one person for it.

'In my case, sovereignty had come within calling distance. But I failed to reach out for it. This man was the reason for that. This Philip Gunavardhane. At that time, he was one of our office staffers. He knew everything about us. He quoted the whole history of the Andrapper family and wrote a letter to the French government harping on our Portuguese origins. Not just that, he argued that the French East India Company had never actually transferred the power to us. He presented 'evidence' for the claim.

'The week in which the power transfer was to happen, when the French Governor asked me about all these things, I was struck dumb. I didn't deny our roots. But they should have considered one thing—the loyalty we had shown to them in the past centuries. They didn't see that. Philip Gunavardhane became big by stomping on me. That's why I said I was waiting for this death. I wanted to see his corpse. To see it lying there didn't make me sad, but happy.'

Valyapapan fell silent for a while.

'Son, now the power has gone much beyond my reach or yours. But someday, some man in our family can win it back. I don't know how long it will take or how many generations we'll have to wait. But that should happen. Every generation should strive for it, and wait for it with hope. This land belongs to the Andrappers. We should get it back. You should do whatever is possible to reach the goal. Future generations should be taught that, they should imbibe it in their blood. Democracy now in Diego is a pretence. A mimicry in the form of authority. However big the ideals that inform them, these institutions ought to collapse. What we had given the people was better than this. It is just that they don't remember it now.'

SUSPENSE THRILLER

I WENT TO Senthil's house after many days. His father, seeing me, ran towards me and hugged me. 'What happened to you, my dear? I called you many times. What happened?'

I didn't know what to say.

Anpu joined us. 'Are you angry with us? Did we do anything wrong? You didn't even answer the phone!'

'I was not here . . .' That was the only excuse I could come up with. 'Some urgent matter . . . Had gone to the mainland . . . Came back just two days ago . . .'

'Oh, so that's the thing. So much for our suspicions!' Appa hugged me again.

'I was afraid you were in hospital or something. We wouldn't have worried so much if you had let us know,' Anpu complained.

'Couldn't do it, Anpu. It was an emergency.'

'What was the matter?'

I stumbled again. What could I say? To hide a lie, a dozen other lies. 'I'm writing a novel. It's being published in Kerala. I'd gone for a meeting with the publisher.'

'Oh, I see, I didn't know. God is with you . . . you'll become world famous . . .', Appa said, all excited. He seemed to enjoy my visit—as if it were the homecoming of a son who had been away. I felt guilty about not visiting them. It wasn't only because of Appa's despair, a pretty girl, too, had been waiting for me! I was such a loser!

'What's the subject of the novel? Can you tell or is it a secret?' Anpu asked with a smile.

'The subject is Diego. A man gets killed. His family thinks it's a natural death. And a writer investigates the death. That's the story.'

'I see. So, it's a thriller . . . When will the book come out?'

'Don't know. It'll take at least three months.'

'I'm booking a copy now.'

'You know how to read Malayalam?'

'Oh, it's not in English?'

'I did my studies in Kerala. I've a soft corner for Malayalam.'

'Okay . . . That's why you keep going to the mainland. Do you also have a girlfriend there?'

'Why are you asking him such questions?' Appa snapped at her. 'Go and get some coffee.'

Anpu knew it was a command imbued with love. She smiled and went inside.

'My dear, you know we had a lot of trouble,' Appa said after Anpu left.

'What's the problem?'

'They had come again. And I made them return a couple

of times. Then I signed all the papers they brought with them.'

I lost my breath for a minute.

'How . . . all those papers were with me.'

'They brought fresh papers. They said if I didn't submit immediately, all the money that was due to Senthil would lapse.'

'So, you signed all the papers?'

'Yes. Is there any problem?'

'Before leaving Diego, I'd shown those papers to a lawyer. He was studying them. I was planning to go and meet him today.'

'What could I do, my dear? I have a girl here. My boy has left me. Now I need something for her. What if Senthil's money is withheld?'

'And did you get something?'

'No. The papers are being approved. I'd gone to their office two days ago. They said the money will be paid by next week. Three lakhs.'

'That large an amount?' That was a big surprise for me. It was three lakh francs. On second thoughts, I felt I shouldn't have said that. What if he thought I was jealous.

'He was in a high position. And he had good insurance. Why would I say no?'

'Yes, yes.' I had nothing more to add to that. I was under the impression that the affidavit I was shown in *Diego Daily* was a forged document. I didn't even consider the possibility of Senthil's father signing the papers. They had made the most of my lethargy. They had shut the last loophole. Better not to talk about it any more.

'Senthil visited Pondicherry often?' I changed the topic.

'Yes, he was like you. He went to the mainland at least

once a month. I suspect he also had a lover there.' The reply came from Anpu, who'd come out with the coffee.

'You! That's all you have in mind. He didn't do anything like that. He was a good person. His visits were official. He was in a high position. He'd be away for two or three days. That's all. Sometimes, he left without telling us, and then would call us from there. That was his nature,' Appa said.

'On that day too, we thought the same. That he must have gone to Pondicherry. So, we were not worried despite not seeing him for two days.' Anpu's face was suddenly filled with sorrow.

'My dear, now my neighbours blame me, saying that I didn't look for him for two days when he was in the hospital. They don't know that it was normal behaviour for him,' Appa complained.

'Anyway, he didn't spend much time at home. He was always with friends. Now, nobody comes this way. No, no need to come. Even if someone comes, I won't let them enter the house . . .' Anpu's face reddened with anger.

I put down the coffee mug and got up to leave.

'Keep visiting, my dear. And please come with me when I go to his office next week. If there is some problem with the paperwork, you can ask them.'

'Yes, please call me. I'll definitely come.'

As I was leaving, for the first time, I touched Appa's feet.

'Why are you doing this, to me you're like my Senthil . . .' He pulled me up and kissed my cheek.

Actually, my promise was an apology. For telling so many lies at a stretch.

BARBECUE

THAT NIGHT, WE had a rare barbecue party in our backyard. The Andrapper house had been filled with joy in the last few days. Valyapapan's return to normal life was a major event. It was a miracle. Something that had never been expected to happen. He no longer locked himself in his room. He went for a morning walk through the palm groves. He stopped to enjoy the breeze at the canal banks. Engaged in chit-chat with workers. He once even took the boat and went to the church! I assumed the party was an extension of the joy.

Pork, lamb, beef, steak, sausages, ribs, appetizers and desserts were stocked in plenty. Papa came back home from work by afternoon. Usually, he delegated all the work, but this time he was out there leading the preparations. By around nine, guests started arriving one by one. Stephen uncle was among the first, then some more relatives, followed by Papa's friends. There were only around twenty guests. No one had brought their families. It was a bachelor party with Mexican music and alcohol flowing, along with the food.

When the party reached a certain stage, Papa got up and requested the family and staff to leave the rest of them to discuss something confidential. Except for Valyapapan, the rest of us trooped inside. The hush-hush meeting went on for an hour. It was then that I realized the party had not been planned for Valyapapan, but for the sake of a clandestine parley.

When the guests left by around midnight, we family members gathered again: Valyapapan, Papa, Momma, Chettan, Chettathi, me.

We were all curious and it showed on our faces. Nobody

asked anything, though. Neither Papa nor Valyapapan
volunteered any information. Prying was looked down upon
by the Andrapper family. We didn't even go into another
person's room unnecessarily. So nobody talked about the
party. The chatter was all about the house. The grandeur
it had in the past. The relatives we have in Alappuzha and
Changanassery. How to organize the next Flag Day better.
How to bring all our relatives here for it.

Flag Day was the commemoration of Hormis Avira
Andrapper's landing in Diego. In my memory, it was usually
a family get-together of about twenty people. I'd heard that
unlike now, it was earlier celebrated with much pomp and
glory.

In the middle of the discussion, Valyapapan dragged in
the topic of my marriage. Papa said it should be only after I
get a job. 'What if he doesn't have a job? Our palm groves
are making enough to provide for him and the girl,' said
Valyapapan. 'Nobody need worry about this, the girl has
already been found,' said Momma. 'It can be arranged any
time,' said Chettathi. 'That's the only way to discipline him,'
said my brother. I was the only one who didn't speak. For
or against. In fact, I didn't know if I should get married. The
talk continued for a while. Then one by one, people started
leaving, till it was only Papa and I who were left.

I thought he'd ask me about marriage or studies or my
novel. But his question was about Senthil.

'What happened to the friend who died? You've been
chasing it for a long time.'

I was amazed. I never thought he took my investigation
seriously. I was under the impression that I did my thing and
he lived in his world. And after I'd ditched my chance of going
to Australia, I thought he'd given up on me completely. I felt

happy all of a sudden. It must have been the joy of knowing that my father had not written me off.

'No progress, Papa. The Public Security says it's a natural death, but I'm sure he was killed.'

'His family knows that?'

'No, that's the worst part.'

'If it's a murder as you say, then there should be other witnesses.'

'There are. But nobody is willing to admit it. I found one person . . . I'll definitely prove it.'

'I realized that you can't continue with your writing till you get this out of the way. That's why I left you to it. Do you think you can get some peace if you are finished with it?'

I didn't reply to that. Instead, I asked him a question: 'What's the connection that the Diego government has with Pondicherry?'

Papa didn't get the question at first. He stared at me, puzzled.

'Do any of our officials have to visit Pondicherry for work? And for what work?'

'There is no connection that I know of. Even if there is, that must be only for the foreign affairs department. Why this question?'

'Nothing. A friend of mine used to visit Pondicherry regularly. I was curious to know what it was for.'

'Must be some business. It won't have any connection with the government.'

'Must be,' I said ending the topic.

Both of us sat there for some more time. We were deep into the night. Across the lake, the lights were still on. The only sound was of the occasional boat passing by. When I got up to leave, Papa held my hands.

'My dear, a father who really loves his son can understand his mind. Your life is now at a crossroads with many roads leading to different directions. If you don't decide which one to take, then we'll have to decide it for you. The job I was talking about was just an excuse. They don't understand your dream. Or my dream for you. Marriage is not important now. Writing is. A single beautiful novel can make you known to the world.'

Many roads. I was thinking about that, lying in bed. A road following Senthil. Another to marry Melvin. The road to politics, as pictured by Daniel D'Silva. The road to my soul called writing. The road to success in writing, as dreamt by Papa. Which one was my choice?

LOVE MARRIAGE

ANPU CALLED IN the morning. 'Appa and I are going to my brother's office today. Will you also come with us?'

'Sure. What time?'

'Around nine.'

'Fine. Wait at Uthukkuli jetty, I'll come there.'

'Okay.'

It was already eight. I quickly got ready.

'Where are you off to?' Momma asked at the breakfast table.

'To an office in Pentasia.'

'Will you be back soon?'

'Let me see.'

She hovered around me, which was unusual. I understood she had something to say or ask. But I was in a rush. So I ignored the rest of her questions as if they were irrelevant, finished my tea and left.

I reached Uthukkuli jetty five minutes before nine. I could see Anpu and her father at a distance.

'You've been waiting for long?' Appa picked up pace on seeing me.

'No, I just got here.'

'Good morning!' Anpu said with a wide smile.

———

We struggled a bit to park the boat at Pentasia as it was office hours. We got a slot far away and that too paid parking. Half a franc for an hour. Wherever there is a chance, the government stares at people's pockets. I didn't have change, so Anpu paid. I felt awkward but there was no other option. The fine was ten francs.

Senthil's office was a long walk from there. We walked slowly amidst people who were streaming ahead to reach the office on time. Appa walked in front, and Anpu and I behind. There was a tantalizing fragrance of jasmine about her. I walked close to her.

Someone who was coming from the opposite direction stopped on seeing Appa. It seemed that they knew each other. Appa's face widened with joy. While they were talking, Anpu and I waited by the side.

Suddenly, the two men turned towards us.

'Oh, isn't that your daughter? She's married . . . what's his name?'

Appa turned pale, not knowing what to say. Anpu was silent.

I told the man my name.

'What is this, sir? Your girl's husband is not from our caste. Was it a love marriage?'

We were dumbstruck.

'Yes, love marriage. I like him a lot. Why not? Should we fall in love only within our own caste?' Anpu intervened.

This time, the man was the one who was taken aback. He bade us a quick farewell.

I looked at Anpu in disbelief. She winked at me and laughed it off. But Appa was feeling awkward to face me. He started walking ahead of us.

Offices in Diego open at nine. But when we reached there at quarter to ten, the employees were still pouring in. We sat on a bench in the verandah. It took another half an hour for Senthil's boss to arrive. Seeing Appa, he greeted him warmly and took us to his room. He made us sit and organized coffee for us. He apologized for his lateness and reminisced about Senthil.

Just as he was about to ask me something, Appa chipped in. 'This is Senthil's close friend. He's like my son. These two are not married.' The officer must have been amused by his panic. I looked at Anpu. She couldn't stop laughing.

Senthil's boss seemed to like me. The rest of his conversation was with me. He explained that the forms that were initially filled had mistakes and that they should be redone. Once they are submitted, the cash will be released in a week, he promised.

He opened a file on his table, and patiently pointed out the mistakes in those papers, one by one. My phone rang. It was Melvin. I was supposed to meet her last evening, but I'd forgotten about it. She was probably calling to check on me. I couldn't take the call as I had to pay attention to the long list of minor errors. The phone rang again after some time. Melvin again. The officer stopped talking and looked at the wall behind us. My eyes followed his. There was a board that said, 'Kindly switch off mobile phones before entering this office'. I apologized to him and turned it off.

I meant to switch it on as soon as I got out, and call Melvin. But it slipped my mind. We don't need reasons to forget; we need them only to remember. It was much later—after we had coffee and got some Ayurvedic medicines for Appa, after I dropped him and Anpu off at the Uthukkuli jetty—that I remembered Melvin. When I switched on the phone, ten missed-call messages beeped in a row. The first two were from Melvin. The rest were from Anita. Melvin and then Anita? What was the emergency? I quickly called back. Anita's reply was a loud howl.

5

Virtual Garden

THE FOURTH PART of *The Book of Forefathers* was a gift to the Thursday Market from me, after I left the hospital. I had neither told anyone about it nor shown it to anyone when they visited me in the hospital. When they asked how I managed to get it despite being laid up in bed, I told them that some things we don't have to chase, they come in search of us. I gave them some theories and fooled around for a while. Then I told them about *Archipelago*, the foreword and Srikumar, and they were suitably surprised.

No one made any deductions or observations after the reading session. Everyone looked at each other, as if asking the other to speak if they could figure out any clue. There was nothing from anyone. Let Benyamin rest, we'll meet later, they said. The Thursday Market dispersed.

After I had recuperated for some more days, I tried once again to return to my novel, *Nedumbassery*. My time in the hospital had given me some good leads to follow. The ideas were there in my mind. And the critical moments that constitute a novel. But I was unable to write. Whenever I sat in front of the screen, *The Book of Forefathers* popped up in my mind. Where could I get the rest of the manuscript? What would it have? What happened to Christy Andrapper while he was writing it? Who killed Senthil? What's Jesintha's role in it? Why did Melvin want to meet Christy urgently? Why did Anita scream? Where did Vinod disappear from the Public Security office? Why did Christy come to Alappuzha? Who among his friends had died at Ernakulam? These were the questions I asked myself. They strangled my *Nedumbassery*. They stopped me from writing. I couldn't get any peace without finding these answers. It became my need more than Andrapper's to find them. I felt angry. I even cursed him for spoiling my peace of mind. Christy, I am not a detective to spend my time identifying your hints and tracing your near ones through such clues. I don't have that kind of an investigative brain. Until now it had been luck and the Thursday Market's smartness. But even they had declared a surrender this time. What could I do?

I convened a couple of more Thursday meetings in the hope that their talents would yield some clues. They shared their thoughts and doubts and possibilities. But no conclusions were reached. Mashu's suggestion was the most practical: 'Andrapper has presented many characters in these four portions we've got. Let's try to get in touch with more of them using our contacts and connections, and get to know about him better.'

First, I called Srikumar. I asked if Andrapper had said anything at all about the other portions of his manuscript. Srikumar said he had written that they were with you. I asked if he knew whose funeral Andrapper had come to attend. 'Some girl. Don't remember the name. Seems like they were closely related,' Srikumar said.

A girl who died? Andrapper's friend? Who could it be? Not Jyoti. She was unwell and in a hospital now, according to Salu. Perhaps it was someone who had not appeared till now? I went over the four sections of *The Book of Forefathers*. Other than Jyoti, there was Leena, Supriya, little Anita . . . Could it be one of them? Anita? But whoever it is, how did they die? I got panicky. The panic of a thirst for knowledge.

Many days went by without anything happening. Then one day, I was riding with Nibu Achachan to a relative's house near Kollam. In a village on the way, there was a huge meeting. Crowds filled the road. Someone loud was on the mike. From the pillion, I looked at the dais. A row of members of the khadi brigade. A large banner read: 'Welcome to Rajanbabu, the pride of Thonakkadu'. I thought it was some politician. But then the words of the orator stopped me: 'Our dear Rajan has completed twenty-five years abroad. This is not a short duration in a human life. Rajan is not just one of the thousands who left their homeland. He is a presence in the place he reached. He always lends a helping hand to the poor. Anyone at any time could run to him. These are not fancy words, there is no one in Diego Garcia today who doesn't know Rajan, or doesn't need his help. Even the rulers crave for his affection and support. He has helped thousands of youngsters from our place and given them a life. There is not a single household here that hasn't got his love. This crowd is a proof of it. Rajan is an exemplary model of what a journalist ought to be . . .'

I touched Nibu's shoulder. Achachan got the hint. We parked the bike in a corner.

We waited there till the function got over. When he was stepping down from the dais, Nibu ran up to him. Whereas I was worried about how to introduce ourselves to him, Nibu was smart. His crisp words were: 'Sir, we are representatives of Pravasalokam.com. We want to interview you.'

He seemed apprehensive.

'We have come from Thiruvananthapuram to attend this function. We heard about it, and inquired about you in Diego. The reports made us very proud of you. The world should know about you. We mostly focus on NRIs who have made it big in life. We are proud that you're one of them.'

He fell for Nibu's praises. 'No problem, no problem, please come home,' he invited us.

We followed his car home. After somehow managing to part from visitors and well-wishers, he sat before us. Nibu took out a notepad and pen from the bike's pocket, and transformed into a serious interviewer. He had the experience of reporting sports for a local daily. I felt bad about fooling such a good man. I consoled myself with the thought that it was for a good cause. Childhood, the circumstances at home, schooling, experiences abroad, and as a journalist . . . Nibu conducted the interview with great professionalism.

'Our idea is to make *Pravasalokam* a platform showcasing the varied experiences of migrants across the world,' Nibu said, concluding the interview. 'Do you know anyone else in Diego whom you would recommend?'

Rajanbabu named some social activists and club organizers.

'Is there a family named Andrapper or something? Are they Malayalis?' Nibu asked.

'It is said they have roots in Kerala. Some say they came directly from Portugal. Whatever may be the truth, they migrated a long time ago. They were once big estate owners in Diego. Now everything is gone. They have nothing.'

'One of them had written a story for our site. Do you know him, sir? His name is Christy Andrapper.'

'Oh, Christy. A brilliant boy. I like him very much.'

'Where is he now?'

'Must be somewhere there. I keep running into him at some function or other.'

'We had got an email from him saying there had been a

murder there and that we should report the news. Do you
know anything about that?'

'Oh, he wrote to you too? He came to me about it. I had
it investigated. It's a manufactured story. Diego is a country
with a strict law and order system. We cannot compare it
with the neighbouring African countries. No one there can
commit a murder and then live in peace. To be frank, that
case was the result of a political game from within his family.
They were once the rulers of Diego . . . that ended a long time
ago. But they still have this craving for power. It comes out as
allegations against Diego. Their intention is to prove the law
and order situation is in a wreck. I've been in that country for
more than twenty-five years now. I know how strict the laws
are. If such a murder had taken place, the criminals would
have been caught immediately. No doubt about it. The new
chancellor, His Excellency Charles Dominic, is very strict in
these issues. I've known him personally for the last ten years.'

'So are you saying such a death didn't happen?'

'A death did take place. But all deaths are not murders.'

'Our site is interested to know more. Sir, please help us to
locate him. We need an interview with him,' I said.

'See, as a journalist, I appreciate involvement in a case.
But this is just a ploy to create news. A mere scandal. Who
will benefit from it?' His face had turned red.

'Not creating news, sir. We only wanted to hear his side of
the story. If his arguments are concocted, we'll expose them.'

'Okay, I'll look for him after I return. But note that I won't
be part of anything that tarnishes Diego's name. The land is
my bread and butter.'

'Oh, thank you, sir. What's your contact number?'

He went inside and came out with his visiting card.

We talked some more and had some tea before we left.

Nibu was fantastic. I had never seen anyone who dealt with such a situation in such a cool manner. The fire in my belly died only after the bike left the premises of Rajanbabu's house.

It wasn't clear whether that visit was fruitful. Meanwhile, something else happened.

One day, I was at a family friend's house. All of us men were gathered in the verandah when we heard his wife shouting at their son. When she was asked the reason for her anger, she said her son hadn't watered the vineyards even though he had been asked to. 'The plants must have died now.' Her anger gave way to tears. We were wondering as to how and when this family—that hated plants and soil and fertilizers—had started loving plants. Have begun to grow grapes? Our friend laughed on hearing the question. 'The farm is not in or near my house, but in Facebook,' he said. And his wife became vocal about getting gifts from friends, building farms, watering land without canals and pumps, reaping profits without wasting effort, and growing cows without stench. I didn't have much clue about it, so I kept mum.

Anyway, that was how I was introduced to the latest social media network called Facebook. I started an account with the idea of owning a virtual farm. Though my garden too died from not being watered, I acquired a lot of old and new friends on Facebook. I gradually moved from Orkut to Facebook.

One day, I got tagged to an Aldous Huxley quote: 'I don't believe for a moment that creativity is a neurotic symptom.' Someone's favourite saying. I registered it as a random quote. But the next day, I got the same line as a message. It struck me that it was the line Andrapper had wanted me to put as my Orkut status. What could it mean? Could this person have any connection to Christy? I looked at his name. Jijo Thomas. An engineer based in Kothamangalam. Interested in music. None of it seemed like a link to Andrapper. Despite that, I replied to the message with four words: The Book of Forefathers. Another question came as the reply: 'Are you the author Benyamin?' Yes, I replied, to which came the response: 'I have to talk to you. Can we meet?'

'Sure, whenever you want. What's the matter?'

'I'm coming to Kottayam next Friday. Can we meet? It's about Andrapper.'

I was roused by that. Andrapper?

'You know Andrapper?'

'I'll tell you when we meet. Can we?'

'Yes.'

'Where?' he messaged.

'Hotel Ambassador, near Manorama.' It was the only hotel I knew in Kottayam.

We exchanged mobile numbers and agreed to meet. All via Facebook. I immediately informed the Thursday Market. Everyone was busy. But I was reluctant to go alone. Finally, Nattapranthan agreed to tag along. Next Friday, early morning, we left for Kottayam in a Superfast bus.

By the time we reached our hotel, it was around eleven in the morning. He was waiting for us at the reception. A fashionable young man with a stud in his ear. Jijo, he introduced himself.

We went inside and ordered some juice.

'Why did you want to meet us?' I asked.

'Christy Andrapper asked me to do so,' he said.

'Why?'

Instead of replying, he opened his bag and handed over a packet to me. I opened it. It was the fifth part of *The Book of Forefathers*. I greedily started reading it right then.

DARKNESS

ANITA ONLY MANAGED to tell me to rush to the hospital. A blade of fear pierced through my spine. Something bad has happened to someone. My god, what could it be? The face of Anita's husband and children floated up in my mind. That increased the speed of my boat. Anita hadn't specified the hospital. I assumed it was City Hospital. When I reached I went directly to Accidents and Emergency. Sudha-chechi was on the verandah, so was Mercy and a couple of others whose names I didn't remember.

'What happened?'

'Nothing. Slipped while getting into a boat. The head hit the plank.'

'Where is Anita?'

'There, she's inside.'

I went into the visitors' room. When she saw me, Anita jumped up and held my hands.

'Did they tell you?' she asked, looking at the people outside.

'Yes.'

'Nothing much. Nothing. Loss of consciousness because of the impact. That's all. That'll be all, won't it?'

'Yes, yes. Nothing to worry. It's just a minor slip . . . Anyway, let me ask.' I gently let go of her hands and walked outside.

I tried to convince the security guard to let me go inside. He wouldn't budge. Neither would the nurses. 'Why do you have to get in? If there is something to be done, we will do it.' They got angry. Suddenly, I remembered Johnny. He might be able to help. But when I checked my phone, his number was not there. I felt angry with myself. How could I have deleted his number thinking he won't be of any use! How can anyone say when people can be of use! I decided to go and find him. I walked a twisted path, following arrows down the long corridors and verandahs. It was as though life had been rewound to the distant past, and was being replayed. Like I had returned to the day when I came searching for Senthil, and I had started my walk from that moment.

The walk was a waste. Johnny was not in at his old seat. Then I remembered his promotion. Nobody there knew where his new office was. Someone suggested I inquire at the Recruitments office.

That was even farther away. Verandahs. Corridors. Stairways. What if Johnny was not there? As I returned to Accidents and Emergency, I heard the wailing from a distance. My throat went dry. I ran. A stretcher lay in the verandah with a white sheet over a body. Anita was down on the floor, with Mercy trying to pacify and lift her. I ran towards them and helped her. With great difficulty, we hauled her up and took her back to the visiting room. A nurse stepped in to ask, 'Anyone else wants to see? We are moving the stretcher to the dressing room.'

Mercy looked at me. 'Don't you want to see?'

I nodded.

She took me to the stretcher and removed the white cloth from the face. I looked. I felt the heaviness of a dark cloud in my head. The darkness thickened. I fumbled to get a hold of the stretcher.

When I opened my eyes to consciousness, Papa was beside me. Curtains formed a wall around me, with a half-empty

IV drip hovering above like a bat. The stench of medicines filled the place. That took me to the source of memories. I tried to recall what had happened. I couldn't. I had told myself, I'm all right, I'm all right. I had tried my best not to fall. But a cold darkness had dragged me down.

Everything is just a dream, I sighed. But my senses did not let me live in the lie for longer than a moment. I had to admit to myself the horror of reality—that death had taken someone close to me into its whirlpool.

The pain slowly spread through my chest. A strange prickling. As if something was stabbing me there. When my eyes met Papa's, tears started flowing down my cheek. I tried to control myself, but failed. They continued to flow, dampening the pillow. Papa pressed my hand, and silently went out of the room.

More than sorrow, it was regret that burnt in me. Till I saw the face I did not allow for even the slightest chance of such a thing to happen. I had decided it was someone close to Anita. It is my habit to imagine a hundred possibilities to anything: Is it this? Or is it that? Could it be . . .? And then become happy or sad or angry. But the reality would be something completely different from my speculations. The same had happened again.

The pain multiplied the more I thought about it. I'd ignored her the past few days. Not intentionally, but it had happened. I'd been pushing our meeting to the next day, or the one after. Who could have thought death would interrupt our unfinished conversation? Melvin, my apologies. If I had known death was only a slip away from you, I wouldn't have treated you the way I did. I would have taken you with me to *Diego Daily*. I would have answered all your calls. I would have come to see you as promised and listened to all you wanted to say.

Whenever you'd sent a scrap in Orkut, you had wished for a boat ride to the seafront or to go shopping. You never insisted though. Even if I didn't have a grain of love for you, I should have agreed to your requests as your friend. But I didn't. I'm one of those out-of-date, antiquated men who think love is not something to be expressed.

In my half-finished novel, a writer goes in search of Diego's heart. He never falls for a girl or loves anyone. Was my life reflected in my work? I saw myself in the novel. Melvin, I've become this person. I can only become this person. What else can I do but apologize?

'Papa, let's go,' I called to him.

'Already? You should stay . . .' Papa came to me.

'It's nothing, Papa. Just a shock, that's all.'

I tried to pull out the drip.

'Someone who faints on seeing a dead body! Lie there for five minutes. Let the doctor come and check on you.' A nurse came in and scolded me.

I hadn't seen a dead body. I saw a face, the face of my dearest. I wanted to say that. But what was the use of telling that to them? I couldn't stay there any longer.

'Papa, please call the doctor. I've to go! I've to go.'

Heeding my panic, Papa managed to bring the doctor with him. I explained that I was fine and ready to leave. I got up to demonstrate.

He reluctantly signed the discharge sheet with 'Against medical advice'.

I ran through the E&A verandah. I had the feeling that Melvin was still lying there. But it was vacant as if nothing had happened. I was about to ask a nurse when she ignored me in her rush to get inside. I tried to follow her, but Papa held me back.

'I have to see her once more, Papa.'

'She is not here. She's been moved to the morgue.'

'So fast? Then, we will go there and see.'

'Not now.'

'Why, Papa? Is it because you think I'll faint again? I won't.'

'We'll go later.'

'No, I have to see her now, Papa. For peace of mind. I'm scared. What if she goes missing like Senthil?'

'Christy, don't be a child. A man's courage and keenness is measured not by his everyday behaviour, but in how he faces extreme and unexpected situations. You have never had to face such a situation before. But this is a chance to test yourself. Be brave. Prove that you're strong enough to face the unforeseen. Tears are not the best love you can give the dead, it's deeds. Think of what arrangements you can make to help send her body home.'

His words snapped me awake. Yes. I should be brave. And strong. Pain should pass through like the wind, affecting only the fringes of the mind. It shouldn't shake it up. What Papa said was right. Tears are not the best love to give the dead. I hadn't done anything for her. At least now I ought to do what I can. Who else was there for her? She shouldn't be lying an orphaned corpse in some cold storage. Melvin, I'll do what is required to send your body home. But you . . . you'll be here with me, right?

EMBALM

WHO COULD HELP me get things done fast? Many names came to my mind. It was when I wanted to call them that I realized

I no longer remembered any of their numbers. There was a time when I knew phone numbers by heart like I knew the multiplication table. When I remembered a face, I used to be able to recall the number that went with it. The mobile had put an end to that. Half my memory had leaked out without my knowledge. What would happen if I lost my mobile phone too? Won't the door to all my relationships be shut in just one swoop? Fortunately, I'd only lost Johnny's number from my phone. The numbers of Rajanbabu sir and Daniel D'Silva were in the contacts list. I called both of them.

Rajanbabu: 'I got news of it. Is she someone you know? Okay, I'll definitely do the needful.'

Daniel D'Silva: 'I'm leaving now and will reach your house within an hour.'

It was a great relief for me.

Papa had already called Stephen uncle to get the papers from the Public Security department.

Though I was born and bought up in Diego, most of my grown-up years were spent in Thiruvananthapuram. By the time I returned, my peers had all left or become absorbed in their own work and life. Because of that, there were only a few in Diego who knew me or whom I knew. Most of the relationships I had, began and ended in literature. There was no humanity in that. When I had a problem, I was unsure of support. I had already faced that in the Senthil case. But this time, it was as though the whole of Diego society was in step with me.

Whatever was on his mind, Daniel D'Silva came immediately and took over. It was great luck that he was familiar with the complicated procedures of transporting a body. Someone new to it would have been totally lost. Death certificate and release certificate from the Ministry of Health.

Then clearance certificates from the Public Security, the Public Prosecutor, the Crime Investigation Department, the Forensic Department, and a paper each from the ministries of Internal Affairs and Foreign Affairs. The record of transferring the salary and other remunerations from the company where she was working to the nearest relative or to the Indian Embassy, and after that the release certificate from the embassy. After everything, papers from emigration, airport, cargo, etc. Each department delayed the proceedings with hundreds of queries. So, he made sure to be everywhere in person to hasten it. Rajanbabu sir called the senior chief at the Ministry of Health to avoid delays in paperwork. Meanwhile, the hospital demanded a post-mortem. Through Rajanbabu, I persuaded the higher-ups not to put Melvin's body under the knife. I wanted it to be sent home as it was. For that an approval letter was required from her parents. Some of her friends contacted them and got it faxed. With that, I wrote a letter stating that nobody in Diego had any complaints. All this while, I had not contacted anyone from her hostel. But updates kept coming and things fell in place somehow. There was help from the congregation at Melvin's church. Formalities that usually take three days were wrapped up in half a day and orders were passed to send the body to India the very next day. On the Mali–Diego–Thiruvananthapuram flight of Indian Airlines at 1 p.m. The body was to be taken out of the mortuary at 7 a.m. and embalmed. At 9, there would be prayers at St. Thomas Ecumenical Church. The body had to reach the cargo section at the airport by at least 10 a.m.

There was a reason for the haste. Diego has direct flights to Thiruvananthapuram only on Tuesdays. Otherwise, one has to go via Sri Lanka or Mali. If any problem cropped up, the body could get stuck in these airports for three or four days. There had been many such incidents before, according to Rajanbabu sir. So, I spent every minute chasing down the necessary papers. Once that was done and I reached home, the sorrows returned. Melvin returned. Till then, I was busy arranging to send a body.

I didn't want to show my pain, and so I didn't face anyone at home. Especially, Momma and Chettathi. I went to my room directly and lay under the blanket. Eyes that were dry until then slowly started overflowing. I mulled over the proximity of life and death. Someone who was so near me yesterday, someone who used to send scraps and messages to me, someone who wanted to see me and tell me important things, she had disappeared in the period between the switching off of a phone and turning it on. Melvin . . . the last call from your phone was to mine. That means even when you were ten steps away from death, you wished to talk to me. Were you sad or angry that I didn't take your call when you were slipping to death? Oh god, why didn't I feel like answering the call? I could have excused myself for a minute to take your call and talk to you. Or I could have stepped out for a minute and called you back. Then you would have waited there till I arrived. You wouldn't have slipped on the boat's step. You wouldn't have gone so far away from me. I desperately wanted to relive the day. To answer the phone while I was in Senthil's office. I actually picked up the phone twice and looked at it. But that moment had passed out of my life. Nothing can bring it back. We are so powerless that we cannot call back a single moment of our lives. Last night, at this time, you might have been waiting for my call. And now, you are in the cold, wrapped in a tight white cloth. I bit my finger and wept without making a sound.

LUGGAGE

IN THE MORNING, a strange scene welcomed me in front of the mortuary. A father receiving the body of a two-year-old girl who had drowned the previous day. He was a Tamil. There was no one with him. He took the cold body from the morgue, held it close to his chest and walked away. Alone. The scene remained etched in my eyes for a long time. How would he have dealt with that loneliness? Oh god . . . what's more horrible than the death of one's children?

Mercy and Jaya-chechi took charge of preparing the body. The first coffin we got had to be replaced with a better model. More cotton, an extra pillow, some flowers and other similar demands had to be met. I stayed at the mortuary to help. Chettathi and Melvin's friends from the hostel were also there. While we were waiting to take the body to the church, Jaya-chechi asked me, 'So, Anita's friend is also going to the mainland with the body, right?'

'Good idea,' Momma said.

'It'll be a relief for them,' continued Jaya-chechi.

I hadn't given it any thought. The confusion was probably evident in my eyes. But I nodded in agreement to pacify Jaya-chechi.

Then another problem arose. Though the body was ready for transport, the mortuary wouldn't release it. It looked as if the hospital staff was delaying it. Finally, Daniel arrived to clarify that the staff had to be tipped. It was one of their own colleagues, but they still needed the bribe! I sent the money through Mercy.

I went up to Momma. 'Did you say that I'm going to the mainland?'

'Oh, you are not going?'

'If I have to go, why are you telling me that so late?' I argued with Momma.

'Why should I have to tell you! Don't you know you ought to go?'

I was uncertain. 'Should he go?' Chettan asked doubtfully.

'Yes, he should go. That's the right thing to do.' Chettathi was firm.

'I haven't booked the ticket. I haven't packed. It's almost ten. How will I catch a 1 o'clock flight?'

'Go now, call someone and get the ticket done,' Momma told me sternly.

Whom could I call? Everyone I knew was busy with something or the other. After dropping my family at the church, I went to the three travel agencies that I knew. None of them could help. The flight was fully booked. Their only suggestion was that I buy a wait-listed ticket and try my luck. If there was any last-minute cancellation, I could board the plane.

I decided to give it a shot. If it was in my destiny to accompany Melvin, then someone was sure to cancel their trip at the last minute.

By the time I collected the ticket and rushed to the church, the ceremony was over. Rajanbabu sir spotted me. 'Where were you?' he asked angrily. I realized that my absence had been noticed. When I gave him my reason, he got more angry. 'You should have just given me a call. Didn't I tell you to call if there is any need?'

I should have done that. But it hadn't occurred to me. I was not in a state of mind to think through anything logically. When we don't remember things on time, most of our actions become follies.

Rajanbabu sir quickly made some calls. 'Okay, go to the

airport directly. There is a Basheer in the Air Lanka office.
Go and meet him. If there is any chance, he'll get it done.'

I said goodbye to him and went inside the church. I could
see why my absence had been noticed. There were so few
people. Two or three from the health department to seal
the coffin. Daniel D'Silva who was supervising everything.
Anita, standing next to the coffin, with tears yet to stop.
Hostel mates grouped in another corner. Not all of them
seemed to be there, the rest were probably on duty in the
hospital. Some others who looked like church staff. Then
Momma, Chettan and Chettathi. That was all. I felt sad. It
was such a small circle she had lived in, with not many to
attend even her funeral.

Someone had mounted a pretty photo of Melvin near the
coffin. I recognized it from her Orkut account. I had admired
that photo a hundred times at least. A hundred times had I
teased her saying a matrimony profile with that photo would
get princes looking for her. But who knew that the fate of that
photo was to smile beside her coffin. That was not a thought
the photographer would have had while taking it, or Melvin's
while posting it on Orkut.

They had closed the coffin and sealed it. I stood there
feeling like a destitute. Melvin, if I can't accompany you today,
this is our last meeting. I couldn't see your face for one last
time. I don't want to see your face frozen in ice. In my mind,
you are the smiling face in the photo.

Anita looked devastated. I didn't see anyone there
affected as much as her. It was the normal silence of death
that characterized the rest of the faces. If you looked more
closely, you could see that they were keen to wind up all of
this quickly and return to their routines. Melvin, life is so
trivial. Yours and mine . . . The loss of it doesn't shake up

anyone, it doesn't cause them to topple over. It just mildly disturbs their routines.

———

I accompanied the coffin to the cargo section. I felt dejected to see how casually they handle the bodies of our dear ones that we leave with tears and from which we part with pain. They see it not as a human body that had a soul, a mind, a heart, that had experienced emotions and feelings, sorrow, laughter and love, but as a 160-pound piece of luggage. As soon as we transferred the coffin, it was hastily weighed and scooped up with a forklift after the address was pasted on it. They paid no heed to my pleas—to be careful in the handling.

I rushed home after that. Momma had packed a bag. I didn't even bother to check what was in it. I just made sure I had my passport and ticket with me. Chettan dropped me off at the airport jetty. Basheer of Air Lanka was waiting for me. He took me to the Indian Airlines' check-in counter. I didn't have to wait for even a minute. No hurdles at all. There was no mention of any waiting list. They gave me the boarding pass. Without waiting for a word of thanks, Basheer went back to his office. Everything was done so quickly. Sometimes it's like that. We might expect a lot of obstacles, but the path is cleared rapidly. Like never before.

The flight to Thiruvananthapuram left exactly at 1 a.m.

THIRUVANANTHAPURAM

I'VE ALWAYS FELT that my biggest weakness is that I worry about a problem only while facing it. Though I'm aware of this shortcoming, I haven't done much to fix it. I don't live a life where I need to foresee situations, and plan and schedule my chores with discipline. I try to do it now and then, but eventually slip into old habits. That was what had happened again. I was a fool. A real fool. A fool who thought that he had the brain and wit of an Investigation Department officer.

Who knew that I was accompanying Melvin's body? I had not informed anyone in the mainland. In case someone from Diego had indeed called up, who would be there to receive me at the airport? How would they recognize me? How would I recognize them? And more importantly, where was Melvin's house? I only remembered her telling me that it was in a village between Ernakulam and Kottayam. How could I find her house with that bit of information? I should have carried the contact number of someone! I didn't even have that. Melvin was that close to me. Though we were just a half-hour boat ride away from each other, we mostly met through emails and on Orkut. We thought that we were only a finger touch away whichever corner of the world we lived in. I've even argued that addresses and geographies will become irrelevant. On the flight I realized that we had failed to know each other. It was a relationship that could have led to marriage. I wondered what it was that we had talked about without touching our home and families. If I tried to locate my sixty-seven Orkut friends outside of the Internet, I probably wouldn't be able to find more than five.

The fact is we have so little knowledge even about someone whom we consider our closest cyber friend. Knowing someone is not just about knowing the person's mind, but also knowing their land.

Ten minutes prior to schedule, at 3.15 p.m., the flight landed at Thiruvananthapuram. Emigration and visa clearance took more time than usual. The queue had passengers from two or three flights. When I finally managed to step out, and taxi drivers surrounded me like bees, I felt like I had walked into a dacoit burrow. They were so aggressive that I was scared they would snatch my bag and run. It was not as though Thiruvananthapuram was new to me. I had lived there for three years. But I'd not seen such an onslaught anywhere else in the city. It was a struggle to get them off me.

I waited at the entrance for a while in the hope that someone might have come to receive me. But I couldn't see anyone. After consulting the inquiry desk, I took an auto and went to the cargo section to collect the body. I was sure someone would be waiting there. By the time I got there, Melvin's family seemed to have taken her body and left. I was baffled. I didn't know what to do next. My only option would be to call Anita or her friends. But I was too embarrassed to do that. I decided to find Melvin's village without anyone's help. After all, I had lived in Kerala for three years. I took it as a challenge.

As people do when they visit a city they had once lived in, I looked up my old friends. I had Sajeesh's number. He was a journalist. He would surely have more investigative sense than me. I called him. But he had left Thiruvananthapuram and joined the paper's Kozhikode bureau. It seemed like he was in the middle of some news report, with no time even to talk. I called my former room-mate, Visakh, next. My bad luck continued. His phone was out of coverage area. My three years in this city had left me with just two mobile numbers. I felt contempt for myself. A person who didn't know how to sustain relationships. My challenge ended there.

I took an auto to the town. My plan was to rent a room, stay there for two days, and return home. After going back,

I'd have to lie that I was part of all the formalities. I'd have to teach the lie to my mind, and live with the lie. There was no other way. Kerala beyond Thiruvananthapuram was alien to me. I could not navigate any major town without the help of someone. How could I presume to find an unknown village? I told myself to let it go. Melvin, our destiny is to part like this.

The auto dropped me off at Thampanoor. I had a headache from the long ride. I wanted a coffee. I went to Indian Coffee House. The memories of my college days blew through like a cool breeze. My literary dreams originated in that place. I used to go to the Indian Coffee House near Statue only to see M. Krishnan Nair who frequented the place. Inspired by his writing, I would search for books in the shelves of the British Library. The pile of books that triumphed over my academic studies led to my writing. It seemed as though that dream had come to an end. Perhaps I can never complete that half-finished novel. My fate was to live unrecognized and die unknown. A name flashed up in my mind: Srikumar. The man who introduced himself as a publisher based in Ernakulam who wanted to publish my novel. There was no one better to help me. And finally I had a stroke of luck—I found his number in my phone. I dialled him immediately.

Srikumar didn't need any reminders. He was excited to hear from me.

'Are you now in Kerala? I have to meet you.'

'And I want to meet you. A friend of mine passed away. I've come to attend the funeral in Ernakulam.'

'Where in Ernakulam?'

'I don't know. I have to find out. I need your help for that. All I know is it's in a village somewhere between Ernakulam and Kottayam.'

'When is the funeral?'

'Tomorrow.'

'What's the person's name?'

'Melvin.'

'Any other details?'

'She was a nurse in Diego. Died in an accident. The body was brought in today's flight.'

'That's more than enough. Get into a train now. Stay in a hotel for the night. I'm in Aluva now. I'll reach Ernakulam by morning. By then, I'll find out the person's house.'

I was taken aback. What confidence! Srikumar's briskness put my anxieties to rest. Even if nothing worked out, at that particular moment, I was grateful to have found someone who offered me relief. That was enough. With that comforting thought, I went to the railway station.

A NIGHT OF CRAZY DREAMS

IT WAS PAST 5 p.m. I got the ticket after waiting in a long queue. When I asked about the next train to Ernakulam, the woman at the counter told me to rush to the fifth platform where the Ernakulam Express was ready to leave. If I couldn't make it, there was the Vanchinad at 5.45. It must have been for me that the train was delayed by fifteen minutes that day. When I found my way to the fifth platform and boarded the train, it started moving immediately. The compartment was crowded. There were more people standing than sitting. The standing seemed to have become a part of their lives. Among them were people standing and reading, standing and writing, standing and playing cards, standing and drinking tea, standing and eating, and standing and chopping vegetables. I felt uncomfortable. I couldn't stand the sound and movement

of the train. Despite leaning on a nearby seat and holding on
to the rod, I kept stumbling. Every journey has a rhythm—
something that the regulars do not notice, and the beginners
cannot manage.

The rhythm of the train would not match with the
rhythm of my body. I was used to water, to boats and
sailing. My body was attuned to the waves. I could walk to
the bow of a boat moving at any speed. I wouldn't fall. No
other form of transport suited my body. During my time in
Thiruvananthapuram, I'd had great difficulty travelling in
buses. I'd vomit if I got into a bus. My head would spin in
an auto. It was like that throughout the three years I spent
there. So I couldn't make any long journeys. My dream
of seeing Kerala didn't happen only because of that. Even
Thiruvananthapuram I mostly saw on foot. My friends used
to call me a miser.

People around me were amused to see someone who
couldn't stand properly in a train. People in Kerala could not
possibly understand my difficulty. They were used to all kinds
of journeys right from childhood. They used boats and motor
vehicles and trains. Their bodies were used to the rhythm of
every form of transport. They might empathize with me only
if they are asked to get into a horse cart or atop a camel.

'Try the chair car. You might get a seat,' someone who felt
bad for my plight said.

'It's four bogies away. Go to the front,' he advised me
again.

I couldn't even stand and then I had to walk! I dragged
myself to the door of the compartment, but when I saw the
pathway between the two compartments, butterflies rose
in my stomach. I took courage and stepped on it twice,
but simply couldn't go forward on the moving surface. I

regretfully watched tea vendors, men, women, girls and even little children crossing over to the next compartment. Just like some old people hesitate at the foot of the escalator, I stood there wistfully.

There was no other choice than to wait there till the next stop. My plan was to shift to the air-conditioned coach. But the train just passed through several stations without stopping. And when it did stop at two stations, I couldn't get down because of the crowd. For almost an hour, till the train reached Kollam, I continued to stand. When the train was nearing Kollam station, a passenger nearby got up. Just when I was moving towards his seat, someone else slipped into it. Later, while I was moving towards the mass of exiting passengers with the plan of getting into the AC coach, three passengers got up together. I dived in. This time I didn't fail. I got a seat. I pushed my bag under the seat and leaned back in relief! I had not felt such relief after any of my recent actions.

I sat back and enjoyed the beautiful view through the window. It was better than what anyone from Diego can imagine. I suddenly remembered the owner of the coffee shop. The man who someday wanted to visit the mainland. He would have been excited by the scenery and felt wonder at the vastness of the world, and its variety. I wanted to continue enjoying the view, but my eyes couldn't cope with the fast-moving images. My head began to feel like it was spinning. I closed my eyes.

I slid into sleep. I was five years old, on a train, with cold winds blowing through the night. I was sitting close to the door and sleeping. Valyapapan was with me. He was standing. I could see only his grey trousers and unpolished shoes. Whenever I stirred awake, I made sure he hadn't left me by looking at his shoes.

'Have we reached Changanassery? Have we reached Changanassery? ' I heard him anxiously asking our fellow passengers.

'Why are you going to Changanassery?'

'A relative died. I'm going for that.'

'Where in Changanassery?'

'I don't know exactly. I've to find out.'

At some point in the night, we got down at a sparsely populated station and took a cab. An old black car with a bald-headed driver. We halted on the way to have tea from a roadside stall lit with a Petromax lamp. Then a long, red bus stopped there. Someone hopped down from it. Meanwhile, Valyapapan was asking for directions from a few people. Then we finally reached a house that had a huge jackfruit tree and a bullock cart beside it. Valyapapan placed a wreath on the body covered in white cloth. He lifted me up to show me the face. I woke up with a start. Splintering through the night, the train was moving at great speed.

'Have we reached Changanassery?' I nudged the person next to me and asked worriedly.

He stared at me.

I repeated my question.

'But this train is not going via Changanassery,' he said.

'Oh, it isn't? I had to get down at Changanassery,' I panicked.

'Don't worry, the next station is Alappuzha. Get down there, and take a bus.'

'Won't it be too far?'

'Not much. You'll get a bus from there,' he said, trying to calm me down.

From being a five-year-old I returned to being twenty-eight. Who had died then? Whose funeral did we go to attend in

Changanassery? I hadn't managed to see the face. But the mystery that had stayed in my mind for so long had come out as a detailed vision before my eyes. Were those images of a dream or were they memories that had been asleep?

Completely forgetting that my destination was Ernakulam, I got down from the train at Alappuzha.

THE GOD OF FOOLS

IS THERE ANYTHING more foolish than believing that dreams are the signposts of human life? But somehow, I became a slave to that belief. I won't admit to it publicly, as I think writers should be free of superstitions and supportive of progressive ideas, but I do have such a belief about dreams. Why else would I have forgotten about all the plans I'd made with Srikumar, and got down at Alappuzha? I was very sure at that point that Melvin's house was in Changanassery. I believed the revelation in my dream! I even felt as if Melvin had told me that once.

When I stepped outside the railway station, I got scared. I'd never seen such a desolate place before. It was only around 8.30p.m., but in Alappuzha, it was like midnight. The little light present was faint. It was like landing in a dark continent a century ago.

I asked an autorickshaw driver to drop me at the bus stand.

'Private or Transport?'

'Wherever it's easy to get a bus to Changanassery.'

'Then, let's go to Transport,' the driver said.

'Is Changanassery between Ernakulam and Kottayam?' I asked.

'No, it is not.'

'No?' I got worried.

'No.'

'Are you sure?'

'It wasn't till yesterday. Now I will have to ask if that has changed,' he said with a mix of irritation and mockery.

'Then, where is Changanassery?'

'Sir, aren't you from anywhere around here?'

'No.'

'Sir, Ernakulam lies somewhere else. Changanassery lies somewhere else. Kottayam has no connection to it.'

I was dumbstruck.

But Melvin had said her house was somewhere between Ernakulam and Kottayam. So, that was not Changanassery? Where was it then? Why did I get down in Alappuzha? Why was I going to Changanassery? Oh god . . . what a blunder I had committed! If I had asked the same questions to someone in the train instead of the auto driver, I wouldn't have got down at Alappuzha. What was I doing behaving like a mad man? Had Melvin's death made me lose my balance? I had no clue what to do now. I was almost on the verge of crying.

'I don't want to go to the bus stand. Please take me to any hotel,' I pleaded to him.

'Because Changanassery is not between Ernakulam and Kottayam, you've decided not to go there?'

'No, not because of that. The place I want to go is . . . No, you won't understand. Please drop me at a hotel.'

He stopped the auto at a nearby restaurant. I had meant hotel as in a place to stay. Before I could explain, he took the 100-rupee note from my hand and scooted off.

Since I was ravenous, I went in and had a dosa and coffee. Chettathi's house was in Cheppadu. I could go there. Again, I had no idea how far it was from Alappuzha. Also, it meant the whole family would come to know about my blunders. No, I couldn't stand the idea of them having fun at my expense. I decided to go back to the railway station and wait for the next train to Ernakulam.

I took another auto and returned to the station. When I reached the ticket counter, another face came to my mind. My classmate Jyoti's. Salu, who had pointed her out to me in that marriage cassette, had said she was a railway clerk in Alappuzha. Would anyone know her? Was that a possibility? While buying the ticket, I asked the person at the counter if he knew anyone with such a name. He did not. I was disappointed.

There were a number of trains to Ernakulam through the night. I could catch any of them and reach there before morning. I had a whole night to find Jyoti. Why shouldn't I try? The regret of having got off the train at Alappuzha left me. I felt happy at the thought that maybe I had to get off because I was destined to meet her. I felt a new wave of energy. I made another round of inquiries at the stationmaster's office. But that failed too. I went and sat on a cement bench. If I could track Salu down, I could find Jyoti. He'd told me she was his neighbour. But how was I to get his number? An answer popped up: Orkut!

BUTTERFLY

I LITERALLY RAN out of the railway station, got into the first auto I spotted and reached the town again. After asking many people, I found an Internet café named Carmel, near the Town Hall. The owner had switched off the lights and was about to close. But when I told him it was an emergency regarding a death, he turned on the system. I opened my Orkut page. Luckily, I found him, right on my homepage. My memory was right. His phone number was there in his profile. I called him up from the café. At first, he mumbled that he didn't know me. When I reminded him about a chat we'd once had, he figured out who I was. There was a reason why he remembered the chat. It was a long conversation about the butterfly dreams of the Chinese philosopher Chuang Tzu. The man dreamt that he had transformed into a butterfly. On waking up, he asked himself: Who am I now—the man who dreamt he was a butterfly, or the butterfly who thinks it is Chuang Tzu? I had sent Salu links of some studies about the human pysche and the subconscious.

'Where are you calling from?'

'I'd come to Alappuzha on some urgent personal matter. I'll be leaving for Ernakulam later tonight. Can we meet before I leave?'

'Oh, sure, why not? Where are you now?'

'Near the Town Hall,' I said.

'I'll be there in fifteen minutes.'

I must have thanked the café owner and walked some ten steps when I remembered that I could also search for Melvin's details on Orkut. I might be able to get her home phone number or an address, or at the very least, the name of her village. I again ran into the café. The owner had switched off the lights and stepped out. I pleaded with him to let me use the Internet again. 'Why couldn't you have checked then? What a pain you're being!' he swore at me. I wondered where his gentle nature had disappeared. Do people change so fast? I told him again that someone very close to me had died and I needed some information about that.

'Died! Is that why you were talking about dreams and butterflies on the phone? Don't think I don't understand anything!' He seemed ready to punch me. 'Even if you are drunk or doped, you should have some control over yourself. You seem to be out to trouble people.' He angrily pulled down the shutter, locked it and walked out into the road.

A smile broke out on my face. What could I tell him? Can't a grieving person talk about dreams or butterflies? There was no way to convince him. I waited for Salu. In exactly fifteen minutes, a bike stopped before me.

'Chuang Tzu?'

'No. Butterfly!'

We smiled at each other.

'How come you ended up here so late?'

'My Chettathi's house is nearby. I was returning from there. I thought about you only after reaching this town.'

If a smart guy is someone who can come up with the right lies at the right moment, I was one. And lucky me. If he had asked for more details about Chettathi's house, I would have been caught.

'I feel thrilled. This is the first time someone whom I've met only on Orkut has come to meet me in person,' Salu said.

'I was thinking how can I not meet you when I've come to Alappuzha. I'm delighted too,' I said. 'I had once asked about a Jyoti, do you remember?'

'Yeah, you first called to ask about that. Jyoti-chechi is my neighbour.'

'I want to meet her too. We were classmates in school.'

'Oh, is that so? Hop on then. Let's go now.'

'Won't she be asleep?'

'Ey, nobody sleeps here in Kerala before the 10 o'clock TV serial gets over.'

While riding pillion on Salu's bike, I thought about the paths a man has to take in life. I wouldn't have imagined such a bike ride even a day ago. I would have laughed if anyone had predicted it. But if I wasn't dead, and not in a dream that had befuddled my senses, I was on the streets of Alappuzha. I was sitting behind an Orkut friend named Salu. I'm going in search of my classmate Jyoti's house! Coincidences. Who decides the paths a man has to take?

We whizzed through many roads and stopped in front of a house which was in darkness. When Salu honked, the portico light was turned on.

'Prasadetta, it is me, Salu.'

A six-year-old boy ran up to the gate and opened it. Behind him came a bald man seemingly in his thirties.

'Prasadetta, you have a guest. I'll go to my house and be back in a jiffy.' Salu dropped me there and drove up to the next house.

'Isn't this Jyoti's house? I'm from Diego . . .'

The man was startled. He had already been unsettled seeing a strange visitor so late in the night.

Hearing of Diego, someone from inside dashed out. 'From Diego? Who's it, Prasad?' There was a peculiar quality to the curiosity. It was Jyoti. Even if she had been somewhere else, in some other situation, I would have easily recognized her. Age usually changes the way people look. But in her case, it looked like she had stopped growing up after Class XII.

'Did you say you are from Diego?' She looked at my face, intrigued.

'Yes.'

'From Diego Garcia?'

'Mm.'

'Come, come inside.' As if Prasad didn't exist, she took

my hands and pulled me inside. Prasad and the boy could only follow us.

'What does my Papa have to tell me?' she asked me.

'What?' I didn't understand.

'I know my Papa has sent you to convey something. Or is it that my Papa or Momma are unwell? Some emergency? Please, what is the matter? Tell me without hiding anything.'

'Nothing. I just came because I was visiting this town.'

'That's a lie! Nobody from Diego has come here all these years. And it's not so close to the centre of town for anyone to come this way or to this house. I know you wouldn't have come unless there was a message from Papa. You definitely have a mission. Please, tell me. I'm dying to know.' Her bizarre talk put me in a spot. It was turning out to be one crazy night. What crazy dream was I dreaming?

'Jyoti, don't you recognize me?'

'Whoever it is, aren't you from Diego? That's enough. Didn't my Papa tell you to convey something? That's enough for me.'

I looked at Prasad's face, feeling helpless.

'Jyoti, this is our Salu's friend. He was visiting Salu's house, so he just came here on the way. He was not sent by your Papa,' Prasad explained to Jyoti.

'So, you are not coming from Papa?' she hesitantly asked me.

'No.'

'So, Papa didn't tell you anything to be conveyed to me?'

'No.'

'No? Then why did you come here? Go! Get out of my house! I don't want to see you. Or him. When you go back to Diego, tell Papa that if he doesn't want me, I don't want him either. Or tell him that Jyoti jumped in front of a train last week. Let him be happy. I don't want any bloody visitors.'

Salu walked into the middle of the brawl. He looked totally lost.

'Come again later,' Prasad told me. There wasn't anything else he could do to help. I walked down the stairs with Salu without uttering a word.

'You can leave tomorrow. Stay at my house tonight.'

'No, I've to reach Ernakulam tonight.'

'Ok, then it's better to take the bus.'

'What has happened to Jyoti?' I asked Salu on the way.

'I don't know. She had come to Kerala for studies and then fell in love and got married. I've heard she never went to Diego again. Sometimes, Chechi acts crazy. Shouts a lot and all. Otherwise, she is nice. Prasadettan is very accommodating. Poor guy.'

I felt a shudder inside me. I didn't know why. Melvin's face suddenly came to my mind.

Salu dropped me at the bus stand. Not long after, I got into a bus to Ernakulam. I reached the city by midnight.

I remember crashing into a bed at a hotel room. I slept the sleep of the dead.

MARTHA MARIAM LITTLE CHURCH

WHEN I OPENED my eyes the next day, it was past nine. I hurriedly got up and called Srikumar.

'Where have you been? I've been in the town since eight. I was wondering why you hadn't called.'

'I overslept.'

'Where are you staying? I'll come there.'

I couldn't remember the name of the hotel. I got hold of

a menu card lying on a bedside table, and I was able to tell him: Hotel Metropolitan.

'I'll be there.'

By the time I had my shower, the bell rang. It was Srikumar. Though I had met him at the summit, I had forgotten his face. If I had been shown photos of two people and asked to identify Srikumar, I would have goofed up. But when I saw him in person, there was no doubt. His face matched with the faded version in my memory.

We hugged each other. I could feel the bundled-up pressure peeling off in that embrace.

'Your visit is totally unexpected,' Srikumar said.

'Like death.' My smile was wan.

'You said the name was Melvin?'

'Yes, did you get anything?' I was apprehensive.

Srikumar opened the paper he was carrying.

UDAYAMPEROOR: Melvin (23), daughter of Kochuvaidyan M.C. Mathew of Valyedathu Veedu, passed away in Diego Garcia. Funeral at 11 a.m. today, after the formalities at home, at the Puthotta Chaldean Martha Mariam Little Church. Relatives and friends kindly treat this as a notice. Mother: Pazhoor family member Annamma. Brothers: Meljo, Merin.

'Read the place name again.'

'Udayamperoor. There is a photo too. Look at it just to be sure it's your friend Melvin.'

'Yes. Udayamperoor. How many times had she told me! That's the place. I'd forgotten . . . I don't want to see her in the obit column.'

'Then get ready fast. It's another ten to fifteen kilometres from Thrippunithura. This is the rush hour.'

How easily had Srikumar found out about Melvin! If I could at least have guessed last night at the possibility of a newspaper obituary, I might not even have called Srikumar. It didn't take more than three minutes for me to get ready. We left.

'Want to have breakfast?' Srikumar asked.

I was very hungry.

We went to a nearby restaurant and had idli and coffee.

'Let's take a taxi,' I proposed.

During the journey, I told him the entire story—how I'd started from Diego and reached Ernakulam. I skipped the incident of getting down at Alappuzha. As for the rest, I could give believable explanations. Our pace was slow till Thrippunithura. From there, it was around twelve kilometres to Udayamperoor. We covered that fast. There were churches throughout the way. At Udayamperoor Junction, we stopped our car before a small shop named Kochupara Stores. Srikumar ordered a lemonade each.

'Must be going to Valyedathu Veedu?' the shopkeeper asked, while stirring the sugar.

'How did you know?'

'Usually people come here to ask for directions. Now that a death has taken place, all visitors will be heading towards that house. Go a little ahead and you will reach Nadakkavu Bhagavati temple. Take the road on its right towards the east, it's hardly two kilometres from there. Anyone will give you directions from there.'

Before reaching Valyedathu Veedu, we asked directions of two more people. There was a turn in between and a steep road. A dog unexpectedly crossed our path, and the driver had to brake suddenly. Srikumar's nose hit the back of the driver's seat. A kilometre down, we saw a long line of vehicles. We parked the car there and walked. We passed a tall brick wall and reached an old, but huge, two-storeyed house. Near the gate, on a mossy stone plate, was the signboard, Valyedathu Veedu. It was clear at first sight that it was an ancestral abode. It was such a huge crowd, as if the whole of the land had flowed to the place. For some reason, I wasn't writhing in pain, but was filled with joy. Melvin was not destined to die an orphan. People had gathered to send her off. It was not just the ten people in Diego who knew her. There was a huge circle of people here who knew her. Her roots were in Valyedathu Veedu, not in Diego.

Srikumar pulled me through the crowd to reach the pandal made of blue tarpaulin. I didn't want to go there or see Melvin. But Srikumar let go of my hand only after helping me get close to her. I had to look at her. Melvin covered in white . . . I'd never seen anyone lying dead look so graceful. There was still a smile left on her face. I felt as though she hadn't walked into her death angry with me or annoyed, but with a joke in mind. The crowd didn't let me stay there for long. I had to move to make space for those who were pouring in.

The ceremonies started at 11. It was a festival, with a bishop and priests. The rituals, songs and chants of the Eastern Church were new to me who was used to Latin ways.

I watched everything with curiosity. After the ceremonies, the bishop made a long speech. There was only a small mention of Melvin in that. It was more about her father. From the speech I came to know that he was the member of an ancient Christian family that had been practising medicine specializing in eye disorders and jaundice for generations. Melvin had never mentioned any of that. Her father's designation as Valyedathu Kochuvaidyan was repeatedly mentioned by the bishop in his speech.

After the speech, it was time to give the final kiss. Amidst the wails and tears, a group of relatives came swarming up. I felt jealous and hostile towards them. It felt like they had stolen away my Melvin. I suddenly felt out of place. There was no need for them. None of them were required. I was enough. Back then, when Anita was standing at the Diego church, I could have bid farewell to Melvin in solemn silence. Isn't that how you should say goodbye? Or was it best with wailing?

I moved back from the crowd. I was worried about what Srikumar would think, otherwise I would have left the place right then.

Then the body was moved inside the house. Some more ceremonies were held there. It must have taken some fifteen minutes. Then the body was moved to a decorated lorry. People walked in two rows in a procession that included local bands, drummers, black flags and ornamental umbrellas.

We took the car to go to the church. After driving through many narrow roads, we reached a church that stood close to a lake. It was a small church which could accommodate not more than fifty people. The board read:

MARTHA MARIAM CHALDEAN LITTLE CHURCH

BELONGS

TO

THE POOTHOTTA VALYEDATHU FAMILY

For the ceremonies inside the church, only relatives were allowed.

By then, from thinking that the presence of these people was not necessary, I had moved on to thinking that I was not necessary. My mind whined that I shouldn't have come. It wasn't necessary, not necessary at all. She had a lot of dear ones at home. They were there to bid her goodbye. I was nobody to her in Udayamperoor. She had wanted me in Diego. In every person's life, and death, others will fit in only at some particular points. On other occasions, their presence becomes inappropriate. Therefore, I didn't go to the cemetery where the body was taken for burial. Instead, I roamed around the vacant church. What I yearned for was the serenity of the church. Its silence offered me great relief. The little church had a grandiose interior with a lot of woodwork. Each and every wood panel signalled the church's ancient past. The expertise of the carpenters and sculptors astonished me. I looked at their work with curiosity. The carvings, which looked like ancient Persian crosses from a distance, were a woman's form inside a fish's mouth. Not easily noticeable unless you linger over the carvings. I couldn't figure out if there was some meaning to it, though.

By the time I left the church, people had begun to leave the cemetery and move towards the food. I whiled away some more time sitting on the verandah of the church.

'Where were you? I've been searching everywhere . . .' said Srikumar as he approached me. 'Didn't feel like pushing with the crowd,' I said.

'But you could have put some soil with your palm's warmth to her sleep?' he said.

I don't know why, tears swiftly flowed from my eyes. Without saying anything, I got up and walked to the cemetery. There were only a couple of workers and supervisors there. The coffin had been covered. I took a handful of soil, held it close to my heart and sprinkled it on her to give her company. A handful of soil that had the warmth of my dreams . . .!

My handful of soil went and fell on the fish-shaped carving on the lid of the box. I stood wondering why there were images of fish everywhere, when someone touched my shoulder from behind. I turned back. A male Melvin!

6

Package Tour

AFTER READING THE portion that Jijo had given me, I felt a sort of regret. It was not born of the knowledge that Melvin was dead. Rather that we had commented on this deceased girl, sent friend requests and been envious of Andrapper's connection with her.

'Isn't there a way on Orkut to identify those who are no more?' I addressed that question partly to myself and partly to Jijo.

'I don't know . . .' Jijo was unaware of the reason behind my question.

'Who has died?' Nattapranthan was anxious to know.

I handed over the sheaf of papers to him. When he started reading, a waiter came with the juice I had ordered. I was famished from our journey, so I drank it to the last drop.

'Jijo, how did you get this bit of the manuscript?' I asked, after regaining some energy.

'Christy sent it to me asking me to give it to you. But I didn't have a phone number or address for you, sir. Till I found you on Facebook.'

'Jijo, how did you meet Christy?'

'First, tell me, how do you know each other?'

'We don't know each other,' I said. 'We haven't met, or spoken, or even exchanged a mail. But for some reason, he trusts me. He chose me to tell his life story. The only connection he has with me is from reading one of my books.'

'That was what I was wondering about all these days,' Jijo

said. 'Why was he telling you all these things? What was his relationship with you? I was reluctant to contact you because of these unanswered questions. But now, after listening to you, I only feel more confused. I've never read anything other than my textbooks. Can a book really earn you such trust?'

'I don't know. It can, I guess. I don't see any other reason for Andrapper to trust me.'

'I'm a distant cousin of the Melvin mentioned in this portion which was handed over to you. When Christy came for Melvin's funeral, I was his local guide.'

'Oh, I see. So I'm sitting with someone who knows Andrapper. Did you see him or contact him after that?'

'We used to mail each other. And when Christy visited Udayamperoor again, we met.'

'Really?! Why did he come again?'

'He came for Melvin-chechi's forty-first day. He also stayed at Valyedathu Veedu for a day. Since then, there's been no news of him. Nothing about where he is or what he is up to . . . Something must have happened there during his last visit.'

'Meaning?'

'There was some reason why he was asked to come to Valyedathu that day. Just think about it. Would any regular acquaintance be asked to come here from abroad?'

'I don't think they were just acquaintances,' I said. 'They wanted to get married.'

'But what's the relationship after death?'

'So, Jijo, are you saying Valyedathu Veedu had something to do with what happened to Andrapper?'

'Yes, and I want to know what it was that happened.'

'How would I know? You're Melvin's cousin, aren't you better placed to know?'

'My relationship with Valyedathu Veedu is distant. I

somehow don't like their age-old customs and ideas. That house is mysterious in nature. Among that family, Melvin was the only one who was somewhat open-minded and interested in being modern. That's why she went to Diego.'

'What was that?' asked Nattapranthan, as if emerging from a dream. He had been completely absorbed in reading the fifth part of Andrapper's manuscript.

'What was what?' I asked.

'His last sentence was "A male Melvin."'

'It's Melvin's brother, Meljo. They were three of them. Merin was the youngest. Melvin, the eldest.'

'Jijo, you must be a friend of Meljo,' I said.

'Ey, no. He is the biggest introvert in the family. He hates even to hear that his sister was in love with a foreigner. When Christy came with Melvin's body, he was the only one who argued that nobody should go to the airport to receive him. Even her Appachan said someone should wait at the airport, but he didn't agree. That is Meljo.'

'How was Meljo with Christy?'

'He didn't ever openly show resentment. But he definitely wasn't okay about Christy's visit. The hatred that local boys have for men who love their sisters! That's why I feel suspicious about Andrapper's disappearance.'

'Jijo, say clearly what you want to say. We aren't getting it,' Nattapranthan said.

'During his next visit, I volunteered to drop off Christy from Valyedathu Veedu to the airport. But he wouldn't agree. Christy went missing after that. He could have contacted me. I've no idea where he went that day from Valyedathu Veedu. Benyamin sir, I've faith in you. You should find out what happened. The Christy I met was a nice guy. We need to know what happened to him.'

'Do you have Meljo's number?'

'Yes, I'll give it to you. But don't tell him that I gave it.
You call him up. Let's see what he says. Christy was a writer.
And you are a writer. It's easy to explain your relationship.
He won't suspect anything.'

Jijo gave us both his number and Meljo's before he left. 'I
came to Kottayam to meet someone. So I've to go now. I'll
be in touch.'

'If I have any doubts, I'll have to call you. It that okay,
Jijo?' I asked.

'24x7, all 365 days of the year. I'm available at this number
all the time except when I'm in the church or the theatre. You
can call me any time. Just one thing. Meljo shouldn't know
that I gave you his number or that we've met. And be careful
while dealing with Meljo. He is a very dangerous man.'

It was all getting more mysterious and complicated. Why
did Jijo say all these things about Melvin's brother? Could
he be such a bad person? What was his role in Christy's
disappearance? There were no easy answers. But the answers
had to be found out. Anyhow, on that day, we returned from
Kottayam filled with the joy of having had a successful trip.

The very next day, I convened the Thursday Market
and updated everyone about our progress. After that, Biju
presented a one-line agenda designating Anil to call Meljo,
and the rest of us passed it by clapping hands.

Anil took up the task and rang the number. The phone
was in speaker mode so that all of us could hear.

'Hello, good evening. Is this Meljo?'

'Good evening. Who is this?'

'My name is Anil. I'm calling from Thiruvananthapuram,
from the desk of a weekly.'

'Ok, what's the matter?'

'We got a story. It's called 'The Book of Forefathers'. Mr Christy Andrapper is the writer. I have some queries about that . . .'

'But why are you asking me?'

'He had written to us from some country called Diego. I couldn't get through to that place. So I called you.'

'Where did you get my number?'

'His covering letter had this number as his contact in India. You are Mr Meljo, right?'

'Yeah, this is Meljo. But I don't know such a person.'

'You don't know him?'

'No!'

'But in the letter, Meljo is referred to as his brother-in-law. Is that a mistake?'

'Looks like it.'

'Well, do you have any contacts in Diego?'

'I don't know anyone there.'

'Oh, okay, sorry. We must have got it wrong.'

'OK. Bye.'

'Bye.'

'He is a super fraud,' Nibu said, as soon as the call ended. 'How coolly he said he didn't know Andrapper. We'll have to sweat it out in order to catch him.'

'If we've to sweat, we'll sweat. But what's the way out?' Mashu asked.

'Let's all go home and think about what crooked tactics will work. We can confer tomorrow or day after,' Nattapranthan said.

'We shouldn't call him for a few days,' Salim said. 'Whatever story we concoct, he'll be suspicious. Let him forget today's call. Then we'll find a way,' he said.

'Okay. Then, here's a devil of a problem for everyone to

meditate on,' Biju said. 'If Jijo had not contacted us and given this part of the book, how would we have got to him? What were the hints that Andrapper had left regarding this portion in the previous bits of the manuscript?'

'So, we have two responsibilities,' Mashu concluded.

'Goodbye till next Thursday,' Salim said and left quickly. The rest followed in Anil's Cultural Ambulance.

There were a few more Thursday Assemblies, but nothing useful came up from them. Meanwhile, Nibu studiously transcribed the interview with Rajanbabu, edited it and got it published in a website named *Pravasakairali*. He also mailed its link to Rajanbabu. That not only removed the doubts he had about us, if any, but also helped Nibu remain in touch with Rajanbabu.

While the search for Andrapper gained momentum through that route, Salim became eligible for a family holiday reimbursed by his company. It was a package trip awarded every two years. This time, he chose Mauritius as his destination. When Salim brought it up at one of the Thursday Assemblies, Nibu suggested, 'Why can't you make the trip via Diego? Then you can visit a country that you've only read about, and we can conduct our inquiries about Andrapper without a middleman.'

Everyone agreed that it was a good idea.

Was there a flight to Mauritius via Diego? Could transit travellers stop over at Diego? Was a special visa required? Would the ticket fare go up? Salim got the relevant information within two days. There were no flights from India to Mauritius via Diego. But transit travellers could get down at Diego and visa-on-arrival was available. The ticket fare was a bit of an issue. Salim's company would only pay for tickets to one destination: either Mauritius or Diego Garcia. One option was to go to Mauritius with the fare paid by the company and then pay for the fare to Diego. The second option was to use the company ticket to visit Diego and go to Mauritius at one's personal expense.

'My head aches,' Nattapranthan said. 'Is life so complicated?'

'Isn't it?' Mashu asked. 'Just think about one day of our lives.'

'So, what have you decided? Are you going to Diego or Mauritius?' Nibu asked.

'To both,' Salim replied. 'With the company ticket to Diego. And from there, I'll pay my way to Mauritius. It's not a huge amount.'

We complimented his decision with loud applause.

'We should make a checklist of things to do there, and people to meet. Else, you'll forget,' said Anil.

'Yes, tell me, I'll note them all down.' Biju was ready with pen and paper.

'People to meet: Mohandas Purameri, Rajanbabu and Johnny for sure, if possible Stephen Pereira, investigator Vijay Mullikratnam, Anita, Sudha, other nurses. And places to go: the Andrapper house, Melvin's hostel, Port Louis. And if possible, Senthil's house in Cherar Peruntheruvu,' I tried to be comprehensive.

'To cover all these, I'd have to spend all of my holiday there!' Salim said. 'I'll do my best.'

In preparation, Nibu sent a mail to Rajanbabu that a friend was visiting Diego, and any help would be appreciated.

Finally, the day arrived. The day we had been wishing for: Salim's departure to Diego. Departing from our routine, all of us went to his house to wish him a happy journey.

'If at least one of you were with me, it would have been easier,' Salim said.

'I do wish for a golden era in Malayalam literature when writers will be able to pay for their foreign trips,' I smiled.

Nattapranthan pointed at Salim's wife Sherly and daughter Janu: 'We are sending two gems on our behalf.'

'We'll take care of him. And we'll return with more details than all of you put together would've got. Fine?' Sherly said pertly.

En route to Mauritius, Salim would spend two days in Diego and another day on his return. We saw them off.

————

Then we waited. Did Salim get there? Was he able to meet anyone? Did he manage to get some details? What was Diego like? Who knows, Salim might bring us a peacock or a monkey as a gift!

We talked about Diego day and night, and waited to hear from Salim. Though I knew Salim's phone would not be active outside of India, I tried calling him. That was the level of my hope and anxiety.

One evening two days after his departure, I got a call from a number starting with 00246. It was Salim.

'Benyamin, I've sent you an email. It has all the details. I'm calling from the airport on my way to Mauritius. Telephone charges are deadly here, so I'm hanging up. Please say hi to everyone.' He said that in one breath. Before I could say or ask anything, Salim hung up.

I ran to the computer. One unread mail in my inbox:

Benyamin,
    The journey was okay. The aerial view of Diego is the most beautiful I've ever seen. Right from the moment we

landed, we began hunting for Andrapper. I called Mohandas
Purameri. He kept talking about his *Archipelago*, so he was
of no use. I think he'll survive on this novel for the next
ten years. He agreed to meet us at the hotel that day, but
didn't turn up, and I didn't bother to call him. I also got
in touch with the Tamil writer Shivasankar, but he was in
Chennai working on a script. Luckily, I got a great taxi
driver (the taxi was a boat): Seyfu, from Africa. There is
no place in Diego that he doesn't know. He took charge
of our two days here. I've never seen such a smart taxi guy
in any of my foreign trips.

First, we went to meet Rajanbabu of *Diego Daily*. I got
a hearty welcome, thanks to Nibu's email. But he didn't
have anything new to give us about Andrapper.

I asked him about the group that had sent a fax to
Diego Daily asking for a probe into Senthil's death.
He was curious as to how I knew. When I said Christy
mentioned it in his mail to web.com, he searched his files
(God, I have not seen any other office with so many files
piled up in columns) and pulled out the fax. Other than
the name 'Uthiyan Cheral Tamil Kazhagam', there was no
other notable detail. There was not even a fax number
from which it had been sent. Rajanbabu told me that
there was no such group in Diego and that it was a part
of Andrapper's political game.

Then we went to Port Louis. It was a haven for coffee
shops! The coffee we drank there was surprisingly good.
We loitered around, took some photos, and left. I couldn't
figure out which was the coffee shop that Andrapper
frequented. I saw some fashionably dressed women,
wearing sunglasses, striding along briskly. I futilely hoped
one of them was Jesintha.

After that we went to City Hospital to meet Johnny. It was difficult to track him down in that huge hospital, but I was determined. He couldn't give me much on Andrapper, but he helped me locate Rajakottaram Hostel where Melvin used to stay. By then it was evening and we returned to the hotel. The night was cold and windy. I left Sherly and Janu at the hotel and went to a few ladies' bars. I've to tell you that when they hear one is from the mainland, the reception is awesome. Must be the islanders' love for the mainland. I went to sleep at 11.

Seyfu came at 8 sharp in the morning. Else, I would have slept till 10. We visited Mariam Church and the Buddhist Sanchi. Took a photo posing in front of the 2000-year-old tree. I broke a bit of a branch and put it in Sherly's handbag. Now you too can touch the Buddha's wisdom tree when I get back! On the way, we also visited a seabird sanctuary, the Chagos temple, Albuquerque Cliff and a peacock-feeding park.

It was almost 11 when we reached the Rajakottaram Hostel. I lied that I was a neighbour of the family of Valyedathu Veedu, and was visiting as per Meljo's instructions. Throughout the trip, it was good to have my family with me! They helped sell the lies better!

Melvin's hostel mates shared their memories. All of them said she was a sweet girl. Andrapper hasn't visited the place after her death. A rich boy with no love or sincerity. Melvin had fallen in his trap. That was the general feeling.

I also tried to ask about Senthil, but they strategically ignored my questions. So we had coffee and left. (Everyone here likes coffee. My attempts to get tea failed miserably.)

From there, we went to Anita's house. Jaya-chechi from the hostel accompanied us. Luckily, Anita was home. She

inquired about Meljo and Appachan. I dodged by saying
all of them were keeping well. If she had asked anything
more, I would have been in trouble.

When I asked about Andrapper, her face turned red.
Since the journey started, I had this intuition which I
haven't shared with any of you: I suspected that Anita
might have the next part of *The Book of Forefathers*. I told
her that Meljo had the first set of chapters and requested
her to hand over the portion she had. I even told her that
I'd come to Diego to collect it from her. But she snapped
at me for even mentioning the name of Andrapper.

We did not spend much time there. We dropped Jaya-
chechi back at the hostel, went to a lakeside restaurant
and had a good lunch with *karimeen* and prawn. We
wanted to return to the hotel and get some rest, but we
were running out of time. So we proceeded to Cherar
Peruntheruvu. It wasn't difficult to find Senthil's house.
We also found a guy standing next to a Periyar statue who
gave us the directions.

Senthil's father, mother and Anpu were there. (What
a beauty! Sherly pinched me twice, finding me staring
at her.) I told them that we were from Pondicherry and
that Senthil used to visit my office regularly. (Benyamin,
after I get back, I want to meet the priest at your church.
I desperately need to confess. I've told so many lies here
in Diego!)

We got a cordial welcome. They cried talking about
Senthil. When I asked about Andrapper, I got an
unexpected response. 'A liar!' That's how Senthil's father
described him. I couldn't get anything else out of them
about him when I probed gently. Finally I gave up.

Then Anpu went inside and came out with something

for me. It was a USB drive. I was surprised. 'Andrapper
came here drunk one day, and gave this to me. He said,
"Someone will come from the mainland looking for it.
Give it to him." Maybe this is something for your office.
Please take it,' she said.

After a quick stop at the hotel to pick up our luggage,
Ṣeyfu drove the boat at 100 miles an hour and dropped
us off at the airport. Such a great driver! He didn't even
accept the tip that I gave him. When we finally made it
inside, we came to know that the flight had been delayed
by two hours! So I opened the USB sitting there. It was
full of songs and some pictures I can't show my daughter.
Towards the end, I found a PDF file. 'The Book of
Forefathers: Part 6'. And sitting at the airport, I finished
reading it.

I'm emailing it to you. My Diego mission is complete!
There were some more places I ought to have visited.
Especially the Andrapper house. I'll do that on the return
trip. I'll have about six hours to manage that.

You can start reading the attachment.

Salim

FAMILIAR ODOUR

NOBODY HAD TO tell me that it was Melvin's brother,
Meljo. So identical were their looks. Not just that; if
Melvin had talked about anyone in her house, it was about
Meljo. I'd often felt that the two shared a heart-to-heart
connection.

'We waited for a long time at the aerodrome yesterday. We
had to return; we were so worried,' he said, holding my hand.

'I took a long time to come out. A minor emigration problem. I came out and only then realized that I didn't know any of you. In the chaos, I'd forgotten to take anyone's number.'

'It was a lot of trouble, wasn't it?'

'Ey, not at all. I had a friend in Ernakulam.'

We reached the church courtyard, Meljo still holding on to my hand.

'This is the person who came from Diego,' he told Appachan.

'Oh, is that so? What happened yesterday?'

I repeated the lies that I'd just told Meljo.

'The girls from the hostel said someone was coming. And we couldn't find him. We all got worried, my dear. But let that be. What actually happened to my girl?' Appachan held my hands and asked.

'She tripped while getting into a boat. Her head hit the plank. No one could do anything,' I said.

A man standing next to us pulled my hand and took me a little further away. 'I'm a distant uncle of the girl's. Let this just be between us. What actually happened there? Did she fall or did someone kill her?'

'Kill her? Melvin? Who would do that?'

'We have so many enemies. How was she there? I've heard some stories about her and someone there. Is there any truth in that?'

'What story? Never. The Melvin I knew wasn't like that.' My voice was trembling.

'By the way, who are you to her?'

I was thunderstruck. I had not expected that question. If I panicked, he'd grab on to it and make up new stories.

'I'm the administrative supervisor at Melvin's hospital. The ministry sent me with the body.'

Sometimes, we have to be good liars. It was one of those moments.

Fortunately, Meljo came to say that Appachan wanted to talk to me, and took me away from there.

Melvin's Appachan was sitting on a chair inside the church. A man who glowed like the sun with his grace and aristocratic demeanour. Someday, if I had to write about him, that is how I'd describe him, I felt at that moment.

I went and took his hand. For a long time, he gazed at my face in silence.

'The girl wasn't supposed to become a nurse. But it was her choice. Like how she went to Diego. When she was a child, the girl used to tell me that she'll someday buy me a boat. When she was angry with me, she'd say that she won't get Appachan a boat. She grew up and it remained the same. Boats and trips by water were always a craze for her. When I asked her why Diego when there were so many countries she could work in as a nurse, she said that it is the only place that has only boats. Who knew it was a place where death had decided to catch her! She went away without getting me a boat. That too in a boat, something she liked a lot. Fate, what else is it . . .'

All the sorrow he had been withholding till then seemed to unleash from his eyes. My heart wept for Melvin. A boat ride with me had been her dream. She had told me about it many times. It was only then I realized that it was more out of love for boats than for me. I never could help her. Oh God . . . I did not seem to be able to understand those dear to me. And I was trying to become a writer?

'You've taken the trouble of travelling such a long distance for her. Thank you. Don't leave today, you can stay in my house.'

'I was able to meet you all. That's enough. I've to return to Ernakulam today. I have some work.'

'Come home for a meal and then decide. Her mother will also want to meet you.'

'Appacha, the car is here,' someone called out.

People were getting into the cars.

'I'm not coming home. I'll leave from here,' I told Meljo. Hearing that, an old man intervened. 'Son, never leave a cemetery without coming home. According to the traditions of us ancient Christians, it is customary to come home after a funeral, and share some food with the family. It's a sign of love for the dead, and comfort and support to the grieving relatives. These days, it has shrunk to the practice of packets of food being distributed at the church. Love and relationships have also shrunk to the size of packets.'

I changed my mind on hearing those words. It seemed unfair on my part not to visit Melvin's home. Unable to find Srikumar, I called him from Meljo's cellphone. He said he'd go catch up with a friend at Chembu, a few kilometres away, and asked me to call him once the ceremonies were over.

Meljo seated me in a car with his cousin Jijo, who was studying engineering at Kothamangalam. A new-generation guy with a ring in his ear. He was warm and friendly, and because of him, later, at Melvin's house, I didn't feel like a total stranger. Jijo introduced me to everyone. The only thing that irritated me was the women staring at me. The irritation multiplied as I felt the looks carried the meaning of what Melvin's uncle had asked me earlier.

The feast was large enough for a hundred people and more. After that, Jijo took me to Melvin's mother. I felt she had come to terms with Melvin's death faster than her father. At least, she seemed strong. She ran around directing people and the cooking in the kitchen. 'He must be tired from the journey. Take him upstairs and arrange a room for him to get some rest,' she told Jijo.

I tried to get away, but Amma and Jijo wouldn't relent. When I entered the room I was directed to, a familiar scent welcomed me.

'Rest for a while. I'll come soon,' Jijo said, sliding the door shut. 'Every other room is full. This was Melvin's room.'

Jijo went downstairs.

Melvin's room! That's why the familiar scent. The scent of her. How many varied experiences did one have to bear with in this life! How did I end up in Melvin's room when Melvin herself was no more? What's the meaning of it all?

I glanced at the room. The dolls she had kept in order. Her make-up. Her notebooks. The mirror that had reflected her image. The clothes that had beautified her. The windows by which she had stood dreaming. The pillows that had cushioned her with love. The sheets that had caressed her fragrance.

Tears began to well in my eyes.

I went downstairs. It was just the guilt of entering a woman's room without her permission. The thought that she might come into the room any time and get scared seeing me. If life had taken another turn, someday Melvin would have brought me to that room. And introduced to me all the things dear to her, one by one. Then told their stories. She would have leant against the mirror and asked me, 'How is my room. Do you like it?'

Jijo and Meljo were downstairs.

'What happened?'

'Nothing. I'm not tired enough to sleep. I'd slept well at night.'

'Oh, your friend called. I told him to leave. That you'll leave only tomorrow.'

'No, I've to go today. Firstly, my clothes are there at the hotel. Secondly, this is the time for you to be left alone, Meljo. My presence will only remind you of the past. Please forgive me. I'll come another time. When I do, I'll stay in this house for at least a day.'

He didn't press me further. He informed the family. Merin's face had turned pale from the weeping. 'You should come visit us again,' that was what Appachan said. 'Don't forget this house,' said Amma.

Meljo accompanied me to the portico. There he broke down into tears. So did I.

Jijo gave me a lift on his bike till Ernakulam.

Though I'd told everyone that I'd visit again, I felt that I'd never take those roads again. So I took in everything. Jijo tried to put me at ease by asking about Diego and talking about his college. I quickly realized that all his queries and chatter had one aim: to gauge my relationship with Melvin. The question Melvin's uncle had asked me to my face had taken a convoluted route via Jijo. I feigned ignorance. We stopped at Thrippunithura to have tea. Then he sat in my hotel room for a while. At last, just before leaving, he lost patience and blurted out what he really wanted to know: 'Are you the one in Diego who was supposed to marry Melvin?'

'Yes, if things had turned out differently, maybe I'd have married Melvin.'

'I know there is no point asking now, but did you agree to the marriage even after getting to know everything?'

'Know what?'

'About Valyedathu Veedu?'

'No, I know nothing. What's the problem?'

'Anyway, it's a closed chapter now. There is no point any longer in me telling you or you getting to know about it. Let it be. May you never know about it.'

He left without saying anything more. That's when I decided that I'd return to Udayamperoor someday.

KOCHI

THERE WAS NOT much time. I called Srikumar, but couldn't get through. His phone was out of range. I checked out of the hotel and roamed around the streets of Ernakulam. After strolling for a while, I felt like visiting Kochi. The taxi driver must have mistaken me for a tourist, for he dropped me off at Mattancheri. The place gave me goosebumps. My ancestor Andrew Pereira had landed at Mattancheri centuries ago. He had built a house somewhere nearby. His son had had a country of his own. The glorious past of my family gave me such an adrenalin rush that I walked vigorously through the streets of Mattancheri. I was so high that I stopped at a shop and inquired where Andrew Pereira's house was. The shopkeeper did not know anything about any Andrew Pereira. 'Where is the headquarters of the Karappuram Madambis?' I asked him. He was clueless. When I walked past an old building, I felt that it could be the house where Andrew Pereira had stayed with his family, and wished I could knock on the door and ask if he was still there. I had fallen in love with Kochi. During the three years I I'd been in Thiruvananthapuram, I'd never visited Kochi. I'd thought of Kochi as a horrible town. I must have been influenced by the public sentiments of Thiruvananthapuram. If the capital city had a grandiose seriousness, Kochi, I felt, had a welcoming simplicity.

Was I lost in the joy of being in a place that formerly belonged to my family? That must be it. Some of my ancestors must have walked these streets with a similar feeling of joy.

When I mention my land of origin, what is the place that I should fondly remember? To which place should I return as an end to my migrations? Diego that belonged to my forefathers? Or Pondicherry where my ancestors lived? Or Kochi where they landed before that? Or Lisbon 500 years ago? How could we know where our predecessors came from? I felt that someday I'd walk through the streets of Lisbon with the same sense of affection.

On the way back, I entered a bookshop in Ernakulam and got some Malayalam books. (Dear author, your book was there among those that I purchased. During the overnight train journey to Thiruvananthapuram, I finished reading it. By the time I reached the end of my journey, I had decided that if someday I have to tell my tale to someone, that'll be to you. And that's how my first email came your way.)

———

I returned to Diego, and the next noon, Anpu called. She asked if I could visit her house. When I reached Cherar Peruntheruvu, some young men stopped me. '*Ennada*? Why are you visiting a house where there are only women?' one of them asked. I pushed him aside and kept walking. 'If we see your face in this street again . . .' another one threatened.

When I mentioned this at Senthil's house, his father fumed with rage. 'If any bastard asks, tell him that I'm giving my daughter to you! What's their problem? Ask them to talk to me.'

'That's okay, Appa. Why did you ask me to come?'

'Just to see you. Why, shouldn't I ask you to come?' Anpu asked in a lighter vein.

I smiled at her.

'We haven't seen you in a long time. Where do you disappear regularly, switching off your phone?' Appa asked.

'Someone close to me had passed away in the mainland. I had to leave immediately. I couldn't let you know.'

'Is that so? I looked for you to . . . for those forms . . . we have to correct them and submit them.'

'Yes, I'd forgotten about it.'

Anpu brought out the forms. I remembered the changes that the officer had asked for, so correcting them was easy. When I asked who should be made the nominee, Appa stammered for a minute. 'My name will do,' he said. I had expected Anpu's name to be added.

The forms were finally filled, but the officer had wanted two new photos of Senthil. Anpu went inside to look for them, and came back after a long time. 'No, not a single one,' she said in despair.

'Useless guy! He didn't even keep a photo,' Appa shouted.

'Please check again,' I said.

She brought out a leather bag and placed it in front of me. 'This is all Anna's stuff. Everything he had is inside this,' she said, unzipping it. The bag was a mess of papers.

'Was he crazy? What are all these papers?' It seemed as though Appa was also seeing Senthil's bag for the first time.

My mind whispered to me that the bag might have the information that could unveil the mystery of Senthil's death. I went through each paper in detail while pretending to look for the photos. Newspaper and magazine cuttings, some other papers—all of them in Tamil. Then credit card bills, telephone bills, hall tickets, certificates, mark lists, and even train and bus tickets. I was looking for a diary. But there was no such thing. However, I decided to keep a sample of each of the cuttings, thinking they might come handy.

'What are these for?' asked Anpu.

'Just like that, to read what Senthil had kept . . .'

'You know how to read Tamil?'

'Of course! I know five languages.'

I dug into the bag one more time, but I couldn't find any photo of Senthil's or anything important. It was then that I randomly opened the side pocket. There was a USB drive in it.

'I'm taking this. He might have saved a photo in this,' I said.

'It won't be there. There'll be nothing in it. He was a useless person,' Appa said angrily. Finally, he gave me a photo, pulled out from a five-year-old certificate, and asked me to make a copy.

'Anpu, go with him to the bay, let's see who wants to pick a fight,' he told Anpu when I scrambled up to leave.

Anpu accompanied me till the jetty. On our way, she suddenly broke into tears. 'I don't even have a single photo of Anna. Nobody will have one. Anna was like that. Look at this. This is all that he has left me.' She showed me her mobile phone. It was some years old. In it was a ten-second video of Senthil laughing.

'I watch this a hundred times a day. Anna laughing,' she sobbed. I didn't know what to say. Words cannot heal pain. I held her hand. She didn't protest.

Before returning the phone, I watched the video once again. In the last two seconds, a face appeared behind him, a familiar one. I played the video twice.

'Who is this?' I showed it to Anpu and asked, my voice trembling.

'Anna's friend. He used to come home every day. After Anna died, he came home and said some of his certificates were with Anna. Searched his bag and took some things. Anna kept everything in order. It was this chap who messed it up. After that, he never came back. Anna had left us. Why would he come?'

'Do you know what are the papers that he took?'

'No.'

'His house?'

'No.'

'Name?

'No.'

I left without even saying bye to her. I was certain that I'd seen the guy in the video. Yes, I'd definitely seen him. He was one of the people who ran away after shooting Senthil.

USB

I REALIZED THAT any evidence of what could have led to Senthil's death was already with those who needed it covered up. Appa and Anpu had been so stupid. How could they be unaware of the importance of a dead man's documents? When someone came asking for some documents, they had opened the entire bag to him. He took all he needed and vanished forever. I was furious that he had got hold of the documents that could have solved the mystery behind Senthil's murder.

I hadn't completely lost hope, though. I plugged the USB to my computer. It was protected by a password. I remembered two of my juniors who owned a computer shop. My Orkut friends. I contacted them. They told me to bring it over. Within minutes, they opened it. I was surprised at how unprotected were the things that we assumed were super-safe, locked by passwords known only to us. There is no privacy in this cyber world. It's impossible. Our secret locks can be easily opened by a lone smart-arse!

There was nothing exciting in Senthil's USB. Most of the files were Tamil song collections. The only thing that confused me was that many of the songs were the same, but saved in different names. I couldn't figure out why. Then there were some nude photos, downloaded from porn sites. Another I couldn't figure out was a file of gossip about Tamil actresses. I read a couple of items out of curiosity:

> Actress Archana who eloped from her shooting location at around 10 a.m. on 10 May 2008, in an Innova with tinted glass windows, was seen today at two shopping malls in the city with young star Faisal Bava from Hyderabad. There are reports that they spent quality time together at Hotel Park Plaza, and that they got into an argument with some people who tried to click photos of the couple in the hotel's parking lot. According to reports, someone named Rajeev had their photos and a record of their conversation on his phone. He is willing to share the photos with anyone interested, Rajeev told Sex Hot News.

> *Hotgirl.com* has confirmed that the person who was seen two nights ago near Pondicherry Arrival Globe under suspicious circumstances is none other than renowned Tamil actress Vinaya. She had gone there to meet Senthil, an extra artist in the Tamil film industry. The two eloped

to Chennai. Vinaya sent him to Chennai Silks to buy clothes, which were later handed over to her mother's driver, Lakshmana, who was waiting at the parking bay. Then the duo discreetly booked a room at Hotel Park Plaza and spent almost two hours there. Vinaya's ex-lover, Veeramani, who somehow came to know of it, reached the hotel and demanded that he, too, get time to spend with her. But according to sources, they couldn't reach an agreement. So, Vinaya escaped from Veeramani, dropped Senthil at the Pondy boat jetty and went to her house. She is relieved that nobody has yet heard of the tussle between Senthil and Veeramani. The rumour is that the couple will not be together again.

There was lots of such low-grade gossip, most of it apparently about B-list actresses and actors. I'd not heard any of those names before, probably because I don't really keep track of Tamil cinema. But many of the names came up again and again.

My image of Senthil was changing from that of a highly intelligent government officer to an introverted psychopath. Until then, I had been under the impression that he must have been killed while attempting to blow the whistle on some malpractice in the government. But after looking at the contents of the USB, I was sure that such a disturbed person couldn't be a whistle-blower. I doubted his intentions in visiting Pondicherry so often. Anpu had quipped that he had a lover there. I felt his love was for the bodies of the red-light district. His lust was evident in the nude pictures and the voyeuristic gossip.

I also went through all the papers I had taken from the bag. Most of them were related to films. I got two more hints that reinforced my suspicions. His credit card had mostly been used to register with and use pornography sites. He had even tried to start such sites, as was evident from the copies of letters he had sent to Europe. There was also a list of the sites he frequented. I tried some of those websites, most of which were banned in Diego. I didn't know how he had managed to browse them. He must have had some technology to break the firewall.

I drew two possible conclusions: Senthil was either a psychopath with sexual anxiety, or he was a pimp or an agent for these sites!

HERO

THE NEXT DAY, I went to the old coffee shop with the intention of meeting Abdul Majid. The shop owner complained that I hadn't kept my word of taking him to the mainland. I promised that I'd take him the next time.

When Majid brought my coffee, I whispered to him, 'We have to talk. That case is still pending.'

'Let's meet at noon,' he said and gave me his phone number.

Just as I finished my coffee, Jesintha appeared in front of me. I was meeting her after a long time. She had gained weight, I felt, and told her so.

'You've lost weight, that's why you think I've put on some! What happened to you?' she asked.

'I was in the mainland. I got back just a few days ago.'

'Oh, I see. You are lucky. You can go anywhere you want at any time. For people like me, to go on a trip, I've to apply for leave first. And my husband has to get leave. The entire family has to get leave. Only then can the trip happen.'

'You're married?' That was news to me.

'Why do you ask? Do I look like I can't settle down? I'm twenty-eight now.'

'Ayyo, no, no, I didn't mean anything like that. I've only seen you with your friends, that's why . . .'

'Like everything else in life, I've a theory about married life too. I don't think that I should end friendships just because I'm married. With men or women. The human mind and soul have a lot of needs. A family is not a one-stop supermarket for all of them. In fact, it is only as big as a small shop. We can't insist that we get everything from there. Some things, we have to go out and get. My husband knows that. I haven't changed the ways of my life after marriage. When I have to go out with friends, I go out with them.'

Suddenly I remembered Bilal's mail. 'Bilal said he saw you in Paris. Were you there?' I asked, looking into her eyes.

'Me? Paris? He must have been dreaming! I've also seen that city only in a dream,' she said without flinching.

'He must have been mistaken, leave it.'

'Why did you go to the mainland?' she asked, as if to change the topic.

'A girl had died here recently, in a boat accident. Did you hear about it? I'd gone with her body.'

'Was that nurse your friend?'

'Yes, she was close to me.'

'So, what I heard is true.'

'What did you hear?'

'Never mind that. The rumours are that the girl had committed suicide. You know anything about that?'

'Suicide? Melvin? Don't spout nonsense!'

'I'm mentioning something that I heard on the streets of Diego. Why are you getting angry?'

'What have you been hearing?' I was in distress.

'That she got into some deals here. Then she got pregnant, and so she jumped from the rooftop.'

'I'll slap you on the face if you talk about dead people in such a manner,' I almost got up to slap her.

'If you want to slap me, then you'll have to slap everyone in Diego. There are at least five other versions of the story of her death.'

I felt like I had experienced a blow. 'None of them are true, Jesintha. Nobody knew her like I did. She was a sweet, very sweet girl. Don't say such things about her.'

'I won't talk. But Diego will talk. It's not the people's fault. If they don't have a story, what will they do? They'll make up new stories and keep repeating them. Anyway, you be careful. In one of those stories, you are the hero.'

'Me?'

'Don't get angry. It's just something that I heard. Not what I believe. It is said that the nurse was the lover of the Andrapper son, and the mistress of the Andrapper father.'

Those were the last words I heard from Jesintha. Like a dead tree shuddering in a storm, I got up and left the coffee shop. I barely heard her calling out from behind.

Oh god, what was this society doing to Melvin? Making an accident a suicide. Making up a dirty story to support it. Then spreading it with pleasure. Do they get excited only when a woman dies? Senthil was shot dead in public. Nobody had a story about that death. Nobody had any doubts. Nobody had even heard of it. That was just a cardiac arrest!

My boat went and stopped at the jetty near Anita's house. I felt like I had to meet her. In such a situation, only her words could have soothed me a little. She had been terribly affected by Melvin's death. She would understand my state of mind.

The gate was open. When I rang the bell, she opened the door. A wan smile welcomed me. But she was not the same Anita I knew—in an instance, I deciphered that she was not pleased with my visit. Perhaps the stories had reached her ears too?

I stepped in without waiting for an invitation. Neither of us said anything for about two minutes.

'You are not at work today?' I finally broke the silence.

'I have a lot of leave left. So, I took a day off. Do you want tea or something?'

'No, I just had some coffee.' When I said that, I remembered the sumptuous reception I got on my first visit. 'I returned from the mainland only yesterday. Everything went well,' I said.

'What do you mean by "well"? Was it her wedding or what?' Anita burst into flames.

I was dumbstruck. Shouldn't I have said that? How else could I describe a funeral that was well organized? Were there better words to describe it? Had my language failed me? That conversation hit an abrupt end. To overcome that, I took up a magazine and began flipping the pages. *Pentasia This Month*. It had a news item that Mohandas Purameri's novel, *Archipelago*, was going to be published in Kerala. A wave of self-contempt swept through me.

I got up after a while.

'Please don't come here again to see me. I don't like it,' she said while I was leaving.

I wanted to know the reason. But before I could ask, she shut the door. Like a refugee kicked out of the last camp of hope, I left.

Oh god, why was the world so cruel? Why were even my dear ones treating me badly? Why couldn't they understand me? Why didn't they know how their behaviour affected me?

Just because I'm a man, how could they think I was heartless and incapable of feeling sorrow?

God, oh my dear god, why have you abandoned me?

MEMORIES

I KNEW THAT alcohol would aggravate my sorrows rather than relieve them. But still, I headed straight to a wine shop. My greatest regret was that I didn't have a friend who would dive with me into the depths of my bared soul. That is when alcohol becomes your friend. Standing in its shadow, I could talk to myself as a friend would to me. The 'other' who would listen to me patiently, absorb my sorrows, lend an ear to my complaints, understand my helplessness, and endorse my innocence. If I had a friend with whom I could unload my pain, I wouldn't have gone to a bar.

When I finally reached home in a drunken state, I found Papa waiting. I fell at his feet.

'I'm a failed writer. I couldn't concentrate on my writing. I wasted days chasing after useless things. Please pardon me. I didn't listen to anything you suggested. I want to go to France. I want to study there. I want to dream big there. Finish my novel. I want to forget everything else.'

He helped me reach my room and put me to sleep. That night, both of us slept in the same bed.

The next morning, before leaving for work, Papa came to my room. 'I hope yesterday it wasn't just the alcohol speaking. Do you really want to go to France?'

'No, it wasn't just the booze. I want to go. I'm fed up of Diego!'

'Okay, then I'll get your papers ready. You said you've a

friend there, right? Contact him and arrange for your stay.'

I emailed Bilal without delay, asking about the opportunities in France, requesting his help on accommodation. He got back to me within a couple of hours: 'You just have to come. Leave the rest to me.'

That night, Papa came with some application forms. I signed wherever he pointed. He wanted a set of copies of my certificates. I gave those to him. He asked for some passport-size photos. I gave those too.

Even then, to be honest, I wasn't quite sure if I'd be going to France. But something happened that sealed my decision. On my way back from the travel agency in Pentasia, I met Vinod on the road. I had last met him at the Public Security office. By the time I came out of Stephen uncle's office where he had scolded me for going to him about such a trivial matter, he had gone missing. I was seeing Vinod for the first time after that day. He ran bang into me, but looked at me as if I was a stranger. He wouldn't respond to my questions. He even acted as though he had forgotten his nickname, da Vinci.

That was when a woman, either his wife or sister, ran up to him and held his hand. 'What happened to him?' I asked her.

'Who are you?' She looked scared.

'We studied together, at St. Joseph's.'

'One day he left the house, saying he was going to the Public Security office. Then for some ten or twenty days, there was no news. We searched for him everywhere. Then we found him lying at our doorstep. Someone had dumped him there at night. Since then, he's been like this. He doesn't remember anything. Has no memories. Bastards. They have killed my brother's brains. Anything can happen in this hell. Who is there to ask?' She guided Vinod away.

A country where anyone can say anything about anyone. A

country where anyone can do anything to anyone. A country where no one is answerable to anyone. Our own Diego Garcia. I didn't have to live in such a place. This wasn't the Diego of my dreams.

After two weeks, I got a call from the French Embassy. I went to attend the interview with an open mind. Four, just four questions. Then I was told to come the next day and get the visa stamped on my passport.

I made all the preparations for the journey. I had even booked my tickets. I was not aware that I was gearing myself up for a trip that would get cancelled, like the trip to Australia. It was that afternoon that I got an unexpected call. It was from Meljo.

'It's Melvin-chechi's forty-first-day memorial this Sunday. For us, it's a family get-together. Appachan wants you to be here. You should come two days in advance. I hope you can come. Can you?'

Fearing that the Diego rumours may have reached Valyedathu Veedu, I had not called them. But this call meant they hadn't heard anything. God, please let them never get to hear any such rumours! And in case they had already heard some stories, they'd suspect me more if I didn't go.

I didn't know what to say. I was supposed to fly to Paris on Monday. A trip to the mainland would take at least three days. Either I had to refuse going to the mainland, or postpone flying to Paris. When I thought of Melvin's parents, and Meljo and Merin, declining their invitation seemed like a sin. Nothing would happen if I delayed my Paris visit. Nobody was waiting for me there. But the mainland was not like that. My mind decided that I should go to the mainland. It would be impossible to convince my parents. 'This is an excuse he has found to cancel the Paris plan,' Papa would sit with a whisky and murmur. Momma would sob, and Chettan would shout. It would all take a while to cool down. Whatever I said, nobody would believe me. So, without telling anyone, I postponed the Paris ticket by another week. I booked a ticket to the mainland. At around 10.30 on Friday morning, I told Chettathi that I was going to the mainland and would be back soon. Before Momma or Chettathi could come up with any questions, I left for the St. Louis airport. To avoid calls, I had already switched off my mobile phone.

The flight was via Sri Lanka. It had two hours of transit there. I reached Thiruvananthapuram by evening. I tried to contact Srikumar as soon as I landed, but I couldn't reach him. I had planned to go to Ernakulam and meet him. But because that didn't work out, I stayed that night in the capital and left the next morning.

I found myself in Udayamperoor once again.

7

The Impersonation

BEFORE SALIM RETURNED from Mauritius, we had a Thursday Market, to read and discuss the part we had got from Anpu.

'Now we don't have to be lenient to Meljo. He's a top-class liar. Christy Andrapper didn't just visit Valyedathu Veedu for a funeral. He had a relationship of the heart with the daughter of the house. And still Meljo said he didn't know Christy,' Anil said.

'He must have forgotten our last phone call. It's time for another try. Does anyone have a better idea than posing as a reporter of a newspaper, weekly . . . ?' Nibu asked.

'I've an idea.' Mashu got up. 'Call him as if you're the relative of some nurse who was with Melvin. He can't ignore that.'

'That's a good idea,' Anil said.

'Then we should prepare our plan well in advance. But we shouldn't stammer during the call,' Motta suggested.

Anil and Nibu made up a clear plan there and then. They narrated it to Mashu in detail. Accordingly, he called Meljo. All of us gathered around him with bated breath.

'Hello, is it Mr Meljo?'

'Who is this?'

'My name is Sudhish. Is it Meljo . . . ?'

'One minute. I'll pass the phone to him.'

'Hello.'

'Hello, Meljo, my name is Sudhish. I'm calling from Kollam. I landed from Diego yesterday. Your sister lived there, right?'

'Yes.'

'I knew Melvin. I'd been to her hostel. My cousin Sudha was with her. They were staying together.'

'Oh, Sudha-chechi. I've heard my sister talk about her.'

'Yeah. Sudha gave me this number, saying I should give you a call.'

'But none of them have called us even once. We lost our sister, and they lost a friend. Now what's there to say?'

'It's not that. What would they talk after calling? Ask you to stay calm? Can fate be mellowed down with words . . .?' Mashu asked.

'Fate! That's it. What else can it be . . . Seems like it's chasing us down. Soon after our sister, we lost our Appachan too.'

'Oh, Appachan? When was that?'

'It's been some two months now. He was very normal. A minor chest pain. But he didn't tell anyone. And then, gone before reaching the hospital.'

'Sorry to hear that. None of us here knew about this.'

'That's fine. Some things we have to face. There is no other way.'

'Yes, that's true.' Mashu's voice had started trembling. Nibu gestured to him to keep going.

'What do you do in Diego, Mr Sudhish?'

'I teach at a school there. At St. Joseph's, Seleucia.'

'Have you been there for long?'

'No, just five years.'

'What's the subject?'

'Malayalam. Oh, that reminds me of something. There was an alumni get-together recently. I met that guy there.'

'Who . . .?'

'Don't you remember Andrapper . . .?'

'Who . . .? Christy!'

'Yeah. We all knew about his feelings for Melvin.'

'Where did you say you met him?'

'At a meeting of St. Joseph's Malayalam alumni. When I said I'll be going to Kerala, he had asked me to convey his regards to you. Do you guys talk often . . .?'

'No. You have his number . . .?'

'Ayyo, no. Met him only by chance.'

'When are you returning, Sudhish sir . . .?'

'I've one month's leave.'

'Please do me a favour. Once you are back, please find Christy for me. And ask him to call me urgently on this number. We've had no news of him for a long time.'

'Oh, sure.'

'Please convey our regards to Sudha-chechi and the others. And please do drop by if possible.

'It's too far for me. And I have a lot to do at home. Yet, I will try.'

'Okay then. Thanks for the call.'

'Bye.'

As soon as the call ended, Sudhi Mashu dropped to his knees. We all got scared for a moment, and rushed to him.

'Damn. You all made me commit this sin. Oh god . . . that was so cruel.' Sudhi Mashu started hitting his head on the floor, crying.

'What's there to worry about, Mashu? After all, it's for a good cause,' Anil tried to pacify him.

'Whatever it is for, I shouldn't have done it. You shouldn't have made me do it. I shouldn't have lied so much to a man who's mourning the loss of his sister and father.'

'You don't have to feel so bad, Mashu. The last time we called, he said he didn't even know Andrapper. How does he know him now? He is also a fraudster. You just have to think that we gave him a dose of his own medicine,' Nattapranthan said. 'I suspect that even his mourning is fake.'

'Anyway, it was not you alone who did it. We all called him together. So we all share the sin. Didn't Salim and Benyamin go to Alappuzha and fool one Salu? I myself led the way in tricking poor Rajanbabu sir. Then Salim went to Diego with his family and bluffed so many people. Even otherwise, there is no cheating or conning in this. We have to impersonate sometimes for a good cause. Then we might have to tell some lies. Mashu doesn't have to feel guilty about it.' Nibu was almost shouting at Mashu.

'Mashu is feeling bad because he is from the old school. These days, on the Internet and places like that, a person has at least some twenty different identities. It's not a sin at all in this new world,' Biju said.

'Mashu, that call would have given him relief, not sorrow. At least, we called; no one else has done so. Look at it as a good deed,' Nattapranthan said. Everyone did his share of mollycoddling to somehow pacify Mashu. But we were all feeling low.

'Let's now meet after Salim returns,' said Anil, as he stepped out.

'We now know that Meljo has no idea about Andrapper. Now I'm wondering why Jijo said that,' Nibu was voicing our confusion as he was leaving.

'Actually, he is hiding some things . . .' Anil said.

'Who? I asked'

'Jijo . . . I think he is the villain in the pack.'

'Ey, I've met him. He is a nice chap,' Nattapranthan interrupted. 'Even if he is hiding something, it'll be out of fear.'

'Okay, whatever it is. After Salim returns, let's call Meljo one more time. If he doesn't pick up, we'll go and meet him,' Anil said.

On that note, all of us dispersed.

———

Salim returned after two days. 'What updates from the trip?' I called up to ask.

'Went to Andrapper's house. Let's meet at my place in the evening. I will tell you everything in detail,' Salim said. That was usual for us. Every time he returned after a trip, we would all gather at his house. To look at the photos. To watch the videos. To listen to the stories from the trip. And to savour a drink from a tinted bottle he would get us from the duty-free shop at the airport.

The last must have been the trigger. Everyone reached his house before the stipulated time. Salim switched on his computer, plugged in the camera cable, and showed us the photos one by one. At the airport, inside the flight, aerial view of Diego, the St. Raphael airport, the reception counter of Hotel Casablanca, boat, peacocks beside the lake, two battling monkeys, Janu with a dancing peacock, the *Diego Daily* office, coffee shops at Port Louis, palm groves, driver Seyfu, City Hospital, the nightlife of Diego, Sherly and Janu hugging in the hotel room, the bars that open to the waters, Mariam Church, the Bodhi tree, George Edward Memorial Seabird Sanctuary, the Temple of Chagos, Albuquerque cliff, Janu in the company of hundreds of peacocks, Sherly feeding one of them, Rajakottaram Hostel, Sherly and Janu with the nurses ('this is Jaya, this one Mercy'), a busy boat route at Pentasia, close-ups of fried fish and other food, Janu licking her finger, Sherly with an African-origin waiter, a board that read Uthukuzhi Padakukuzhi, a scene from Cherar Peruntheruvu, and a statue of Periyar.

Then the location shifted to the beachfronts of Mauritius. We took our eyes off the monitor.

'Sho, still Salim-ka, you didn't click a photo of that pretty girl Anpu,' Nattapranthan sulked.

'Ya, go and try your luck. Then you'll know,' Sherly said, while keeping on the table the tinted bottle and glasses.

'Though it burnt my pocket, it was a beautiful trip. Diego is awesome. Mauritius is double awesome,' Salim started his travelogue. 'Seven days in Mauritius went in a flash. On the return journey, the flight landed in Diego at 7.30 in the morning. We were back in the same hotel. We checked in, took a shower, had breakfast and called Seyfu. Left then itself to Pentasia. Saw a few places such as Cornish, Senate Centre and the Diego Monetary Agency. I will show those photos later. Then the memorial where Andrapper had come, what's its name, Sherly? Ah, Arch of Diego. Their St. Antony's Catholic Church. It's only as big as our chapel, but for them, it's pretty big. And it's ancient. That must be the reason.

'Then we went to the Seleucia North Public Security Office. I tried my best to meet Stephen Andrapper and Vijay Mullikratnam, but that didn't work out. From there, we left for the much-anticipated Andrapper House. Janu, get me that video.' We started watching the video.

From the boat sailing through the lake is a long shot of a huge mansion on one bank. The closer it gets, the majesty and grandeur of the house becomes clearer. There are three jetties to the house on various sides. One waterway extends to the compound. Every entrance has an iron gate. Salim gets off his boat at the main gate and walks towards a locked gate.

The camera zooms to the courtyard and the top floors of the house. Sherly and Janu stand beside the gate and pose as if for a photo. The camera shakes while changing hands. Salim also joins them to pose. Then, like a TV reporter, he walks towards the camera, saying, 'We are now standing in front of the famous Andrapper House in Diego. Our hopes to meet Christy Andrapper, for whom we have been searching for a long time, or any of his relatives, have been blocked by these gates and latches. It's time for us to return to Kerala. But we'll still be on the chase. For Thursday Market, Salim and family reporting from Diego's Andrapper House.'

The video ends there. We all clapped.

'After that we wrapped up and returned to the hotel. The flight was scheduled for 1 p.m. Luckily, we called the airport from the hotel and came to know that it's been delayed by two hours. But we didn't feel like going out again. So from the hotel, I started phoning people one by one. Mohandas Purameri, Rajanbabu sir, Johnny . . . just to say goodbye. We also called Sudha-chechi and Anita. It was like Anita was waiting for our call. "I want to meet you again. Can you please come to my house once?" she asked. I told her there was not much time left for the flight. "Just ten minutes," she said. "Please." We packed our bags and left for her place. She was waiting for us at the dock. Took us inside and gave us lemonade. She asked us about the Mauritian trip in detail. Still we were in the dark as to why she wanted to meet us. Finally, I had to raise the topic.

'"After you left, I called up Meljo. He said he knows you well and that you should be treated well." I only remember her saying that much. To tell you the truth, Mashu, I was peeing in my trousers! Has anyone caught a cheat red-handed in such a manner? Sherly and Janu must have been squirming.

'But Anita handled the situation well; she showed a maturity beyond her years. She didn't get worked up. Didn't do any cross-questioning. Didn't hurl any accusations. "Now please tell me, who are you? What do you want?" She asked only these two questions, very politely.

'I didn't have any option other than to succumb. I confessed to her, narrating all the incidents that had happened till then. She didn't seem to believe me completely. But I got a little lucky. The USB that I had got from Anpu was lying in my bag's side pocket. I took the laptop from Janu, and showed Anita what was in the USB. Her face turned pale. Are all these things true, I asked her. She nodded in acceptance. Then where is Andrapper now, I asked. She had no clue.'

We didn't have much time to spend there. She accompanied us till the dock. When we got into the boat, she said, 'Just a minute, I'm coming,' and ran to the house, returning with a packet.

'"After the last time mentioned in that book, Andrapper had come to my house one more time," she said. "He gave me this on that day. I was not sure if I should be giving you this or not . . . But I'm unable to hold it back. If this can help you find Andrapper, then let it be that way."

'She gave the packet to me. Janu, bring that packet.' When Janu came with it, Salim unwrapped it and showed us: papers.

It was the seventh part of *The Book of Forefathers*!

CHALDEANS

AT AROUND 2 P.M. on Saturday, I got down at Vaikom Road railway station. I was in a private bus to Udayamperoor, when a board with 'Poothotta' written on it whisked past me. I yearned to go to the church and see Melvin before heading home. So I got down at the stop. Bought a packet of candles and a lighter from a wayside shop, took an autorickshaw and got down at Martha Mariam Church. The gate wasn't latched. I got in and walked to Melvin's cemetery. The flowers had started withering off the wreath. Saplings were peeping out of the loosened soil. It seemed like Melvin was reaching out of her burial place eager to see the world. Dear little weeds, are you her eyes . . .? Are you the ones who tell her the tales of the earth? I asked them. They nodded yes. Will you tell her that I've come . . .? We will, we will, the leaves unfurled. I spent some time with her quietly, looking at her eyes. Then lit the candles . . . the light of love. When I was returning, the weeds wept asking me to come again. I, too, wept.

The church was open. I walked inside. There was an old priest lost in prayers, who turned to me hearing the sound of my footsteps. He looked nervous seeing me. Hiding it, he quickly waved his hands at me. When I went close, he held my hands and made me sit beside him. And then continued his silent prayers. I felt a strange power of tranquillity flowing towards me.

When he finished his prayers, I introduced myself. I told him that I had come to Valyedathu Veedu. When he heard I'm from Diego, he was curious. He asked a lot of things about the islands. Especially about Mariam Church. I told him all I knew.

'I've also heard about the church. As far as I know, it belonged to the first-generation African slaves. It was then abandoned. Whoever etched Mariam's history to it so craftily deserves a pat,' the Father said.

We walked till the church courtyard, stopping at a

board that read: 'Martha Mariam Chaldean Little Church. Poothotta. Belongs to Valyedathu Family.'

I don't know why, but I suddenly felt that this was the right person and occasion to ask a question that I'd been carrying for a while.

'I don't follow the church or its beliefs. I have no clue about its traditions and customs. Please don't take this in any other way, but what's the difference between a Catholic and a Chaldean . . .? Doesn't everyone believe in the same Christ?' The question was also triggered by the curiosity of seeing a Catholic priest in a Chaldean church. He stood silently for a few minutes. Then he placed his hands on my shoulder and said, 'In the past ten years, this is the first time a youngster has asked me this question. I keep wondering at this generation. I don't even understand their thoughts. Everyone is a great believer. They go to church, to mass, pray, do everything. If someone criticizes their church or belief, they are forever ready to fight too. But what are the basics of these beliefs? What's Christian theology? What are the contradictions in it? That nobody wants to know.' He took me back to the church, and we sat on a bench.

'The difference lies in the theology itself. But it's too vast to be explained in a day or two. For now, I'll only answer what you'd asked, son. About the Chaldean faith. The evolution of Christian theology runs parallel to history. It actually has only a distant relation to the Bible and the belief in Christ. Instead, the heart of theology lies in the interpretations. During the course of history, people interpreted Christ and his divinity in various ways. Every account was received by some and denied by some others. That naturally led to a conflict, and to the various cults that exist today. Nobody can claim that their faith is the right one; because nobody knows who was the real Christ. That's the first and last mystery of Christianity. Fortunately or unfortunately, the views of the majority were regarded as correct down the ages. It's not always necessary that the majority is right. Also, the masses have always been submissive towards people in authority. That means the words of the powerful were always written as history. However, history also always had people who rose to fight for the defeated side, to guard its secrecy, to face the wrath of the authorities and to die as martyr. The sacrifices are astonishing. They remind us of certain things which humans value more than their lives. That's why we now have various cults in Christianity. There is another interesting thing. Sometimes the majority became the minority, and vice versa. Those that were thought to be extinct came back to life. Those thought to be timeless faded away. That's the thrill of knowing and learning history. At first sight, every cult seems to follow Christ, but the insights are extremely different. A common man won't be able to grasp them. It's difficult even for a believer. The only way to know is with a deep understanding of theology.

'Christian theology evolved and progressed during the third and fourth centuries. And two schools of thought played a crucial role: the Alexandrian and the Antiochian. It can be said that the story of the disputes and struggle for dominance between these two factions constitute the history of the Eastern Church.

'In fact, it was from the second century that Jesus's mother, Mariam, came to be referred to as the Mother of God. But in the first half of the fifth century, Nestorius, the Archbishop of Constantinople, rejected the long-used title. He also emphasized that there were two separate hypostases in the Incarnate Christ, one divine and the other human. But this

Nestorian theology faced strong opposition from Patriarch Cyril of Alexandria.

'To decide on the issue, a general church council was summoned at Ephesus in 431 AD. Cyril was at the helm of the council, which apparently deposed Nestorius and declared him a heretic. In retaliation, the eastern bishops, who were supporting Nestorius, convened their own synod and deposed Cyril. Both sides then appealed to Emperor Theodosius II. The emperor was with Cyril, so he issued an edict that exiled Nestorius first to Antioch, and then to the Great Oasis of Hibis, near Libya. Nestorius spent sixteen years in the island and breathed his last there.

'Now let's walk and talk.' He closed the church door from outside and strolled out with his shoulder bag. I followed him.

'It can be said that after the Council of Ephesus, the Christian theology split into two,' he said, while walking through the corridor. 'Nestorius's supporters were chased down by the Roman Empire. The bishops of Antioch who rallied around his doctrine were removed from their sees. By the end of the emperor's regime, every one of the Nestorian churches was shut down. However, the doctrine that was believed to have been crushed by the iron hands of power bloomed and blossomed in Persia. Nestorian Christians relocated from Rome to Persia, and the thought became ingrained in the native community. The school of Edessa shifted to the Persian city of Nisibis, which later became a centre of Nestorianism. Also, in 486 AD, a Persian council congregated and accepted their total allegiance to the Nestorian faith. See, a doctrine that was believed to have become history surprisingly regained its full glory! Those Nestorian followers are now known as the Chaldean Church.'

'How did the Church come from Persia to Kerala?' I asked.

'The Christian theology again had differences in opinion, and further divided into many sects, but in all the historical records I've seen, the Malankara Church in Kerala had totally followed the Chaldean beliefs from the fourth to the fifteenth century. It came due to the ancient connections with Persia. The other sects spread here only after that. The Portuguese, Antiochians, the British, all spread their own beliefs. And all of them tried to suppress and sabotage the Chaldean Church. But none could do it. It has survived the storms of history. It has had to go underground at times. But it never lost its continuity. Somewhere or the other, it was protected. That's the wonder of the wonders of history!'

We had reached the main road. A bus was coming from afar. He waved his hand.

'Okay then. Someday, I'll come to Diego to visit Mariam Church. We should definitely meet.' He bid farewell to me.

'Father, you didn't tell your name,' I reminded him.

'I didn't ask your name too, son, because we have neither met here nor talked about anything. Isn't it like that?' he said and laughed.

The bus came to a halt. He got into it and left. I felt rather strange. Why did he not introduce himself . . .?

I walked towards the next junction to catch an auto. Suddenly, a Scorpio car came and stopped beside me. It was Meljo.

'Hah, where are you coming from?' I was amazed.

'That's what I also have to ask. How did you land here?'

'I just came to the church.'

'Okay, come.' Meljo opened the car door.

We left to go to Valyedathu Veedu.

PHOTOCOPY

'ACTUALLY, I WAS planning to leave for France the day after tomorrow. I cancelled it and came here only because you called me,' I told him on the way.

'France? For what . . .?'

'Higher studies. I've been planning to go for a long time. Now I decided not to delay it any further.'

'Ayyo, if I had known that, I wouldn't have insisted on you coming here.'

'Nothing will happen if I push it back another week. Also, I felt like meeting all of you once again before leaving.'

'Your last visit was a relief for all of us in the family. As you yourself came to tell us what really happened, others could also be pacified. Otherwise, this place would have been full of gossip.'

While stories were dying here, new ones were spreading in Diego, but I didn't tell Meljo that.

'But that day, how did you recognize me in the crowd? I had wished to leave without letting anyone know.'

'I knew about you through Melvin-chechi. At home, she used to open up only to me. Her dreams, wishes, everything. Merin and I are only one year apart, but I gelled more with Melvin-chechi, who was three years older.'

'You were the only family member Melvin had talked about. Even the fact that Appachan was a doctor I came to know only after coming here.'

'Melvin-chechi was like that. She took time to start talking. By the way, how did you recognize me? That day, when you called me by name, I was surprised.'

'What's the surprise in that?' I asked. 'You two look very similar. Even a child who'd seen Melvin could recognize you.'

'Yeah, everyone says that. Some have even asked if we were twins. The joke was that I was photocopied from her. Now the original has gone away, leaving this photocopy behind.' Meljo broke into tears.

I, too, could not stop my tears.

'Is it possible to delete another person's Orkut account . . .?' Still in tears, Meljo asked out of the blue.

'Don't know. Might need the password. Why . . .?'

'Many friends who don't know she is no more, are still sending her greetings and scraps. What'll I do . . .? I'm yet to come to terms with it. How will I tell another person?'

'No, Meljo. Don't tell anyone. Don't also delete her account. Like in our minds, let Melvin live in that virtual world too. Let us also send a message to that once in a while. With a hope that she must be reading all of them from somewhere.'

Then, till we reached home, both of us were lost in our own memories.

My entry with Meljo grabbed quite a few eyeballs from the family members. 'We knew you were coming, but how come you two are together?' one of them asked.

Meljo narrated how he met me on the road.

Appachan inquired about the journey, and Amma, about food. Many relatives had already arrived. They did some small talk with me. Then asked Meljo to help me take rest.

He took me upstairs and opened Melvin's room. The same room. Nothing had been moved out of it, everything was intact, prim and proper. A beautiful photo of hers was the only addition.

'Only this room has an attached bathroom facility. Is that fine?' Meljo asked.

'If I'm staying in this house, I would rather prefer this room.'

'Take a shower and freshen up. I'll be back,' he handed over a soap and towel, and went downstairs.

I was tired. Shower was a good option. In the bathroom, there was a photograph of a young Melvin on the mirror. I stumbled for a minute. That was a very old photo of hers. It was as if she was gazing at me. I felt ashamed to undress in front of her. I covered the photo with a towel. Still I felt that she was looking at me through the strands of the towel. Maybe it's written in my destiny that I've to take shower in her bathroom, in front of her photo, when she is no more.

When Meljo came with coffee, I was standing in the room, sniffing a doll.

'Not just the room, every object here has her scent,' I said. 'I feel her silent presence here.'

'These are all Chechi's collections since childhood. These dolls were her companions. Nobody has used this room other than her. Then how will it not smell of her ...? God willing, you two would have spent your lives here,' Meljo said.

'Our lives ...?' I stared at him, confused.

'In the Valyedathu tradition, the eldest girl shouldn't be sent away after marriage. We adopt the guy. Appachan had come like that. Actually, Melvin-chechi wanted to tell you about that tradition before she left. She knew everyone there loves her. But she wasn't sure if they would accept it. A day before she had called me too, and told me that she couldn't meet you to tell you. Here, wedding inquiries were in full swing. Her plan was to tell Appachan only after Andrapper agreed. Otherwise, she wouldn't have gone back to Diego.'

'Hello, when did you arrive?' Jijo walked in, putting our discussion to a halt.

'This afternoon.'

'I see. I had to go to college. From there, I came here directly.'

Jijo asked me more questions and I replied to all of them, but my mind was somewhere else—on the issue that Melvin had wanted to discuss with me. A kind of adoption. Would I have agreed . . .? It is only recently that I'd come to know of Udayamperoor and the Valyedathu family. Even then, I would have thought twice before deciding to stay here forever. At a time when all these people were as alien to me as a distant patch in an African forest, if Melvin had raised such a demand, would I have agreed? No, for sure. Then how would have Melvin reacted? Would she have stayed with me in Diego? Or would she have left me and returned to Valyedathu? From what I could gather from Meljo, Melvin had decided on the latter. But if I had explained my part, maybe Melvin would have changed her decision. Or after listening to her, I would have changed my mind. If not, would I have lost her?

I didn't know why I was worrying about things past. Sometimes, the mind is like this. It won't take the route of logic.

'Shall we go for a walk?' Jijo's question took me back to normalcy.

'Oh yes, let's do that.'

I got ready in a jiffy. We called Meljo too, but he said he was stuck with some preparations for the next day.

It was beginning to get dark. We talked about Jijo's college and my Diego days as we reached the main road. We had tea from a wayside stall.

'Why are guys adopted at Valyedathu Veedu? I asked Jijo while returning.

He stopped walking. 'Have you seen Udayamperoor Old Church?' he asked.

'No.'

'It's a historically relevant church. You shouldn't miss seeing it after coming all this way. Shall we go?'

We turned back. Jijo said it was close, but it didn't seem so. I'd never walked so much in Diego. There are only short walks in Diego. And short walks in the mainland are long distances for us islanders.

THE OLD CHURCH

TWO CHURCHES IN the same compound. One old and the other new. A plank next to the gate proclaims that the Synod of Udayamperoor took place on 20 June 1599. It has the images of two saints, with garlands. A caption below it reads: 'St. Gervasius and St. Protasius, please pray for us'. An archaic stone cross stood next to it. Keeping guarding on its four sides were a winged lion, vulture, ox and human forms. The old church has been made a memorial.

The evening mass had just got over at the new church. Some people were loitering around.

When we tried to get into the memorial church, the priest was initially reluctant, saying that the visiting time was over and that it would be difficult to get a guide. I told him I'd come from very far and had to go back the next day, that we didn't need a guide; then he called up someone to open the church. We went through a narrow door leading to a dark room. There was a big granary. In earlier days, the church treasures were kept in it, said the guy who opened the door, acting like a guide. The right wall of the room had three stone relics. I tried to read them and failed. They were in old Malayalam. The door next to it opened to the church. Inside, it was dark and smelled its age. There were lights blinking here and there like fireflies. We slowly walked around, looking at things. This church seemed to be an excellent example of Kerala's traditional architecture. Considering when it was built, it's a relatively big church.

'It is one of the oldest churches in Kerala,' Jijo assumed the role of a guide. 'Believed to be built in 510 AD, this church has much relevance in the history of Malankara Christians. The Synod of Diamper (former name of Udayamperoor), during which the Portuguese Padroado gained control over the Malankara Church, took place here.' Seeing that Jijo had taken over his place, the man with us slowly pulled back.

Many memorials of the synod were preserved in the church. The first glass box had a model of the synod. The next one had the model of a decree by which the Kerala Christians banished the Portuguese authority after fifty years. Then there were priests' cassocks, zucchettos, candle lamps, prayer books, clerical utensils, a tomb, and such things.

What made me the most curious was a raised platform from where everyone could hear the speaker at a time when the microphone was not invented.

There were no pillars to support the church's ceiling and roof. As it was dark, I could not see the ceiling clearly. But from whatever was visible, the architecture could beat the best of present-day sculptors in Kerala. It's doubtful that anyone can dream of such a work in Diego, forget making it. The roof had motifs of elephants and horses, the rafters had forms of angels, fish, birds, flowers, leaves, and the smaller planks were full of floral woodwork.

'Have you ever heard of Thoma of Villarvattom?' Jijo asked while moving away from the architecture.

'No. Who it is he?'

'Villarvattom is the only Christian dynasty in Kerala's history. The kingdom's capital was none other than Udayamperoor!'

I was surprised to see a young, smart engineering student quickly transforming into a well-read history teacher. The change was reflected in Jijo's expressions, voice and body language. 'Chendamangalam, Malyankara and Udayamperoor were the borders of the kingdom. Chendamangalam was the first capital, but after the Arab invasion, the power centre shifted to Udayamperoor. For over 1000 years, all the Christians of Malankara were under the rule of the Villarvattom Thoma kings. Like the Pope in Rome, the right to decide the archdeacons for Malankara Christians vested with the Villarvattom kings. The old church where we stand now was the royal church during those days.

'Once, the kings were buried inside this church. You remember the three epitaphs we saw? One of them says: '*Chennongalathu partha Villarvattom Thoma rachavu naadu neengi 1500 Kanni 2-nu*' (King Thoma of Villarvattom from Chennongalathu passed away on the 2nd of the Kanni month, 1500). It's in the old Malayalam script. Not easy to say which king's it was. It was a custom with the Villarvattom dynasty to not use their original names. Every one of them was called King Thoma. Anyway, after the last king passed away, Paliath Achan assumed power in a coup and merged it with the Kochi kingdom.'

'Was Mariyam his daughter . . .?'

'Yes. She fell in love with a Hindu prince and married him. But Paliath Achan cheated them. That's how the regime ended.'

'Amazing. Are we standing in the church of that Thoma king and Mariam?'

'Why, have you heard of this before . . .?'

'There is a church in Diego believed to be built by Mariam. I realize it only now that she was a princess of Udayamperoor. That church has a huge following of women. I used to take my Chettathi there regularly. That's where I first met Melvin.'

'Oh I see . . . And yet, Melvin had never told you these stories?'

'No.'

'Nothing about Mariam?'

'No.'

'About Thaikkattamma?'

'Thaikkattamma?

'No.'

'Oh, I thought she would have told you something. That's why I was asking earlier whether you'd decided to marry her even after knowing all about Valyedathu Veedu.'

'Jijo, you have not replied to my question. Why do men have to be adopted into this family?'

'Come, I'll tell you.'

We waded through the darkness.

THAIKKATTAMMA

'IF WE GO east from here, there is a chapel called Thaikkattu Palli. Thaikkattamma is the deity there. Jesus's mother Mary has many local forms across the world. You must have heard of Manarcad Mathavu, Velankanni Mathavu, Koratti Muthi, etc. Like that, people here call her Thaikkattamma. Every universal figure has regional interpretations. The locals have a special affection for these deities. An affection rooted in their faith. Shall we go there?'

'Yeah, sure,' I said.

It was only a short distance away. A beautiful little chapel. The crowd was bigger than at the Udayamperoor church. They were lighting candles, pouring oil, and praying in front of a statue believed to have stuck in a fishermen's net at sea.

I, too, lit a candle, for Melvin. 'Oh dear Thaikkattamma, the graceful one, please accompany Melvin in the lonely journey of her soul.'

'This church, too, has a huge following of women,' Jijo said as we were leaving. 'There is a custom of pregnant women offering paddy here. People come from distant places. As I was saying, the general belief is that Thaikkattamma is the Virgin Mary, but a faction of the people secretly believes she is Mariam, daughter of the last Thoma king. But many people here aren't aware of that.

'Though Paliath Achan betrayed her, deposing her husband to Ceylon, and merging her land with Kochi, she stuck to her beliefs till her death. At least some still believe that Mariam was a saint, that she had magical powers, and that prayers to her can help get any deed done. It is said that it was due to such prayers and powers that Paliath Achan's last days were grim; all his wealth was confiscated. To those who believe in her, she can be very kind and bestow all kinds of blessings; but to those who don't, she'll fume with fury. Like the Chathan Seva Mutts, there are still at least four families in Kerala that use Thaikkattamma for rituals to ward off enemies and evil forces.

'There is a secret ritual in some houses that worship Mariam. The prayers and chants are in the ancient Pali script. It's called Mariam Seva. But it's very difficult to please Thaikkattamma. It needs a lot of patience and prolonged efforts to get her to grant your wishes. For that, a girl from the family has to be offered to Mariam. The girl has to follow a long list of customs, fasting, abstinence and sacrifices. Once offered, the girl can't be taken away from her. She has to spend her whole life with the family that does the seva and be part of the rituals. But there is no issue in her getting married or leading a normal life. In fact, Thaikkattamma likes her more if she is married, as she herself is longing for her husband. If the seva is disturbed or the customs are not followed, the girl could end up being a lunatic or mentally disturbed, or even dead.

'I don't know which are the other three families in Kerala that do Mariam Seva. But I know the fourth one: Valyedathu Veedu! In the name of treatment, what Meljo's Appachan actually does here is Mariam Seva. And the girl from this generation who was offered to Thaikkattamma was none other than Melvin!'

We had reached Valyedathu Veedu. In the dim light, the house looked like a ghost inn.

THE SONG

AFTER WHAT I'D heard, everything at Valyedathu Veedu looked strange and mysterious. It was not the same house I'd seen before. I started observing every nook and corner of the house with a new set of eyes. I found an uncanny element in everything I saw, every picture and in every room. Some pictures in the verandah, some carvings in the rooms, a prayer room similar to the one in Hindu houses, a stone cross, the obscure etchings on it, prayers in front of a lighted lamp . . . everything seemed bizarre and out of place. When we reached, the evening prayer was on. Two or three priests and a lot of relatives. We, too, joined them. But I didn't understand a word of their chants. I felt a strange fear for the first time.

Mariam Seva! I'd never heard of it before. Does that really exist? It must. The prayer room of this house is adding to the belief. This is not a normal house; it's a den of mystery.

When the prayers ended, Appachan scolded Jijo for taking me out at dusk, when snakes comes out to prey in the dark. Then he held my hand and took me to the next room, saying he had not had time to talk to me the last time, and that he doesn't get anyone to talk to these days. News of Diego, about my house, about my father and mother, and about Melvin's death . . . he asked about everything in detail. As the gentle and soft conversation proceeded, his simplicity and affectionate attitude grew. I was studying him the entire time. Are his gentle eyes hiding a vicious evil-worshipper . . .? Are his soft fingers secretly writing the mantras . . .? Is this the tongue behind the chants . . .? The hands that invoke Mariam . . .?

While talking, he suddenly grabbed my hands. 'Son, it was my daughter's wish to make you part of this family. Thaikkattamma didn't let it happen through her. But now you are part of our hearts and this house. Now there can be no separation. Let me ask: will you marry Merin and be part of this house . . .?'

I was sweating, I did not know what to say. My hands started shaking. No. No. Merin is not Melvin. I can be part of this house. But I can't marry Merin. I can't. I can't. I wanted to scream that out aloud, but no voice could come out. It felt like he had tied my tongue. I didn't say what I wanted to say, but what he wanted to hear.

I'm willing, I promised him. He held me close and kissed my forehead. 'My daughter is lucky. This house is blessed.'

He broke into tears. Me too.

It was only when Merin came and invited us for dinner that we got up. I was totally tired and exhausted by then. I only remember going up to my room after dinner. And falling into Melvin's bed. I slept like I'm dead.

Sometime at night, a song woke me up. A group song. It reverberated, like the sound of waves from a distance. I first thought it was a dream. So, lying down, I enjoyed it for a while. Then I realized that it was not a dream, but reality. The song was coming from somewhere close.

I slowly got up and sat on the bed. A thick blanket of darkness surrounded me. Groping, I switched on the light. The song was coming from the ground floor. I checked my mobile phone. It was past one. Hasn't anyone gone to sleep here? Why is there singing now . . .? I went to the door anxiously, removed the latch and tried to open it, but it would not open. I tried again and again, but no, it was not opening. Then it stuck me that someone had locked it from outside! A shiver ran through my spine. What are they doing after locking me in this room . . .? My anxiety and fear increased. I ran around the room like a mad cat. There was a window that faced the next room; I tried to open it, but that too was locked. Fuming with anger and dismay, I sat on the bed. I'm a guest in this house. I came here because I was invited. Then why have they locked me in? What secret do they have to guard from me? Or are they doing what Jijo had talked about—Mariam Seva? I was so angry that I wanted to break open the door and go downstairs. But one part of my mind was telling me that it would be dangerous to do anything rash. If they have locked me in, that means something is taking place that they wish to keep hidden from me. So, if I come to know of it, they might do anything with me. I've been trapped in a den of the worst evils. I've to act cautiously. Not emotionally—tact is required here. I got back to my bed. Outside, the song had reached its height. There were bells ringing. Suddenly, I spotted a small ventilator above the door. It was covered with glass. I pulled the table close to the door, and got on top of it. Luckily, that hadn't been latched. I opened it slowly and craned forward to see. The hall on the ground floor could have been seen clearly were it not for a money plant hanging near it. I tried to lean and look from various angles, but the view wasn't clear. I felt so sad, angry and helpless. After a while, the song stopped. It felt like everyone was dispersing.

What Jijo said is right. There is Mariam Seva here. After Melvin died, Merin must have been offered to Thaikkattamma. That must have been the function, which took place now. I felt so angry at the house and at Appachan, who was always gentle. He did all this pooja and seva, and got one daughter killed. But he's still not content; now he wants to offer his next daughter. Melvin wanted to run away from this ghost house. That's why she had gone so far to Diego. And fallen in love with me. And wanted to marry me. I felt bad that I couldn't save her. I need to at least help Merin out of this hell.

I heard someone climbing the stairs. I was still standing on top of the table. I jumped down, dragged the table to the previous spot, switched off the light, ran to the bed and pulled the blanket up. There was the sound of unlatching. I snored as if I was in deep sleep. I could feel someone coming close to the bed. I slowly opened one eye. It was too dark to see anything. But I knew the person was walking around the bed making sure I was asleep. Then he came right up to me and tried to wake me up. I purred in sleep. After a while the footsteps receded. When the door opened, I quickly turned to see who it was. In the light falling from outside, I had a glimpse of his face. It was the Catholic priest whom I had seen at Martha Mariam Church that afternoon!

JOURNEY

MELJO WOKE ME up in the morning. It was around eight. My eyes were still heavy with sleep.

'Last night, I came up thinking of chit-chatting with you, but you were in deep sleep. Must have been tired with all the travelling, right?' Meljo asked.

'Yeah, totally tired,' I got up and sat on the bed.

From last night's hurried pulling of the table, some of Melvin's dolls had fallen to the floor. Without asking anything, Meljo picked them up and put them back in their place.

'This must have happened when I went to the loo in the night,' I tried to explain.

'Okay, get up now and get ready. It's time to go to the church.'

I quickly freshened up and went downstairs. Everything looked normal there. Everyone was busy getting ready.

Merin came to me with coffee. 'Did you sleep well last night?' she asked. She was unusually shy. 'Yeah, but I had some bad dreams. Some chaos and songs or something.' I was observing her keenly.

'Must be because of the change of place,' she said without a change in expression. Merin knows how to lie and how not to give anything away. Or maybe, she developed the skill as a child in this family.

'You also look sleepy. Did you go to bed late?'

'After Melvin-chechi's death, nobody sleeps here properly. Appachan and Ammachi just act as if nothing has happened.

And yesterday, all the relatives and all . . . yes, I slept late. Must be because of that.'

No. She doesn't seem to stumble at my queries. A cat knows how to fall. It doesn't matter who throws it down.

That was the first time I was really talking to Merin. I inquired about her studies and college. She was in the final year of her degree programme, at Ernakulam. After that, she wanted to do a BEd.

'Where is Jijo? I haven't met him this morning.' I looked around.

'There was not enough space for everyone here. We have another house nearby. So, he is there. He will come here soon.' She took the empty cup and left.

Umm. So that's how it is. Jijo was not here last night. He was also kept away so that he won't know what's happening here. Jijo is a close relative. But even he was filtered out of the guest list last night. That shows how secretive it was.

Two Scorpio cars had been making round trips to the church since morning. When Jijo came, I got into the car with him. He also gave the same reply that Merin gave me about the sleeping arrangement. He added that he had come to take me also to the place, but then as I was sleeping, he let it be.

Before leaving, I will ask Meljo directly. I knew everything that had happened last night. Let me see what lies he tells.

Qurbana was halfway through when we reached the church. There wasn't much crowd; only a few close relatives. We stood outside, talking. Before the prayer at the cemetery, I went there and chatted with Melvin's saplings. Appachan had hinted about something last night, what should I do? I asked Melvin. 'Say yes, say yes,' the flowers nodded. Not for Valyedathu Veedu, but I'll agree for the sake of Merin, I promised her.

The reception at Udayamperoor Panchayat Community Hall was a full house. The local MLA, a state minister, panchayat members, politicians, heads of other religions, priests and all such important people had come. I could see people fighting to win the favour of Melvin's Appachan. I felt they could be the secret visitors and clients of Valyedathu Veedu. Amidst all the bustle, everyone seemed to have forgotten Melvin. It's the same with every death. Nobody will be remembered beyond forty-one days. By any one.

It was around 11 when the people left. I had expressed my wish to leave. There was a Kingfisher flight from Nedumbassery to Chennai at 3.55. If I could catch it, I would get a connecting flight to Sri Lanka that goes via Diego. I could also avoid a train trip to Thiruvananthapuram, and save a day. I'd booked the return ticket, considering that.

'It's only at four; there is a lot of time,' Meljo insisted. Ammachi asked me to leave after lunch.

No, I don't want anything. I've to leave now. This is my last and final visit to this house. I'll never come again. I'll never contact any of you. This is a house of superstitions and witchcraft. I've had enough of all of you. This is what my mind was saying, but nothing came out in words. In this house, not just Appachan, everyone has some power that clips the tongue of others. In this house, I've become feeble, unable to speak my mind. This time too, I did what they said. There are not many occasions on which I have been such a slave.

So I had to stay on at Valyedathu Veedu till lunchtime. As much as I was trying to go away from the house, some powerful forces of fate seemed to pull me closer. Some believe that for forty-one days after a person's death, his or her soul remains on the earth; only then does it go to the netherworld. If that's true, today is Melvin's last day on earth. As she leaves

this place forever, is it her wish that I have to be with her
dear ones . . .?

After lunch, Jijo was planning to drop me at the airport
on the way to his college. I thought then I could discuss last
night's event with him. But that didn't work out. Some group
from Angamali offered to drop me in their car. Appachan
said that would be better than a long bike ride. Neither Jijo
nor I could oppose him. We looked at each other helplessly.

Jijo left alone.

Forgoing all that we could have told each other, I bid
farewell to all and joined the Angamali group for the airport.
But I was still hoping that I could call up Jijo and have a
long chat.

8

Wednesday

'THIS IS VERY weird ... this actually happens here ...?' asked Sudhi Mashu.

Anil smiled. 'It's only here that this happens even now! We have the new-generation churches, then we have evil worship, we even have *mashinottam*, then something as new-fangled as pulse diagnosis. Kerala had become a centre of the black school of mysticism long ago ... And among them there's Mariam Seva. Nothing to be surprised about.'

'These kinds of prayers and beliefs are not part of one particular religion. Every religion practises them,' Salim said.

'Till recently, the Christians in Kerala were part of the Hindu ethos. Most of their customs followed the Hindu style. Whatever was followed by Hinduism was also observed by the Christians. This must be one such instance. How will we get at the truth?' Pattar Biju asked.

'If we believe that Andrapper has been truthful till now, then this too should be true. There is no need for him to lie only about Valyedathu Veedu,' I said.

'Why are we struggling so much? Jijo, whom we had met that day, is a cousin of these people. We can ask him,' Nattapranthan suggested.

'That's correct. Call him right now,' Anil told me.

I dialled the number. As soon as it started ringing, everyone surrounded me without a word. Jijo took the call at the very first ring. Not just that, he quickly recognized me from my voice. After some small talk, I got into the topic.

'By the way, there is some progress on the Andrapper issue. I've got some more parts of his book, *The Book of Forefathers*.'

'Any idea where he is now?' Jijo asked.

'No. But he has mentioned some other important things. Especially about Valyedathu Veedu.'

'What is it . . .?'

'Should I tell you? Don't you know?

'I didn't get you.'

'About Mariam Seva.'

'Oh . . . that. That's not a secret. Everyone in Udayamperoor knows that such a custom takes place at Valyedathu Veedu. Not just that, people from across Kerala come there to do it.'

'Actually, what is this Mariam Seva . . .?'

'Something like Chathan Seva, to put it in simple terms. Mariam is invoked and beseeched to do things.'

'Is it the Virgin Mary whom they invoke?'

'Valyedathu Veedu has Thaikkattamma. At some other places, Mary is invoked.'

'Does it actually yield results?'

'It must be. Isn't that why more and more people are coming? But I don't have any faith in all this.'

'Who does it at Valyedathu Veedu?'

'Their Appachan. But he passed away recently. Now Meljo does it.'

What's Merin's role in this?'

'She has been offered to Thaikkattamma, that's all. She doesn't take part in the seva or the pooja.'

'Then what was it that Christy heard and almost saw? Was it the ceremony of offering her to Thaikkattamma?'

'When . . .?'

'Christy had written that while he was in the house,

there was a celebration at night. I was asking about that.'

'At Valyedathu Veedu . . .? Ey, no chance. The offering takes place at the church.'

'Then what might have taken place there that night?'

'I've no idea. What has Andrapper written?'

I gave him a short account of what had been written.

'This is very interesting. There can't be such a ceremony at Valyedathu Veedu that I know of. But I can't believe that Andrapper got it wrong.'

'So what's the way of knowing what had happened?'

'Did you call Meljo?'

'Yeah, but he keeps things to himself. He was saying he doesn't even know any Andrapper.'

'I've told you earlier also. He's a master cheat. You'll have to sweat it out to get anything out of him. I still strongly believe that he had a hand in Andrapper's disappearance.

'Anyway, let us think of a way. Jijo, please try to figure out what ceremony took place that night.'

With that, we ended the conversation.

But the talk had only put us in further confusion. Yes, there was indeed Mariam Seva. Jijo accepted it. But what was the ceremony that took place that night? Andrapper says it was the ritual in which Merin was offered to Thaikkattamma. Jijo says that's not how the ritual is usually conducted. Who among the two is right? Who is wrong? Or is there a truth between these two? How can we figure that out . . .?

The Thursday Market had many inconclusive discussions. Finally, we came to this decision: We have to call Meljo one more time.

'We should confront him boldly. It will have to be a strong move in which he will have to accept his relationship with

Christy. From there, we should be able to find out the inside
story of Valyedathu Veedu,' Anil said.

'The call shouldn't be based on a rash reason. Each of us
should go home, make time and think. We should concoct a
good reason to call him. We can, we are smart,' said Salim.

'Okay. Then, let's leave this topic for today. Only the liquid
treat is left,' declared Nibu.

That day we wrapped up after finishing the bottle that
Salim had got and listening to his Mauritius stories. Next
week, we met again. Though each of us presented ideas to
call up Meljo, nobody could come up with a convincing one.
Everyone slowly slid into silence and our own thoughts.

'Has anyone of us seen Mariam Seva?' Anil asked as if
woken up suddenly. A silence followed, indicating that no
one had.

'I've also not seen it. But I'm going to see it,' Anil said.

'No. Anil, that's too much of a risk. Meljo already has
doubts about us. We should be cautious about landing in
such places. They have the support of big gangs of goons,'
Mashu advised Anil.

'What Mashu says is absolutely right. I've had direct
experience. One guy went to Bangalore to see Nagamanikyam.
There is a five-lakh-rupee fee just for seeing the stone. He got
beaten up, and lost the cash. That's how these goons function.
So, all the investigation till now is good enough. Let's not
complicate it,' Nibu seconded Mashu.

'To get to the soul of a matter, it has to be sliced through
the middle. I'm going to that house to see Mariam Seva.
Maybe, I'll lose a bit of money. Or get beaten up. But I'll
catch the lion in its own den. Who has the guts to come with
me?' Anil asked.

'I'm ready!' I piped up in the excitement of the moment, despite my usual cowardice.

'So, how can we attend a Mariam Seva? What are the procedures? Benyamin, call up that Jijo now and get the details,' Anil said.

I phoned Jijo.

It has to be booked in advance, Jijo said. He also gave me a number for it. Anil tried the number. There was some cross-questioning from the other side, asking who we are, where we were calling from, and how we came to know about Valyedathu Veedu. When he gave the proper answers, the fees and procedures were explained to him. Thus, Anil's name was booked for a Mariam Seva for a day the following week. Then the wait started. A week-long wait. Finally, the day came. Today. Wednesday. Anil and I left for the house in the early morning.

That's how we landed in Udayamperoor. We didn't have to ask for directions. Andrapper's *The Book of Forefathers* had the precise details.

EVIDENCE

'IT'S A LIE! Whatever you've said are lies. Andrapper has not written a book like that. Even if he has written it, it's all lies. Who are you trying to fool? Me? What exactly do you want? Is it money? Or something else . . .?' Meljo's face was shaking in fury.

'Hello, Meljo, cool down. Who are you getting angry with? Us? There is no need for that. Because, none of this is our imagination. These are the descriptions in a book that we had got, which we then toiled to assemble. If you are angry with Andrapper, there is no need to take that out on us. We are less close to him than you are, you must have understood that by now. So let's stop the drama and get to the point. Tell us from the point where the story has reached. What happened to Christy Andrapper after he left for the airport with the Angamali family?' Anil asked in a composed, yet sharp, tone.

'You came here unnecessarily following a story, that too a story written by a fraud who tells lies, and cheats. You are not going to get anything from here. I've nothing to help you with. He has never contacted me after he left. I don't know the reason. And I don't know where he has gone,' Meljo reiterated his stand.

'Meljo, you keep repeating the word, "lies, lies". Please tell me, which part of Christy's writing is a lie? Is your sister Melvin's death a lie? The affair they had, was it a lie? Is it a lie that he had been to your house many times? Srikumar, Jijo, Anita, Sudha-chechi . . . all lies? Is Udayamperoor a lie? This Valyedathu Veedu? Is Mariam Seva also a lie?'

'I don't know if the others are a lie. But the treachery he did to us is enough to prove that he is a total cheat.'

'What did he do to you? Leaking the secret of Valyedathu Veedu?'

'Look, dear friend, unlike what you think, there is no big secret about this house. Valyedathu Veedu is an open book. Everyone in this area knows we do Mariam Seva here. People come here for it. It is a gift handed to us by tradition. Thaikkattamma comes to our prayer room and blesses us. We share the fruits of the blessings with others. There is no dark secret in that. And it's not a crime in India.'

'Then let me ask openly. What was the celebration that took place that night? We know that that's not the way how a girl in the family is offered to Thaikkattamma. Then what was that ceremony about?' Anil was persistent.

'Ha ha ha . . . that's what I, too, don't know,' Meljo burst into laughter. 'Such a celebration never happened here that night. How can I say what it was when such a thing never took place? Even otherwise, less than forty-one days since my sister's death, how could we have a celebration? He must have been hallucinating. That's why I call this one a Book of Lies.'

'Okay. So everything except that celebration is true. But after he left that day, has he never contacted you? He had promised to come back, he had promised to marry your younger sister, he was about to be adopted by the family . . . Didn't you search for him?'

'Look, friend, I told you at the beginning of our conversation that he is a fraud. After listening to all these stories, I still stand firm on that. He had left promising to come back. That was not a promise given to me, but his word to Appachan, who cared for him a lot. But he never returned. Or called. He once wrote me a letter giving the reasons—that he was living in fear and that the police would catch him any time. I believed for a long time that he was right. Then I came to know that he was lying and that he was walking about freely in Diego. Many people who saw him there called up and informed me.'

'Who had seen him there? Can you give us one name? We want to contact the person,' I said.

'Why are you so sure that he is not there?'

'Meljo, one of our friends had gone to Diego as part of our search. The Andrapper house had been closed for a long time, that's what we came to know through him. It's not a rumour, we have an eyewitness.'

'Your friend must have got it wrong. Sudhish, a teacher

from Diego, who came on leave recently, also told me that
he had met Andrapper not long ago.' We didn't know what
to say. Meljo was talking about Sudhish's prank call! If we
reveal it, we could get into trouble, and so we kept mum.

'There is more proof. Recently, someone called me from
some weekly saying they had got a story from him. Similarly
many more called, saying that they knew Andrapper.'

That had to do with Anil's prank call! That too we couldn't
reveal.

'Okay, Meljo, we trust you. Do you have the letter that he
wrote saying he was afraid and that the police was after him?'

'No. I lost that a long time back.'

'That means you have nothing with you to give us which
could lead to Christy, right?'

'What will you do after finding him? What you wanted
was his novel. That you got. Let him get lost now.'

'We can pacify ourselves like that. Our relation with him
was through a story. But you two were not like that. Wasn't
he a part of this house, one who would have become husband
to your sister? Shouldn't you be helping us in finding out what
happened to him?

'Relation! We don't have any relation. Valyedathu Veedu
doesn't have to make a relationship with such a pathetic family.'

'On what evidence are you saying this?'

'On the evidence of his confession . . .'

'We don't get you.'

'I was thinking of never showing it to anyone. That he
and the history of his family should perish without anyone
knowing about them. But he betrayed my sister's love. He
betrayed this family and its privacy. So why should I protect
him? Let everyone know about the great Andrapper house.
This is the best revenge I çan take on him.'

Meljo got up and went inside. After some minutes, he returned with an envelope. 'This he had sent me. Read it and tell me who is right and who is wrong. Aren't you a writer? You should not only read this, but also write about it. Let everyone know about his history. You can keep this. We don't need any holy leftovers of Andrapper here. And nobody should ever come here again mentioning his name!'

Meljo got up. That was a hint that we shouldn't hang around.

'When you leave, please take the cash on that plate. Valyedathu Veedu has failed to get your wish granted,' Meljo said. Then he turned quickly and stomped inside.

Like Adam who was thrown out of Eden, we stood there baffled for some time. Then knowing it was useless, we slowly stepped out.

During the return journey, I started reading the chapter of the Andrapper biography that Meljo gave.

PARK PLAZA

WHEN I REACHED Nedumbassery, I came to know that the flight was delayed by two hours. To wait was the only option. It landed another half an hour after the estimated time. Before taking off, there was a half-an-hour wait at the runway for reasons unknown. Finally when it reached the Chennai airport, the Sri Lankan flight had already been one hour in the air. I tried to fight with the manager at the airport, hoping at least to get a hotel arranged to stay. But it didn't work out. He said he was helpless. 'We don't have any connection with Kingfisher. Their delay is not our mistake.' The only saving grace was that I managed to book a ticket for the next day. Now I had to find a hotel to spend the night in Chennai. When I took a prepaid taxi and asked the driver to drop me at a decent hotel, he took me to Hotel Park Plaza in Egmore. Not a bad one. So, that night, quite unexpectedly, I slept in Chennai.

Next morning, an idea struck me. The gossip items in the USB found from Senthil's bag had some mention of this Park Plaza. That was the first thing that came to my mind when I woke up. I've no clue how I'd thought of it at that particular moment. It just occurred, that's all. But why would I have thought of it at all? Was it predestined that my flight would get delayed, that I would miss the Sri Lankan plane, a taxi would take me to this hotel, and that I would remember Senthil the moment I woke up? I wouldn't call it sixth sense, but intuition it certainly was. As if there was some relationship between Senthil and this hotel.

For a long time, I was immersed in these thoughts. The boy who came with coffee was a simple guy. I asked him about breakfast. We talked a bit—about his job, the hotel, its staff. I found out that there was a Malayali at the reception in the shift that would start at 9 a.m. When I went down to have the complementary breakfast, I casually went to the reception and got pally with him. Manoj Thomas. From Balussery. Suddenly, I remembered our Sseri mashu. Sseri sseri, Balussery . . . When I said I was from Diego, he got excited. One of his uncles apparently works with Diego's airport service. He also wanted to go to Diego. By telling him that Diego has a lot of opportunities in the hotel business, that I've a lot of friends there, and that I can easily find him a job, I completely bought him. But I need a small favour, I said, and he agreed without any qualms. After going to my room, I called up the reception. I introduced myself as an officer from Diego's vigilance department. I told Manoj not to speak about this conversation to anyone.

'Can anyone stay here in a fake name?' That was my first question.

'No, especially since there are terrorist issues, it's mandatory to take a photocopy of the identity card before we give anyone a room. It's a strict order from the Chennai Police.'

'So do you keep details of everyone who has stayed here?'

'Yes, at least for three years. After security issues popped up, that too became compulsory.'

'Okay, then what's the way to know if one Senthil from Diego used to stay here regularly?'

'That I can't tell you. It's management policy.'

'What policy? I won't be telling anyone else. This is just between us,' I gave him my word, but that too didn't work.

'Okay, not for free. In return, I promise you a well-paying job at a nice hotel in Diego. How about that?'

Poor guy. He fell for that.

'What's the issue? Was he a criminal there?' Manoj asked.

'Ey. Some swindling of government finances. That's all. A small vigilance inquiry. No big deal.'

'Sure I won't be in any trouble?'

'What trouble . . .? Nothing of that sort. Why should Manoj be scared of some issue in Diego?'

He half-heartedly agreed to let me call him after ten minutes. But I didn't have to; he called me. 'No, nobody in that name has stayed here in the past three years.'

'You must be saying it without checking,' I tested him out.

'No, no. Everything is in the computer. It just takes a three-minute search,' he confirmed.

I was sad that my intuitions were all going wrong.

'Then, please see if anyone from Diego had recently stayed here?' I decided to try one last time.

'Let me see.' After another five minutes, he called again. 'Not recently. But one Faisal Bava had stayed here. Many times.'

'You must be having his photo ID. What's the way to get that?'

'I don't think I would be able to get it for you. From reception, everything gets shifted to the office. A lot of files would have to be searched.'

'Can't that happen if you want to?

'Difficult. I don't have any duty at the office.'

'No, but Manoj knows how to get it done, whom to contact.'

'The office has a peon. I'll have to tell him.'

'Not just tell him, also offer Rs 1000.'

'But I can't get it done soon.'

'No problem. I'll be here for two more days. Within that time, please.'

'Okay.'

I then remembered I had to reschedule the Sri Lankan ticket. I took a shower and went downstairs.

'Sri Lankan Airways has three offices in Chennai,' Manoj said at the reception. 'Kodambakkam, Nungambakkam, and the airport office at Meenambakkam. From here, the closest will be Nungambakkam.'

'Can you please arrange a taxi for me?'

'Why not!'

By the time I flipped the pages of the newspapers at the reception, the taxi had come.

It was my first time in Chennai. I felt suffocated by the city's crowd and traffic. I realized how peaceful Diego was.

'Sir, should I take you to some tourist place too?' the taxi guy asked on the road. It was then that I realized that possibility. What will I do for two days? Even thinking of getting into this crowded mess scared me. I should escape out of this town. There is no need to return today. But I didn't want to go to memorials, parks, beaches and museums, all of which will be crowded. Where else will I go . . .? Somewhere that could turn useful. Suddenly, Pondicherry came to my mind. A place frequented by Senthil. In Anpu's words, to meet his lover. No, I wouldn't follow that trail. How about visiting the house of the coffee shop guy, Abdul Majid. There is no better way than that to know more about Senthil. Since the morning, Senthil has been with me, as if he won't go till I find his secret. Why else will I remember Majid now? Fortunately, I had his number saved in my mobile phone. I called him. He recognized me easily.

'I'm going to Pondicherry now. How can I meet your Amma and Appa?'

'Pondicherry . . .? You . . . You'll meet Amma and Appa?' he asked as if he had got a shock. 'You don't have to go all the way to Pondicherry, it's before that. Ask for Kottakuppam Juma Masjid. Ten houses from there, near Yasar's shop. Nobody will know my name. Appa's name is Sadur. Ask anyone. They'll know. 27 Shalai Street. Kottakuppam post. Villupuram district. Tamil Nadu, 605104. That's my house address.'

All of it came out in one breath.

After collecting the new ticket from the airlines, we left for Pondicherry.

PONDICHERRY

WHILE PASSING THROUGH the arid landscape of Tamil Nadu on our way to Pondicherry, I was mulling over how generations travelled from one land to another. Quite unexpectedly, I was going to another ancestral place of mine. I'd never thought of a Pondicherry trip. But some twists of fate were leading me there. If the flight had not got delayed, if the taxi guy had not taken me to Hotel Park Plaza, if this guy had not asked me at the start of this journey if I would like to go to some tourist place, if I had not then remembered about Pondicherry— then this trip would not have happened. Even when I said Pondicherry, it was not in my mind that this is an ancestral place of mine. I remembered it midway through the drive. This was such a predestined journey. A destiny that I have to be there at every place that my forefathers had been to.

Had my ancestors, who at some period lived in a small street in Lisbon, ever thought of the roads their future generations would be taking? A journey that started in Lisbon to Kochi, then via land to Pondicherry, now rests at Diego. Will this be the final stop . . .? Everyone, at some point, would think that he is at the last point of his journey. In my case, whatever be the pressure of circumstances, I could never thinking of moving away from Diego. Wherever I go, that'll be for a maximum of two years. Then I have to return. I was born and brought up in Diego. I can't leave it for any other place. But now when I think of it, it's all just a romantic feeling. No land belongs to anyone. People move from one place to another. One flows towards favourable circumstances. Even someone as adamant as me might also go. Or my children will go. Or their children. Every baggage of thoughts is temporary. Generations should flow from place to place like a river. Nostalgia doesn't work. My ancestors had realized it. They might have seen every place as a temporary base. When new opportunities came up, they left the old ones and moved forward. No relations chained them to any land. Otherwise, how could Andrew Pereira have moved out of a big city like Lisbon and migrated to a small town like Kochi? Would Hormis Andrapper have abandoned a great granary in Pondicherry and set sail to the marshland of Diego? They must have dreamt of the returns from the new lands. Success is only for those who travel to tomorrow's lands. The Andrapper dynasty knew that.

I felt like calling home. Momma must be worried that there was no news from me. I was supposed to go to France today. They didn't know that I rescheduled the ticket. They might suspect that I've run away this time too. The repercussions of which I've to face when I return.

When I called, Momma was furious. 'Where the hell are you . . .?'

'Chennai. Your Madras. From there, I'm slowly moving in a black Scorpio to the dreamland of our ancestors—Pondicherry. Within minutes, I'll reach the land of promises. Momma, what should I get you from here? Gems? Pearl? Emerald? Tusks? Pepper? *Karinthali* . . .?'

'Wherever you are, just come back here fast. There are some issues here.' When Momma said that, she was close to tears. There was a shadow of fear in her voice.

'What issues, Momma?' I panicked. 'Is Valyapapan all right?' 'Will tell you when you return. Take the next flight and come. Don't delay it.' Before I could ask anything more, she disconnected the phone.

I couldn't continue the journey after that. The fear and worry in Momma's voice had shaken me. Momma is usually

not a feeble heart. This must be some big issue. I asked the
driver to return. 'Why now? We are almost there, it's only a
short while from here,' he said. I didn't listen. In one minute,
Pondicherry had disappeared from my mind. Somehow or
the other, I wanted to reach home.

After reaching the hotel, I checked out immediately. When
Manoj asked, I said I'd got an urgent call from the office and
that I would be back in a week. There was a Mali flight in the
afternoon via Diego. Though there was no seat available, due
to a last-minute cancellation, I could get on it.

I knew the boat guy who took me from the airport to home.
Other than the regular small talk, he didn't ask me anything.
From his conversations, I didn't feel like some big tragedy
that could get public attention had taken place at my home.
Otherwise, he would have talked about it. Could it have been
Momma's drama to make me return? I was suspicious.

But when I stepped into the house, I realized that
something unusual had indeed happened there. This was not
the house familiar to me. It had become dead silent. I could
feel the heat of a tragedy from it. Every house has a character.
Its movement, light, sound, behaviour . . . Even a small change
can be felt by the residents. Before anyone tells them. Only
they will understand it.

Momma held my hand and made me sit on the sofa. She
didn't say anything for a long time. I didn't ask anything
either. But my mind was preparing itself to listen to a tragic
piece of news.

'Your Papa . . .' Momma only said that much.

A splinter passed through me. I stared at her face. Is he dead?

That was the meaning of the stare. I guess she understood it.

'Papa has been missing for the past few days.'

'Missing . . .?'

'Yeah. The day you left, he came rushing in around the afternoon, packed up some necessary things in a suitcase. "There are some issues. I'm moving away for a while. Don't look for me." That's all he said. Then no news.'

'Didn't you ask what the issue was?'

'I asked, but he didn't tell. I'd never seen him so frightened.'

'And you guys haven't looked for him anywhere?'

'Your Chettan has been trying for the past three days. Nobody knows anything. Some say it's about some money dealings at the office. I don't know what to do or whom to ask. I'm really scared, da.'

I, too, had no idea what to do. Fate was taking me through some life moments which I'd never experienced or thought of. Some moments to which I hadn't learnt how to react. The moments that make me distinct from other people.

I went to Valyapapan's room. He was lying under a blanket, unusually.

'What happened?' I went near him.

'Not well, feeling cold.' His voice revealed the fever.

'Should I get some medicine?'

'No, it's okay. I just had a *chukku kappi*. It'll be fine.'

'Did Papa tell you anything before leaving? Like where he was going . . . or something . . .?' I came to the topic.

'He didn't even tell me he was leaving. But I think there is nothing to worry about. Wherever he goes, he won't forget us. Once he is safe, he'll call. I'm sure about it. For a long time now, I've been having a feeling that it's time for us to leave this Diego. He must have felt the same.'

'What makes you feel so, Valyapapan?'

'We are rulers and traders. When we lost both, our ancestors never stayed put. That's our Andrapper family history.'

Without asking anything, I left the room. For me, his words resembled the ramblings of a hopeless dreamer. They had no connection whatsoever with our present lives or events. They won't help to find Papa.

I took the boat and did a round. There was no particular destination. My confused days are always like this. Just keep rowing for a while. The journey will find the destination all by itself. This time, it stopped in front of the North Public Security office.

After getting a verbal thrashing from ID Stephen Andrapper last time, I'd consciously avoided all possible meetings with him. I'd successfully avoided him during Philip Gunavardhane's funeral too. Embarrassed about recommending a fraud to him. But if I continued to cling to my fear, it wouldn't be possible to trace Papa.

Luckily, Stephen uncle was in his office. And he was not busy. I didn't have to say anything. He had heard about Papa. They were very close and shared all secrets. Stephen uncle knew more about Papa's private life than I did. But he, too, had no idea why Papa had left. He suspected that Papa must have left the country. But not by air. Stephen uncle had already checked that. There was no inquiry against Papa from the government's side. 'Papa is not a swindler. He is a synonym for discipline and detail,' Stephen uncle said clearly. 'All other news are made-up ones.' Then, where is Papa? Why did he leave . . .? Both of us got stuck before these questions.

'I'm doing everything possible from my side. Don't worry. Nothing will happen to him. We'll find him,' Stephen uncle tried to assure me. I sat there helplessly for some more time, and then got up in disappointment.

ART OF LIVING

THAT NIGHT, FOR the first time, I went to Papa's office room. When everyone in the house, living in the shadow of sadness, went to their bedrooms, an idea struck me. To open and see Papa's room. To see and feel the secrecy of the room, which I'd never entered for the past twenty-eight years. He must have left at least a clue, even if unintentional. As far as I've heard, it was not a planned exile. It was only a reaction to a sudden situation. If there was some secret behind it, then he wouldn't have had the time to hide it. So I was hoping to find something in the room that could lead me to Papa.

As a kid, I had not been allowed to enter the room. And not just me, everyone in the house. Though Papa had never said so, still everyone observed it as an unwritten rule. When I grew up, the room faded away from my memory. Like a strange, dark hole in the house, the room was blank to me. Now I stood in that room with the curiosity of getting introduced to a new man. I'd never seen an office room kept so neat and tidy. Papers and files were in order. A clean table. Two or three pens in a cup with a picture of a kangaroo. A small globe. An old pager. A tiny bell. A notepad. A three-in-one smoking set. A table calendar. A picture of St. Antony. A rosary. A small doll. Some finance, politics and law books on the table and the shelf. On the wall, a wooden Buddha seated on a snake. On top of the shelf, a small pharaoh.

Instantly, I felt high regard for Papa, and a little jealousy. I've never thought such a civilized way of life existed in his character. I was of the opinion that he was a wealthy, coarse man who lived immersed in his accounts. Even an aspirational writer like me didn't have such a beautiful table. On my desk, you would only find scattered papers, old books, cap-less pens and empty tea glasses. I realized that there existed another Papa beyond my comprehension. A Papa whom I did not know. I went through every paper and book in the room searching for the new Papa. I was in the room till past midnight. I found an old diary in his drawer, about three years old. With curiosity, and the guilty feeling of overhearing a confession secret, I flipped the pages one by one . . . Most of them were accounts about cash transactions. From insurance amount to electricity bill, everything had been recorded in it. The diary showed me that he had done bigger dealings with people than I expected. Most of the names were unknown to me. Names that never figured in regular conversations at the dinner table. These must have been contacts outside his friends' circle. I wondered what business Papa was doing to be able to handle so much money. He had some investments in the share market. Other than that, I never thought he and the Andrapper family would have these many movable assets. The diary said nothing about his daily life. So, it wasn't a book that revealed Papa's life. I combed the room further, and stumbled upon a few photo albums. I was seeing them for the first time. It was customary to call a photographer during every function at home, but I never knew where these photos were kept. I was under the notion that the exercise was just a show-off act and the photos never got collected afterwards. But Papa's discipline in arranging the photos surprised me. His account book and the photos justified his right to shout at my laziness.

I went through each album carefully. It was a huge collection of photos old and new. It could be called a visual archive of the Andrapper family history. If Valyapapan had collected history through books, Papa did it through these photos. It had images of all the major events and functions.

With dates and captions for each. Starting with a few tattered images of Valyappachan and Valyamooma, it moves on to Papa's childhood pictures. Various stages of his growth. The glory days of the Andrapper family are engraved in the photos. Photos of celebrations, get-togethers and parties with a lot of people; photos of leisure trips to various countries; photos of the Andrapper house hosting famous world leaders; photos of weddings, baptisms and holy masses; photos of deaths and funerals . . . A long period of time was floating in front of my eyes. Through these photos, I was seeing many events in my life for the first time or remembering them after a long time.

'My first love' read a black-and-white photo among them, of a young girl. Someone who was ten times prettier than Momma! It opened before me another secret door to Papa. Oh God, there was a lover in Papa too? He had a heart that could fall in love? I couldn't believe it. What had happened to that lover? Why didn't that marriage take place.? Was he living all these years holding that love inside? Where was this girl now? Is she still inside his heart? A bunch of questions that were like riddles. For a minute, I even thought that he might have eloped with her after all these years.

Other than the private and family photos, the rest were party pictures taken at night. I tried anxiously to find out whether his friends who were not known to me would be there. But there was no one in them whom I didn't know or had not seen before. I was disappointed. Without any oversight, Papa had hid those who he had to hide. I was almost wrapping up my search. But the photos in an album that I got from the corner of a shelf really shocked me. It was of a party at a hotel terrace at night. With a glittering pool as a background, Papa was raising a wine glass, saying cheers, and with him I found a familiar face, smiling, and this started burning me from inside. Dr Iqbal! Papa and him? What's the relationship? They must have some connection, something that I missed, I tried to pacify myself. But the next photos shattered me. It was easy to recognise another face. With a wine glass in hand, it was a half-naked Jesintha! In the next photo, papa was holding her close! In another one, Papa and she were saying cheers to a stranger. Another one had more unknown people—to me—with papa. Then women posing with Papa. Visuals of them sharing booze with him. Of them sitting on his lap. I got worried whether what Jesintha had said might be true. The last photo was the one that struck me the most. Papa and Jesintha at a dinner table. Opposite them, the guy who was there in Anpu's phone video!

PHONE BOOK

NEXT MORNING, WITHOUT any notice, the Public Security raided our house. Officials of the law department and vigilance barged into the house without asking permission and started searching. It surprised us that Stephen uncle was also among them. He ignored us and even Valyapapan, and acted like an honest officer. When I had gone to meet him yesterday, he had told me there was no probe against Papa. Now he himself was at the helm of it. If he had come to know about it only this morning, he could still have called and told us. Not for anything, but just to prepare the mind. But he didn't. Okay, let it be. We have nothing to hide. Andrapper House is an open house. Anyone can walk in any time. But Momma was perturbed. Valyapapan's expression was that of a total loser's. This must be a first in their lives. A Diego law officer coming to them with an order! They have only seen officers who obey. It took a while to pacify them. The officers took everyone to a room and checked the house for hours. They spent most of the time in the Room of the Forefathers and Papa's office. They came out with lots of diaries from Papa's room that I'd missed yesterday. From the ancestral room, they seized documents of the Andrapper family history and of the deals with the French government. Valyapapan, in a feeble voice, tried to stop them from taking the official records of the family, but the officers didn't pay any heed. From Chettan's room, they took the laptop and some CDs, calling them 'suspicious'. From my room, they couldn't get anything incriminating. So, in a fit of anger, they took Theogin's *A French Ship's Journey to India 1642* and *Kanyabhogasooktham*. The other books of mine were all literary. Who wants them? But I was left wondering from where they got the *Kanyabhogasooktham* that had been missing for some days. Luckily, I had taken Papa's diary that I had read and the photo albums to my room. When the officers came, I had thrown them in the laundry basket. So they were not found.

After the swoop had gone on for four long hours, Stephen uncle came to our room with other senior officers. Their faces were not familiar. 'None of you should leave Diego. The country is confiscating your passports. If Mathew Andrapper calls you or if you get any news of him, you should inform the Public Security immediately. Nobody should try to act over-smart. Remember that everyone is under our observation,' said Stephen uncle.

'What did he do?' asked Momma. They replied with just a harsh stare. A long while after that, the house was numb. The kitchen maids who had left the house during the raid stood panicked at the steps and the compound. Nobody understood anything. What was happening or what could be done. None of our relatives or friends came or called. We didn't want help from anyone, but we wanted to know what the charge was against Papa. But nobody came forward with anything. That's how friendships are—for good times.

I survived those moments when time stood still by going through my mobile's phone book. The names that appeared were not mere names. They were memories. They were long relationships. They were time periods. They were dreams and hopes and promises. But I didn't bother to renew any relationship or promise. But then came Daniel D'Silva's name. My fingers stopped there. After thinking for a long time, I decided to call him. I needed to know what exactly was happening here. But he seemed to know of it only when I told him. So that means not many have come to know of it in Diego. Fortunately.

'I'll call you back in ten minutes,' he said. But after half an hour when he didn't call, I got annoyed and called him. He didn't pick up. I realized he was avoiding me. The contempt I felt for myself! Why did I call, I thought. After a while, a message came—from Daniel. 'Sorry, I can't tell you that. Be careful. Don't contact me again.'

That message worsened my confusion. The photos that I saw yesterday, Jesintha's words that Papa was a womanizer, and this message from Daniel D'Silva all put together had started to give me a sore head. What crime could Papa have committed that he couldn't reveal it to me? Did he steal something? Kill someone? Rape? I wanted to share my thoughts with someone. But with whom? Chettan was weaker than me. Momma and Valyapapan were already miserable. Who else was there? A friend? A girlfriend? No, no one. Oh God. After twenty-eight years on this earth, when I needed to share my worries during a crucial time, I found myself so lonely. Why did I have to live this long? If I had failed to make a single good friend, how could I be called a human being?

I pulled out some photos from Papa's album, stuffed them into my pocket, and left for Port Louis. Jesintha was my target. She was the only route left to reach Papa. I had to find her even if she avoided me or hid from me. On the way, I called her. I thought she wouldn't pick up, but she surprised me again. When I told her I wanted to meet her, she agreed to be at the regular coffee shop in half an hour. On my way, I told myself a thousand times that this time I wouldn't stumble over my words, that I would see through all her designs. Halfway to the coffee shop, I remembered Abdul Majid. I'd told him that I would go to his Pondicherry house, now what will I tell him? What excuse can I give? So I went to a shop on the other side of his. I sat in the corner so that I could see Jesintha from a distance, and ordered coffee. Suddenly, someone patted me on my shoulder. I shuddered and turned around. It was Vijay Mullikratnam!

He grinned.

'Dude, long time. What's up? No new cases?' he asked, as if making fun of me.

'Of course. A missing-person case. Why, can you find him for me?' I retorted with some bite.

'Oh God . . . again a missing case? I'm fed up with you. Okay, give this to me in writing. Within two days, I'll find the person. Nobody has understood the real Vijay Mullikratnam,' he said, stretching his chest.

'OK then, take this. My Papa has been missing for the past few days. Are you capable of finding him?' I didn't relent.

'Who? Your father? That nice man? What happened to him . . .?' he appeared surprised.

'I told you. Missing. Just missing. You are a smart officer. Can you find him?'

'Are you serious? Or are you making fun of me?' He was not convinced.

'Actually, I was making fun of you. But what I said is true. Papa is missing.'

'Your Papa? He was one of my best friends. What happened to him?' He seemed not to believe it.

'Best friend? Still the smart officer doesn't know what has been going on? What a pity!' I poked him further.

He didn't reply. He sat brooding for a while and then went out and rang up someone. Then he rang up more and more people. At first I looked at him with contempt. But this faded when I saw him making so many calls and the changing expressions on his face. My heart was beating furiously. I understood that he was getting some serious information.

'What has happened, sir?' I went to him.

He put his hand around my shoulder and took me to a secluded place. 'Junior Andrapper, I have been on suspension for the past one month. I didn't know a thing. The department thinks that I've taken a bribe from some group in India to settle the Senthil case. I have not taken any money from anyone. I don't need to do it. The person who asked me to settle the case is your relative, Stephen Pereira. He is still a favourite of the department. Welcome to Diego.'

'Tell me what has happened to my Papa . . .'

'You really don't know that yet?'

'No, I swear!'

'Don't panic. Some four days ago, he was arrested from Diego airport!'

'Arrested? But Stephen uncle said . . . Papa was . . .' I fumbled for words.

'I don't know about that. As far as I know, he is in some jail.'

'For what? What crime did my Papa commit?'

'Dude, I'm really sorry. I am under suspension!'

He left me there and walked away. I felt all alone, as if I was the only man on earth.

CRIMINAL

JESINTHA HAD CALLED me at least three times before I took her call. I was numb.

'Where are you? After saying this was urgent and all . . .?' She was angry.

I took her to the coffee shop where I had been sitting.

'What has happened to you? You look like you have some disease,' she said.

It was true. I felt exhausted, ill.

'What has happened to my Papa?' I asked, leaning on the bench.

'Your Papa . . .? How do I know . . .?'

'You know. You know. I won't let you go unless you tell me.' I grabbed her like a mad man.

'Are you drunk?' she asked and shoved me away.

'Jesintha, you've fooled me in the past saying many things. This time I won't leave you. I won't fall for your words. Tell me, where is my Papa?'

People at the coffee shop started noticing us. Some of them gathered around us and started being protective of Jesintha. But she discouraged them, saying it was a private matter. She then took me out for a walk. 'I know you aren't drunk. Tell me, what has happened to you?' She held me as if I were a patient and made me sit on a roadside bench.

'You know why my Papa ended up in jail. Jesintha, please, you should tell me . . . Please.'

'Your Papa in jail? I don't even know him, da. Really. How will I then . . .?' There was genuine helplessness on her face.

'You don't know him for sure?' I asked her.

'No.'

I took the photo out from my pocket and threw it in front of her. 'Now say again that you don't know my Papa.' She took it and sat looking at it for a long time.

'You don't know him?' I repeated the question.

She sat there staring at the photo, without uttering a word.

'You don't know him even a bit?' I asked her again.

'I know . . .' she broke the silence. 'But I didn't know he was your Papa!'

'Jesintha, please. Again, you're playing games. We are stuck in a terrible situation. I've come to know that Papa is in jail. I want to know the reason. At least now you should tell me the truth. How did you come to know Papa? What's the relationship between the two of you?'

'The relationship between a smuggler and a customs officer! The kind of ties the two of them can have, we have all of them!'

'Smuggler? My Papa?'

'Yes, he is!'

'I will never believe it.'

'I will not insist you believe me. But it's the truth. He is one of the notorious but intelligent criminals in this island!'

'Jesintha, don't make a fool of me. He's the most perfect gentleman I've ever seen. To evade my questions, don't think you can say anything you want.'

'That means I know him more than you know him,' Jesintha said with confidence.

'What proof do you have?'

'The photo you've bought to trap me is more than enough.'
Suddenly, I felt crestfallen.

'What does he do?'

'Anything that can get him easy money. He exports arms from land to land . . .'

'Since when did you know about this?'

'I know that he has been in this business for over twenty years. We two know each other for at least five years.'

'Five years! And still when you hear he is in jail, why are you not feeling even a tad of pain, or even sympathy?'

'For what?' She laughed. 'Our only connection had to do with making money. Nothing more. Even the hug in the photo you brought was in celebration of a multi-crore deal. Those who do these kinds of businesses sometimes become successful. Sometimes they get caught. Some stay in jail for some time and then get out using influence. Everyone knows about these things. There is nothing to worry about. Go home and get good sleep.'

'You can say that. He is just one of your many business partners. But for me, he is my Papa.'

'Being your Papa doesn't make him above the law. Anyone can be caught any time. That's natural. But I'm sure about one thing. Whoever has caught your Papa now has not done it for this business, but for something else . . .'

'How do you know?'

'If this was the matter, the CIDs should have come for us a long time ago. Nothing of that sort has happened.'

'Then what is the reason behind this arrest?'

'I know only a small part of that man's life. The rest is a blank for me. To arrest someone in Diego, there don't have to be a lot of reasons.'

'I don't disbelieve you. Every time I've thought I shouldn't trust you, you've beaten me with your words. This time too. So just one more question. What's the connection between Senthil's death and my Papa?'

'Sorry, I don't get you.'

'Does my Papa have a hand—direct or indirect—in Senthil's murder?'

'Definitely no.'

From my pocket, I took out the photo which had Jesintha, Papa and the murderer, and showed it to her.

'One of the guys who shot down Senthil was him. I'm sure. What do have to say now?'

'I stand by what I've said,' she said, returning the photo. 'He's just an ordinary criminal who can be bought off and used.'

'What proof is there that my Papa hasn't used him?'

'He might have used him. Many times. But not in Senthil's case. According to your Papa, Senthil was a marked man. But before he could get it done, someone else did it. Your Papa himself had told me this.'

'Then who was it?'

'I don't look at issues that don't affect me.'

'You don't look at them, but you know about them, right?'

'No, Christy. Even in Senthil's life, there are areas which I don't know about.'

I got up to leave. She, too.

'Jesintha, one last question. The girl who died. The nurse Melvin. Was her death natural or a murder?'

'I shouldn't be talking about things I don't know about. But I'll tell you something I've come to know. She had put her feet on the boat and someone shook the boat at that time. That's how she slipped and fell. He was a criminal. I don't know on whose orders the person did that.'

I didn't wait to hear the rest.

BETRAYAL

JESINTHA HAD GOT the better of me again—either with a great lie or with pure truth. I didn't have enough of an arsenal with me to dig deeper and know the real picture. She was too tall a wall for me to vault over. I had no other option but to believe her. Like a ferocious wave that slammed itself to death on a rock front, I returned helplessly.

Nothing had changed at home. But the assumption that the whole thing was connected to Papa's monetary issues at the workplace had got stronger. I didn't bother to correct it. Let it remain so. Otherwise, I would have to do a lot of explaining. And even if I do, who will understand? Believe? But I knew that there was one person in the house who would know everything. Valyapapan! He's hiding it on purpose. He's acting as if he is ignorant. I have to make him speak.

I went upstairs determined to do it. Valyapapan was not in his usual recliner. I could hear a slight whimper. I walked around. I followed the sound and reached the room of the forefathers. Its door was closed. I slowly pushed and it opened. The scene I saw! I was shattered. The room looked as if an earthquake had hit it! This was what remained of the Public Security raid. God, how many years and generations and layers of memories got wrecked in a single day! Books were lying scattered, historical records destroyed, untied palm tree manuscripts, broken plates of handwritten signs, torn paintings of ancestors, smashed pieces of their favourite objects . . . and on top of it all, Valyapapan lying and weeping like an orphan!

Nobody could wipe away his tears. It was the squall of someone who has lost everything to the sea. I could only sit with him as he cried. Once or twice, I tried to lift him, but he clung harder to the destroyed objects, and continued lying there. He cried and cried, and after he was finished with his tears, he slowly got up. I helped him get back to his chair. Both of us were feeling desperate, but neither he nor I talked about the Room of the Forefathers. Instead, I told him: 'Papa is in jail!'

There was no response from him. His face was expressionless as if he had known it for a long time.

'You know the reason for it. What is it?' I asked.

He remained silent for a long time.

'I want to know. Valyapapan cannot avoid this question,' I said firmly.

'Treason! Betrayal! Coup! Isn't that enough for anyone to be jailed?' Valyapapan said at last.

'Treason?'

'Yes. For them. But for us, it was an attempt to recover. If it had worked out, the crown would have been on my head now. The new flag of Diego would have fluttered atop this house.'

'When did these things take place?' I asked.

'It has been in the making for the past twenty years. We have been preparing for it, using my influence and your Papa's strategies. Each barbecue party held at the backyard of this house arrived at a new decision. But . . .'

'But?'

'This time, too, an Andrapper betrayed us.'

'Who was that?'

'Another Andrapper. I.D. Stephen!'

I felt as if someone had shot at my head.

When I was about to walk away, Valyapapan held my hand. 'Whatever is to be done, do it urgently. Our moments are also numbered. Nobody knows where the secret jails in Diego are!'

My walk led me to my writing table. The rest of that

day—and the entire night—I wrote without wasting a single minute. I didn't even get up to have a drop of water. Memories were flowing into my mind. I didn't have to wait for a single word. The only issue I faced was of the pen not keeping pace with my mind. I wrote and wrote and wrote, and by morning, I fell asleep.

MADNESS

I JUMPED OUT of sleep at some point and started scanning all that I'd written. I was still sleepy. I vigorously scanned a lot of pages. But I got scared about the pending ones. I didn't know what I had written about myself. I divided the scanned section into two and send the first part to the writer Benyamin. The second one I sent to Bilal. The rest of the parts I divided and kept them to be sent to my close friends and dear ones. My plan was to give one part to Anpu and another to Anita. But considering it would be dangerous to leave it at Anpu's house which was frequented by the Public Security, I scanned the part quickly and saved it in Senthil's old USB drive. I decided to send the last part to Meljo. I also wrote a covering letter for each of them, mentioning the content and to whom they should hand it over. I inserted them into envelopes and left home right away. I had not taken a shower. Or brushed my teeth. I had not done any of the morning routines. Not combed my hair. Or changed clothes. Half conscious and half sleepy, I left the house. I took my boat and drove some distance; then I realized that CIDs could be shadowing me. So I left the boat at a jetty in Seleucia and dissolved into the crowd. I moved randomly from street to street, trying to shake off anybody following me. Then I took a line boat and got down at a bay

in Pentasia. From the central post office there, I sent all the
parts of the work, except the last one for Meljo. After that,
I took another boat to Uthukkuli jetty and went to Senthil's
house. On the way, someone tapped me on my shoulder
and asked, 'Why are you coming this way drunk?' I walked
forward without responding. I didn't have the energy to retort.

I knocked at the door of Senthil's house. It was Appa who
came out. He looked at me rather strangely. 'What do you
want?' he asked derisively. 'Appa, I don't want anything. I
just came here to see you people for one last time,' I said. 'To
come here, is this your wife's place?' Appa asked; he seemed
ready for a fight. Actually, I got scared. Why is Senthil's Appa
behaving like this? This was not the way he used to behave
with me. Or is it because he has not recognized me?

'Appa, don't you recognize me? It's me. Senthil's friend.
Your kannan.' I broke down.

'Whose kannan? I had one kannan. He left me. I don't
know you. Leave this place,' Appa dismissed me. 'Appa, I
don't know if I'll see you again. This is my last visit. Before
leaving, I want to tell you one thing. Our Senthil . . . He didn't
die of a heart attack. He was killed!'

'Son of a bitch, you knew it, right? You knew it, right?'
Appa grabbed my neck. 'Then . . . then . . . you . . . You cheated
us all this time. *Poda*, just leave this house. I don't want to
see your face again. You and your Andrapper family will be
plagued for twelve generations!' Appa shouted and pushed
me out. Anpu came to us. She, too, was hostile. She took
Appa inside forcefully.

'Anpu, why is Appa like this?' I asked.

'You go. Here everyone knows that your Dad killed my
Annan. Now don't come here again.' Her tone was harsh.

'My Papa? No . . . Anpu, that can't be true.'

'Please go. Nobody knows what Appa will do next.' She turned back.

'Anpu, one minute,' I called out to her. She stopped. 'This is your Annan's USB. I had come here to return this. One day, someone from the mainland will come here looking for it. Please give it to him. Don't show it to anyone other than him. It has such an important matter. It has Senthil's and my life in it. Someday, he will tell you my true story. It'll be the suspense thriller you once wanted to read.'

I gave it to her. Then, like a lunatic on the prowl, I returned from Cherar Peruntheruvu.

LIFE

FROM THERE, I went to Anita's house. She, too, treated me with contempt. She shouted why I had come there drunk. I gave her the envelope that I had kept for her. Then, like I'd done with Anpu, told her that there was truth in it and to hand it over only to the person who would come from the mainland. After that, I left quickly. I reached Seleucia's post office and sat at the visitor's lobby, writing out all that had happened since I left home in the morning.

Sitting there, I introspected about my life. I think I'm someone who wanted to be somewhere, but reached somewhere else. The place I'd dreamt of and the place I've reached are vastly different. I sometimes felt proud of myself for having a great dream (if becoming a writer is a great dream). Often, I had sympathized with my friends and classmates for failing to realize their ordinary dreams and living ordinary lives. All that time, I'd never tried to look at things through their eyes. Or look at me through their eyes.

There are many friends who have ridiculed my great dream of being a writer. Bilal and Rahim were among them. A loser with paltry dreams, that's what they think of me. To those who believe that money and a rich lifestyle are criteria for greatness, how will I convince them that my dreams are great?

I'd always thought that there was nothing greater than being a writer. But is being a writer the greatest dream? What is a great life? Which is a great life? For Babu, his underworld life is first-class social service, so, isn't that a great life? What about a politician's life ? Or a company owner's who gives jobs to ten people? Won't they, too, be thinking that their lives and their aims are great? That way, isn't the life of anyone who has no regrets great... If one has become what one wants to in life, if one is content with it, that's the greatest life! Nobody then has the authority to sympathize with him or judge him on that.

The only relevant issue is how one remains true to one's life. Jyoti has become a railway clerk and Anita a pharmacist to meet some or the other of their dreams. So, what right do I have to feel pity for them? I couldn't achieve my friends' dream of becoming Diego's chancellor. My dream was something else. Isn't that the case with everyone?

Is my life a success or a failure? At what point of time do we measure it up? The present me is a failed writer. That means I've failed my dreams too. Friends expected me to be a chancellor. On that note too, I'm a failure. If somehow, tomorrow, I succeed in some other way, then how will I be judged? What is the right time to judge the success and failure of life? When uncertainties hang like a pendulum till the last moment of death, who can judge at any particular time whose life is a success and whose isn't?

If a failed attempt to pen a novel puts me in the losers' list (like how my Papa saw it), then the sum total of my short life, experiences and travels should place me in the winners' list. My dear writer, the one who is going to analyse my life in detail . . . what do you have to say after hearing all this . . .? Readers, what do you think? How will you judge me?

I wanted to ask myself more questions and write a lot more. But two people have been watching me for some time now. Maybe it's just my fear. Since a crucial part of my biography is unsafe with me, I'm not taking any risk. Before they can come to me with questions, let me post this to Meljo.

9

Rajaji Nagar

FINALLY, WHEN THE story ends, the narrator and the listener share a sense of vacuum. A despair that there is nothing left to hear or say. We were all immersed in such a sorrow. Till now, our lives were made exciting by the investigation, the search for hidden messages, observations, assumptions, information and debates. All those meetings were thrilling. But nothing remained now. Nothing. Like a bottle deserted by a genie, Andrapper's book lay in front of us. It had no more budding surprises for us.

'After listening to the whole story, whom do you think was right? Andrapper or Meljo?' I asked, breaking the silence.

'There is no ultimate right,' said Mashu. 'Sometimes, there are many rights. And more than one truth. The right called Andrapper is not negated by the right called Meljo. Now it feels like everything came to a close suddenly.'

'We should have got to know about everything after some more time.'

'That's true! I was hoping that at least Meljo would have put us in major confusion, and that we'd have a well-planned operation to enter Valyedathu Veedu and grab Andrapper's book in a hard-fought adventure. It would have been thrilling. Now Meljo has spoilt everything. He also fell for Anil's words,' Biju shared his hope and despair.

'The so-called brave people are all cowards. They cannot even withstand our words. I knew for sure that he would fall for it,' Anil said.

'The thrill and fear and anxiety that these two, Anil and Benyamin, faced at Valyedathu Veedu . . . ho, I also wanted to be a part of it,' Nattapranthan said.

'If you really want to experience it, then we should go to the field again. Who's ready for that?' Biju asked.

'Another twist to this story? What's that?' Nibu asked.

'I've never met him, but after all these days, it feels like Christy Andrapper is one among us. He ditched his novel to take up a responsibility. One which he could never fulfil. We should complete it now. We should find out the killers of Senthil,' Biju said.

'We are just the readers in this story. Beyond that, we don't have any responsibilities to anyone. We haven't given our word that we'll complete what Andrapper left midway.' Nibu became furious.

'Whether we are liable or not, there are some things that I'm curious to know. What is this Uthiyan Cheral Tamil Kazhagam? What were the original data in Senthil's USB drive? Why did Senthil often go to Pondicherry? Who is Faisal Bava, the regular visitor at the Park Plaza? What's his relation with the gossip stories? Does it have any connection with Senthil's murder? If we believe in Andrapper's version that his father was not behind the killing, then who did it?' Nattapranthan asked.

'In this case, we have a responsibility to ourselves, directly or indirectly, that's what I feel, said Mashu.

'Me too. As a person who has been to Diego, I am a bit more excited about this entire thing,' Salim said, supporting Mashu.

'Then let's start from the first question. What is Uthiyan Cheral Tamil Kazhagam? Who can give us the details?' Anil asked.

'It'll be better to start with the second question. Since the USB is our property now, it'll be easier to start with that and then move to Tamil Kazhagam,' Biju suggested.

'Okay, then that's decided. I'm hereby handing over the USB drive to you guys and launching Operation Diego Garcia Part II,' Salim said, and the Thursday Market members clapped and cheered the decision. We moved to the computer there and then and started opening the files one by one.

As Andrapper had written, most of them were nude pictures, and Tamil news and songs. None of us could decode anything suspicious from them. As nobody among us could read Tamil, even the details Andrapper had given about the news couldn't be independently verified.

'This won't help us to know more about Senthil,' Salim said. 'For that, we need to prepare for another journey. To Pondicherry. We have one address left. 27, Shalai Street, Kottakuppam Post, Villupuram District, Tamil Nadu, Pin 605104. Abdul Majid's residential address. That's where we should start our hunt for Senthil.'

'No, it shouldn't be from there,' Nibu interrupted. 'I think we should start from Hotel Park Plaza. From the receptionist Manoj!'

'Will that be possible?' Biju asked.

'Why not? If Andrapper can travel alone from Diego to that place, why can't the seven of us do the rest of the miles?'

'Okay, we'll travel. But who among us?'

'The one looking for a thrill. Let Nattapranthan go,' Nibu suggested.

'I'll go,' Nattapranthan agreed. 'Who'll join me?'

'I'm ready.' I took the responsibility of being the writer.

'Me too,' Salim said.

Thus we decided. According to the plan, two Saturdays

later, on a weekend, which was followed by a public holiday, three of us started out on our trip to Chennai and Pondicherry.

Our plan was to stay at Hotel Park Plaza and start our investigation from there. But once we heard of the room tariffs at the Park Plaza, we dumped the plan. We booked a cheaper hotel nearby and tried to start the probe. But then we came to know that Manoj Thomas, the receptionist who had promised to help Andrapper, had shifted from the place. We approached the boy who had replaced him and asked about Faisal Bava, but he was a pain, not responding to sweet talk or threats. So we had to call off the attempt.

The next day we set off for Pondicherry via Mamallapuram. We roamed around the Pallava temples there for about two hours. That was also fated to be part of the trip.

It was past noon when we reached Kottakuppam. Shalai street was obviously a Muslim neighbourhood. We didn't have to sweat much to find the Juma Masjid and Yazar's shop nearby. When we asked about the house of Abdul Majid who works in Diego, a boy accompanied us to the house. It was a big two-storeyed bungalow. Nobody would imagine that a waiter in a coffee shop in Diego was the owner of the house. It was so palatial. When we said we had come from Diego to tour Pondicherry and that Abdul Majid had told us to come here, his Appa showered us with love. 'He is the blessing of this house. He married off his three sisters. Jobs for five brothers, this house, car, everything we owe to the money he sends from Diego,' Appa proudly presented all the good deeds that Abdul Majid had done for the family in the past twenty years.

When we asked about Senthil who used to visit them regularly from Diego, he screamed, '*Ada paavi*', and slammed his chest. '*Ennada ungalude* Diego, such a gentleman got killed and you couldn't find the killer!' he bawled.

'Did Senthil come here regularly?' Salim asked in broken Tamil.

'Once a month for sure.'

'What was the purpose of his visits? What business was he doing here?' I asked.

'Some official purpose. Who knows!'

Just then, his youngest son, Kabir, who studied in college, came home. We asked him too about the purpose of Senthil's visits. He didn't know the name of the office, but he knew that it was in Rajaji Nagar. That was all we wanted. After having *pakku vada* and tea that Majid's mother affectionately served us, we left the house. Rajaji Nagar was our next target.

'If there are some ten offices there, how will we figure out the right one?' I shared my doubt with the others while in the bus from Kottakuppam to Pondicherry.

'Then we'll go to all ten offices. We'll ask at every place if they knew of one Senthil from Diego,' Salim said with his usual self-confidence.

My worries about Rajaji Nagar turned out to be true. The street was full of office complexes. We walked reading each office name plate. Mother's Service Society, Saraswati Shanmugham Charitable Trust, Urvasi Foundation, Children's Action Trust, Amar Seva Sangham, Vivasayangal Urpathiyalar Sangham, Raj Foundation, Association of Non-traditional Employment, Bhagavan Mahavir Foundation, Tamil Deseeya Pengal Viduthalai Izhakkam, CDDP, ACIK, Dhan Foundation . . . So many non-profit, charity and NGO offices!

'God, we have so many social workers and still India is struggling with poverty and inequality,' said Nattapranthan, placing his hand on his head.

Even Salim, who was confident that we would 'ask at

every place' got discouraged by the number of offices. We were confused where to start our search from. But after two or three turns, when we reached the third street, we saw a board in English and Tamil, in front of which we stood dumbstruck for around ten minutes.

Uthiyan Cheral Tamil Kazhagam!

Excited with the find, Nattapranthan hugged me. 'This is the real snake we were hunting down!'

But I was feeling uneasy. A fear about what kind of trouble we were getting into. Salim led us inside, as if ready to face any consequences. We followed him.

There was one peon there. We struggled a lot to converse with him because of his indecipherable Tamil. Somehow, we made him understand that we needed to meet some senior person. The boy called up the office secretary. He came within ten minutes. Luckily, he knew some Malayalam!

When we told him we were tourists from Diego and that we had heard of this organization before and wanted to know more, he took us to his office room. He gave us brochures and described the activities of Uthiyan Cheral Kazhagam.

'It is a non-profit organization that works for Tamils across the world. Anyone can work with us, no matter what his religion or caste or group or politics. Our main aim is to protect orphans and widows. Also, to nurture the basic talents of people, encourage them to be good citizens, help them succeed in life. . . we work for all that. We also do career-development courses, facilitates the conducting of IQ and aptitude tests, and promotes Tamil language and culture. Last year, we did an aptitude test for around eight lakh children across the world. We have adopted 120,000 orphaned kids. Last year, we distributed forty tonnes of rice among the poor. All this was possible thanks to God Almighty . . .' he kept talking.

'Do you have any branches in Diego Garcia?' I asked, interrupting his discourse.

'Not just Diego, we have branches in all countries. Local clubs and societies help us with that. In Diego, a group called Madras Tamil Munrum is affiliated to us,' he said after checking a long list.

'One Senthil used to come here from Diego regularly. What was that for?' Salim asked.

'Senthil . . . Who is that?' He didn't seem to know.

'The same Senthil who was shot dead in Diego!' When I said that, he was taken aback. But he recovered quickly.

'Why, you don't know Senthil?' I asked in a serious tone.

'Actually, who are you guys? What do you want?' That question showed that he knew Senthil.

'We work with a newspaper in Diego. The fax you had sent was to our paper.'

'That was a while ago. Why are you asking about it now?'

'It is now that the Diego police have started looking at it. One police officer has already been suspended. Our *Diego Daily* wants to do a follow-up story. Please tell us the details you know about the case,' said Nattapranthan.

'When you write your newsreports, please don't put our name. It's bad for an organization like us that does charity work. That's a request I have for you.' He was almost begging us.

'Yeah, we agree to that,' Nattapranthan said. 'Under no circumstances will we use your name or the organization's name. Tell us all you know.'

'Udiyan Cheral Tamil Kazhagam has an agent in every country. They come here once in a while. There is nothing special about it. That's just part of their social commitment. When I heard such a nice person suddenly died, I had some doubts. So I sent the fax . . .'

'What's the reason for you having those doubts?'

'He was working there in the tax office, right? He always used to say that he had a lot of enemies.'

'Who were those enemies, did he ever tell you?'

'Who knows! Must be those who didn't want to pay tax, who else . . . You have to find out who they are.'

'There are many stories in Diego linking Uthiyan Kazhagam with the murder. Do you have anything to say on that?'

'People can make up stories. For a social organization like ours that is running well, there will be a lot of stories written about us. We don't care,' he said with contempt.

'Do you have anything more on Senthil to tell us?'

'No, this is all I know.'

Knowing that we would not be able to get more from him, we left. The rest of the day, we roamed around Pondicherry. Late in the night, we returned in a bus to Ernakulam.

Later, the Thursday Market called the trip the most non-productive trip we've ever had. Salim opposed it, saying that we should not expect every trip to be totally successful or that it should reveal a trove of secrets. But all three of us regretted that we didn't discover more during the trip.

'Next time, we'll bring a bomb that'll surprise you all,' Nattapranthan challenged.

Though he said that in jest, such a challenge was in my mind too!

CELEBRATION

I WAS IN that daring state of mind when I got a call from Jijo quite unexpectedly.

'Sir, the matter you had asked me to find out, that ceremony . . .'

'Yeah, yeah, any details of that?' I hurriedly asked.

'No, but there is one thing. There is some event planned next week at Valyedathu Veedu. I overheard Appachan here telling Ammachi. I asked them, but they didn't tell me much.'

'You have any idea what it is about, Jijo?'

'My engineering brain tells me that there is only one speciality for the day that Appachan was talking about. It was the same day, a year ago, that Melvin's forty-one-day ceremony was carried out. If there is celebration on that day, that means the ritual Andrapper had seen will be repeated. I am guessing this, what do you think?'

'Full marks to your engineering brain. I guess you are right. Even in science, such assumptions lead to the truth. We have to somehow find the truth this time. Can Appachan be swayed?'

'Don't think so. He is tough.'

'What's his weakness? We'll use that.'

'I've been trying to find that out for the last ten to twenty years. He's a difficult catch.'

'OK. Let me discuss this with my Thursday Market. I will call you back.' That day itself I gathered the gang and presented the matter. Nobody had any idea how to buy off Jijo's Appachan. But everyone agreed that this chance should not be wasted at any cost.

For that, it was decided that two of us would go and meet Jijo and make a plan for the crucial day. To restore the pride lost in the Pondicherry trip, Salim and Nattapranthan volunteered to go. Accordingly, they went to Kothamangalam College to meet Jijo. Knowing that he had our support and help, Jijo's excitement increased. During their meeting, a plan came up. On the morning of the day of celebration, Jijo goes to Valyedathu Veedu as if on a casual visit. He'll hide a camera without anyone noticing. Salim promised to get a small movie camera that could hold its charge for around twelve hours. After planning to meet on the appointed day at Udayamperoor, they dispersed.

None of us had such a camera. Salim contacted one of his friends in Bangalore and got a camera that could retain its charge for a decent time. With that, we arrived Udayamperoor. Salim, Anil and I were in the team. As decided, Jijo arrived in front of Udayamperoor's Old Church at 5 p.m.

We had tea at a nearby restaurant and discussed the itinerary.

'Look, Jijo, it's our responsibility to protect you in this operation. We'll even die, but won't betray you. You have to trust us. This is a joint operation. Success is our common aim,' Anil said.

'The visuals we shoot will be attributed to Andrapper. So we should capture them from where he had stayed before: Melvin's room on the second floor. To be precise, the money plant that obstructed his view should still be there. If possible, we should place the camera among its leaves. Then we are safe,' Salim said.

'Now, let Jijo go to Valyedathu Veedu to get a feel of what's happening there. Let's think of the camera later,' I suggested.

'No, give me the camera. I'll do things according to the circumstances.' Jijo appeared confident.

Salim handed the camera to him and explained its settings and operation. 'Okay, then. We'll be right here. If you need any help, please call.'

We went to the Old Church and walked around it. Then went to Thaikkattamma's chapel. It had been renovated through the donation of some believer in the Gulf. We thought of going to Poothotta to see Martha Mariam Church and Melvin's grave, but then Jijo called. 'I'm coming. Please wait.' Within ten minutes, his bike came and stopped in front of our car. We got out anxiously. 'What happened?'

'I've placed it.' His hands were shaking while he said it. 'Some three or four Appachans and Ammachis have come. When he was busy talking to them, I went upstairs. I kept it where you wanted it to be kept. Now that money plant has grown bigger. Nobody will be able to spot the camera. Now it just needs to be switched on.'

Anil hugged him to make him relax.

'If no issue pops up, I'll stay there tonight. Then I can also see the whole thing in person,' Jijo said, kick-starting his bike.

'Either way it's okay. But call us.' We bid him goodbye with a thumbs-up gesture.

To avoid any suspicion, we also started our car and drove away.

It was around seven in the night. Eight. Nine. Ten. There was no call yet from Jijo. When we tried to call, it said he was out of coverage area. In between, there was a string of calls from Nibu and company to know about the developments. The more time passed without any news, the more worried we became. 'Shall we go there?' Salim asked. 'No, he is smarter than us. And bold,' Anil stopped him. We waited till midnight. Then we lost all hope and returned to Ernakulam. We took a hotel room. None of us could sleep. Our thoughts were all about Jijo. A gnawing fear that we had put him in trouble. Nobody said it aloud, though.

I dozed off sometime in the morning. When the phone rang, I jumped up from the bed. It was Jijo. I was so angry. 'Where the hell were you till now? Why didn't you call?'

'I will explain in detail. Where are you guys?'

I told him the hotel's name.

'Okay, I'm coming there.'

I woke up Salim and Anil. Within an hour or so, the room bell rang, and all three of us rushed to the door.

'Are you all right?' That's the first thing we all asked when Jijo entered.

'All good. Operation successful!'

'Then why didn't you call? You know how worried we were . . .?'

'I couldn't call. I'll tell you in detail,' he sat on the sofa. We sat around him.

'When I arrived at night, a lot of people were there. All familiar faces—relatives and near ones. Around fifty of them. Meljo panicked when he saw me. He asked me why I had not left. I lied that my bike had a puncture on the way, so I came back.

'Why are so many people here,' I asked. "Oh, you forgot . . . tomorrow is Chechi's anniversary," he told me a big lie. In between, he took my mobile phone saying he'll return it soon. Then it went missing. "I had kept there, I'd given it back to you, the kids must have taken it . . ." and such other excuses. He also made sure that I wouldn't stay there overnight. He led me to a room at a nearby guest house.'

'So did our camera plan fail?' Anil asked.

'No, let me continue. I got an opportunity during dinner. I quietly went upstairs and switched it on. It was good that we had concealed it there beforehand. It would have been impossible to get it there at night. I prowled around the house twice at night, hoping I would get to hear something. But not a single sound was audible.'

'What would have taken place there?'

'That's what we have placed the camera there for,' Jijo

said, taking out the camera from his pocket. Anil snatched it with excitement. Salim brought his laptop and connected the camera.

'Then, where did you find your mobile?' I asked him.

'That's the joke. In the morning, when I had gone to retrieve this camera, the phone was lying there on the sofa. Switched off. Meljo blamed the children again.'

'The Appachans who had come left in the night itself?'

'No, no. They are having a mass at the church for Melvin, for name's sake.'

By then, the video started playing. All of us became silent. There was not much in the beginning. Images of people walking here and there. But to know that the camera had indeed worked was a relief. Then slowly, people started gathering in the courtyard. Excitement gripped us. After some time, Meljo came and placed a lamp in the middle of the hall. People sat around it and started clapping hands and singing. The audio was not very clear. Two priests came towards them.

Suddenly, everything turned dark. We were shocked. Oh God, what's this! We all slammed our hands on our heads. When we checked again, it was a leaf that had fallen on the camera.

With hope and curiosity, we forwarded the entire video. But nothing more was there in it. In the dark-green vagueness created by the leaf, we could only get some audio of the songs and ringing of bells. We were all depressed. For a long while, we couldn't talk to each other. Out of sadness, our words got stuck in the throat. My eyes were filled with tears. Jijo started crying.

'This is more than enough . . . to suck the venom out of that snake. Leave it to me,' Anil said after a while, with some plan in mind. We stared at him, wondering what he could mean. 'Benyamin and I are going to meet him again,' Anil said.

'Today itself?' Jijo asked.

'No, another day. Benyamin, you call him up and make an appointment.'

I called Meljo. When I said I wanted to meet him, he tried to avoid me at first, but then agreed, saying that I could meet him after two weeks.

'Okay then. Let's disperse now.'

We said bye to Jijo.

THE FALL

WHEN WE REACHED Valyedathu Veedu yet again. Meljo was busy with a seva. After some time, he came out with someone whose face looked familiar. I whispered to Anil asking who he was. Anil said he was an upcoming politician and reminded me of the TV discussion that he had participated in.

After seeing him off, Meljo came to us. 'What new problem have you guys brought?' He was visibly irritated by our visit, but we were not bothered.

'We have not come to ask you annoying questions. The other day, we got a video. We want to confirm its contents. We'll return soon without hindering your sevas and ceremonies,' Anil said.

'We could have shown it to others and clarified it, but since we two have become close, we thought that should be avoided,' I said.

'Someone from Diego had sent it. With the caption that it was from Andrapper's mobile phone,' Anil said.

'What video are you talking about?' Meljo was getting angry.

'About the celebration that took place that day!'

'When?'

'We had asked about it the last time we came here. But Meljo, you avoided it tactfully. You asserted that Andrapper was a liar and that no such celebration had taken place.'

'God is not blind, Meljo. He won't erase anything without leaving proof. Otherwise, we wouldn't have got this video.'

'If you think you can blackmail me like this, you're mistaken. I think you still don't know whom you're playing with. You guys go and do something better, I've other work.' He stood up and started walking towards the inside.

Suddenly, Anil got up and held his hand out. 'Stop, Meljo. Just one minute. You see this and then decide. You'd said this house has no secrets. That there was no celebration that night. But this camera has every visual of that night. Andrapper had shot them with his mobile camera.'

Anil took the camera from his bag and showed it to Meljo.

I was startled. The visuals in it could easily be laughed off as a general gathering or an evening prayer.

But it wasn't Anil who got the calculations wrong, but me. With Amit's daring move, Meljo tumbled over.

'I don't want to see it. I knew that he would cheat,' Meljo said in a worn-out tone.

'Then tell me, what are these ceremonies ?'

'Who all have you shown this to?' It was evident from his tone that he had succumbed.

'We have a friends' circle. Five to six people. Only they have seen it till now,' Anil said, about to put the camera back in his bag. Meljo quickly snatched the camera out of his hand. But Anil didn't panic. I was surprised with the way Anil was handling the situation.

'No use, Meljo. Don't think we are such big fools that we'd come here with just one copy of the video.'

Meljo gave back the camera to Anil, and fell back on the sofa. It was the fall of someone who had missed his last stride.

Anil came and sat next to him. 'Tell us, Meljo, what was it?'

But Meljo wouldn't reply.

'We have to know about it for sure. And we'll go to any extent to know it. If you don't tell us, we'll have to ask other people. Not one, but many people. From common men to historians. We'll have to post these video in public forums—Internet, mails, blogs, newspapers, YouTube, everywhere. That means the secret that you want to hide from us will go out to a lot of people. Isn't it better that you yourself tell us? It's for you to decide!'

Those words had an effect on Meljo. He slowly got up.

'Tell us, Meljo. You can start from where Christy had stopped . . .' Anil encouraged him to speak.

'If you promise that you won't show this video to anyone else, I'll speak.'

'Yes, it's a promise. We won't share the visuals in this camera to anyone. I swear in the name of Thaikkattamma!' Anil said.

Meljo looked at me. I nodded, meaning he could trust us.

'If I talk about the ceremony without giving an idea about Villarvattom Swaroopam, you probably won't understand. The same thing had happened to Christy.' Meljo began, taking us outside to a bench on the verandah.

VILLARVATTOM

'THE VILLARVATTOM THOMA kings were a Nasrani dynasty that has a history and tradition of about 1000 years. The estate was a vassal of the Chera kings, and it had its capital at Mahadevapatanam for a long time. Later it was shifted to Udayamperoor when the Arabs invaded the island.'

'This is a myth we have kept hearing for ages. Do you have any concrete proof to show that such a dynasty existed?' I asked Meljo.

'The first proof is the Udayamperoor church which is still there, and the cemeteries of the Thoma kings. The Udayamperoor Old Church was a royal cathedral built by the Chaldean bishops, Mar Sabor and Mar Proth, who came from Persia in 510 AD. For a long time, the church was known after the Chaldean bishops, but with the arrival of the Portuguese, their names were removed since they were seen as anti-Christs, and the church came under the Catholic priests of Mar Gervasius and Protasius. Another strong proof is a letter written by Pope Eugene IV in 1439, before the advent of the Portuguese. The pope accepted this dynasty as the real Christians, and sent the letter through an envoy. Unfortunately, the messenger couldn't reach here, but a copy of the letter is still in the Vatican records.

'"To my most beloved son in Christ, Thomas, the Illustrious Emperor of the Indians, Health and the Apostolic benediction. There often has reached us a constant rumour that Your Serenity and also all who are the subjects of your Kingdom are true Christians." That was the content of the letter.

'Then what changes did the Portuguese make to the Villarvattom Swaroopam?'

'Actually, the first group of Christians from Europe were cordially welcomed by the Nasrani king, Thoma. When they landed in Kochi, King Thoma received them, along with Unniramavarma Koyi Thampuran. He expressed his joy by handing over his royal sceptre to Vasco da Gama. He also helped them set up trading facilities in Kochi. It was the scholars of Villarvattom who taught Malayalam to Andrew Pereira. But when they came to know that the Thoma kings were Chaldean, the mentality of the group, including Vasco da Gama's, changed. They wanted the entire authority of Villarvattom to be handed over to the Portuguese. Da Gama interpreted the handing over of the sceptre as transfer of power. So, in the first visit itself, the Portuguese were at odds with King Thoma. That's how they made the trade deal with only the Kochi kings, and returned. Later on, at every visit of da Gama and Cabral, there were attempts to invade the Villarvattom Swaroopam. But King Thoma held on to his fort. When the attempts to seize the land failed, they tried to invade with faith. That's how the Roman Archbishop Alex de Menazis was sent here. It can be said that Menazis, to a certain extent, succeeded in imposing the Catholic faith over the Malankara Chaldean faith. Except four families, including ours, everyone was a willing convert from Chaldean to Catholicism. That's how the Synod of Diamper was held in 1599 and the Malankara church fell under the control of the Pope. At that time, Menazis tried to burn all the Malankara prayer books and literature in the Pali language in front of the Udayamperoor church. He succeeded to an extent. And he stopped all prayers and ceremonies in the Pali language and initiated the Latin system. More than a difference of faith, it was a revenge on King Thoma.

'That incident ignited the anger of the Malankara king, Thoma. "I would have forgiven everything, but these Parangis destroyed the language of my ancestors. I won't forgive that. If it's war, let it be war." That's how King Thoma responded to the destruction of the Pali books.

'Since then, he defied every compromise move of the Portuguese and he organized the Malankara Nasranis against the Menazis, and declared war. An army of more than 50,000 Nasranis were his strength. King Thoma's move succeeded in no time. That's how in 1653, the Coonan Cross Oath, a public avowal by members of the St Thomas community and the Malankara Orthodox Syrian Christians, excommunicated the Roman clergy. Without the leadership of a strong ruler like King Thoma, would the poor people of Malankara even have thought about such a fight against the Portuguese? But King Thoma could only free them from the clutches of the Romans. He couldn't bring them back to their Chaldean faith. That's how the Chaldean faith, which had been very strong in Kerala from the fourth to the fifteenth centuries, dwindled to a few people.

'However, that ended the Portuguese's yearning for the Villarvattom Swaroopam and they got edged out to the Kochi fort and surrounding areas. Unfortunately, the Villarvattom Swaroopam survived only for 50 years after the Coonan Cross Oath. On 9 February 1701, the last Thoma king passed away. You have already heard of what happened to his only daughter Mariam. A thousand years of rule by the Thoma kings ended with the betrayal by Paliath Achan.

'Okay. But what is the relation between what we wanted to hear and this narration?' I asked.

'Paliath Achan could only steal power. But we retained our beliefs. We retained our tradition. We made sure the chain wasn't broken. The bloodline of King Thoma's daughter Mariam still lives on in Kerala! For us, the order of King Thoma has still not lost its power. From then till now, the first-born girl of every generation sits on the throne of Mariam and rules us. In that lineage, the latest queen was my sister Melvin!

After her death, Merin took over. Villarvattom Swaroopam
has transformed to become Valyedathu Veedu!'

'Then, that ceremony was to crown Merin?'

'Yes. That's what had taken place that day. On the forty-
first day after the death of a queen, the next one is enthroned.
It's a ceremony where only the elders in the family are invited.
Every consecutive day of the year, there will be celebrations.
In the generation before us, one of the sisters of my mother
was on Mariam's throne. But she didn't have daughters. That's
how Melvin got the chance. But she was unlucky. In Thoma
history, she probably held power for the shortest tenure. I
pray that Merin is not that unfortunate.'

Suddenly, Meljo broke into tears. We were baffled. From
the brave and bold Meljo, we had not expected this reaction.
Anil approached him and patted him on his shoulder.

'I just remembered my sister. We were very close. There
was nothing we didn't talk about,' he said, wiping his tears.

'We can understand that.' Anil hugged him. In the comfort
of that love, Meljo softened. I wondered if this was the same
sombre guy who had done all those nasty things to us.

'There is one thing that Andrapper has noticed and noted
many times. The sign of the fish that's at many places. What
does that signify?' I asked after he regained his composure.

'That's the symbol of Villarvattom Swaroopam. It is not
a woman gulping fish, as Andrapper puts it, but a woman
originating from a fish's mouth. That's Mariam!'

'There is something strange in this story. The Portuguese
had tried to sabotage this tradition. Then still, why were you
willing to marry off your sister to one of their lineage? Or
was it because you didn't know his bloodline?' Anil asked.

'I'll tell you. I had inquired about his family. Though da
Gama, Kubral and Menazis had eyes on the Villarvattom

Swaroopam, Christy's forefathers—Andrew Pereira and Diego Pereira—were kind to our dynasty. You were asking what proof is there that the Villarvattom Swaroopam is the truth; come, let me show you one thing.'

He took us inside the house. We passed through several small doorways and dark rooms. In between there was a granary. Then we climbed stairs twice, and descended once. That was when I got a vague idea about the size and complexity of Valyedathu Veedu. It didn't look so big from outside. I felt fear. From our interactions till now, Meljo had emerged as a person who would do anything to guard his secrets. Was he leading us to another of his traps? We finally stopped in front of a big room. Its lock had to be opened with four keys. A peculiar lock. Some had to be turned right, and some left. Another round of turning it twice to the left and once to the right. Another door awaited us inside. It had an ancient number lock. Like Rubik's cube. Meljo opened it turning some wooden blocks multiple times to the left and right, top and bottom. I watched curiously as the numbers changed in the lock. I couldn't figure out a thing. Only someone who had mastered it could open the lock.

'This is the most sacred room in this Valyedathu Veedu. More sacred than the prayer room in which Thaikkattamma is invoked. This could be the first time anyone outside the family is seeing it. I'm trusting you guys that much,' Meljo said, opening the door. We walked in to a dim light. It reminded me of the description of the room of the forefathers at Andrapper House. At the same time, it was equipped with a high-tech CCTV camera, a burglar alarm and a firefighting system.

He took us to a corner of the room. There he opened a box and took out a rod. It was a red wand with two silver knots at the top and three bells hanging from it.

'This is more than 1000 years old,' Meljo said. 'This was the royal sceptre that King Thoma handed over to da Gama.'

'How did it come here?' I asked, wide-eyed.

'That's why I was talking about the kindness of the Pereiras. This sceptre that went from da Gama to Andrew was later returned by Diego to King Thoma when he was the landlord. Also, some of the Chaldean documents in Pali that Bishop Menazis had tried to burn on that synod day was secretly shipped by Diego Pereira with the help of some priests at Udayamperoor church and later returned to Valyedathu Veedu. That's his kindness. So, all the leaves and rolls and books you see in this room are all historic documents that were once believed to be lost forever!'

I looked at them in astonishment. The documents that everyone believed were lost to the cruelty of Menazis were retained here with great reverence. I felt a mixed feeling of fear and joy about the significance of Valyedathu Veedu.

'But why have you not told anyone, Meljo? Why has this been kept as your private property? Don't you realize the historic worth of these books? Shouldn't you be keeping them safely in a museum and not let them rot here?' I asked.

'It won't rot here, Benyamin. This is the soul of Valyedathu Veedu! We know how to guard them in all sanctity and secrecy,' Meljo said. 'And there are many reasons why we don't show them in public. Many of the Chaldean texts go against the popular Christian beliefs in our society. If this reaches a nouveau believer who has no idea about the birth and evolution of faiths, he'll become another Menazis.' Meljo showed the works one by one. 'Look, this is *The Book of Prahan*. It says Joseph had other wives and children before marrying Mariam. This is the *Gospel of Thomas*, this the *Gospel of Magdalene*, and this one, the real *Gospel of Judas*. Here, you won't find the same Jesus you find in the Bible.'

He showed us more books, reading aloud their names. '*Anpathu Nombinte Udir Prarthana, Subade Namaskaram, Idara, The Songs of Kameez*, this is the *Enkartha* book, *Nuhura, The Book of Vavukatte*, this is *Parsiman*, this one *Margasesha*, this *Yohannan vara Kaldosa*—it says Christ and the Son of God are different people. Now, this is the book of the forefathers that describe the history of the Nestorian clergy, this one's *The Book of Pavizham*, this is *Machamoth*, then you have Mishiha's *Thirubalapusthakam* that describes the childhood of Jesus; here's *The Book of Synods* that talks about the synods and the Malankara faith, then there's the *Letter from Heaven* and the *Book of Narsaye*.

'The rest are records, certificates and declarations. It was none other than Diego Pereira who rescued them from the fire of Menazis, a total illiterate in history. Appachan believed it was destiny that one person in that bloodline fell in love with a girl in this family and decided to get adopted to this house,' Meljo said, walking us out of the room.

'In such a great tradition, how did something like Mariam Seva get in? That doesn't fit in with the history,' Anil said as we proceeded to the living room.

'One Appachan who got adopted to this house was from the Kadamatathu family. Even Kadamatathu Kathanar, some believe, was a Chaldean priest who migrated from Persia. Anyway, Mariam Seva came to his house through that Appachan. We still continue it as a mysterious ritual, which protects the hidden secrets. When people inquire about this house, they come to know about Mariam Seva, while the rest remains a secret.'

'Do you believe that the Villarvattom dynasty will ever

return to power?' Anil asked while we were taking our camera, bag and other stuff.

'Which royal dynasty in India doesn't believe so? Everyone keeps announcing their heir . . . for what?' Meljo retorted.

We didn't have an answer for that. That moment, I felt that India is a beauty of the night who sleeps over a pile of collated dreams. Someday, if the dreams get broken? During the return journey from Udayamperoor, that was the thought that muddled my mind.

10

Appendix

THE LAST THURSDAY MARKET

IT WAS THE first Thursday Market after the publication of *The Yellow Lights of Death*. Other than the usual discussions, it was also a book release function. It was Biju's suggestion that the book should have a 'private' release. Nobody opposed the proposal. Sudhi Mashu, who was the eldest in the group, handed over a copy to Salim. Anil read a chapter of the novel. 'We can have a discussion now,' I said. As they were also characters in the novel, there were only casual comments. None of them came up with any major critique of the novel.

It was Nibu who raised the issue: 'What happened to Andrapper after that?'

'It is not the novel's responsibility to find that out, so we don't have to worry about it,' I said.

'Maybe the novel doesn't have the responsibility of providing the answers, that's the author's call. But we, as human beings, have that responsibility.'

'It's sheer stupidity to go outside the novel and look for a character, or worry about what happened to him after the events of the novel.' I stuck to my argument.

'I'm not getting the point at all.'

'Nibu, characters are created for the sake of the novel. So, even if they are real, there is no need to look out for them outside the text. The author is also not accountable for the expenses the characters incur!' Anil said.

'This is against human values. True fiction holds a mirror to life. I don't agree that life is irrelevant outside fiction. Whatever be your opinion, I feel obliged to find out what happened to Andrapper afterwards. I am going to start my search from this very moment. Does anyone want to join me?'

Biju and Nattapranthan raised their hands.

'The majority is still on the other side,' I said.

'This is not a decision to be taken by the majority. Even if I'm alone, it has to be done. For that, I don't need the support of any author. I call it Operation Diego Garcia Part III, and I'll start on it now. Not just that, it's difficult for me to continue with a Thursday Market that thinks we can confine ourselves within the limitations of fiction. I don't see life like that.'

Nibu walked out of the group. Biju and Nattapranthan followed him.

That was the last-ever Thursday Market.

AN EMAIL FROM ARAVIND

BENYAMIN, I'VE JUST finished reading your new novel. You can have your serious discussions of it with your writer colleagues and critics. My quick mail is to let you know my opinion on a very particular matter.

About the person called Senthil and the photos in his USB drive, I wish to come to a different conclusion. I don't think he frequented pornography websites because he was a porn addict or had a sleazy curiosity about explicit images. I don't know if you're aware of it but such porn sites are the safest communication platform available now for terrorists across the world to transfer messages. They embed their secrets into the photos without anyone noticing anything. They can sit in any corner in the world and safely surf the sites and decode the secrets—in the pictures or in their captions. The information they decipher could be about what kind of weapons to use, which route to take, whom to contact, etc. Even if someone else stumbles upon these images and the messages they carry, he won't be able to understand them.

This process of hiding messages in digital images, in audio and video files, is called steganography. Only if we scrutinize the audio files and video links of Senthil's USB will we be able to find the hidden messages in them. I'll do it for you someday when you visit. Please tell Salim and Biju to keep the drive safe with them.

And you keep writing novels. I'll keep emailing you.

Aravind

SHANMUGHAN

WHEN I FIRST met Shanmughan, he was creating a scene at the entrance of a hotel in Delhi. He was standing in front of me in a queue for security check. I was there to attend a literature festival. When the hotel security guard asked him something in Hindi, he started screaming back in English and Tamil. 'You better talk to me in Tamil or English, don't even utter a word of Hindi'—that was the meaning of his outburst. The security guard must have been stunned. He didn't say a word.

As we went up to our rooms in the same lift, he was still fuming. 'Why are they so hell-bent on teaching me Hindi? Let them learn Tamil!' We reached the seventh floor, and lo, our rooms were adjacent. It was while opening the doors that we introduced ourselves to each other. When he heard that I was a writer, Shanmughan was full of respect. He had come to participate in an NRI global conclave. 'We'll meet later,' I said and slipped into my room.

The journey had exhausted me, so I had dinner early and was lying on the bed when the bell rang. It was Shanmughan. He was a bit tipsy. I invited him into the room. He was from Malaysia where he managed a huge textile showroom. His family had settled there ages ago. He hadn't forgotten his motherland. He had Person of Indian Origin status and visited Tamil-Nadu twice a year. His children attended a Tamil-medium school. It was his greatest desire to come back home someday.

He frequently quoted couplets from the *Thirukkural*. He believed that Thiruvalluvar was a greater poet that Valmiki, and Paranar a better one than Kalidasa. Not only did he love Sangam literature, he had a good knowledge of it. He knew well the classic texts, he knew all about *thinai* (he liked *mullai* the best) and preferred *puram* poems to those of *akam*.

I asked Shanmughan about the new generation of Tamil writers. He didn't seem to know much. Let a greater poet than Thiruvalluvar be born in India, then let's see—that was his opinion. According to Shanmughan, Tamil was the most ancient language in the world. The Cheras ruled the one true empire. And their capital city, Vanchi Muthur, was the centre of the world.

When I asked Shanmughan what was his ultimate desire in life, he blushed and named a famous actress. He wanted to spend a night with her. When I asked if that was the reason for his regular visits to India, he said that he had a bigger dream, but couldn't talk about it. I tried to get it out of him, but he didn't yield. I opened my bag and took out a bottle and two glasses. Shanmughan flattered me by praying to the bottle that it was his great luck to have a peg with a writer. He even kissed my hands. And after two rounds, more *Thirukkural* began to flow from his tongue.

When Shanmughan was in his element, I forced him to reveal his dream. He got up and briskly walked out to his room. I thought he wouldn't return, but he did and spread out a roll of paper in front of me. It was an old map.

'This is our dream!'

I didn't get it at first. Then, when I studied it carefully, I understood that it showed the first Chera dynasty that had spread across the entire peninsula. 'That ancient nation of the Cheras ought to be re-established. That's our dream!'

'Our dream? Whose dream is that?'

'Tamizhaka Odukappatoor Viduthalai Izhakkam, a group started in the 1980s by a school teacher named Pulavar Kaliyaperumal. Former Naxalite Tamizharasan, Anpazhakan, etc. were part of it. At that point, its name was Tamil Nadu Liberation Army. In 2002, the Indian government banned the group. After that we split ourselves into various groups such as Tamilina Viduthalai Kazhagam, Vivasayangal Urpathiyalar Sangham, Tamil Desiya Penkal Viduthalai Izhakkam, Orumai Koruvar Orungamaippu, Tamil Nadu Ayyangar Peravai, Uthiyan Cheral Tamizhar Kazhagam and Tamizhaka Odukappatoor Viduthalai Izhakkam. If you inquire, you'll find that each is a well-organized political, social, non-profit charity organization. But each organization's aim is to unite the Tamils across the world and fight till we achieve victory.'

In the list, I had noticed the name 'Uthiyan Cheral Tamil Kazhagam . . .! The Pondicherry one. The office Senthil had visited frequently. That means Senthil . . .?!

'You think something like this will work out? In a country like India? It's just a fantasy. Even after a hundred years of activism, you won't be able to realize even the least bit of your dream.' I bid him goodnight with a little ridicule and a lot of anger.

'I'll leave now, but we will fight till we attain victory!' He left, reciting a classical poem.

I couldn't sleep that night.

LEENA

I RECEIVED AN email from an anonymous source proving that there was more to Andrapper's life than we had discovered, and that there were more portions to the manuscript that had to be uncovered. This is how the mail read:

I was sitting on the terrace of my house when I saw a boat draw to a stop at the entrance. A young woman climbed up the stairs. I couldn't recognize her. Assuming she was one of Chettathi's friends, I went back to the novel that I was reading.

Momma called out after a while, 'There's a visitor for you!'

When I went down, I was stunned. Leena! Leena who sat next to me in the class photo. I had been searching for all my classmates and Leena had come in search of me.

'How come you're here?'

'Why, can't I come to see you?'

'Oh no, it's not that. How did you find my house?'

'You think it's difficult to find the Andrapper House in Diego? Tell any boat driver and he'll drop you here blindfolded.'

'Where are you coming from?'

'From City Hospital. I had gone to meet Anita. She told me that you'd be here.'

'I see, what did she say?'

'You'd gone to meet her once or twice, right?'

'Yes, yes. About a case.'

'About the murder that you mention in your novel?'

'How do you know about that?'

'Anita told me.'

'Ah! I'd once showed her a portion of my manuscript. Our classmates appear in it.'

'What have you written about Anita in that?'

'What have I written? Why?'

'Idiot. Should I tell you what you wrote? That she had grabbed your hand and had given you her children's photograph. She told me nothing of that sort had happened. Anyway, she is not very happy with what you've written, okay? She also knows your intentions in going to meet her often. You should remember that she is a married woman. You are still a daydreamer!'

'I've no such feelings. I just visited her about the murder and . . .'

'Oh, as if I don't know! We all knew! Anita, Supriya and I have laughed about it. Leave it, she never liked you. Never.'

It hurt me, but I recovered quickly. At that point it was not Anita who interested me, it was Leena. She seemed the same. She talked the same way she used to. There was no unfamiliarity. She was not affected by the long gap since we'd met. She chatted with me as if we had met the previous day. No wonder we called her 'the advocate'.

'Did you actually become an advocate?' I asked.

'Ha. Do I have to fulfil the dreams of my classmates? I did my higher studies in Cape Town. After that, Paris for a while.

I'm now in Geneva, a small job in the UN.'

'The UN?'

'Yes, the United Nations.'

God, another surprise. Leena had blossomed beyond my imagination.

'Actually, when I heard about the story of your novel, I, too, felt the same desire that you had—to meet our old classmates.'

'I'm really happy that you came. And that you feel this way.'

'Was Senthil really murdered?'

'That's the truth. But I don't have any evidence to prove it. What can I do?'

Momma came with apple juice and biscuits, and sat down to chat with Leena. When she heard that Leena was a UN official, she was full of admiration.

'Look at her. She was in your class. Look at where she is now! My dear, we told him to go to Paris, he didn't listen to us. Instead he went to Thiruvananthapuram. Now he is writing a novel and roaming around like a loafer.'

After Momma left, Leena looked at me and smiled.

'Sorry, Mommas are like that. They always want to see their sons rich. But I think you should never veer away from your writing. Some of our classmates have become doctors, some nurses, some businessmen, some high officials, some rich people. But I feel more respect for you than for any of them. That's why I came to meet you even though I've very little time this trip.'

She got up to leave. I accompanied her to the stairs of the jetty. There was an official boat waiting for her. Before she got into it, she held my hand.

'You'd written that Anita held on to your hand. Let her go.

I've held you in real life. I hope that's enough? Then again, I can't gift you a photo of my children as I'm not married. So you've a chance,' she laughed and patted me on my shoulder.

'Our Senthil . . . he is not a story in a novel, he is a human rights issue. Can't you do something?' I asked.

'I know. But I have limitations. You can at least protest through a novel. I don't have that power.'

She boarded the boat. It created a few ripples in front of me and vanished from sight. When walking up the stairs, I opened my wallet. It still had the photograph of Anita's children.

AFFIDAVIT

(RAJANBABU SENT THIS with the note: 'I got it from the Public Security.')

I have come to know from the Public Security department that a book has been published in Kerala titled *The Diaries of Christy Andrapper*. Christy Andrapper is my son. There is no evidence that it was actually written by my son. My family and I strongly suspect that the stories have been manufactured to malign the Andrapper family and Diego Garcia. In fact, this book has been published without the knowledge of and permission from any of us. Benyamin, in whose name it has been compiled, is not related to or acquainted with anyone in the Andrapper family. We have not given him the rights to publish such a book.

If such a book has brought disgrace to our Diego Garcia, its government or its sovereignty, as the mother of the author, I tender my sincere apology to this land.

I don't believe this country or its government has any hand in the disappearance of my son. The Andrapper family believes that he might have voluntarily migrated abroad, or committed suicide. I hereby certify that he was clinically depressed since his childhood, and was unstable and liable to episodes of mania like his grandfather. I am writing this in sound mind, by my own hand and not under the influence of anything or anyone.

Jai Diego Garcia!

Sincerely,

Janet Maria Andrapper

NEWS REPORT

MALAYALA MANORAMA 13 SEPTEMBER 2010

Major plantation companies in India and abroad are all set to invest in African countries. It is feared that the effects of climate change in countries such as India, Sri Lanka and Malaysia, and the dearth of labourers would result in huge losses to the sector in the coming years. This has been attributed as a reason for the companies' latest move. Ghana, Ethiopia and Cameroon are the top three choices. Other than big firms such as Harrison Malayalam, Tata, Kannan Devan, Unilever and Manjusri Plantations, some individuals and Almaya forums of some Christian groups are also investors. These companies will set up estates of tea, rubber, sugar cane, cotton, coffee and coconut. Andrapper and Co., the multinational company known for its investments in the plantation sector, has already bought thousands of acres of land in Ethiopia and begun developing estates. Other companies will follow.

Meanwhile, in a press conference, Andrapper and Co. denied reports that the influx of plantation companies to

Africa would be a threat to them. 'We have an edge over the others because of our experience in setting up plantations in various countries and during different periods in history. The entry of other players in the sector is not a threat to us,' Jeffrey Andrapper, the spokesperson of Andrapper and Co., told journalists in Addis Ababa. He added that the company had withdrawn all their investments in Diego Garcia and that their new headquarters would be Gore in Ethiopia.

AUTHOR'S ACKNOWLEDGEMENTS

Courtesy, love, thanks to—

Friends in reality and fiction: Anil Vengode, E.A. Salim, Sudhi Mashu, Nibu, Biju and Nattapranthan, aka Saju.

The friend who gave me the dope on Mariam Seva.

The essay titled 'I, the Joan of Arc' (*Bhashaposhini*, December 2005) by V.K. Sriraman, which had details about the Andrapper family history.

The websites that had a wealth of information about terrorist outfits; and the annual report of the Union Home Ministry.

The many Nasrani documents.

The residents of Udayamperoor.

All those who love my words.

And to you, of course!